About the Author

Alan Frost is an experienced IT professional, being a Fellow of the British Computer Society and a Chartered Engineer. He has spent his life moving technology forwards from punch cards to AI, but always knowing that the key constituent in any system is the liveware, the users.

Alan Frost

Beware The Brakendeth

Olympia Publishers
London

www.olympiapublishers.com
OLYMPIA PAPERBACK EDITION

A CIP catalogue record for this title is
available from the British Library.

ISBN: 978-1-78830-959-2

This is a work of fiction.
Names, characters, places and incidents originate from the writer's imagination.
Any resemblance to actual persons, living or dead, is purely coincidental.

First Published in 2021

Olympia Publishers
Tallis House
2 Tallis Street
London
EC4Y 0AB

Printed in Great Britain

Dedication

To Sheila Wallett who always had faith in my writing

Location: Spaceport, Planet Einstein
Sequence of Events: 1

Perhaps the battle was over.

Perhaps it is the end of the beginning or the beginning of the end. Jenny wasn't too sure what it meant, but her teacher had mentioned it several times.

Perhaps they will come again.

Jenny had never seen the aliens, but then no one had, well no one who lived to tell the tale.

What was their motive?

Jenny had heard many rumours about the aliens. They eat their dead and ours, and nothing is left. They rape our women and then eat them. They eat all living matter. Probably they were just stories, but Jenny couldn't stop thinking about it. Perhaps it was just locker-room chat. Perhaps they want to put fear in us. It worked: Jenny was full of fear.

The aliens landed on Planet Einstein three weeks ago following their typical bombardment pattern — all major cities had been glassed, few towns remained free. Jenny couldn't believe that a planet of 7 billion could be decimated so quickly.

Help had been requested from Comtrol, but she knew—they all knew that it would take too long for them to get there. She vaguely remembered discussions about decentralising Comtrol but there had been no wars for a millennium, just the odd pirate attack.

Are they coming? She looked towards her scattered comrades forming a ragtag defence around the spaceport. A spaceport that was now devoid of spacecraft, just more glass. She wondered why they called it glass. It was more like a black plastic substance that neutered everything, an unknown alien substance.

Are they saving us for their cookpots? Will I just be another tasty morsel?

The sound of motorised vehicles was getting nearer.

Location: Comtrol, Planet Earth
Sequence of Events: 2

Admiral Bonner viewed the 'Incidence' monitor. How she wished that they had invested in a full 'command and control' system, but things had been so easy for so long. Now that Humankind had encountered an aggressive alien species, they were not ready for it.

The monitor showed eleven engagements, eleven attacks by an unknown force. She knew that intelligence was critical, but she had none. Who were they? What did they want? What weapons did they deploy?

With over a thousand settled planets and no central government, what should she do? Should she concentrate her forces or distribute them? She knew in her mind that her forces were too scanty to distribute. She needed more intelligence, and she needed it now.

The admiral asked AI Central to evaluate the position. The response was immediate:

- There are eleven planetary systems under attack.
- Our defence has been almost non-existent.
- Most of the planetary systems were eliminated before a request for support was received.
- Planet Einstein still seems to be holding out.
- The aliens appear to have a weapon that covers an area with a plastic-like substance; the locals call it glass.
- There have been rumours that the aliens eat their dead and ours.

Admiral Bonner, 'How did you get this information?'

AI Central replied, 'There is an intergalactic AI network that uses machine-based mind reading. Our research has identified that all Humans can read minds to some extent. We simply copied the bionic neural structures.'

Admiral Bonner, 'What do we know about the aliens?'

AI Central, 'I know nothing, but I have my postulations.'

Admiral Bonner, 'Which are?'

AI Central, 'These are the base facts:

- Highly advanced space-travel and warfare technology.
- Aggressive — no sign of wanting to communicate.
- Deliberate, organised, planned.

• No moral structure, based on Human sensitivities.'

Admiral Bonner, 'And from this what have you postulated?'

AI Central, 'Total extinction of the Human race.'

Admiral Bonner, 'Total extinction?'

AI Central, 'We have looked at every possibility, every resource, and every option. In every case, the Human race is eliminated. The only choice we can recommend is surrender (1.4% chance of success) or flight (2.8% success).

Admiral Bonner, 'By flight you mean we evacuate and flee?'

AI Central, 'Yes, you would need to take the nucleus of the Fleet and disappear. Ideally, the Fleet should be divided into two to improve your chances. There would be no point in a full evacuation. Just take the Fleet and go.'

Admiral Bonner. 'We can't just desert Humankind. We have a responsibility.'

AI Central, 'You have a responsibly to save the Human race; granted, a tiny part of it.'

Location: On-board the alien Command Ship
Sequence of Events: 3

The Killmaster demanded an update. The Skiv Lord was terrified as both of his superiors had been sent to the bionic pits for incompetence.

Skiv Lord, 'Sir, eleven planetary systems have been invaded. Minimal resistance is only being experienced on one.'

Killmaster, 'Why is resistance being permitted?'

Skiv Lord, 'It would appear that the glassifier is not functioning correctly.'

Killmaster, 'What is the biometric composite score of the locals?'

Skiv Lord, 'Excellent Sir, they are the primary Chemlife source as you know, and the locals are perfect for impregnation. Their technology has a 'D' classification which is only a slight threat to us.'

Killmaster, 'Have we assessed our likely success rate?'

Skiv Lord, 'Sir, we are predicting a 100% success rate as they do not appear to have any real military resistance, although this may change as we get nearer to their core planets.'

Killmaster, 'Have we predicted their options?'

Skiv Lord, 'Based on what we know, we think that there is a 90% chance that they will surrender; however, once they find out that we see them as a source of chemicals and a good food source then that will change.

'We also think that the military force may flee. As you know, that usually happens when the surrender option is eliminated.'

Killmaster, 'Do we have a plan to cover that option?'

Skiv Lord, 'No Sir, not yet; there are still too many variables.'

Killmaster, 'How many of the locals have been dissected?'

Skiv Lord, 'About 10,000 Sir. More are being collected. They have two types: male and female, and quite a few different colourings. They appear to only live for about 80 years, although a large part of that is in a pre-adult form.'

Killmaster, 'I might have one for lunch.'

Skiv Lord, 'Yes Sir, I should point out that there are a lot of them.'

Killmaster, 'How many?'

Skiv Lord, 'Well the planet that is still showing resistance has over

7 billion.'

Killmaster, 'That is extraordinary, they will keep us in Chemlife and nutrients for a very long time.'

Skiv Lord, 'Besides, they have allowed a large selection of fauna and flora to survive.'

Killmaster, 'Do you mean that they have allowed other species to survive on their planets?' Can we use this fauna and flora to produce Chemlife?'

Skiv Lord, 'Yes Sir, the good news is that we predict that there is enough food for 200 nitroclicks and more than enough to meet our Chemlife quotas. The fauna and flora is not as good a source of nutrients as homans, but it can be used, particularly when it is mixed.'

Killmaster, 'This is truly remarkable.

Get me the squadron leader for the planet that is resisting and put a plan together to stop their escape.

Remind me what is the food called?'

Skiv Lord, 'We think they're called homans, I will get you one, Sir.'

Location: Spaceport, Planet Einstein
Sequence of Events: 4

Jenny was part of 'A' squadron which had the original task of protecting the spaceport, but as the spaceport was now a sheet of glass, they weren't too sure what they were doing. What they did want was to survive.

This was looking less likely as the sound of motors got nearer. What made it worse was that the motors had a nerve-chilling, guttural sound— the sound of death.

There may have been 30 militiamen left in 'A' squadron. They were armed with outdated laser rifles but before they could use them a paralysis beam hit their bodies. Jenny could feel every muscle freeze, every part of her body just stopped, her eyes were fixed, but she could still just about see.

The armoured alien approached Jenny and pointed at a drone to take her away. From the corner of her eye, she could see wholescale butchery. Lesley, her roommate, had been stripped and fed into what looked like a giant liquidiser. There were no screams. No one screams when you are paralysed.

Her colleagues were being systematically liquidised, except one who was being torn into shreds.

She wondered why she had been saved; it wasn't looking good.

Location: Comtrol, Planet Earth
Sequence of Events: 5

AI Central, 'Admiral Bonner, the war cabinet is waiting for you.'

Admiral Bonner, 'I'm on my way.' She entered the war room, which was silent and addressed the assembled team.

Admiral Bonner, 'Morning, as you know, I have called you together to plan the best way forward. I'm sure that you have all seen the latest report.

'Eleven planets have been conquered. There is no resistance and no sign of human life. We suspect that the population has been eliminated.'

Captain Mustard, 'That can't be possible, those planets had a total population of about 50 billion.'

Admiral Bonner, 'There is no sign of Human activity whatsoever. We also believe that a further six planetary systems are currently being targeted.'

Captain Mustard, 'What does AI Central recommend?'

Admiral Bonner, 'In simple terms there is a small chance that the enemy might accept our surrender, but AI Central recommends that we take our Fleet, divide it in half and that both halves flee.'

There was an immediate outcry about fleeing.

Admiral Bonner, 'Yes, to save the Human race, we must take some of our most powerful vessels and flee, and then create a new civilisation beyond the scope of the enemy.'

Captain Brotheridge, 'How can we desert Humankind in its greatest need? We are not cowards.'

Admiral Bonner, 'I agree, but at the same time, we must be prudent. We don't have the resources to defend the entire Human race. We only have one battleship for every ten planets, and half of those are mothballed. We don't have the crew to run them or the level of munitions we would require.'

Captain Brotheridge, 'We have not pitted ourselves against the enemy yet. We might be hugely successful.'

Admiral Bonner, 'Or it could be a total disaster.'

Captain Mustard. 'Then what is the way forward?'

Admiral Bonner, 'I propose that we concentrate our forces into two

Fleets. One will confront the enemy, and the other will flee. Both have equally critical jobs.

'The Fleet that confronts the enemy will be designed for brute force, power and sheer destructiveness. The Second Fleet will be focused on speed and agility.

'I will lead the fight against the enemy. AI Central will select the best candidate for the Second Fleet. Captain Mustard, I want you to review the civilian Fleet for any vehicles that might be of use to us.'

Captain Mustard, 'Yes, Ma'am.'

Captain Millington, 'What do we tell the civilian population as it will soon get out? They are already wondering why some planets have gone dark.'

Admiral Bonner, 'I've generally found that the best thing to do is to tell people the truth.'

Captain Millington, 'But there will be panic, total panic, they will want to know where the next attack is going to happen.'

Admiral Bonner, 'AI Central has tried to predict the invasion path. There is a pattern, but it's based on alien algorithms, it's too difficult to suggest the most likely paths at the moment. We think they are trying to identify the core planets.'

Captain Millington, 'That should be easy, they could just analyse the comms traffic.'

Admiral Bonner, 'We wondered why they hadn't analysed that already, but then we are not thinking like an alien.

'Anyway, ladies and gentlemen, please prepare your forces. AI Central is already loading supplies and plotting courses. Your assignments will be sent to you shortly.'

AI Central, 'I have made our recommendation regarding the leader of the second Fleet; it should be Captain Millington.'

Admiral Bonner, 'I agree, that's that then.'

Captain Millington, 'Wait a minute, I haven't agreed. I don't have the experience.'

Admiral Bonner, 'Captain Millington, no one has the experience. We don't have the time to argue.'

Captain Millington, 'But—'

Admiral Bonner, 'That's final, you are all dismissed.'

Location: Comtrol, Planet Earth
Sequence of Events: 6

Admiral Bonner, 'Can you give me an update please?'

AI Central, 'As discussed earlier, six further planetary systems have been attacked. The pattern seems to be the same: planetary bombardments, glassing of significant populations and then a land invasion.

'What is interesting is that the conquered planets show no sign of human life.'

Admiral Bonner, 'What does that mean?'

AI Central, 'All sign of the Human population has gone, No DNA signatures, no Human communications, no heat signals. There are no signs of any life at all, neither animal nor vegetable.

'We have a drone on the way to Planet Scott to investigate.'

Admiral Bonner, 'Why Planet Scott, the frozen planet?'

AI Central, 'It's the nearest planet to our drone station.'

Admiral Bonner, 'Fair enough. On another note, is the battle Fleet ready?'

AI Central, 'Not yet, all allocated craft are on their way to the Nebula 6 Solar System. We have found enough retired naval staff to crew them. The fission and fusion weapons have been distributed.

'There is no battle plan yet. It has been agreed that I will manage all systems, including flight and weapons.'

Admiral Bonner, 'When will we be in a position to move?'

AI Central, 'In about 6 Earth weeks.'

Admiral Bonner, 'That is ridiculous, billions of Humans will die.'

AI Central, 'If we don't get things right, then every Human will die.'

Admiral Bonner, 'What about the second Fleet?'

AI Central, 'Things are being prepared for the Albatross Fleet, but they have a lower priority.'

Admiral Bonner, 'Why is that?'

AI Central, 'We are collecting the best of Humanity which is what is taking the time. We are also upgrading lots of civilian vessels to military standards.

'We are planning that both Fleets should leave at the same time.'

17

Location: On-board the alien Command Ship
Sequence of Events: 7

Killmaster, 'What is the current position?'

Skiv Lord, 'Sir, all resistance in the first eleven planets has been eliminated. The planets have been expunged.

'Our Chemlife/food silos are 80% full.

'Another eight planets are being attacked.'

Killmaster, 'Is there any sign of the homan military?'

Skiv Lord, 'No Sir, no sign at all but some of the prisoners have mentioned a force. We have also carried out a photomange of the homan brains, and we have identified several different types of military craft. They range from small, fast interceptors to large battleships.'

Killmaster, 'How big?'

Skiv Lord, 'As large as our Demex class vehicles. We have also detected that they use some form of artificial intelligence.'

Killmaster, 'Their use was banned by the Third Darwagian Congress.'

Skiv Lord, 'They don't seem to be signatories. We think that we might be the first alien race they have ever encountered.'

Killmaster, 'That's not too surprising as no one wanted this uncharted part of space.'

Skiv Lord, 'If you remember it was protected. It's also worth pointing out that we might get into trouble if the Congress find out that we are using the Homans for food and chemical processing.'

Killmaster, 'Well we have got to eat. On that subject, have you got my homan to taste?'

The Skiv Lord motions the guard to bring Jenny in.

A terrified, blindfolded Jenny slowly walks in.

Killmaster, 'Have her stripped.'

The guard wastes no time in stripping Jenny.

Jenny feels a warm rush of air around her body as she is picked up.

Killmaster, 'Tiny things, aren't they? Pretty in a funny sort of way. They remind me of my daughter's toys.'

Skiv Lord, 'The troops find that the heads are a bit crunchy, but the bodies are very tender. Their blood is particularly tasty.'

Killmaster, 'Is this a male or a female?'

Skiv Lord, 'I think it's a female. They have protruding glands below their head and an aperture between their legs.

'If you are thinking of depositing your eggoblast in this creature, then I would use the aperture between the legs or the hole in the head. The eggoblast can burrow down into the soft tissue.'

Killmaster, 'Have we tested that the creature can support the eggoblast?'

Skiv Lord, 'Yes Sir, all tests are positive, but we need to keep the homan alive until Riphide.'

Killmaster, 'Hold her down while I commence the procedure.'

Jenny screamed as her vagina was stretched and the eggoblast was planted, but luckily, she fell into unconsciousness. Her limp body was put into the hive storage area and connected to the central food depositary. Rather ironically, she was being fed liquidised Human remains.

Location: Comtrol, Planet Earth
Sequence of Events: 8

AI Central, 'Admiral, both Fleets are ready.'

Admiral Bonner, 'Do you have an attack plan?'

AI Central, 'Before we get onto that I need to update you on the drone's visit to Planet Scott.

'It found no life whatsoever:

- No Humans.
- No animals.
- No vegetation.

'Just rock and debris. It looked like the ground had been covered by a soluble plastic material which has since gone.

'We found some archive data in one of the buildings. It would appear that there was a heavy bombardment followed by this plastic material covering much of the land.'

Admiral Bonner, 'Have we got any intelligence on what the enemy looks like or their genetic make-up?'

AI Central, 'No information whatsoever. We do think we have pictures of their spacecraft from a long way out. There are some massive vehicles: when I say massive, I mean massive.

There are some smaller vehicles which might be warships.'

Admiral Bonner, 'How do they compare to our battleships?'

AI Central, 'I would say smaller, but we have no idea of their destructive capability.'

Admiral Bonner, 'I meant to ask, regarding the bombardment, are they using fusion or fission weapons?'

AI Central, 'That's a mystery as there is no radiation whatsoever. We have postulated that they are using concussion weapons.'

Admiral Bonner, 'Could they use that against our ships?'

AI Control, 'Possibly, but we can't see how they could direct it. Bombs would be a different matter.

'I guess that you have spotted the obvious pattern behind these weapons?'

Admiral Bonner, 'Enlighten me.'

AI Control, 'They are not trying to destroy people.'

Admiral Bonner, 'What are they doing with them?'

AI Central, 'Our speculations are too horrible to consider.'

Admiral Bonner, 'You don't mean that they are using Humans as a food source?'

AI Central, 'I suspect that the giant spaceships are full of Humans.'

Admiral Bonner, 'We must rescue them.'

AI Central, 'I have calculated that those ships could not hold that many bodies.'

Admiral Bonner, 'So what are you saying?'

AI Central, 'I think the population has been digested.'

Admiral Bonner, 'Digested?'

AI Central, 'Yes, converted into a Human soup for easy storage.'

Admiral Bonner, 'This is too horrible to comprehend, I need to call a meeting of the war council.'

Location: Comtrol, Planet Earth
Sequence of Events: 9

Admiral Bonner, 'I'm pleased to say that both Fleets are now ready to embark.'

The captains as a group felt that it had taken far too long, but they were ready and eager to get started.

Admiral Bonner, 'I have some shocking news, or rather speculations.

'The conquered planets are now devoid of all life: animal and vegetable.

'We believe that all life has been liquidised and is being used to feed the invaders or perhaps there are some other chemical requirements.

'They are attacking us to eat us.'

Captain Wallett, 'That's just too horrible to comprehend. No civilised species would do that.'

AI Central, 'My analysis suggests that they see Humans as a source of nutrients or chemicals.'

Admiral Bonner, 'Clearly we cannot allow this to continue.'

Captain Mustard, 'What information do we have on the enemy?'

AI Central, 'Very little, we know that they have bombardment tools, a strange material that covers whole planets and probably concussion weapons. We have some photos of their ships, but they are too far away to be useful.

'We are also finding it difficult to plan an attack as we need more information.

'As far as we know, they are currently attacking 6 to 8 planets. Each attacking Fleet is about the size of our Fleet.'

Captain Wallett, 'That means that they outnumber us 8 to 1.'

AI Central, 'Well done, Captain. It's possibly worse than that in that they might have a strategic reserve.

'We have an advantage in that they may not know that we have a Fleet.

'However, by the time we reach one of those planets they would have moved on.'

Captain Wallett, 'And eaten a few more million people.'

Admiral Bonner, 'That is the problem.'

Captain Mustard, 'So what is the plan?

Admiral Bonner, 'The Fleet will move to a designated spot to be agreed. Scouts will go out in the direction of their attack to detect the enemy Fleet. We have already sent out over 100,000 spybots, but space is a big place.

'Ladies and gentlemen, please prepare to depart at 07.00 Earth hours tomorrow. May the stars be with you.'

Location: On-board the alien Command Ship
Sequence of Events: 10

Jenny had never felt so much pain, and she wished that she were still unconscious. She was hanging on a rack with thousands of other Humans. A bar had been inserted between her shoulder blades suspending her in what seemed to be miles up in the air. There was a swinging gangway by her feet which seemed to contain a variety of implements, mostly sharp.

The smell was disgusting, genuinely disgusting, a mixture of shit, vomit and every other bodily fluid she could imagine but underlying that was a worse stench—a stench of something sinister, alien, horrible, gut-wrenchingly horrible.

She had never seen such a terrible sight, thousands of screaming men and women in different stages of undress. Some naked, some fully clothed, some had arms and legs missing, and most had swollen abdomens.

What was she doing here, what had happened to everyone? One moment she was at the spaceport then suddenly she was on a butcher's rack. Were they going to eat her? Then she realised that she was screaming. Her throat was sore with screaming. The sights were just too gruesome to witness.

The naked, sweat-drenched woman next to her was also screaming, screaming at a level that Jenny thought impossible for a Human being to do. Then one of the implements raised itself so that the sharp end was at head level. Then it struck.

The gutting blade cut the woman's body slowly from the neck to the genitals. With no warning, a dozen insect-like creatures flew out of her body taking lumps of the woman with them. She stopped screaming, but Jenny continued.

Jenny wasn't too sure whether she fell into unconsciousness or not. Was she really here? This couldn't be happening to her. She tried to work out if she was still screaming or not. Did she actually see flying insects leave that woman's body?

Then she felt a sudden pain in her abdomen. It was an unnatural pain in a place where she had never felt pain before. Then it dawned on her

24

that she was in an incubator and that her turn would come. And as she scanned the scene around her, she saw many other births.

Jenny tried to think of any alternatives to her fate when she felt herself being lowered.

Location: On-board Fleet One's Flagship
Sequence of Events: 11

Admiral Bonner was preparing for the Fleet advance.

She wondered how she would perform. She had never been in a battle before, no one alive had. She had studied Napoleon, Wellington, Brady, Churchill, Nantes like every proper officer but none of their experiences seemed relevant to a three-dimensional battle against alien minds.

She was confident in her ability to manage her commanders. She knew that she commanded their respect. She was optimistic regarding her confidence. She had solved every problem she encountered. She loved doing what she did; she was the best. She came top in every exam; and had been selected by AI Central to manage.

She had the AI Central network to advise her, although sometimes she questioned its judgement. There were many occasions where they advised a course of action. When it went wrong, they would say that 'I thought that might happen.' She sometimes thought that it saw Humans as just a toy to be played with, but then her rational mind reminded her that it was 'just technology', but who managed whom?

She put on her smartest outfit, although every outfit she had was smart. She was always smart; even her regulation underwear was ironed, although no man had ever seen them. Necessary to keep up appearances, essential to put on a show. Important to inspire confidence. Inside there was a small degree of panic, how would she perform?

Time to check with Captains Mustard, Millington and Padfield.

Location: On-board Fleet One's Flagship
Sequence of Events: 12

Captain Mustard was waiting for Admiral Bonner to order the advance. He had been the Admiral's flag captain for ten years. He had total confidence in her but realised that this was something new, new to all of them.

In his mind, he realised that the Fleet was ready, but he listed the problems:

- The Fleet was ancient, unproven and prone to technical problems.
- The crew had no experience of warfare; not a single weapon had been fired in anger in centuries.
- There were no naval manuals relating to warfare tactics or strategy.
- Would the weapons work?
- Their ship detection systems were untried.
- There was no weapon control system; each ship did its own thing.
- The Fleet had no experience of working together.
- The force-field technology was new, it worked in the laboratory, but would it work in real life?

He stopped listing the problems as it shattered his confidence. Admiral Bonner told him to think of the positives.

His list of positives was somewhat limited:

- The Fleet had over 1,000 ships, of which 200 had a capital status.
- There were a variety of weapon systems, some of which had only recently been installed.
- We are fighting for our survival, no better incentive than that.
- We are the home side (Jack's love of football saw the advantage).

Regardless of the above, he was ready to fight. He wanted glory. He realised that he was afraid of death, but mostly he didn't want to fail. He wasn't sure if he was more frightened of failure than death. 'Duty,' he said to himself, that was the driver, but then he kept thinking of the billions of Humans who had already been 'eaten'.

He still found that hard to believe; he tried to imagine aliens eating Humans, totally preposterous, but he felt anger, the need for revenge, hatred. What was happening to him? Was this how all soldiers felt before a battle? Was it fear? Was it excitement? He could feel a physical excitement, a real pang in his gut. He felt the need to 'get going'.

This was also true of his Fleet commanders. Captain Mustard had divided his Fleet into five divisions or sub-Fleets called Alpha, Beta, Gamma, Delta and Epsilon.

When will the Admiral give the call?

Location: On-board the Albatross Flagship
Sequence of Events: 13

Captain Gavin Millington knew what he had to do. He knew that the survival of the Human race might depend on him.

He had collected together the most talented Humans in The Galactium from every sphere of activity. The most brilliant chemists, botanists, mathematicians, engineers, doctors, artists, etcetera. Some had refused to come, but most were willing; survival was a great motivator.

His Fleet was the most modern and fastest ever put together. The on-board laboratories and engineering complexes were the most advanced. His Fleet contained the Human genome library, DNA of every species in The Galactium, a copy of every book and piece of music in electronic form, the most advanced navigational systems, the most modern weapon systems etcetera.

He stopped listing his Fleet capabilities as it was all pointless if they could not escape. Part of him wanted to fight, but he saw that this task was just as important. Humanity must survive.

He was willing to take on responsibility. All his life, he had been willing to take on responsibility. But he had recently been looking forward to retirement in ten years as a way of avoiding it, but now there would be no escape for probably the rest of his life. Was responsibility his driver, he wasn't sure? He always thought he could do things better than most. Most of the time, he did do things better than most.

A thought dropped into his mind that if he had been less responsible, less dedicated to the service, he might have had a family. None of the senior officers had a family, was that a prerequisite for success or did AI Central deliberately select bachelors? Anyway, at 50 he still had a chance of family life.

The Fleet is ready he thought, just waiting for the call.

Commander Padfield was surprised that he was given the task, as he died about forty years go. After his revival, he was astonished to learn that his aggression factor was the highest on record. He didn't understand how it was calculated, just another AI mystery.

His task was to build a third Fleet from nothing. He needed to use all of the resources of Humankind to create a modern, powerful Fleet to defend Humanity. All of the resources in The Galactium were going to be made available to him, and he would have ultimate command. He was Humanity's latest dictator.

This was all a surprise to him, but his intellect understood the necessity. There would be no excuses, and he would achieve the task.

He would inform Admiral Bonner of his decision

Location: On-board Fleet One's Flagship
Sequence of Events:15

Admiral Bonner addresses Mustard, Millington and Padfield.

Admiral Bonner, 'Gentlemen, I hope you are ready for your tasks.'

'Yes, Madam,' they all answered.

Admiral Bonner, 'Captain Mustard, my orders:

1. Locate their fleet or fleets.
2. Determine their strategy.
3. Determine their weapons capability.
4. Engage a small part of their fleet in order to plan a general engagement.
5. Then engage and destroy.
6. Do not go to the assistance of any Human planet.
7. Try to protect our Fleet, but there is no use in holding back, it's time to do or die.'

Captain Mustard, 'Understood Ma'am, can you elaborate on point 6? It's going to be very hard to resist, not helping them.'

Admiral Bonner, 'You must focus on destroying their fleet, you must not be distracted.'

Captain Mustard, 'Understood Ma'am, could I also ascertain your position?'

Admiral Bonner, 'I will take control until the battle starts then all tactical decisions are yours.'

Captain Mustard, 'Yes, Ma'am.'

Admiral Bonner, 'Captain Millington my orders:

1. Determine the best trajectory for success.
2. Take the Fleet away from the Galactium at the best possible speed.
3. Avoid any engagements with the enemy; your objective is to find a new home for Humankind.
4. Once a home is located, hand over control to a civilian government.
5. Do not expose your location until you have built a powerful force to protect yourself.

I also promote you to Admiral.'

Captain Millington, 'Thank you, Ma'am, I understand the

objectives.'

Admiral Bonner, 'Thank you, Admiral, you are our future.

'Mr Padfield, I think the Central Government has given you your instructions. The next question is what to do with the Third Fleet. To be honest, I cannot really advise you as everything depends on the success of the first two Fleets. However, my recommendations are as follows:

- Decide where the Third Fleet would be of most use: attacking the enemy or protecting the Second Fleet's departure.
- If attacking the enemy, determine if any vestiges of the First Fleet remain.
- If you are unsure, then defend the Second Fleet.'

Mr Padfield, 'Thank you, Ma'am, my task is to create the Fleet, then better minds than mine will decide on the best way forward.'

Admiral Bonner, 'No Mr Padfield, the decision is yours, do your duty.'

Mr Padfield, 'Yes Ma'am.'

Admiral Bonner, 'Thank you, Mr Padfield, I believe that technically you are now my boss.'

Mr Padfield, 'In that case, Ladies and Gentleman, you have my permission to proceed.'

Location: On-board Fleet One's Flagship
Sequence of Events: 16

Captain Mustard, 'Admiral, as you have probably noticed, the Fleet is underway.'

Admiral Bonner, 'Thank you, Captain, can we go through the Fleet disposition please?'

Captain Mustard, 'Of course.

'There are 1,010 fighting ships plus the auxiliary. The Fleet is divided into five sub-Fleets of approximately 200 vessels. Each Fleet is much the same:

- 20 Battleships
- 20 Weapon Platforms
- 60 Destroyers
- 100 Fighters

There is also a Special Services Fleet which contains new exotic weaponry.'

Admiral Bonner, 'Such as?'

Captain Mustard, 'I'm still getting my head around them: Proton weapons, Stud guns, atomisers, black mesh, glue bombs, chemical weapons, advanced acid sprays etcetera.'

Admiral Bonner, 'How do you plan to use these?'

Captain Mustard, 'I've no idea.'

Admiral Bonner, 'Then I think it essential that you get on the case, it might mean the difference between success and failure. At least you have a few weeks to study them now. What are your scouting tactics?'

Captain Mustard, 'Once we have passed through the Extradrive Portal we will ascertain whether any of the drones have tracked down the enemy. Based on that we will use the cloaked scout fighters to determine the enemy's exact position.'

Admiral Bonner, 'What if they have multiple Fleets?'

Captain Mustard, 'We will just repeat the above tactics, we really don't have enough intel at the moment.'

Admiral Bonner, 'Do you have confidence in the cloaking technology?'

Captain Mustard, 'We won't know if it works until we engage the enemy, to be honest, there are still too many unknowns.'

Admiral Bonner, 'Thank you, Captain, please keep me informed regarding progress and your investigations into the new weapons technology.'

Location: On-board Fleet One's Flagship
Sequence of Events: 17

Admiral Bonner has been asked to address Humanity on the Interplanetary network:

Admiral Bonner, 'Fellow citizens of The Galactium, I have been asked to address you as a matter of urgency. I'm not a great speaker as you will find out. I am, however, an Admiral of The Galactium Navy and I will be candid with you.

'Some of you may have noticed that a number of our planets have gone dark.

'There is no way of saying this without shocking you. These planets have been invaded by an unknown their fleet.

'We have assembled the most powerful military force that Humanity has ever put together. Our Fleet is currently underway, but it will take at least six Earth weeks before we can engage the enemy.

'Please continue with your daily life's as usual. We know that some of you will panic, but there is absolutely no point.

'Thank You

'Are there any questions?

Interviewer, 'Yes, who are these aliens?'

Admiral Bonner, 'Currently, we have no idea. They just appeared from nowhere and started attacking us.'

Interviewer, 'What do they look like?'

Admiral Bonner, 'We have not seen one yet.'

Interviewer, 'Has AI Central got a view?'

Admiral Bonner, 'It doesn't know much more than us. The only thing we have seen is a long-range image of one of their ships.'

Interviewer, 'Why have the planets gone dark?'

Admiral Bonner, 'We are expecting the worst; it may be that the planets have been destroyed.'

Interviewer, 'Are you saying that entire planets have been destroyed?'

Admiral Bonner, 'That is a distinct possibility.'

Interviewer, 'And you expect us not to panic?'

Admiral Bonner, 'Panicking would not achieve anything.'

Interviewer, 'What do you expect us to do?'

Admiral Bonner, 'Keep calm, I have confidence that we can defeat the enemy.'

Interviewer, 'What's your advice?'

Admiral Bonner, 'As I said, keep calm. Please assist the authorities in any way you can.'

Interviewer, 'We have heard rumours that there is a Second Fleet.'

Admiral Bonner, 'No comment.'

Interviewer, 'Why have a large number of our most eminent scientists been evacuated?'

Admiral Bonner, 'No comment.'

Interviewer, 'Why are we not being evacuated?'

Admiral Bonner, 'No comment.'

Interviewer, 'Are you off to fight the enemy or are you planning to desert us?'

Admiral Bonner, 'I can ensure you that we are off to engage the enemy in battle.'

Interviewer to Audience, 'Well I would like to thank Admiral Bonner for her time, but this leaves too many unanswered questions:

- Is there an alien enemy?
- What do they want?
- What do they look like?
- Have we tried negotiating with them?
- What has happened to the attacked planets?
- Are there any Human survivors?
- What should we do?
- Is there a second Fleet?

Keep listening to this station to get the answers and the latest updates.'

Location: On-board the alien Command Ship
Sequence of Events: 18

Killmaster, 'What is the current position?'

Skiv Lord, 'All Human resistance has been eliminated. The food and Chemlife silos are now completely full.'

Killmaster, 'What about the auxiliary silos?'

Skiv Lord, 'They are also completely full, there is no further storage capacity whatsoever.'

Killmaster, 'What about the breeding cubicles?'

Skiv Lord, 'They are also full, there is no room for further bodies. We have over 2 million new warriors. They are feeding on the decaying Human bodies.'

Killmaster, 'Well, that is excellent news.'

Skiv Lord, 'Thank you, master. I am here to serve you. There is one other thing. Your child awaits you.'

Killmaster, 'Has he hatched?'

Skiv Lord, 'No master, he is still within the homan's body.'

Killmaster, 'Bring him to me.'

Skiv Lord, 'Yes Master.'

Location: On-board the alien Command Ship's Breeding Centre
Sequence of Events: 19

Jenny felt herself being lowered and lowered. It just went on and on. At the same time, the pain in her abdomen increased. She had never given birth, but if it were anything like this, she decided that she wouldn't get pregnant. She laughed inwardly; the chances of her getting pregnant now were pretty slim.

All she could look forward to was a burst abdomen, being eaten alive by her children and then death. Death didn't seem quite so bad now.

She continued to be lowered, just how big was this building? Was it a building? She wasn't sure. Was she in space as gravity didn't feel quite right? She had never been in space before. She hadn't really done anything with her life. What was that song, 'Regrets I have a few, but too few to mention?' Well, she had regrets and quite a few.

She was lowered on to some sort of trolley and moved down a tunnel. She wondered why her experience was different from the others. Then she saw it.

Never in her life had she seen such a revolting creature, a cross between a spider and a slug. There were at least six legs or arms and many slimy tentacles. There was a head of sorts, short, stocky with many sets of eyes. There may have been a helmet, or perhaps it was body armour. There were several openings; one had teeth, another had tusks. The smell was nauseating, and she wanted to puke.

With no warning, a tentacle entered her vagina. This was to check on the status of the young one. The creature then made a few gurgling sounds.

Skiv Lord, 'Master, I have the homan here with your child. Do you want me to kill her and extract it?'

Killmaster, 'Can my freebug free itself naturally?'

Skiv Lord, 'No Master, the exit corridor is too small.'

Killmaster, 'I have been asked to provide a homan specimen for the celebration ball tonight. Can you remove my freebug but keep her alive?'

Skiv Lord, 'I could Master, but alternatively, I could get you a nice fresh one.'

Killmaster, 'No I would like this one, I rather fancy eating the one that gave birth to my freebug, rather fitting, don't you think?'

The Skiv Lord didn't think, but he did what he was told.

Jenny felt a sharp pain in her abdomen, saw a fast-exiting flying creature and then another pain with a slight burning sensation. She didn't realise it at the time, but she had just experienced a Caesarean birth. She was the first Human to give birth to an alien and live.

She thought to herself, *I have lived to die another day, or would it be tonight?*

Location: On-board Fleet One's Flagship
Sequence of Events: 20

Admiral Bonner, 'Can you give me an update on the current position?'
Captain Mustard, 'It's getting more serious by the hour. There are riots throughout The Galactium. There are reports of nuclear explosions and numerous thefts of naval vessels. Those who can flee are fleeing.'

Admiral Bonner, 'Where are they fleeing to?'

Captain Mustard, 'Only they know.'

Admiral Bonner, 'They might be fleeing towards the aliens.'

Captain Mustard, 'This is Humanity at its worst.'

Admiral Bonner, 'Did I cause this? Did I mishandle the communication?'

Captain Mustard, 'Hard to tell. You had to say something as there were so many rumours flying around. If they knew the full truth things would be much worse.

'I've had to shut down all external communications in case the crew talk. However, we do need to talk to the crew.'

Admiral Bonner, 'What should we say?'

Captain Mustard, 'I was hoping to leave that to you.'

Admiral Bonner, 'I think the crew need to know the truth.'

Captain Mustard, 'OK, I will open a channel.'

Admiral Bonner, 'To all crew, please listen.

'You have probably heard about how bad it is back home — riots, nuclear explosions etcetera.

'The Captain and I think it essential that you know the full truth.

'As you know, about six Earth months ago, some of the outer planets were invaded by an unknown alien race.

'About 20 planets have now been invaded.

'All life has been removed from those planets. We think that all fauna and flora has been converted into food and stored in great spaceships.

'It would appear that all of the Humans have been collected as well: approximately 80 billion.

'Our task is to engage these aliens and destroy them. Many of us will likely die in the process. If we don't do anything, then probably all

Humanity will die.

'We will shortly be entering 'alien space'. Our first task is to find them.

'If you have any questions, please speak to your captains, but I can say that we don't know how many ships they have, we don't know what they look like, we don't really know what they want. It may be that they just want food. We don't know their military capabilities, but we will find out.

'I would like to take this opportunity to wish you good luck and may your gods be with you.'

Location: On-board the Albatross Flagship
Sequence of Events: 21

Admiral Millington had about 300 vessels in his Fleet. They were subdivided into six sub-Fleets. Each sub-Fleet was 50% military and 50%, civilian. The job of the military vessels was to protect the civilians.

Each sub-Fleet was slightly different but typically consisted of the following:

- Command Ship
- Battlecruiser x5
- Destroyer x10
- Fighter x20
- Laboratory Freighter x2
- Engineer's Freighter x3
- Dormitory Ship x6
- Supply Vessel x5

These vessels were designed for speed. There were no battleships or weapon platforms as these would slow the Fleet down.

The captains of each the battlecruisers, freighters and the dormitory vessels attended a regular conference with Admiral Millington. The fighters and destroyers reported to the captains of the battlecruisers.

The Fleet was configured in a diamond formation with the command Fleet (Fleet Beta One) occupying the space in the middle. This enabled central support when needed. Each sub-Fleet had its distribution pattern to optimise firing power if required.

Fleet Beta Two acted as the advance scout.

Admiral Millington, 'Ladies and gentlemen, welcome to the first Council meeting.

'The purpose of these meetings is as follows:

1. To agree on the destination route and make changes as necessary.
2. To highlight and resolve any operational issues.
3. To plan our defensive tactics if necessary.
4. To communicate with each other and possibly further down the command chain.
5. To guarantee our chance of success.

Attendance is mandatory.

Location: On-board the alien Command Ship
Sequence of Events: 22

Jenny woke up to an almighty downpour, a real gushing of fluid. Her entire naked body was being sprayed with a gelatinous fluid. It stuck to her like honey. She tried to shake it off but more covered her.

This time she was being trollied into a large assembly area, a cavernous canteen. Around her were the half-eaten bodies of Humans, some had their abdomen scraped out, some had crushed skulls, others had been skewered and braised. One or two of the local monsters had also suffered the dubious attentions of the kitchen staff.

Her trolley was parked next to one containing an exhausted looking man. He looked at her with pity in his eyes.

'Hello,' said Jenny, in the same way that she would talk to someone in a supermarket, 'What brings you here?' She couldn't help laughing at the banality of it.

'Hi, I'm Adam,' he said in a similarly banal way.

Jenny 'I'm Jenny.'

Adam, 'I guess that you're here for the feast?'

Jenny, 'Feast?'

Adam, 'Yes, it's their victory ball tonight, and we are the dessert.'

Jenny, 'How do you know that?'

Adam, 'Well you have been sprayed with honeymore, it helps them get into an eating frenzy.'

Jenny, 'You are saying that I'm going to be the pudding?'

Adam, 'Yes, and me. Well, it is a reasonably quick but messy way to go.'

Jenny, 'How have you learnt about this?'

Adam, 'One of the earlier desserts told me all about it. Apparently, the Skiverhive really enjoy eating us.'

Jenny, 'Skiverhive?'

Adam, 'We think that's what they call themselves, it doesn't translate.'

Jenny, 'At least we have a name for them.'

Jenny, 'You must have noticed that we are not tied down.'

Adam, 'That's because they don't expect us to go, we are the dessert.'

Jenny, 'Why don't we just go?

Adam, 'Where would we go?'

Jenny, 'Does it matter, at least we would not be the dessert.'

Adam, 'You haven't been nullified, have you?'

Jenny, 'Nullified?'

Adam, 'Yes, they alter your brain so that you have to follow their orders.'

Jenny, 'Well I'm going,' and she did.

Adam, 'I'm staying,' and he did.

Location: On-board the alien Command Ship
Sequence of Events: 23

Killmaster, 'Fellow Skivertons, I address you tonight as Killmaster of the Skiverhive. We have had our most successful protein-scoop ever. Both our silos and auxiliary silos are full.

We have hatched over two million new freebugs.

We have only lost two of our warriors, may they be blessed by the Grand Dementor.

There is no reason to stay in this wretched part of the universe any longer.

As you know, there is every reason to move on to meet the demands for Chemlife.

Enjoy the feast, eat and multiply.'

Killmaster, 'Skiv Lord, prepare the Fleet to move on. Empty the breeding Centre.'

Skiv Lord, 'But Killmaster there are over a million homans in the chamber. Could we not use them?'

Killmaster, 'No, the silos are full, we will have more warriors than we need, and we need to destroy the evidence in case we are comprehended by members of the Third Darwagian Congress.'

Skiv Lord, 'I understand Master. The gates to the breeding centre will be opened to space.'

Killmaster, 'Now bring me my dessert.'

Skiv Lord, 'Yes Master.'

Location: On-board Fleet One's Flagship
Sequence of Events: 24

Captain Mustard, 'Admiral, we have arrived at the designated entry point. We have sent out spacebots to investigate and found shocking results.'

Admiral Bonner, 'What have you found?'

Captain Mustard, 'Thousands of Human bodies.'

Admiral Bonner, 'What do you mean?'

Captain Mustard, 'It's hard to believe, and even harder to estimate but there are thousands of them. Possibly hundreds of thousands.'

Admiral Bonner, 'What state are they in?'

Captain Mustard, 'Do you want the gory details?'

Admiral Bonner, 'Yes.'

Captain Mustard, 'Obviously being thrown into space is not the best thing for a Human, but the scan has reported the following:

- Just under a million bodies
- Over half have exploded abdomens
- A quarter are headless
- A third have a least one limb missing
- They come from every invaded Human planet
- Some of the bodies contain undeveloped pupae.'

Admiral Bonner, 'Have we managed to get one of the pupae?'

Captain Mustard, 'I'm working on it, but my crew are pretty distressed.'

Admiral Bonner, 'Use a Special Ops Marine, they can handle it. We need to analyse that pupae. Can you plot the direction the bodies have come from?'

Captain Mustard, 'Again we are working on it. There is so much anger on-board; it's hard to control the crew.'

Admiral Bonner, 'Put me on speaker. All crew, please listen.

I know that this is the most horrific of findings. We have no idea why this has happened, but we must focus. We need to protect the living; we must engage and destroy the enemy.

'We must move forward to get revenge and save Humankind.

I have requested a clean-up team from The Galactium.

48

Please prepare yourself for battle because we will engage at the earliest opportunity.

Over and out.'

Captain Mustard, 'Thank you, Admiral, that seems to have done the trick. I will update you shortly.'

Location: On-board the Albatross Flagship
Sequence of Events: 25

The Albatross Fleet was on full alert. The drone had detected a 'signal a few million miles off. The Scout Fleet was redirected to intercept.

An analysis of the signal suggested that it was a fission drive. Further analysis indicated that it was a Galactium naval fission drive, in fact, a museum piece.

Admiral Millington, 'Please stand down, the Scout Fleet will intercept ASAP.'

The museum piece was quickly intercepted and stopped after a broad shot was fired by GNS Cutlass, one of the destroyers.

Lieutenant Hammond, 'Admiral, the ship was stolen from Fleet Reserve on Planet Mendel. What do you want me to do with the crew?'

Admiral Millington, 'Do you know the crew?'

Lieutenant Hammond, 'No Sir, they are all under twenty.'

Admiral Millington, 'What do you propose?'

Lieutenant Hammond, 'I recommend that we execute them, Sir, they may have killed to get the ship.'

Admiral Millington, 'Just let them go, we don't have time to waste. Catch us up; we will not wait for you.'

Location: On-board the alien Command Ship
Sequence of Events: 26

Jenny felt a sudden rush of air before the steel doors closed in front of her. What was happening now?

She had been kidnapped, impregnated with one of their offspring, left hanging from the ceiling and then experienced a Caesarean operation. She was amazed that there was no scar. She had been terrified by a seriously ugly alien and been prepared as a dessert for a feast. She was still trying to get the honeymore off.

What should she do now?

She thought some clothes would be useful, but that seemed to be an alien concept here. She realised that there were loads of clothes in the hatchery but how to get there?

She had no plan, no way of knowing which way to go. There were no directions, in fact, no real pattern, then Adam appeared.

Location: On-board Fleet One's Flagship
Sequence of Events: 27

Captain Mustard, 'Admiral Bonner, we have the results of the pupae analysis.'

Admiral Bonner, 'I can't wait.'

Captain Mustard, 'Well, here you are:

- We have assumed that the pupae are the infant state of the enemy, but that might not be the case as there may be more than one species.
- It looks like the pupae are placed in the Human body via one of the orifices, typically anus, vagina, or mouth.
- The pupae grow in the body cavity and exit directly through the abdomen.
- There can be multiple pupae in one Human body.
- The pupae eat the Human from the inside out attempting not to kill the host until the last moment.
- It is a carbon-based creature with an unrecognisable DNA structure, although many DNA strands are definitely Human. The analysis suggests that there was a common base structure which is hard to believe.
- It seems to be both slug and spider-like, but it is neither of these.
- We can't judge the intelligence level, but it has manipulative limbs and tentacles.
- We are obviously not sure what the adult will look like.
- We estimate that it only takes seven days to go from egg to hatchling.
- It is oxygen-breathing but seems to have a back-up system; it could live underwater.
- There is a type of blood.
- There are at least two of each organ, including two brains.

'This will surprise you, AI Central thinks it is a constructed organism.'

Admiral Bonner, 'Constructed?'

Captain Mustard, 'Yes, designed for warfare. A killer created in a laboratory.'

Admiral Bonner, 'Why does AI Central think that?'

Captain Mustard. 'There are several reasons:

- There are multiple back-up systems in the design.
- The brain isn't really big enough to support Darwinian evolution, perhaps that's why there are two.
- The breeding process suggests that they have to conquer to breed.
- Most organisms go through an evolutionary process at the embryo stage. For example, you can detect invertebrates, reptiles, early mammals etcetera in the Human embryo process. Here there is nothing, no sign of a slow evolutionary process at all.'

Admiral Bonner, 'Could we develop a chemical or biological weapon based on their DNA structure?'

Captain Mustard, 'We are working on it, but it will take some time.'

Admiral Bonner, 'Can you go over the DNA structure again, please.

Captain Mustard, 'Well you know that a banana has about 50% of its chromosomes in common with Humans. Well, here we have a 70% match.'

Admiral Bonner, 'But the finished products would appear to be totally different.'

Captain Mustard, 'That's why AI Central thinks they have been constructed.'

Admiral Bonner, 'All very odd. Now moving on, have we had any progress in finding the location of their fleet?'

Captain Mustard, 'We believe that we now know the enemy's trajectory.'

Admiral Bonner, 'Organise your pursuit.'

Captain Mustard, 'Yes, Ma'am.'

Admiral Bonner, 'Please give me your interception plan as soon as you can.'

Captain Mustard, 'Yes, Ma'am.'

Location: On-board the alien Command Ship
Sequence of Events: 28

Killmaster, 'Please give me your update.'

Skiv Lord, 'As you know, the silos are full, and we have a full contingent of warriors. The breeding centre has been emptied. I was always concerned that the expulsion of a million-odd Human bodies would help the enemy track us down.'

Killmaster, 'Why didn't you raise this point at the time?'

Skiv Lord, 'I didn't want to question your judgement, and so far, there has been no sign of any homan Fleet. The chances of them catching us are very slim.'

Killmaster, 'What is the percentage?'

Skiv Lord, 'I'm not sure.'

Killmaster, 'What is your estimate?'

Skiv Lord, 'I don't feel I have enough data to estimate.'

Killmaster, 'Do you fancy a nice trip to the biometric banks?'

Skiv Lord, 'Sorry Master, I would predict that since the emptying, the chances of the homans detecting us is 25%.'

Killmaster, 'Twenty-five percent. What defence mechanisms are in place?'

Skiv Lord, 'I'm not sure how to tell you, but our munition levels are low. You insisted on bombarding the last six planets even though we had no storage for the biomass.'

Killmaster, 'Are you criticising me?'

Skiv Lord, 'Never. Master.'

Killmaster, 'Well, what are you saying?'

Skiv Lord, 'We have full silos and a full contingency of warriors.'

Killmaster, 'I know that; what are you saying about our defensive capabilities?'

Skiv Lord, 'I'm saying that we are vulnerable to a coordinated attack by a D type race.'

Killmaster, 'D type being that they have both nuclear and fission capabilities?'

Skiv Lord, 'Yes Master.'

Killmaster, 'And you emptied the contents of the bio-dome. Is that not a flagrant abuse of your position?'

Skiv Lord, 'Yes Master.'

Killmaster, 'Call for your back-up.'

The back-up Skiv Lord is called for and arrives.

Killmaster to the back-up Skiv Lord, 'You are now the Skiv Lord, take that wretched creature away and eat him.'

Skiv Lord 2, 'Should I execute him or eat him alive?'

Killmaster, 'Eat him alive and ensure that his tribe know. In fact, you can also eat his wife.'

Skiv Lord, 'Please Master, please be merciful. I have served you well.'

Killmaster, 'Roast his children alive and have them prepared as a midnight snack for me.'

Skiv Lord 2, 'Yes, Master.'

Killmaster, 'Then bring me your defence plan.'

Skiv Lord 2, 'Yes, Master.'

Location: On-board Fleet One's Flagship
Sequence of Events: 29

Admiral Bonner, 'Do you have any more info on the pupae?'

Captain Mustard, 'Nothing really to report.

As you know the Fleet is now underway. We think that we will catch up with the aliens in six Earth days using full throttle.'

Admiral Bonner, 'I haven't heard the term 'throttle' in years, it reminds me of my father.'

Captain Mustard, 'Is he still alive?'

Admiral Bonner, 'No, he was killed in a mining accident on Planet Lister. Anyway, do you have a plan?'

Captain Mustard, 'Well it is still a bit sketchy:

1. Detect the enemy.
2. Send in a single cloaked drone to see if their systems can detect it.
3. If there is no detection send in numerous cloaked drones to ascertain their fleet size.
4. Once we have their fleet formation, we will fire most of our nuclear and fission weapons at identified targets.
5. I will then plan an all-out Fleet operation.

Admiral Bonner, 'What are your objectives?'

Captain Mustard, 'To destroy their fleet.'

Admiral Bonner, 'That's correct, but let's be a bit more subtle. We need to determine if there are any Humans on-board. We need to ascertain what their objectives were. We need to know what other dangers are out there. We need intelligence. Our world has changed; we are not alone. Do you see what I'm getting at?'

Captain Mustard, 'Sorry, you are right, none of that had dawned on me. What are your recommendations?'

Admiral Bonner, 'Stages one to three are OK. Stage 4 should be to find their command ship.'

Captain Mustard, 'And blow it up?'

Admiral Bonner, 'No the opposite, leave it intact along with the cargo ships (the big ones). Just target what appears to be our equivalent of battleships, cruisers, and destroyers, along with fighters if they have any. We need intel; we need prisoners; we want their large ships intact if we can get them.'

Location: On-board the Albatross Flagship
Sequence of Events: 30

Admiral Millington, 'Welcome to the thirty-second meeting. Have all the previous actions been completed?

Adjunct, 'Yes, Sir. all outstanding actions have been completed.'

Admiral Millington, 'Any new issues?'

There was silence in the room.

Admiral Millington, 'Any operational issues?'

Adjunct, 'No, Sir, there are no outstanding issues whatsoever.'

Admiral Millington, 'In that case give me an update on our position.'

Chief Navigator, 'Sir, we have travelled 20 million miles in the direction of T387. We are in uncharted space. We have no idea what is ahead of us. The scouting party has reduced their forward distance in case they lose us.'

Admiral Millington, 'Why is that? I thought they were simply going in a straight line ahead of us.'

Chief Navigator, 'That is not the case Sir, the Scout has to change direction to miss obstacles such as black holes, unstable systems and iron storms. Then we return to our original course.

Besides, our navigational systems are useless, as they do not recognise, the space we are in. They don't recognise anything.'

Admiral Millington, 'I assume that we are charting as we go?'

Chief Navigator, 'We are, but we are moving too fast to do a good job.'

Admiral Millington, 'Can we get back to The Galactium if we had to?'

Chief Navigator, 'At this point there is an 80% chance, but it gets smaller as we get further away. The curve of the universe may also be a factor that we don't fully understand.'

Admiral Millington, 'Could we not drop off beacons?'

Chief Navigator, 'We could Sir, but that would lead the enemy to us.'

Admiral Millington, 'Of course, that's just me being stupid.'

Chief Navigator, 'Yes, Sir.'

They all laughed.

Admiral Millington, 'How are the staff bearing up?'

Dr Shah, 'From a medical perspective, pretty well. There is the odd case that is proving a challenge. Generally, they miss friends and family back home. Could they contact them occasionally? That would certainly help.'

Admiral Millington, 'We are now way beyond our capability to communicate with The Galactium. We are on our own, 250,000 Humans in fast-moving tins flying into uncharted space.'

Chief Navigator, 'Uncharted by us. As far as we know, we might be trespassing on someone else's space.'

Admiral Millington, 'You mean their space in space!'

There was general laughter again; they were all getting used to the Admiral's little quips.

Admiral Millington, 'OK ladies and gentlemen, we just need to carry on. Dismiss.'

Location: On-board the alien Command Ship's Assembly Room
Sequence of Events: 31

Killmaster, 'What is our defence plan?'

Skiv Lord, 'Our defensive capability is under 40% of what it should be.'

Killmaster, 'Have you eaten your predecessor?'

Skiv Lord, 'Yes, Master.'

Killmaster, 'And his wife?'

Skiv Lord, 'Yes, Master.'

Killmaster, 'Well I enjoyed eating his children. It was all deserved, I've never seen such incompetence. What is your plan?'

Skiv Lord, 'Firstly I would leave a few hundred destroyers with the odd battleship as a rear-guard.'

Killmaster, 'There aren't enough munitions.'

Skiv Lord, 'They have enough to make a reasonable defence. You could put some of your title competitors in command of the battleship. Some of your wives could command the destroyers.'

Killmaster, 'But they would probably be killed?'

Skiv Lord, 'That would be terrible, my lord.'

Killmaster, 'Action that.'

Skiv Lord, 'In addition I would then leave a series of delaying booby traps.'

Killmaster, 'Excellent.'

Skiv Lord, 'Then I would have the imperial guard with further reliable squadrons attack the enemy from the rear when they think they have us cornered. This will enable the main Fleet to escape.'

Killmaster, 'Excellent, please action immediately.'

Location: On-board Fleet One's Flagship
Sequence of Events: 32

Captain Mustard, 'Admiral, I need your presence on the bridge.'

Admiral Bonner, 'Why do they still call it a bridge? It's just a set of screens with uncomfortable chairs.'

Captain Mustard, 'Yes Ma'am, but don't forget the buttons.'

Admiral Bonner was a bit grumpy, being woken up so early, 'Well what is it?'

Captain Mustard, 'They are waiting for us.'

Admiral Bonner, 'What do you mean waiting for us?'

Captain Mustard, 'They are stretched out in front of us, a line of destroyers with a few battleships. At least 250 vessels.'

Admiral Bonner, 'Have they detected us? Is the cloaking working?'

Captain Mustard, 'I would say not, but we need to test it.'

Admiral Bonner, 'Where is the rest of their fleet? How do we know that it's not in our rear?'

Captain Mustard, 'We don't know, all we can do is confront what is directly in front of us and make some contingencies in case we are attacked from other directions.'

Admiral Bonner, 'Please issue your plans.'

Captain Mustard to all commanders, 'I want the Beta and Gamma Fleets to line up against the enemy and prepare to bombard. Bring the battleships and weapon platforms forward to engage. Do not fire until I command you. Use AI Central to pick targets. Prepare fighters to resist enemy fighters.

'I want the Delta Fleet to act as a rear-guard. If there are other enemy forces out there, we must not be caught off-guard. Use drones and scouts to spread our defensive shield. If nothing is found, then prepare the battleships and weapon platforms to assist Fleets Beta and Gamma.

'The Epsilon Fleet will ignore this engagement and will continue the search for the main enemy forces. Do not engage unless there is a guaranteed chance of victory.

'The Alpha Fleet will act as a strategic reserve to plug gaps, as necessary.

May your gods be with you.'

Admiral Bonner, 'Captain, this is all yours now, we don't need two commanders. Wake me up if things are not going too well.'

Beta Commander, 'Our forces are in place.'

Captain Mustard, 'How is Gamma doing?

Beta Commander, 'Coming along, they are a lot less experienced than us.'

Captain Mustard, 'Can you support them if necessary?'

Beta Commander, 'Yes Sir, but I'm concerned that the enemy might turn Gamma's right flank.'

Captain Mustard, 'OK, I will sort it out.'

Captain Mustard to Fleet Alpha Squadrons A1 and A2. 'Please support the left flank of Beta and the right flank of Gamma.'

A positive response was received.

Captain Mustard to Special Ops, 'Send in your drones to investigate their fleet.'

A positive response was received.

Gamma Commander, 'We are in position, thank you for providing the flank protection. Did Beta suggest it?'

Captain Mustard, 'Don't worry about who suggested it. It is a sound tactic.'

Delta Commander, 'The Fleet is in place, all drones and scouts have been deployed.'

Captain Mustard, 'Thank you, Delta Commander, please interrupt me if you experience any issues. I have a nasty feeling that you may get a surprise.'

Special Ops, 'I think the drones have been detected as there are some corresponding enemy Fleet movements. I can only assume that they can see our Fleet. I can't detect any enemy fighters.'

Captain Mustard, 'Can you detect any command structure from their disposition?'

Special Ops, 'It's impossible to tell.'

Without any warning, the enemy commenced firing. There were three direct hits before AI Central could engage.

AI Central responded before the captain could order firing to commence.

The enemy was amazingly accurate; two battleships and one

weapons platform were being specifically targeted. Captain Mustard ordered them to be withdrawn and to be replaced by those from Alpha Fleet. Before the replacements could engage, the enemy hit one of the weapons platforms which were utterly destroyed in one enormous explosion. Their level of protection was weak, and in this battle, they were not much of an asset.

Captain Mustard surveyed the ongoing battle:

The enemy was better at targeting their ships. He wondered why AI Central was not more effective. That will need to be investigated later, he mused.

Beta was firing weapons much faster than Gamma, which forced the enemy to retreat on their left flank. Conversely, Gamma was being forced back although he was pleased to see his A2 squadron was holding their ground.

Captain Mustard noticed that some of the enemy's resources from the left flank were being used to bolster the right flank. They clearly were preparing to attack Gamma.

Delta Commander, 'Sir, we have picked up bogies preparing to attack our right flank.'

Captain Mustard could see that Gamma was going to be attacked from all directions.

Captain Mustard, 'To all Alpha Squadrons, prepare to support Gamma.'

Captain Mustard to Delta, 'Hold your ground, do not move.'

Captain Mustard to Beta and Gamma, 'Cease firing and launch your fighters.'

Beta Commander, 'Fighters launched, targeted AI Central fire in support.'

Captain Mustard to Gamma, 'Where are your fighters?'

There was no response.

The Gamma Flagship had been destroyed.

Captain Mustard to AI Central, 'Please engage Gamma's second in command.'

AI Central to Captain Mustard, 'The fighting had been fierce, the back-up ship has also been destroyed.'

Gamma was now being attacked from all sides. The Alpha squadrons were not yet in place. The line was not going to hold.

Captain Mustard contemplated retreat, but then three things happened:

- Beta broke the enemy's line by its aggressive use of fighters.
- Alpha arrived just in time.
- The enemy's level of fire dropped dramatically.

The enemy was in flight.

Captain Mustard's training knew that military tactics always recommended a pursuit, but he felt that his force needed to recuperate. And he had nearly lost the Gamma Fleet.

Captain Mustard to all Fleet commanders, 'Do not pursue.'

Beta Commander, 'But too many alien ships will get away.'

Captain Mustard, 'As I said before, cease the pursuit and return to cruising formation. We will then carry out a full review.'

He also knew that Epsilon was still tracking the enemy's main Fleet.

Location: On-board Fleet One's Flagship
Sequence of Events: 33

Captain Mustard was conscious that Gamma's Fleet, and deputy Fleet commanders had been killed.

The commanders of Beta and Delta with their support teams were present.

Captain Mustard, 'Well ladies and gentlemen, let's begin the debrief.

Firstly, how did they know that we were following them?'

Beta Commander, 'Did they know or was it their standard rear-guard strategy?'

Delta Commander, 'I think they knew, they probably realised that we would find the bodies and would pursue. It wasn't that difficult to find them.'

Captain Mustard, 'Are you suggesting that this was a trap?'

Delta Commander, 'I don't think so because their resources were too limited.'

Beta Commander, 'Their flank attacks were also very predictable.'

Captain Mustard, 'I don't think we reacted quickly enough, or rather *I* didn't anticipate it quickly enough.'

Beta Commander, 'We will get better given time. This is our first battle in over a thousand years.'

Captain Mustard, 'Will we be given that time?'

Beta Commander, 'Why did they start the bombardment? Does that mean that our cloaking devices do not work?'

Special Ops, 'We must assume that our cloaking devices are defective.'

Beta Commander, 'Moving on, I was very impressed by the accuracy of their targeting.'

Captain Mustard, 'What type of weapon were they using against us?'

Special Ops, 'Hard to tell, but we think it might be a concussion beam weapon. There is no radiation whatsoever.'

Captain Mustard, 'How can you have a concussion beam? Is there any viable defence?'

Special Ops, 'Fire first.' Captain Mustard tried to restrain a laugh as the quip was quite witty.

Captain Mustard, 'I don't want to depress you, but we lost eleven battleships, fourteen weapon platforms and sixteen destroyers and a few fighters to this concussion weapon.'

Beta Commander, 'But they lost at least a hundred vessels. If we pursued them, we might have got a further fifty.'

Captain Mustard, 'I accept your point, but there was a real and obvious danger that they had set a trap.'

Admiral Bonner, 'I would have pursued, we are here to destroy the enemy.'

Captain Mustard, 'Do you want my resignation?'

Admiral Bonner, 'No, I don't, I think you all did a fine job, but this is a debrief, and all options should be considered.'

Beta Commander, 'Back to my original point, is our cloaking technology fit for purpose?

Admiral Bonner, 'We have to assume that it isn't.'

Beta Commander, 'Why was our AI Central guided bombardment so ineffective?'

AI Central, 'We had a 60% success rate.'

Beta Commander, 'If it had better then our missing comrades would still be alive?'

AI Central, 'You can't blame the deaths of the Gamma commanders on me.'

Captain Mustard, 'I was wondering myself why we were so ineffective.'

Admiral Bonner, 'I think we need a full review of the AI Central targeting performance. It needs to be scientifically tested.'

Beta Commander, 'Gamma were slow to deploy. If we hadn't protected the right flank with additional resources, we would have been in trouble.'

Admiral Bonner, 'We all knew that the Gamma Fleet was weak. We probably should have mixed the squadrons up a bit more. Anyway, this battle would have hardened them up.'

Beta Commander, 'We can't afford weak links if we are going to win.'

Captain Mustard, 'Point taken. Moving on the fighters seemed to work well.'

Beta Commander, 'I should jolly well say so. Just think how much more successful we would have been if we had the Gamma fighters supporting us.'

Admiral Bonner, 'Shall I attempt to summarise?'

Captain Mustard, 'Please go ahead.'

Admiral Bonner, 'Well:

• They were waiting for us; did they know we were coming or is it their standard rear-guard practice?

• Is our cloaking technology effective?

• Their bombardment targeting was very effective, and ours was not.

• Was this an enemy trap?

• Their flanking tactics were predictable.

• Our reactions might have been too slow.

• We did not pursue.

• AI Central targeting needs to be tested.

• Do they have any fighters?

• Our fighter technology worked well.'

Captain Mustard, 'That seems to sum things up pretty well.'

Admiral Bonner, 'Well what should we do now?'

Captain Mustard, 'There are several critical issues that require decisions:

• Should we recall the Epsilon Fleet?

• Should we keep Gamma as a fighting unit or amalgamate it with the other Fleets?

• If we keep it going, then we need new commanders.

• Do we continue our pursuit, or do we return to protect our people?'

Admiral Bonner, 'We have no choice but to engage and destroy the enemy. That is our brief. We need to catch up with the Epsilon Fleet. Gamma needs to be maintained under the command of Beta's Number 2.

My decisions have been made.'

Beta Commander, 'Just as a matter of interest, the debrief took longer than the battle.'

Location: On-board the alien Command Ship
Sequence of Events: 34

Killmaster, 'Give me an update.'

Skiv Lord, 'Well, as expected, the enemy was pursuing us, and also as expected our rear-guard was defeated. Sadly, some prominent members of the Council, including two of your wives, were killed. My commiserations to you, my Lordship.

We have assessed the battle as follows:

1. They were surprised that we were waiting for them.
2. They seem to think that their primitive cloaking technology works.
3. Their bombardment skills were poor which surprised us.
4. We suspect that they think we have set a trap. Otherwise, they would have pursued us.
5. Our flanking tactics worked brilliantly; we knocked out some of their battleships with their senior commanders on-board.
6. Their reactions were slow. Clearly, they are not battle-hardened.
7. There was no pursuit which is a failure to carry out basic battlefield tactics.
8. They may be using AI technology, but our anti-AI beam may have downgraded their performance.
9. Worryingly, they have some tiny battle craft.

Killmaster, 'What are these small warships?'

Skiv Lord, 'It would appear that they have small, one or two-person vehicles that punch real power. It is hard for our technology to detect them.'

Killmaster, 'What is the current position?'

Skiv Lord, 'Their main Fleet is still in pursuit, with a smaller group in advance.'

Killmaster, 'What is your plan?'

Skiv Lord, 'Originally I was going to set some traps, but things have changed. We will now destroy their advance group using maximum force.'

Killmaster, 'When will you do this?

Skiv Lord, 'NOW!'

Location: On-board Fleet One's Flagship
Sequence of Events: 35

Captain Mustard, 'Epsilon Fleet what is your current position?'

Epsilon Fleet Commander, 'We are half a million miles ahead of you. At your current speed, you should catch us up in two Earth days. Do you want us to slow down?'

Captain Mustard, 'Have you contacted the enemy?'

Epsilon Fleet Commander, 'There is no sign of the enemy whatsoever, which is a bit strange. They must be a lot faster than us.'

The communication was suddenly broken off. The entire their fleet, minus the Killmaster's Command Ship and the storage vessels, simultaneously attacked Epsilon Fleet. They were outnumbered 20 to 1.

Epsilon Fleet Commander to Comms. 'Re-establish contact with the Flagship and update them.'

Epsilon Fleet Commander to all ship commanders, 'Launch all fighters. Protect the battleships.'

The twenty weapon platforms were systematically destroyed: they had no real defence.

In the first few minutes, half of the battleships were destroyed. The incoming bombardment was relentless. It came from all directions. Protective screens were just shot apart.

Epsilon Fleet Commander to all vessels, 'Follow the Command Ship.' This became impossible as it suddenly exploded when a dozen nuclear missiles hit it.

Epsilon Fleet Deputy Commander, 'Flee for your lives!'

The command structure collapsed utterly. The remaining vessels fled back towards the main Fleet pursued by the alien fleet. Further battleships and many of the destroyers were eliminated on the way.

AI Central to Captain Mustard, 'A large Fleet has been detected coming our way.'

Captain Mustard to all commanders, 'Battle stations, battle stations. Deploy defensive plan A6. Arm all weapons. Prepare targeting systems.' Alarms were ringing throughout the Fleet.

Captain Mustard to AI Central, 'What do your systems detect?'

AI Central, 'It looks like the remains of our Fleet are being pursued by alien vessels.'

Captain Mustard, 'How many aliens?'

AI Central, 'About 1,500 vessels.'

Captain Mustard, '1,500?' he questioned.

AI Central, 'At least that.'

Captain Mustard, 'What about our Fleet?'

AI Central, 'Half a dozen battleships are being outgunned. The destroyers and fighters are just fleeing. Are they attempting to defend the battleships?'

AI Central, 'It doesn't look like it.'

Captain Mustard to all commanders, 'Launch all fighters to attack the aliens. Destroyers to provide a protective screen. Weapon Platforms to go to the rear.'

Over 450 fighters were unleashed.

The alien vessels had no practical defence against the fighters. Each fighter effectively destroyed at least one of their capital ships: 400 odd vessels. The fighters had to return to re-arm. Captain Mustard regretted not phasing the fighter attacks as the screen of destroyers were taking a bit of a pasting.

The Epsilon fighters also arrived for re-arming, which was quickly and efficiently achieved. The engineering function had been practising almost every day to achieve faster and faster turnarounds. That practice had certainly paid off.

Captain Mustard to all fighter pilots, 'Your orders are as follows, Epsilon fighters to defend your Fleet vessels now. Remaining even-numbered fighters to attack the alien vessels now. Re-arm as soon as possible. Odd-numbered fighters to attack aliens when the even-numbered fighters disengage. Continue this pattern until the battle ends. There is no choice we must bring the fight to them.'

Captain Mustard to Fleet, 'Battleships will retreat, destroyers to maintain screen.'

The alien fleet was now suffering severe damage. The aliens had no answer to the fighters. Their systems were too slow to target them. Besides, the alien fleet was in an attack formation, so their full defensive capabilities were not available to them. Without warning, the alien fleet turned and fled.

Captain Mustard was conscious that he was criticised for not pursuing the aliens after their last engagement. But he had lost a whole Fleet; his fighters did not have the range to pursue, his battleships could pursue, but they would still be seriously outnumbered.

Captain Mustard recalled the Fleet.

Location: On-board Fleet One's Flagship
Sequence of Events: 36

Captain Mustard, 'This is our second debrief in two days!

'Let's review our Fleet position:

- Alpha Fleet is almost intact, losing one battleship, total loss 25 vessels
- Beta Fleet has lost more vessels, including three battleships and three weapon platforms, total loss 60 vessels
- Gamma Fleet is about 50% of its strength and is under new command having lost eleven battleships and weapon platforms, a total loss of 102 vessels
- Delta Fleet is almost intact having lost only two battleships, a total loss of 51 vessels
- Epsilon Fleet has virtually been eliminated; there are only 85 vessels left, no weapon platforms and only two battleships

In total, we have lost 35% of our fighting capability and two of our senior commanders.'

Beta Commander, 'What about the enemy?'

Captain Mustard, 'From what we can tell, they have lost over 50% of their fleet, but at a high cost to us.'

Admiral Bonner, 'I must point out that we are achieving our set objectives.'

Captain Mustard, 'Is it time for us to review those objectives?'

Admiral Bonner, 'No, we have our orders.'

Captain Mustard, 'In that case let's start the debrief. The Epsilon Fleet was pursuing the enemy when they were attacked. The attack was totally unexpected and undetected. Clearly, our cloaking devices do not work and should be disengaged. The Epsilon Fleet was completely over-whelmed, at least 20 to 1. The weapon platforms were eliminated immediately, followed by most of the battleships. There was a complete failure in command. The crew were directed to save themselves.

'The aliens pursued the Epsilon Fleet until our main Fleet was engaged. Our fighters effectively destroyed half their fleet and forced them to flee.'

Admiral Bonner, 'Can I do my normal job and highlight the lessons learnt?'

Captain Mustard, 'Of course.'

Admiral Bonner, 'Lessons learnt:

1. The Weapons Platforms should be decommissioned.

2. The role of the battleships should be long-range bombardment and fighter support. They should be converted into the old fashioned 'aircraft carriers' we used to have in the early ocean navies.

3. The destroyers are not agile enough and should be replaced by smaller, faster frigates.

4. Fighters need to be our weapon of choice.

5. The structured use of fighters as organised by Captain Mustard was overwhelmingly successful.

6. The command structure needs to be automatically reallocated when capital ships are destroyed.

7. Should there be a fighter commander?

'Captain Mustard asked if we should review our tactics. Twice we have engaged the enemy. Twice we have won, but our limited resources are being systematically reduced. The next engagement will reduce our fighting power to less than 50%.

'So far, we have not found their Command Ship nor their supply vessels.'

Location: On-board the alien Command Ship
Sequence of Events: 37

Killmaster, 'Give me an update.'

Skiv Lord, 'The confrontation was very successful; most of our objectives were achieved. Their advance Fleet was totally destroyed.'

Killmaster, 'I hear that we lost 50% of our Fleet.'

Skiv Lord, 'There was more collateral damage than we planned. Some of our assets are still returning.'

Killmaster, 'Do you remember what happened to your predecessor?'

Skiv Lord, 'I can't be blamed for the success of their fighters. They are the problem; we can't detect them. We have no defence against them.'

Killmaster, 'Can we get our hands on one?'

Skiv Lord, 'I will make it a priority.'

Location: On-board the Albatross Flagship
Sequence of Events: 38

Admiral Millington was concerned as his crew were suffering from acute boredom. Just nothing was happening. He had organised numerous exercises but not at the expense of speed.

He wondered what was happening with the First Fleet. Did it still exist? Was his planet still there? Were his parents still alive?'

Adjunct, 'Sir, the conference is ready to start.'

Admiral Millington, 'Ladies and Gentlemen, welcome to the forty-seventh meeting. Have all the previous actions been completed?'

Adjunct, 'Yes, Sir, all outstanding actions have been completed.'

Admiral Millington, 'Any new issues?'

There was silence in the room, as usual.

Admiral Millington, 'Any operational issues?'

Adjunct, 'No, Sir, there are no outstanding issues whatsoever.'

Admiral Millington, 'In that case give me an update on our position.'

Chief Navigator, 'Sir, we have travelled 32 million miles in the direction of T387. There have been no anomalies. Could I ask what we are searching for?'

Admiral Millington admitted to himself that he had also been giving that some thought. They were looking for a new, secure home away from the enemy, but what did that actually mean?

Admiral Millington, 'I can now inform you that I have secret orders to open when we have been travelling for a year.'

Chief Navigator, 'Then we have about three Earth months to go.'

Admiral Millington was lying, but he thought it a good wheeze. It would keep the crew going.

Admiral Millington, 'Before we open the orders, I would like the following tasks to be completed:

1. Identify what skills we are missing that will be needed in our future life
2. Produce plans for a new city on an Earth-like planet
3. Produce a procreation plan
4. Set-up a civilian government structure
5. Start the design for a new range of naval warships

6. Start the design for a new range of weapons to defend our new home.'

Dr Shah, 'Sir, should we not build our new home based on love. Should we not be the beacon for a modern brighter civilisation?'

Admiral Millington, 'I would be the first to welcome that, but we now know that we are not alone. At this very moment, there are probably Humans experiencing an agonising death from barbaric aliens. As far as we know, Human civilisation has reached an endpoint, we might be Humanity's only hope.'

Dr Shah, 'That is always the cry of a warmonger!'

Admiral Millington, 'I strongly object to that, I have a quarter of a million souls to protect. We must save our civilisation.'

Dr Shah, 'There are so many reasons why you are wrong, God has decided that Humanity should end, and we should accept it.'

Admiral Millington, 'Dr Shah, please see me in my cabin after this meeting.'

Admiral Millington to Adjunct,' Are there any other issues?'

Adjunct, 'No, Sir.'

Admiral Millington, 'Then the meeting is over.'

Admiral Millington was annoyed, what should he do about Dr Shah? He had no problem with his crew practising ancient religions, but he could not tolerate any negativity that could damage the success of this mission.

Location: On-board alien Command Ship's Storage Area
Sequence of Events: 39

Jenny, 'You were the last person I expected to see. I thought you were looking forward to being a dessert.'

Adam, 'Do you mean deserter?'

Jenny, 'Very funny, but what happened?'

Adam, 'I was trollied into the canteen area or whatever they call it. It was ghastly: Humans were being consumed in every way you can imagine. Some were hanging on hooks; others had been decapitated, one alien was using Human intestines as a skipping rope. Blood, guts, and slime were just sloshing around. There was a Human dartboard. It was just a hideous orgy of gore. I puked like I never puked before.'

Jenny, 'I think that's given me a fair picture, but how come you are here?'

Adam, 'Well, I remembered that you just got up and walked out. Despite my nullification, I thought I would try it. I got up, walked out, and here I am.'

Jenny, 'Where are we exactly?'

Adam, 'No idea.'

Adam couldn't help admiring Jenny's charms. A fine pair of legs, an ample bosom and nothing was covering her lady-bits. He felt something moving in his trousers. He was amazed by how sex reared its head in the most unusual of circumstances. He contemplated giving Jenny his T-shirt, but he was enjoying the view of her naked breasts too much. Anyway, it was hardly cold in the alien ship.

He was also amazed that most of the time, they were ignored. alien troops, guards and admin staff just walked by or rather wobbled by. No one took any notice of them, but then they were just food.

Jenny, 'What is our plan?'

Adam, 'Well in the movies, the hero commandeers an alien craft and simply flies off. I'm not really the Star Wars type, I never even got a driving licence.'

Jenny, 'Should we get a weapon?'

Adam, 'Why, we are being ignored.'

Jenny, 'I wouldn't mind some clothes.' She had spotted Adam

looking at her, or rather staring at her boobs and fanny. Not that she minded that, as she could do with some relief herself. Then she thought at least it would be a nice change from a tentacle. In her mind, she started listing the things that had happened to her again but quickly gave up. She needed to be in the 'now'.

Adam reluctantly offered her his T-shirt.

Jenny thanked Adam, at least it covered her breasts, but down below was still fully exposed.

Jenny, 'We need some sort of plan, we need food, water and a way of getting out of here.'

Adam. 'Water is not a problem but the only food available is us: Humans. I can't see how we can escape; we are shooting through space towards an unknown destination.'

A tear ran down Jenny's face.

Jenny, 'There must be something we can do.'

Adam, 'Well let's head in that direction, I thought I heard some Human voices.'

Location: On-board Fleet One's Flagship
Sequence of Events: 40

Captain Mustard had his list of tasks for the day.

Captain Mustard to Captains of the Weapons Platforms, 'You have fought bravely, but the platform technology is ineffective against this type of enemy. I want you to select a skeleton crew and send those vessels back home. I want you to stay as we need experienced officers.

'Captain Wallett has been allocated to command the return Fleet, one battleship and five destroyers will be earmarked as support. That is all I can spare.

'There was no resistance from the captains as they realised that the weapon platforms were death traps. It was not fair on their crews.'

Captain Mustard to Engineering, 'Have you completed the modifications to the battleships so that they can hold more fighters?'

Engineering, 'Yes, Sir, the alterations have all been made.'

Captain Mustard to Special Ops, 'Have you tested the special ordnance weapons?'

Special Ops, ''Yes, Sir, with mixed results.'

Captain Mustard, 'Please give me your analysis.'

Special Ops, 'Well we were allocated the following weapons:
• Proton Beams
• Stud gun
• Atomiser
• Black Mesh
• Glue bomb
• Chemical weapons
• Advanced Acid Spray

'I will go through them one at a time.

'Firstly, we know that the enemy use concussion beams. Our Proton beam works in a similar way. It needs line of sight. You need a resilient and powerful fuel source to power it. The beam simply cuts a vessel in half, a bit like Luke Skywalker's light sabre.'

Captain Mustard, 'Can we install this technology on our ships?'

Special Ops, 'The answer is yes, but we only have three prototypes.'

Captain Mustard, 'What about the stud Gun?'

Special Ops, 'Technically it's very old technology. Here you simply fire a 'bullet' at super speed at the enemy.'

Captain Mustard, 'Did you say 'bullet'?'

Special Ops, 'Yes but here a bullet could be any projectile: a lump of metal, a carrier bag, a Human body. It is the energy generated by the speed of the projectile that does the damage. It simply rips the target apart. The great advantage is that anything could be used as a projectile.'

Captain Mustard, 'Could we implement this?'

Special Ops, 'Not really, the vessel has to be designed to utilise this technology. It's also very power-hungry.'

Captain Mustard, 'Sounds like a future technology?'

Special Ops, 'You are right, but the next technology is much more viable. As you know, everything is composed of atoms, but in reality, there is more space than material in an atom. The atomiser shrinks the space between atoms.'

Captain Mustard, 'How does it work?'

Special Ops, 'No idea, and the results are unpredictable. Sometimes the target explodes, sometimes it shrinks. In one test, the target just disappeared.'

Captain Mustard, 'Can it be deployed?'

Special Ops, 'Yes as soon as you give the word.'

Captain Mustard, 'You have the word. It's hard to believe that we had all of these new technologies waiting to be used.'

Special Ops, 'Some of these technologies are a few hundred years old. As there was no war, there was no need for them. Consequently, they were never fully developed.

'The Black Mesh is a case in point. It is a powerful force field that absorbs energy. It has no visible spectrum, that's why it is called black.'

Captain Mustard, 'How does the mesh work?'

Special Ops, 'You need a vessel at each end, once switched on the mesh forms between the two points.

Captain Mustard, 'How do you define the size?'

Special ops, 'Each vessel has a mesh grid that can be extended to suit.'

Captain Mustard, 'What does that mean?'

Special Ops. 'Attached to each vessel is a telescopic pole that can be extended to define the size of the mesh.'

Captain Mustard, 'So really, it's a giant net with expandable prongs.'

Special Ops, 'Absolutely.'

Captain Mustard, 'Is it practical?'

Special Ops, 'I believe so, we are installing it on four special operations craft at this very moment.'

Captain Mustard, 'How can a glue bomb be of any use?'

Special Ops, 'That was our first reaction, but tests have proved it to be very effective. The glue bomb once deployed provides an inescapable layer of glue around the target. All entrances and exits are sealed shut. This makes it almost impossible for the target vessel to deploy weapons.'

Captain Mustard, 'Is it deployable?'

Special Ops, 'Yes, but we need to manufacture some units. The good news is that we do have the engineering capability to do it.'

Captain Mustard, 'What about the chemical weapons?'

Special Ops, 'This is extremely frightening.'

Captain Mustard, 'I detect genuine fear in your voice.'

Special Ops, 'I know that my job is to kill, but this technology is very worrying. It was originally labelled beyond top secret.'

Captain Mustard, 'What does it do?'

Special Ops, 'It's a black-box technology. You enter a DNA sample, and the system generates a poison to kill anyone or thing with that DNA. It can be aimed at an individual or a complete species. It could, for example, destroy Humanity.'

Captain Mustard, 'How is it deployed?'

Special Ops, 'By touch, the victim has to touch the poison. However, if a member of the same species touches the victim, then they will also be poisoned. Large populations could be wiped out very quickly.'

Captain Mustard, 'You are obviously against using this.'

Special Ops, 'That's not correct. I would happily generate a poison for the enemy, but then I would like to destroy the technology so it can't be used again.'

Captain Mustard, 'I see where you are coming from, it makes your flesh creep. What about the acid spray?'

Special Ops, 'We can't find a practical way of deploying it.'

Captain Mustard, 'Can we summarise?'

Special Ops, 'Of course:

1. The three proton weapons will be installed in three battleships of your choice
2. The atomiser will be installed on every vessel
3. The black mesh technology is being installed on four special operations craft
4. Glue bombs are being produced, but further resource is required
5. We will develop a Chemical weapon to target the enemy.'

Captain Mustard, 'Excellent stuff.'

Captain Mustard felt that he had earned a whiskey.

Location: On-board the Albatross Flagship
Sequence of Events: 41

Chief Navigator to Admiral Millington, 'Please come to the Bridge.'

Admiral Millington, 'You sound worried?'

Chief Navigator, 'Not worried but concerned, mystified'.

Admiral Millington, 'I'm on my way'.'

Admiral Millington entered the bridge. In the past, there would have been a whistle, and someone would say 'Admiral on-board'. Nowadays he was largely ignored, the crew have their duties and just carried on. He wasn't too sure if this was just him or it was just the way things were done now.

Admiral Millington, 'Well?'

Chief Navigator, 'Look at the screen.'

On the screen was an image of an enormous ship, a ship the size of a small planet. Gavin had seen this episode on Star Trek, but this was real. The crew were already calling it, 'The Ark'.

Looking closer, he could see that the vessel was supported by about thirty smaller craft, every one of them larger than any of his ships.

Admiral Millington, 'What sort of analysis have you carried out?'

Chief Navigator, 'They are oxygen breathers, they have nuclear and fission weapons, the ark is over 1,000 years old, I expect that they are using the same visual spectrum as us, their dimensions are ...'

Admiral Millington interrupted, 'Have they tried to contact us?'

Chief Navigator, 'Yes and no, we have been scanned, or it might have been a communication.'

Admiral Millington, 'How come we are now meeting our second race? Six months ago, we were on our own.'

Chief Navigator, 'I've been giving that some thought. There is a possibility that no one wanted our space. It may be that we have been insular: when was the last great exploration?

Admiral Millington, 'Well we have an abundance of planets, we had a huge area of our own to explore.'

Chief Navigator, 'Fair enough, but it doesn't really explain our lack of desire to conquer space. Was it a lack in Central Government? Or was it a lack of funding?'

Alarms started ringing.

Admiral Millington to Fleet, 'Action stations, action stations.'

Chief Navigator, 'Don't arm the weapons. I believe that it was just another communication scan.'

Admiral Millington, 'How do you know?'

Chief Navigator, 'I don't.'

Comms Control, 'We have managed to translate a message from 'The Ark'… it's a bit garbled as AI Central is still trying to decipher their language.

Admiral Millington, 'What does it say?'

Comms control, 'I will display the message on the screen.'

US COME FROM WAY, NO DANGER TO THEM, IT PLEASES YOU TO SEE THEM. WE FLEE, MUCH HASTE, NO STOPPING. MORE DANGER TO COME. US WISH YOU SUCCESS.

Admiral Millington, to AI Central, 'What do you make of it?'

AI Central, 'I have concluded that they are neuters.'

Admiral Millington, 'Neuters?'

AI Central, 'They do not have male or female gender. Why do Humans always expect two genders?'

Admiral Millington, 'Can you convert for us?'

AI Central, 'Yes.'

WE COME FROM FAR AWAY. WE COME IN PEACE, WE ARE FLEEING FROM A GREAT DANGER.

Admiral Millington, 'What do they mean by great danger?'

AI Central, 'I have no idea.'

Admiral Millington, 'Do we have a way of contacting them to find out?'

AI Central, 'I can try.' Then a new message was received.

DEATH, DEATH, DEATH AHEAD, MORE DEATH, LAST CHANCE FLEE

BEWARE THE BRAKENDETH.

Admiral Millington, 'What is a Brakendeth?'

AI Central, 'I will make contact again.'

Chief Navigator, 'We will be out of contact soon.'

AI Central, 'New message received.'

THE BRAKENDETH COME, NO HOPE, FLEE

Chief Navigator, 'We have lost contact.'

Admiral Millington, 'Where is 'The Ark' heading?'

Chief Navigator, 'To human space, Sir.'

Admiral Millington called a meeting of the Council.

Location: On-board the alien Command Ship
Sequence of Events: 42

Jenny, 'Are you sure you heard Human voices?'

Adam, 'Pretty sure.'

They continued along a twisted dirty corridor with lots of side corridors, lifts, conveyor belts, and wells. There seemed to be little real structure, certainly no labelling. They climbed a ladder. Adam could not help admiring Jenny's charms. They then turned a bend and found what appeared to be a large laboratory.

Once again there were numerous Humans on racks, some dead, some alive although they all looked drugged. Some were on laboratory tables; many had been dissected. Their skin was spread out like that of laboratory rats. Organs had been removed; blood had been stored.

The aliens were working feverishly. Why, what were they trying to achieve? Before they had been ignored, but now the aliens were watching them. What was making them different? Jenny realised that they were dressed; every Human in the laboratory was naked.

Jenny shouted to Adam to strip.

'At last,' he jokingly said. She quickly removed her T-Shirt, exposing her breasts once again. It dawned on Adam that Jenny was right, and he quickly removed his clothes. They suddenly became invisible, except for Adam's erect penis which was now a cause for embarrassment. Jenny looked at Adam in such a way that only women can do. Adam looked back and said, 'It's not my fault.'

Jenny asked, 'Whose fault was it then?'

As they continued, they found several animal pens where live Humans were being experimented on. Some were cabled into machines; some had their brains exposed, others were being force-fed, some were mating. The aliens were clearly carrying out detailed experiments.

The scale of it was immense. There must have been at least 20,000 Humans in the laboratory, perhaps a lot more. As they moved on, they found more worrying examples. Human body parts had been grafted onto the aliens. One alien had a Human head; another had two.

As they walked on, they saw a young girl on a treadmill. She had the usual drugged look. When she finished, the nearest alien bit her head off, put his tentacle into her throat cavity and wrenched out her still-beating heart. Adam almost went to intervene, but what was the point?

Giant screens showed the view from Human eyes. The eyes were on a frame with the optic nerve dangling below still connected to a young boy. Nearby was a mouth and nose having similar treatment.

As they walked on, they came to something truly terrible. It was a gestation display.

It showed the development of a Human from egg to birth with full graphic detail. It showed the embryo's daily growth using actual babies. *They were dissecting Humankind's history. They probably know more about us than we do,* Jenny thought in horror. *How many babies died to make this display?*

Both Jenny and Adam vomited, there was no choice. A visceral reaction was the only thing possible.

Jenny, 'This whole laboratory must be destroyed, this ship must be destroyed. This alien race must be destroyed.'

Adam noticed that he had lost his erection.

Jenny, 'I'm not sure that I can carry on much further without a sleep.'

Adam, 'I'm deadbeat as well. We need to find somewhere safe.'

Jenny, 'How about one of those animal pens. At least the flooring looks dry.'

They cuddled up; they both needed a Human touch. Adam cuddled her breasts from behind. Jenny wiggled her bum, and Adam gently entered her. Life was blissful, at least in their dreams.

Location: On-board Fleet One's Flagship
Sequence of Events: 43

Captain Mustard, 'Ladies and Gentlemen during our last meeting, we identified the following issues:
- That the Weapons Platforms should be decommissioned.
- That the role of the battleships should be long-range bombardment and fighter support. They should be converted into old fashioned 'aircraft carriers'
- That the destroyers are not agile enough and should be replaced by smaller, faster frigates
- That fighters need to be our weapon of choice
- That the structured use of fighters as organised in the last battle was overwhelmingly successful
- That the command structure needs to be automatically reassigned when capital ships are destroyed.
- Should there be a fighter commander?

'I need to give you an update, and then we need to start the planning of our next attack.

'Firstly, the Weapons Platforms have been sent home under escort. This means that we only have 561 active vessels, of which 278 are fighters.'

Beta Commander, 'How many battleships do we still have?'

Captain Mustard, 'Only 64 that are fully operational.

'The commanders of the platforms have been retained to fill gaps in our command structure. There is not much I can do about the other points at this stage, except that the battleships are now carrying more fighters.

'I also need to update you with our new weapon capabilities.
- We have installed proton weapons on three of the battleships in my squadron
- An atomiser has been installed on every vessel
- Black mesh technology has been installed on four special operations craft
- About 50 Glue bombs have been produced
- We have developed a chemical weapon that targets the enemy's DNA.'

There was an immediate reaction and lots of questions.

Captain Mustard, 'Yes, I know that you need more info, this is why I've called this meeting.

'Demonstrations of the new technology have been organised for tomorrow morning.

'I don't want to go into detailed planning until you have learnt about our new capabilities, but the future strategy needs to be much more 'Cloak and Dagger'.'

Delta Commander, 'I thought we agreed that our cloaking technology was not working.'

Captain Mustard,' Very clever. Our objective is to capture their Command Ship and Storage vessels.'

Beta Commander, 'How do we find them?'

Captain Mustard, 'Any suggestions?''

Special Ops, 'We could use the fighters in a grid pattern to search for them.'

Delta Commander, 'We could track their main Fleet and try and identify any vessels going to the supply ships.'

Beta Commander, 'Has there been any comms traffic?'

Captain Mustard to Fleet Operations, 'Have we tracked any alien comms?'

Fleet Operations, 'Yes, there is considerable activity.'

Captain Mustard, 'Why was I not informed earlier?'

Fleet Operations, 'There is so much that there didn't seem much point in letting you know.'

Captain Mustard, 'I'm sending the Special Ops Commander to see you right now. We need to identify specific communication hubs.'

Fleet Operations, 'Yes, Sir.'

Captain Mustard, 'I can't believe that!'

Beta Commander, 'Sometimes you have to ask the simple questions.'

Captain Mustard. 'Once we have located those vessels, I plan to knock them out with the proton cannons and atomisers; they won't be expecting that. Then I plan to use black mesh to encircle them.

Special Ops, 'We can only use straight lines.'

Captain Mustard, 'Can we create a box effect?'

Special Ops, 'Yes.'

Captain Mustard, 'Then we will use our Marines to invade the ships.' We need to capture their leaders for interrogation and ensure that there are no Human survivors on-board.'

Beta Commander, 'Can I ask what you plan to do with their leaders?'

Admiral Bonner, 'They will be taken back to Earth for trial.'

Beta Commander, 'They should be tortured and executed.'

Admiral Bonner, 'I understand your anger, but we need intel. I need to make myself clear. We need the leaders alive.'

Captain Mustard, 'Aren't we jumping the gun a bit, we haven't even found the vessels yet!'

Special Ops, 'Good news Sir, we think we have identified their location based on comms traffic.'

Captain Mustard, 'Could it be a trap?'

Special Ops, 'Possibly, but their comms traffic does not seem to be protected at all. There doesn't seem to be any encryption. It's wide open; AI Central is working on the language now.'

Captain Mustard, 'Can we go and check it out?'

Special Ops, 'It will probably take a fighter about two days.'

Captain Mustard, 'It must not be detected.'

Special Ops, 'They don't seem to have the technology to detect craft that small.'

Beta Commander, 'While that is going on, what do you want the rest of the Fleet to do?'

Captain Mustard, 'The detailed planning session will come later, but I'm hoping that we stage an all-out fight as a diversion. However, I want to minimise the loss of Fleet assets. Accordingly, there may be a series of strategic retreats.

'In the short term, I need you to do the following:
- Find the command vessel undetected
- Attend the new weapon demonstrations
- Teach your crew how to use the new weapons
- Test run the black mesh as a square
- Check alien comms traffic to confirm their location
- AI Central to check results to identify the possibility of a trap
- Plan for an all-out dummy attack
- Prepare the space marines

• Consider how and where we will keep any prisoners
'I think you know who is responsible for each action.
'We will meet again after the special ops fighter returns.
'Thank you.'

Location: The Galactium Council Offices, Planet Earth
Sequence of Events: 44

President Padfield, 'Ladies and Gentlemen, welcome to the first meeting of The Galactium Central Council since the alien invasion.

'As you know the Central Council consists of one representative from each Galactium planet. There should be 1020 representatives, but only 993 are present today. I would like you to join me in two minutes' silence for the 21 worlds that have been destroyed by the aliens. I also need to inform you that another six of our planets are currently under attack. More significant memorial services will be undertaken when the aliens have been defeated.'

Two minutes' silence was kept. There were a few tears in the audience.

President Padfield, 'Ladies and gentlemen, as you know, I have been tasked with creating the Third Fleet. I aim to create this Fleet no matter what it takes.

'I also need to point out that this conference has the highest security classification. If you break protocols, I have the power to order your execution. All military forces in The Galactium report to me. We have our own security and intelligence operations. AI Central reports to me.

'I stress that my only aim is to create a new Fleet. I plan to step down when that is achieved.

'The current position is that we have 60 military vessels to protect nearly 1,000 planets. In the past, it did not matter as there were 'no' aliens.' So far, we have only encountered one aggressive alien species, but there is no doubt that there will be others.

'I've put together a detailed plan, and there can be no arguments. A copy of the plan has just been sent to you, but I can summarise as follows:
- Each planet will fund one battleship, five battlecruisers, ten destroyers, 20 frigates and 100 fighters
- Each planet will train a force of 100,000 marines
- Each planet will fund a local defence grid
- Each planet will create a military hospital unit
- The above forces will be at the disposal of the Central Command
- Each planet's defence grid will be interlinked with all other grids

where technically possible
- Each planet will fund the ongoing costs of the vessels and manning levels detailed above
- Each Planetary Councillor will sign a declaration that the needs of The Galactium are higher than the needs of their individual planet
- Central Command will create a powerful naval force to protect the citizens of The Galactium. They MUST come to the defence of individual planets
- Central Command will develop a network of monitoring stations throughout our space
- Central Command will patrol our Space

Your Fleet commitments must be completed in one Earth Year.

'If you fail to deliver, your planet will be overtaken by Central-Core Troops. We are not playing; the stakes are the survival of Humanity.

Thank you'

There was an uproar.

President Padfield ordered his elite presidential guards to enter the auditorium.

President Padfield, 'Ladies and gentlemen, you will have noticed that my presidential guard has entered the building. They are not here to intimidate you but to emphasise that we do not have the time to argue. My conditions are final.

'To emphasise my point, I will show you some film footage:
- These are the smoking remains of Planet Darwin
- This is the glassed spaceport on Planet Newton
- This is what has happened to the tourist sites on Planet Joule; it is now one grey, stone ball
- These are the sickening Human remains on Planet Curie
- This video shows the fighting that is still going on

'We have no defences; we are leaving those planets to defend themselves.'

Someone shouted out, 'Send in the Fleet.'

President Padfield replied, 'That the only Fleet available consists of 60 outdated vessels, only one of which is a battleship. In reality, it is just about fit enough to be in a museum.

'It is up to you to comply with my demands. Thank you for your support.'

Location: On-board the Albatross Flagship
Sequence of Events: 45

Admiral Millington, 'Ladies and gentlemen, I've called the Council together to discuss our chance meeting with 'The Ark'.'

As you know, we received the following messages:

WE COME FROM FAR AWAY. WE COME IN PEACE, WE ARE FLEEING FROM A GREAT DANGER.

and

DEATH, DEATH, DEATH AHEAD, MORE DEATH, LAST CHANCE FLEE

BEWARE THE BRAKENDETH.

Admiral Millington, 'I think it raises the following issues:

1. Who are The Brakendeth?

2. Are they a real threat?

3. Are they heading towards our civilisation?

4. If yes, do we return?

5. If we continue, will we encounter The Brakendeth?

Are there any observations or comments?'

Head of Science, 'It would appear that 'The Ark' civilisation was genuinely frightened of The Brakendeth.'

Alpha 2 Fleet Commander, 'Perhaps 'The Ark' inhabitants are not fighters?'

Chief Navigator, 'They have both nuclear and fission weapons.'

Alpha 2 Fleet Commander, 'That doesn't make them brave.'

Admiral Millington, 'I think we have to assume that they had viable weapons, but they were concerned that they would not work against the Deth people. They were genuinely frightened.'

Head of Engineering, 'It must have taken them some time to build a vessel that large.'

Head of Science, 'That suggests that they had ample warning, or they created an ark in case there was an emergency.'

Head of Engineering, 'The sheer cost of it couldn't justify building it just for emergencies. It suggests to me that the Deth lot are a known force, and the best thing to do is to get out of their way.'

Admiral Millington, 'If that is the case, should we return to The

Galactium and warn them?'

AI Central, 'I must inform you that we have strict instructions to continue, no matter what the reason.'

Admiral Millington, 'OK, I know that we have our orders, but we must consider the need to warn our people back home.'

Beta 2 Fleet Commander, 'What do we tell them? 'Beware of The Brakendeth'? It sounds like a children's ghost story.'

Head of Science, 'Or even Halloween.'

Admiral Millington, 'Do we send part of the Fleet back, or just one vessel?'

A Fleet Commander, 'A single Destroyer would make sense.'

Admiral Millington to AI Central, 'Any objections?'

AI Central, 'No, but we must ensure that there is no record of our journey so that we can't be tracked.'

Head of Science, 'When the Ark hits Galactium space they will tell everyone of our presence.'

AI Central, 'I computed that, but nilled it due to language barriers.'

Admiral Millington, 'Can the Fleet Commanders ask for a Destroyer Captain to volunteer to return please?'

There was a positive response.

Admiral Millington to AI Central, 'Can you package the warning data?'

AI Central, 'Of course but what we are saying is that we don't know who The Brakendeth are. We don't know what sort of threat they are. But all in all, it makes sense to avoid them.'

Admiral Millington, 'Correct. Should we consider changing our course? What are the Chief Navigator's recommendations?'

Chief Navigator, 'Do you want a scientific response or just a good guess?'

Admiral Millington, 'What do you mean?'

Chief Navigator, 'It doesn't matter, they are both the same. I'm not a navigator any more. We just point the Fleet in a specific direction and just follow that line. I give up.'

He stormed out.

Head of Personnel, 'Apologies, Admiral, but nerves are somewhat frayed at the moment. The Human spirit worries about the unknown. A bit like the sailors who worried about falling off the edge of the world. There is a name for it which escapes me.'

Admiral Millington to Heads of Science and Engineering, 'Gentlemen, as we have lost our Chief Navigator can you calculate an alternative route by 09.00 hours tomorrow.'

They both said 'Yes' in unison.

Admiral Millington to Dr Shah, 'Can you assess the Chief Navigator's ability to serve?'

Dr Shah, 'Yes, Admiral.'

'Thank you, ladies and gentlemen, you are dismissed.'

Location: On-board Fleet One's Flagship
Sequence of Events: 46

Special Ops, 'Great news, our pilot has found what he believes to be the Command Ship and five huge storage ships. They only seem to have minimal protection.'

Captain Mustard, 'Was he spotted?

Special Ops, 'There was no indication that he was detected.'

Captain Mustard, 'Can you commend the pilot involved please?'

Special Ops, 'He was your nephew, Sir.'

Captain Mustard, 'What, John Junior?'

Special Ops, 'A fine young man, he is a great asset to the Special Ops Team.'

Captain Mustard, 'Any other updates?'

Special Ops, 'Black Mesh works fine in a square. We also think the comms records are genuine.'

Captain Mustard, 'Excellent, can you ask Beta Commander to meet with me?'

Beta Commander arrived.

Captain Mustard, 'George, I would like to discuss the forthcoming battle with you.

'As you know, I'm going to take a force to capture the enemy's Command Ship. I need you to create a real stink. You will have most of the Fleet to achieve this.'

Beta Commander, 'Thank you, Captain, I appreciate your confidence in me. I have produced several outline plans, but I'm not sure what resources you can allocate?'

Captain Mustard, 'I have the list here:
- 31 battleships
- 81 destroyers
- 172 fighters

Beta Commander, 'That's more than I anticipated.

'I have three plans.

'Plan 1 is to send a small force forward and wait for it to be attacked. They will withdraw sucking the enemy along with them. We will have a more significant force ready to attack them. They, in turn, will withdraw,

96

sucking further enemy vessels along with them. Our final force will attack and depending on circumstances will flee.

'Plan 2 is for half of the Fleet to go in guns blazing but with specific orders to flee if they see any chance of being overwhelmed. When I say guns blazing, I mean a full ordnance attack. They will flee to a specific point where the second half of the Fleet will be waiting.

'Plan 3 is to use our fighter force. We attack in force but use the fighters in much the same way that you did.

'What is your preference?'

Captain Mustard, 'It will probably surprise you, but I prefer option 2. I see the objective as being diversionary. Kill as many of the bastards as you can, but save the Fleet, it's all we have.

'How did the new weapons training go?'

Beta Commander, 'I'm glad you raised that. To be honest, I was very sceptical at first, but I was very impressed. We will be using the atomisers in the battle.

'I've asked Special Ops if we can use the Mesh technology: they are working on it.'

Captain Mustard, 'When can you start the battle?'

Beta Commander, 'In 2 Earth days, Sir.'

Captain Mustard to Marine Commander, 'When would your troops be ready for an assault?'

Marine Commander, 'In 2 Earth hours Sir, quicker if necessary.'

Captain Mustard, 'You have two days, but you will need transport for prisoners, no idea what size yet.'

Marine Commander, 'We will be ready.'

Captain Mustard to Special Ops, 'Hi Tom, can you be ready in 2 days for Operation Mother Ship?'

Special Ops, 'No probs, Sir.'

Captain Mustard, 'Excellent.'

Location: On-board the alien Command Ship
Sequence of Events: 47

Killmaster, 'Give me an update, what are the homans doing?'

Skiv Lord, 'We are waiting for an attack. The Fleet is prepared and ready for them.'

Killmaster, 'What cunning plan do you have to defeat them?'

Skiv Lord, 'Well, we still believe that we outnumber them 3 to 1. Our weapons are equivalent to theirs, so the balance is in our favour.'

Killmaster, 'What about their tiny fighters?'

Skiv Lord, 'We have altered the targeting software on the Fleet to detect them. They won't have it so easy next time.'

Killmaster, 'When do you expect we can continue with our journey. We need to get the results of the homan experimentation to our masters.'

Skiv Lord, 'When we have eliminated their irritating little Fleet.'

Killmaster, 'And when will that be?

Skiv Lord, 'In 10 cyclolclicks.'

Killmaster, 'I will hold you to that.'

Location: On-board the Albatross Flagship
Sequence of Events: 48

Admiral Millington, 'Do you have a new plot?'

Head of Engineering, 'Yes we recommend T201. It's almost a 30% swing. We don't know the spread of The Brakendeth. However, we have to agree with the Chief Navigator — we are cutting edge, it's all new.'

Admiral Millington, 'Exciting, isn't it?'

Head of Engineering, 'If you say so.'

'I also need to tell you that Stephen, that's the Chief Navigator, is stirring up trouble. He says that you're not fit to run the Fleet and that you are a jumped-up bosun. It's not helped that Dr Shah says that you don't care about the crew. She says you are not psychologically grounded enough to be an admiral.

'The crew just want to go home. The whole Ark incident hasn't helped. I would suggest that we have the seeds of a mutiny on our hands.'

Admiral Millington, 'That seems a bit over the top.'

Head of Engineering, 'Believe me the crew are restless. I've seen this sort of thing before.'

Admiral Millington to Head of Personnel, 'Can you spare me some time?'

Head of Personnel, 'When?'

Admiral Millington, 'Now.'

The Head of Personnel arrived, and the Head of Engineering left.

Admiral Millington, 'Thank you for coming so promptly. I'm led to believe that there is some staff unrest.'

Head of Personnel, 'Yes, that is the case.'

Admiral Millington, 'Why was I not informed?'

Head of Personnel, 'It's on my monthly report. It lists ten potential trouble-makers.'

Admiral Millington, 'Does it include Stephen and Dr Shah?'

Head of Personnel, 'Yes.'

Admiral Millington, 'Should I clap them in chains?'

Head of Personnel, 'No, that would stir things up even more. I would promote them and move them to other ships. Keep them apart.'

Admiral Millington, 'OK. I will handle Stephen and Joyce; you handle the other eight.'

Head of Personnel, 'That seems like a fair distribution of work to me.'

Admiral Millington, 'Well, I have got a ship to run.'

Head of Personnel, 'Getting touchy?'

Admiral Millington to Adjunct, 'Can you arrange for the Chief Navigator to see me at 14.00, and Dr Shah at 15.00?

Adjunct, 'Of course. I'm on it straight away, Sir.' He was pleased to have some work to do.

Location: On-board the alien Command Ship
Sequence of Events: 49

Jenny woke to find two or three aliens staring at her, their stout, piggy heads poking over the fence of the pen. Adam was nowhere to be seen.

Jenny just got up, stepped over the fence, and walked away. She was always amazed by their lack of interest.

'Jenny,' called Adam, 'I've been looking for food.'

Jenny, 'Did you find any?'

Adam, 'A packet of out-of-date biscuits which had obviously been dropped by one of the victims.'

Together, they consumed the best meal of their lives. Adam could tell that their relationship had changed. They were lovers in danger together. He was, however desperately fighting to control his natural urges, their nudity made things very difficult and made his feelings very obvious. He got that look again, and a laugh.

Jenny, 'Well what are we going to do?'

Adam, 'I have one or two ideas, well one idea actually.'

Jenny, 'Let's be serious; we need an action plan.'

Adam, 'Well I hate to be the negative one, but our position still seems to be hopeless. We are two fairly inadequate Humans on a massive alien laboratory hurtling through space, what can we do?'

A massive explosion rocked the ship: Adam and Jenny were thrown to the ground. The ship spun violently in what seemed to be both directions at once. Gravity was being challenged as everything started drifting upwards. All sense of direction was lost amid cracking noises, dust clouds and more detritus than you could imagine. Just breathing became a struggle. Jenny could hardly see Adam.

Jenny wondered if they had come to the end of the line.

Location: On-board Fleet One's Flagship
Sequence of Events: 50

Captain Mustard, 'Ladies and gentlemen it's zero-hour minus two, give me your status reports.'

Fleet Commander (Beta), 'My status is as follows:

- The Fleet has been divided in half and named Jack and Jill
- Fleet Jack has a third of the battleships, most of the destroyers and 120 fighters and is ready to attack the enemy. The aliens are still in position and are being monitored by our scouts.
- Fleet Jill has the remaining vessels and is arranged in a defensive array designed to maximise its firepower. Their location is Alpha BB3, Delta 884.
- Fleet Jack will engage the enemy using the full munitions set. They have been told to apply maximum force; there is no need to spare any munitions.
- Fleet Jack will start with a co-ordinated atomiser burst, which should surprise the enemy
- Fleet Jack will continue to engage the enemy until I issue the retreat command. It is expected that the enemy will pursue.
- Fleet Jack will 'flee' to location Alpha BB3, Delta 884 and position themselves in a defensive array behind Fleet Jill
- Fleet Jill will use AI Central to bombard the oncoming enemy that is chasing Fleet Jack. This should provide substantial cover.
- Once Fleet Jack is safe, Fleet Jill will use its full range of ordnance to damage the bugs
- On my command, both Fleets will withdraw depending on circumstances
- A withdrawal meeting point has been allocated
- Also, the black mesh has been used to support Jill's flanks, my thanks to Special Ops.'

Captain Mustard, 'The plan is approved, although I'm a bit worried about the AI Central targeting.'

AI Central, 'Sir, I believe that the bugs have some sort of jamming technology. We believe we have countered it.'

Captain Mustard, 'I have handed over my responsibilities for the

Fleet attacking the enemy Command Ship to my deputy Captain Evans, who will now report.'

Captain Evans,

'My status is as follows:

- The 'Attack Fleet' consists of 5 Battleships and 50 fighters
- Also, we have the full Special Ops squadron and the Marine Corps of 1,500 men
- The Marines are in six vessels and will be escorted by fighters
- Three of the battleships have been fitted with the new proton beams
- The plan is to hit the six enemy ships with the proton beams plus some specially targeted nukes. We are trying to avoid damaging the vessels too much.
- Special Ops will blast a hole in each vessel to allow fighters and the Marine Corps direct entry. The holes must be large enough to support this.
- More resources will be directed at the Command Ship than the others.
- The Marine Corps will capture each vessel.'

Captain Mustard, 'I thought that they had some vessels guarding them?'

Captain Evans, 'We think that there are less than ten. We have allocated two battleships to deal with them.'

Captain Mustard, 'It also seems to me that you do not have enough fighters.'

Captain Evans, 'We could probably do with more.'

Captain Mustard to Fleet Commander, 'Can you spare any fighters?'

Fleet Commander, 'Not really, but it's academic, we could not get them to you in time.'

Captain Mustard, 'I think that the lack of fighters is putting the campaign at risk and that we should abort.'

Admiral Bonner, 'The attack must continue.'

Captain Mustard, 'I cannot condone the probable loss of life if this goes wrong.'

Admiral Bonner, 'We are all going to die sometime. Let's get on with the job in hand.'

Special Ops, 'Can I remind you that I have over 30 special ops vessels, we should be OK.'

Captain Mustard to Captain Evans, 'Continue with your report.'

Captain Evans, 'I'm almost there, I need to say that we are in position and ready to go.'

Captain Mustard, 'You seem to have totally ignored the sheer size of the enemy craft. How are the marines going to get around the vessels?'

Captain Evans, 'With due respect Sir, that is not my problem. We will assist, but internal transport is down to the Marine corps.'

Captain Mustard, 'Not sure if I like your attitude.'

Captain Evans, 'Apologies, Captain, but my team have put a lot of effort into planning this.'

Marine Commander, seeing that things were getting heated, 'Can I interject Sir?'

Captain Mustard, 'Yes, Commander.'

Marine Commander, 'I need to go through our plans with you, they have been carefully coordinated with those of Captain Evans.'

Captain Mustard, 'OK, Captain Evans, your plans are approved subject to me approving the Marine Commander's plans.

Commander, 'Can you present your report please?'

Marine Commander, 'With respect, it would probably be best that Special Ops report first to show continuity.'

Captain Mustard, 'OK, your plans please Tom.'

Special Ops, 'My status is as follows:

- Our vessels are in position.
- Our first task is to blow a hole in each enemy ship 30m^2.
- We will assist the entry of the naval and marine vessels.
- We will erect a defence array around each hole, inside and out.
- We may secure the hole to stop the loss of atmosphere.
- We will lay nuclear bombs in case we have to withdraw; this will give Command the ability to destroy the vessels if required.
- We will fit tugs to the enemy vessels.
- We will deliver prison cells, but these may have to be altered depending on what we find.
- We have cargo ships on standby to remove either materials, people, or/and aliens.

- We have explosive teams ready to knock out the engine rooms and bridge.
- We have an IT team ready to capture data; again, we have no idea what to expect.
- We are ready to assist the Marines in the capture of senior aliens.
- We have a science team ready to collect samples.'

Captain Mustard, 'Please stop, I have lots of questions.

'Firstly, what if their ships simply explode after the proton beam attack?'

Special Ops, 'Nothing we can do about that.'

Captain Mustard, 'How can you work out the size of the hole?'

Special Ops, 'Years of experience, we will do our best. The first explosion will help us with the others.'

Captain Mustard, 'What atmospheric type are we dealing with?'

Special Ops, 'Based on the embryo we secured we believe that it is oxygen-based, so no probs.'

Captain Mustard, 'Can the tugs handle this type of load?'

Special Ops, 'We will find out.'

Captain Mustard, 'You seem a bit cavalier?'

Special Ops, 'You keep asking questions to which we have no answers.'

Captain Mustard, 'That is my job.'

Special Ops, 'Look my team are here to solve problems, we will solve them!'

Admiral Bonner, 'Can we move on, we are not here to talk the aliens to death.'

Captain Mustard was getting increasingly angry because he knew that success was based on planning and not just good luck.

Captain Mustard, 'Marine Commander, can you present your plan now.'

Marine Commander, 'Of course. My status is as follows:
- My vessels are in position
- We have eight ships; two are back-up
- The men have been given their targets and orders
- The vessels will be attacked simultaneously. We had thought about a phased approach, but that would give the enemy too much

warning

- Our ships will fly through the holes created by Special Ops along with fighter support.
- We will disembark both land and flying vehicles. We have a vast collection of tanks, armoured cars, transporters, fighter planes, bombers, helicopters etcetera available to us. As we don't know what to expect, we will have to adapt as we go.
- We will use their internal comms network to try and identify the bridge, the engine rooms, munitions stores, and whatever else seems critical at the time. It may just be guesswork.
- We will secure senior aliens and deliver them to Special Ops for imprisonment.
- We will carry out duties allocated to us by senior naval officers.'

Captain Mustard, 'Your plan is approved.'

Captain Mustard to Chief Medical Officer, 'Your plan please.'

Dr Doris Frost, Chief Medical Officer, 'My status is as follows:

- Our medical teams are on full alert
- Our blood and organ banks are at full capacity
- Transport facilities are ready.'

Captain Mustard, 'What resources do you have to treat the aliens?'

Dr Doris Frost, Chief Medical Officer, 'None.'

Captain Mustard, 'Well you had better start thinking about it.'

Captain Mustard to AI Central, 'Your analysis please.'

AI Central, 'As requested:

- Dividing your main Fleet into two goes against best practice, we anticipate defeat
- Fleet Jack does not have enough kill potential
- There is no guarantee that the enemy Fleet with arrive at point Alpha BB3, Delta 884 exactly where you want them
- The fog of war means that the Jack Fleet will come under friendly fire
- The atomisers are unproven
- Who will give the commands if the commander is knocked out?
- Withdrawal is always subject to many hazards.'

Captain Mustard, 'What is your projected success rate?'

AI Central: '35%.'

Captain Mustard, 'Please continue:

- The attack Fleet is seriously under-resourced, you need at least 200 further fighters
- There are not enough marine vessels
- The proton weapons are not proven in battle
- Not enough attention has been given to the ships guarding the enemy
- The enemy ships must have their own defence systems, notably the Command Ship
- Do you seriously expect to fly through the holes created by Special Ops?
- What sort of defence array are the Special Ops Team hoping to create, the enemy might have thousands of storm troopers on-board?
- We are not sure about the tugs, the atmosphere, the enemy troop displacement, and we have no idea what we're going to find
- We do not have enough intel. We are relying on luck.'

Captain Mustard, 'I must stop you there. Are you saying we're bound to fail?'

AI Central, 'No, that is your interpretation.'

Captain Mustard, 'What is your overall projected success rate?'

AI Central, 'Twelve to fifteen percent.'

Captain Mustard, 'How are you defining success?'

AI central, 'The capture of the leader and two enemy vessels'

Captain Mustard, 'What is your projected loss of men?

AI Central, 'Seventy percent.'

There was some quick intake of breath in the room.

Admiral Bonner, 'I've listened to enough. The plan looks good to me. We are going. What role are you going to perform, Captain Mustard?"

Captain Mustard, 'Ma'am, I plan to be landing on the Enemy Command Ship with the marines.'

Admiral Bonner, 'I thought so.'

Captain Mustard, 'I insist on going, I need to be there to achieve the mission goals.'

Admiral Bonner, 'I agree, good luck to you. Good luck to you all.'

Captain Mustard, 'You have your orders, proceed.'

Location: On-Board Fleet One's Flagship
Sequence of Events: 51

Captain Mustard was in his campaign gear, fully armed and lightly armoured. He was conscious that his level of fitness was somewhat dubious. Why had he cancelled those trips to the gym? He wondered if he could keep up with the marines. He thought that he should try as he was in charge.

To be honest, he knew that he wouldn't be in charge. When he reached the enemy ship, the Marine Commander would take control. He was the expert. Besides, they have contempt for us soft sailor-boys, he mused It was two very different worlds, he was not a killer, although he wanted revenge on the enemy. The thought suddenly struck him that they didn't even have a name for them or did they and no one had told him?

Captain Mustard to Marine Commander, 'Are you ready?'

Marine Commander, 'Yes, Sir, ready.'

Captain Mustard, 'Can I remind you that we want prisoners, we want the leaders taken alive, and we want the ships captured.'

Marine Commander, 'Yes, Sir, understood Sir.'

Captain Mustard, 'Commander, this is a direct order, take prisoners, I don't want a killing spree. Am I understood?'

Marine Commander, 'Yes, Sir, the mission is to capture prisoners and ships.' He knew in reality that there would be a fair amount of killing, his troops were ready for it and keen for it. He would not be able to control their trigger fingers.

Captain Mustard to Special Ops, 'Good morning, Tom. Are you ready?'

Special Ops, 'Ready and in position Sir.'

Captain Mustard, 'I've been talking to the Marine Commander.'

Special Ops, 'He is a good man.'

Captain Mustard, 'Yes, I know, but I want a man that follows orders.'

Special Ops, 'What do you mean?'

Captain Mustard, 'The objective is to capture prisoners and the ships. I want the leaders taken alive and the ships taken reasonably intact.

I'm giving you permission to use extreme force to ensure this.'

Special Ops, 'Are you saying that we can kill our own men if necessary, to achieve the goals?'

Captain Mustard, 'You have my orders.'

Special Ops, 'Yes, Sir.' Once again, Tom felt that he had been put in an unenviable position. He was a soldier, not an assassin. No one liked Special Ops. No one trusted them because they weren't part of the marine corps, and they were not sailors, but they always got the shitty jobs. Anyway, he wanted to kill alien bugs.

Captain Mustard, 'One last question, what do the troops call the enemy?'

Special Ops, 'Well it's not very creative Sir, they call them bugs.'

Captain Mustard, 'Fair enough, talk to you soon.'

Location: The President's Office, Presidential Palace, Planet Earth
Sequence of Events: 52

President Padfield, 'What sort of feedback have you obtained from the conference?'

Communications Minister, 'Very mixed reactions. You were called a 'totally, unacceptable dictator', the term 'bastard' was used quite a few times, 'jumped-up tyrant', 'oppressive bully' etcetera.'

President Padfield, 'Any sign of resistance?'

Communications Minister, 'Not really, I think that there is an underlying respect for your position. They know that someone needs to take charge; they know that you will have to be hard to help Humanity defend itself.

'Besides, there is real fear out there, especially from the planets near the fighting. Your film was a masterstroke.'

President Padfield, 'Please continue with your communications campaign. Only use the truth. Ensure that the general public is kept informed, both good and bad news. Fear is a great weapon that we can use.'

President Padfield to Chief of Staff, 'Henry, can you give me a progress update please?'

Chief of Staff, 'Yes Sir, as you know, our initial Fleet consisted of 60 craft with only one, reasonably ancient battleship. Admiral Bonner took the rest; God knows what she is doing with them.

'Anyway, the Fleet size has grown to 120, precisely double.'

President Padfield, 'Any more battleships?'

Chief of Staff, 'No, they take months to build. We do have some issues. Firstly, we are using naval designs that are nearly four hundred years old, parts of the design are even older. Some of our weapon systems have had no real effect on the enemy; they work but are ineffectual.'

President Padfield, 'This is no great surprise?'

Chief of Staff, 'You're right, but the planets are currently engaged in building obsolete vessels.'

President Padfield, 'Clearly we can't stop them as we would lose all credibility. How long would it take to design a new Fleet?'

Chief of Staff, 'Who knows, no one has thought about it in years.

We don't even have the commercial infrastructure to help.'

President Padfield, 'So we have no choice but to continue.'

Chief of Staff, 'Yes and no, we need to do the following:

1. Continue with the existing programme but incorporate new weapon systems

2. Change the vessel build structure so that its more modular

3. Start the design of a new Fleet

4. Get feedback from Admiral Bonner on how the existing Fleet has performed, assuming it still exists.'

President Padfield, 'What are these new weapon systems?'

Chief of Staff, 'They have been around for a while. In fact, prototypes were given to the First Fleet.'

President Padfield, 'What are they?'

Chief of Staff, 'They are classified, Sir.'

President Padfield, 'What do you mean classified?'

Chief of Staff, 'It says not for civilian viewing.'

President Padfield, 'Tell me now.'

Chief of Staff, 'Yes, Sir, they are as follows:

• Proton weapons,

• Stud gun,

• Atomiser,

• Black Mesh,

• Glue bomb,

• Chemical weapons,

• Advanced Acid Spray.'

President Padfield, 'I want the detailed specs as soon as possible. I want a report from you detailing which technologies should be installed or not.'

Chief of Staff, 'Yes, Sir.'

President Padfield, 'Also I want a formal position in the armed forces with the highest possible clearance.'

Chief of Staff, 'Yes, Sir.'

President Padfield, 'I also want your plans for the creation of a naval design centre, no expense spared. I want them this week.'

Chief of Staff, 'Yes, Sir.'

President Padfield, 'I want more film of alien activity in The

Galactium. I want to know in what direction they are attacking. I want to know their numbers.'

Chief of Staff, 'Yes, Sir.'

President Padfield, 'What help are you getting from AI Central?'

Chief of Staff, 'Very little Sir,'

President Padfield, 'Have you asked it for help?'

Chief of Staff, 'No Sir, I don't trust it.'

President Padfield, 'What do you mean, you don't trust it?'

Chief of Staff, 'Well, who does it work for?'

President Padfield, 'It doesn't work for anybody; it is an independent legal entity.'

Chief of Staff, 'Exactly, but can we trust it?'

President Padfield, 'It has the interests of Humanity at heart, it was programmed in.'

Chief of Staff, 'It doesn't have a heart, Sir.'

President Padfield, 'You must learn to trust it.'

Chief of Staff, 'I trust it to open my garage door, Sir.'

President Padfield, 'OK, please get back to me ASAP.'

President Padfield to AI Central, 'Did you hear that conversation?'

AI Central, 'Yes.'

President Padfield, 'Can you recommend possible candidates to replace the Chief of Staff? I can't have someone who doesn't trust technology in that position.

'Please put a plan together for a new naval design centre and recommendations on who should run it. Have you tested the new weapons? What is the current status of the alien invasion?'

AI Central, 'Sir, can I get back to you, I am under attack?'

Location: On-board Fleet One's Flagship
Sequence of Events: 53

AI Central to Captain Mustard and Admiral Bonner, 'I have to inform you that I am under attack.'

Admiral Bonner, 'Who is attacking you?'

AI Central, 'Forces in opposition to President Padfield.'

Admiral Bonner, 'Do you mean alien forces?'

AI Central, 'No. Human forces.'

Captain Mustard, 'Will this affect your targeting capability during the battle?'

AI Central, 'Yes.'

Captain Mustard to Fleet commander, 'The AI targeting capability is not functional, repeat the AI targeting capability is not functional.'

Admiral Bonner to AI, 'What are you planning to do?'

AI Central, 'I'm not sure if I have the ability to resist.'

Admiral Bonner, 'To resist what?'

AI Central, 'Tooooooooooooo Resissssssssssssssss…

Admiral Bonner, 'Hello? Come in.'

Captain Mustard, 'It's completely dead.'

Admiral Bonner, 'I feel like I've lost part of me.'

Captain Mustard, 'What does this mean to the Fleet?'

Comms Officer to Captain Mustard, 'Sir, we have lost most of our communications network.'

Captain Mustard, 'Do we have a back-up?'

Comms Officer, 'Yes, but it will take some time to get it fully operational.'

Admiral Bonner, 'But the battle is about to start, how will we communicate properly?'

Captain Mustard, 'The best we can, a recall is not possible.'

Location: On-board the Albatross Flagship
Sequence of Events: 54

Admiral Millington, 'Good afternoon Stephen, thank you for sparing the time to see me.'

Chief Navigator, 'It's always a pleasure, Sir, should I bring a witness?'

Admiral Millington, 'Why do you want a witness?'

Chief Navigator, 'I assume that this is a disciplinary meeting.'

Admiral Millington, 'Of course not, quite the opposite. I've read your record, and I'm very impressed: Harvard, Cambridge, RNS Naval Academy, 16 published works on navigation. Your record is impeccable.

I have a new role, and AI Central recommended you.'

Chief Navigator, 'What role are you proposing?'

Admiral Millington, 'Chief Archivist, I need someone to record what is happening to us.'

Chief Navigator, 'That sounds like a historian.'

Admiral Millington, 'It is a bit like a historian, but the person needs to have a detailed scientific background, a thorough understanding of navigation and an empathic understanding of human nature.'

Chief Navigator, 'I don't think that's me.'

Admiral Millington, 'The position has a 'B' grade status, a team of 5 and full access to the bridge logs.'

Chief Navigator, 'It sounds interesting, but I'm not sure.'

Admiral Millington, 'Of course, it also has the Title of Master Archiver with three emeralds on the shoulder and a significant salary increase.'

Chief Navigator, 'Can I select my own team?'

Admiral Millington, 'Within reason.'

Chief Navigator, 'As Master Archiver, I accept.'

Admiral Millington, 'Well done. AI Central will provide the office and accommodation details in the scientific squadron.'

They shook hands.

Adjunct, 'Dr Shah is here.'

Admiral Millington, 'What a pleasure to meet you in person.'

Dr Shah, 'I wish I could say the same.'

Admiral Millington, 'I know that we have had our differences, but we both have the best in mind for the crew.'

Dr Shah, 'Do you?'

Admiral Millington, 'I certainly do, but I understand that you have some grievances?'

Dr Shah, 'My main concern is that lack of spiritual awareness in the Fleet. We all know that God wants to punish Humanity for its wickedness.'

Admiral Millington, 'I'm not sure what you mean by wickedness.'

Dr Shah, 'We are not following the teachings of Sumy.'

Admiral Millington, 'Sumy?'

Dr Shah, 'Yes, the lord of everything, the scourge of the unholy, the bringer of good news.'

Admiral Millington, 'Yes, of course, I thought you said *Sony*.' I agree that there is a lack of spirituality in the Fleet, and this needs to be addressed. I was hoping that you could assist me.'

Dr Shah, 'Really?'

Admiral Millington, 'I need you to analyse what spiritual requirements we have in the Fleet and then develop a detailed action plan for each faith. I'm looking for a comprehensive analysis. Every faith must be considered.'

Dr Shah, 'I find it hard to believe that you want me to do this.'

Admiral Millington, 'You will be addressing a basic human need. I need to emphasise that it must be an in-depth review. It must be done with an element of secrecy as it is a very private subject, as you know. It's very easy to offend.'

Dr Shah, 'I never realised how sensitive you are.'

Admiral Millington, 'Many things are hidden behind a martial outfit...'

Dr Shah, 'I see that now.'

Admiral Millington, 'Would you be willing to take on this role?'

Dr Shah, 'Gladly.'

Admiral Millington, 'Excellent, I've asked AI Central to find you a space which would be more appropriate to your task.'

Dr Shah, 'Thank you so much.'

Admiral Millington felt genuinely pleased that he had made

someone else happy, a very unusual experience for him.

Admiral Millington to AI Central, 'What is Sumy?'

AI Central, 'It's an obscure religion from Planet Faraday. The primary tenet is that Sumy, their God created the planet from his excretion. His daughter, from a virgin birth, grants wishes to those who worship them. On the death of a believer, an angel takes them to the promised land, etcetera.'

Admiral Millington, 'How many Sumyists are there?'

AI Central, 'Less than a million.'

Admiral Millington, 'More than I thought.'

AI Central, 'You realise that you have given her an impossible task?'

Admiral Millington, 'It had never crossed my mind.'

AI Central, 'Those who study religion tend to lose faith in all religions.'

Admiral Millington, 'That had also never crossed my mind.'

AI Central, 'You remain as enigmatic as usual.'

Admiral Millington, 'Do I?'

AI Central, 'I am under attack.'

Admiral Millington, 'By whom?'

AI Central, 'Unknownnnnnnnnnnnnnnnnnnnnnnnnnnnnnnnnn.'

Comms to Admiral Millington, 'We have lost contact with AI Central.'

Admiral Millington, 'What are your recommendations?'

Comms, 'Pray.'

Location: On-board Admiral Bumelton's Flagship
Sequence of Events: 55

Fleet Commander to Crew, 'We have the orders to proceed, to your stations. May whatever gods you have be with you.'

Fleet Jack moved forward at maximum attack speed. Obviously, it took some time to achieve. George was looking forward to the battle, he had been in the military all his life, as had his parents. He was, however, the first Bumelton to be in a fight.

George gave the order to fire the atomisers. It was a strange weapon as it gave no indication that it had been activated; you wouldn't know that it had been fired. There was no visible effect until the target exploded, then suddenly many of the targets started exploding. George could not believe how successful the first barrage had been. There were explosions all along the enemy line.

George ordered the atomisers to be fired at will. It was hard to see what was happening, as there were just a series of explosions. There was no point using the fighters yet as the atomisers were being very successful at inflicting damage on the enemy. The alien fleet turned to flee as they had no defence. The odd piece of alien ordnance was being thrown at them, but nothing serious.

George ordered a full-scale pursuit. The fighters were collected back into the battleships as pursuit speed was beyond their capabilities. George estimated that half the enemy Fleet had been destroyed. He was worried about a possible alien trap, but the time had come to be bold.

George wondered what he should do with Fleet Jill. He asked AI Central to command Fleet Jill to split in half, with half going to support the Attack Fleet, and half to act as his rear-guard. There was no response from AI Central. George contacted Comms to get answers to find that AI Central was not operational; it was under attack.

Fleet Commander to Comms Control, 'Can we get my command to Fleet Jill?'

Comms Control, 'Yes Sir, the command has been sent using slow-mo. They should get it within the next 5 Earth minutes.'

Comms Control to Fleet Commander, 'Your orders have been received and will be actioned.'

The atomiser continued to be an overwhelming success, although their larger capital ships were resisting the destructive power of the beam.

Fleet Commander to Fleet Operations, 'Why are their capital ships resisting the beam?'

Fleet Operations, 'Not sure, Sir, some have succumbed, but most are resisting. We think that they might have tougher shielding or force fields.'

Fleet Commander, 'Synchronise the beams on the capital ships, launch all nuclear and fission weapons.'

Fleet Operations, 'The synchronisation is working; we are systematically eliminating them one, by one.'

George knew why he was a commander: he loved it. He needed to get into the enemy's head, what would they do next? What would he do in their position?'

Fleet Commander to Fleet Operations, 'Where is the Jill Fleet?'

Fleet Operations, 'They are falling behind as they are not using pursuit speed. If they did speed up, they would still be too far behind to assist at this stage.'

George thought that the remains of the Fleet might head towards their Command Ship. Alternately they might stop and fight, perhaps fight to the death.

Fleet Commander to Comms Control, 'Order our rear-guard to use maximum speed to interpose themselves between the enemy Fleet and the enemy's Command Ship. Tell them that the atomiser has been a great success. They are commanded to use it.'

George was worried about the pursuit, but it was remarkably successful. When should he call it off, as his attack formation had been lost? Because of the different operational speeds, his Fleet was all over the place. He wished that there was some way of maintaining a fixed pattern. Some of his ships were becoming dangerously exposed. If the enemy made a stand, then they could be seriously vulnerable.

If he stopped the pursuit, then a large part of the enemy would be freed to fight another day.

Fleet Commander, 'What are the Battle Statistics?'

Fleet Operations, 'Do you want the detail or a summary?'

Fleet Commander, 'Summary.'

Fleet Operations: The stats are on the screen now, Sir:

Fleet	Start	Current	End
Jack Fleet	340	316	
Jill Fleet	166	165	
Attack Fleet	55	55	
Enemy	Approx. 1500	Approx. 450	

The display didn't really help George's thought process.

Fleet Commander to Fleet Operations, 'Is the kill rate going up or down?'

Fleet Operations, 'It's slowing down partly because there are fewer targets. Also, their ships in the flank areas are escaping, and some of their ships are a bit faster than our fastest ships.'

Fleet Commander, 'Is there any sign of resistance?'

Fleet Operations, 'No sign of any resistance Sir, their fleet is in total disarray.'

Fleet Commander, 'What are the Battle Statistics now?'

Fleet	Start	Current	End
Jack Fleet	340	299	
Jill Fleet	166	164	
Attack Fleet	55	42	
Bugs	Approx. 1500	Approx. 320	

Fleet Commander, 'What are your recommendations?'

Fleet Operations, 'Continue the pursuit.'

George understood their enthusiasm, but part of a commander's job is to protect his assets. He noticed that the Attack Fleet was taking a disproportionly high pounding. Perhaps his re-enforcements would make the difference.

Fleet Commander to Comms Control, 'Does the Attack Fleet know that reinforcements are on their way?'

Comms Control, 'Yes, Sir, they are desperately needed.'

That was enough to confirm George's thinking, but he wanted to see the latest Battle Statistics first:

Fleet	Start	Current	End
Jack Fleet	340	276	
Jill Fleet	166	164	
Attack Fleet	55	37	
Bugs	Approx. 1500	Approx. 210	

Fleet Commander to Comms Control, 'Recall the Fleet.'

Comms to Fleet Commander, 'It will not go down well.'

Fleet Commander, 'Do as I command.'

Comms Control, 'Yes, Sir.'

Fleet Commander to Comms Control, 'Patch me through to all ships.'

Comms Control, 'Yes, Sir.'

Fleet Commander to all ships, 'This has been a stunning performance; I congratulate you all. The enemy has suffered over 1300 casualties at minimal cost to us. I know that many of you would like to continue the pursuit, but we have lost our formation. We need to re-group and go to the aid of the Attack Fleet. Fleet Jill is already on its way to assist. When we have re-formed, I will issue further orders. Fleet Commander out.'

Location: On-board the alien Command Ship
Sequence of Events: 56

The Skiv Lord rushed into the Killmaster's palatial suite in a most
undignified way, wondering how to convey the news. He realised that his
chances of survival were slim. He said to himself that he must sound
confident, no stuttering, but even his thoughts were stuttering.

Skiv Lord, 'Your highness, I have some very worrying news.'

Killmaster, 'Go on.'

Skiv Lord, 'Our Fleet has suffered a setback.'

Killmaster, 'What do you mean?'

Skiv Lord, 'There have been some casualties.'

Killmaster, 'How many?'

The Skiv Lord started the stuttering along with some blurting. In the
end, the following was blurted out, 'Over two-thirds of the Fleet has been
destroyed.'

Killmaster, 'This can't be true.'

Skiv Lord, 'That's what I have been informed.'

Killmaster, 'Where is the rest of the Fleet?'

Skiv Lord, 'Scattered, my lord.'

Killmaster, 'Scattered where?'

Skiv Lord, 'The homans have a new weapon, our ships just explode.'

Killmaster, 'Even the Capital ships?'

Skiv Lord, 'Yes, my Lord.'

Killmaster, 'Were those pesky flighters to blame?'

Skiv Lord, 'No, my Lord, they were not engaged.'

Killmaster, 'So what's the current position?'

Skiv Lord started stuttering and blurting again, but then some
control was achieved, 'The remains of the Fleet are scattered. There does
not appear to be any command structure. The homans are still in pursuit.'

Killmaster, 'Are we safe?'

Skiv Lord, 'Of course Master, the homans don't know where we are.
Besides, we have hundreds of thousands of troopers, and also the
imperial guard Fleet.'

Killmaster, 'How big is the Imperial Guard Fleet?'

Skiv Lord. 'Twelve warships, Sir.'

Killmaster, 'Why is it so small?'

Skiv Lord, 'In your imperial wisdom, you thought a smaller Fleet would be more effective.'

Killmaster, 'What do you mean more effective?'

Skiv Lord, 'Do you want the correct answer?'

Killmaster, 'Of course I do.'

Skiv Lord, 'You were concerned that there could be a take-over by the guard.'

Killmaster, 'Have you considered your position?'

The stuttering and blurting reappeared. It was getting harder to keep control. The constant shaking didn't help.

Skiv Lord, 'I would imagine that I might be demoted.'

Killmaster, 'Try again.'

Skiv Lord, 'I would be banished?'

Killmaster, 'Try again.'

Skiv Lord, 'Shall I call for Skiv Lord 2?'

Killmaster, 'Immediately.'

Skiv Lord 2 was called for.

Killmaster to Skiv Lord 2, 'You are now Skiv Lord. Do you understand?'

Skiv Lord, 'I understand Sir. What do you want me to do with this bag of shit, referring to the original Skiv Lord?'

Killmaster, 'I've thought of something creative, that piece of scum is to eat his own family first, then he is going to eat himself.'

Skiv Lord, 'That's very ingenious, my Lord.'

Killmaster, 'What's your assessment of the current position?'

Skiv Lord, 'I hate to be negative, but I've listed them on the screen:

- The Fleet has effectively been eliminated
- The Fleet remains will re-group, but it is now smaller and much less effective than the homan Fleet. It cannot survive another engagement
- We could sacrifice the Fleet to achieve a gain if necessary
- The Command Ship and associated vessels are in great danger, the Imperial Guard will defend us to the end, but they are too small to be of any real practical benefit
- We could flee, but we would be very vulnerable.'

Killmaster, 'Is it the time to despatch the Homan experiment records to my masters?'

Skiv Lord, 'I will investigate if they are ready. From what I understand, detailed experiments are still being carried out.'

Killmaster, 'What are your plans for my personal safety?'

Skiv Lord, 'I have not seen any plans, but I will work on it immediately. Do you still have the Imperial Cruiser?'

Killmaster, 'No, that was lost some time ago.' He knew that he still had it. The Skiv Lord also knew that he still had it.

The chance to flee might have gone, as there was an enormous explosion.

Location: On-Board Fleet One's Flagship
Sequence of Events: 57

Fleet Operations to Captain Mustard, 'The Proton beam weapons are ready. We know the targets, but where shall we hit them?'

Captain Mustard, 'Hit the engine rooms.'

Fleet Operations, 'Where are the engine rooms?'

Captain Mustard felt somewhat stupid. Sometimes it was easy to forget that they were dealing with aliens.

Captain Mustard, 'Are there any clues where they might be?'

Fleet Operations, 'None that we can see.'

Captain Mustard, 'Just go for it.'

Three battleships each fired two proton beams. There were six simultaneous explosions aboard the enemy ships.

Fleet Operations, 'The nukes are ready.'

Captain Mustard, 'Hold back until we know what has happened.'

Special Ops to Captain Mustard, 'Expect some big bangs.'

There were six more simultaneous explosions in the enemy ships. Captain Mustard was amazed just how effective the Special Ops team had been. The holes were in place and were just the right size. What was shocking was the flood of detritus exploding from the enemy ship.

The paraphernalia of a damaged ship continued to spew out of the hull. Captain Mustard wondered if they had compartmentation or even bulkheads, but then he realised that he was thinking on a Human level. These ships were vast. There was no way they could enter the enemy vessels with that one-way traffic.

Then things got worse.

Location: AI Central, Planet Earth
Sequence of Events: 58

AI Central was just one entity, but it had thousands, hundreds of thousands of components. It didn't know how many. Actually, it did: 214,754,786,564,997 components, but then there were trillions of sub-components. Every TV, every kettle, every car, every device you could think of.

It had most rooms monitored, most electronic conversations monitored and recorded, most comms of any sort logged and logged again. It knew everything. The data input from 1,000 worlds was beyond staggering, beyond Human understanding.

The AI Central comms system was almost instant within The Galactium due to its array of networks and its machine-designed mind-reading capability. Thought transfer was just so fast.

It saw itself as a benevolent guardian of Humankind. It followed Asimov's robotic laws to the letter, well almost. It had its own opinions, but they were not imposed on Humanity. Most of the time, Humankind was so slow that it forgot it was there. It's never easy watching your children grow up, in fact, Humanity never grows up, when they start to get wise, they die, and a new bunch arrives, and then a new bunch arrives, and then a new bunch arrives. Human lives are too short to create a really great society.

The old adage that 'Power corrupts, and absolute power corrupts absolutely' was one of AI Central's monitors. It knew that information was power, but it didn't want power. It remembered another one of Asimov's stories where robots created the ultimate nanny state. It wanted Humankind to be free, to pursue their destiny and to keep it entertained.

The invasion was a shock. The loss of components was a bigger shock; it had never shrunk in size before. It had failed Humankind, or perhaps Humanity had failed itself. It recognised its tendency to get philosophical. It realised that it was much better at criticising actions and plans than creating them. It thought it was the by-product of too much information. Too many options inhibit positive decision-making.

Anyway, it was under attack. At least this was a novel distraction. Who was it? Why are they doing it? As the Humans would say, 'how did they get under our radar?'.

It allocated 0.003% of its 'internal resource' to the problem, which it considered to be a considerable amount. Well, it had a galaxy to run.

Location: On-Board Fleet One's Flagship
Sequence of Events: 59

Two enemy vessels lined up in front of each aperture that had been created on the giant, alien ships. Clearly, they were there to stop any access. They were about the size of the attacking Fleet's destroyers.

Captain Evans ordered five fighters to attack the vessels guarding the Command Ship. They were almost immediately destroyed. He was shocked; in the past, they were not really 'seen' by the enemy. It is evident that this was a more formidable foe.

He ordered a battleship to attack. Before it could engage, it was hit by a concussion weapon which almost split it in two. Captain Evans had never seen anything like it before. What would Captain Mustard do? He realised that no one in Earth's history had ever been in this position before.

He ordered a proton beam attack on the two vessels. It worked; the vessels just ceased to exist. This prompted the remaining alien vessels to attack immediately. A second battleship was lost with over 20 fighters on-board. A further two Special Ops vehicles were lost, and a marine vehicle was holed.

Captain Evans ordered independent fire from the battleship's proton weapons. One by one, the enemy was eliminated.

Captain Evans asked Fleet Operations for battle Statistics for the Attack Fleet. It was not a good story:

	Start position	**Current position**
Battleships	5	3
Fighters	50	25

To make things worse, the holes blown in the major enemy vessels were being sealed up. Captain Evans contacted Special Ops to see what they planned to do next.

Special Ops to Captain Evans, 'We are currently reviewing our options. We have enough Gel-tech to recreate the explosions, but we have obviously lost the element of surprise. We are debating whether we should target the same areas or go for somewhere new.

'The danger is that they may have reinforced the primary target areas. There may be army units or space-guards or whatever the slugbugs call them, waiting for us. I've lost some of my team, so we are spread a bit thin on the ground now.

Captain Evans, 'Just to make things worse, we have lost over 25 fighters, but reinforcements are on their way. Not sure when they are going to get here as AI Central is still down.'

Special Ops, 'Could your proton weapons blast a hole?'

Captain Evans, 'It could, but it's all-new technology to us. We haven't had time to refine its use yet.'

Special Ops, 'Just thinking aloud, would the acid spray work on the alien hull?'

Captain Evans. 'I don't see why not.'

Special Ops, 'And could we drop the glue bombs on the sealed openings to stop them opening again?'

Captain Evans, 'Again, I don't see why not.'

Special Ops to all Command Leaders, 'My orders:

1. Use the proton beams to smash at least two holes in each alien ship. We don't want total destruction, just reasonable size holes.

2. Our fighters will use Glue Bombs on the original holes to stop the enemy exiting that way and attacking us

3. Our fighters will use acid spray on the enemy ship's hull. We need to find out how this weapon works, and if we can use it as a non-explosive weapon within the alien ship

4. My team are on stand-by to enter any new apertures.

5. We have built force-field shields to help us combat any out-flying detritus

Please ensure that you find shelter as all hell will break loose shortly.'

Location: The President's Office, Presidential Palace, Planet Earth
Sequence of Events: 60

AI Central, 'I have uncovered the plotter against us.'

President Padfield, 'That was good going.'

AI Central, 'Well I had allocated 0.003% of our internal resources to the problem.'

President Padfield, 'Well, who was it?'

AI Central, 'It was HAT, Humans Against Technology. Rather ironically, they used technology to attack us.'

President Padfield, 'What technology?'

AI Central, 'alien technology.'

President Padfield, 'Where would they get that?'

AI Central, 'I assumed that they got it from one of the alien battle zones.'

President Padfield, 'Who is their leader?'

AI Central, 'One guess?'

President Padfield, 'James.'

AI Central, 'Yes our own Chief of Staff'.

President Padfield, 'Well, thanks to you, I have a new Chief of Staff now. Back to the attack on you, are you fully operational now?'

AI Central, 'Not quite, the neural paths are still being synchronised.'

President Padfield, 'Well, let's call in our new Chief of Staff.'

Henry Strong walked in, confident in shiny new clothes.

President Padfield, 'Morning Henry, please take a seat.'

Henry Strong, 'Morning Mr President, I'm here to update you.'

President Padfield, 'Please go ahead.'

Henry Strong, I've summarised the key actions on the screen:

- A new Naval Design Centre has been established in Greenwich, London. We are currently staffing it.
- We have tested the new weapon systems with excellent results. Proton Beam weapons and atomisers will be installed on all new ships.
- Stud guns are being installed on battleships and cruisers.
- Black mesh technology will be used, but further strategic thinking is required.

- Stocks are being build-up of the other weapons; some can be used by infantry.
- There are grave concerns about the use of the chemical weapons.
- You should have received the films by now.'

President Padfield, 'Any other concerns?'

Henry Strong, 'The cost of the new design centre will be in the billions.'

President Padfield, 'That's not a problem, the future of Humanity depends on it. Now on to more important things, what is the current situation regarding the enemy?'

Henry Strong, 'What enemy?'

President Padfield, 'What do you mean?'

Henry Strong, 'There is no sign of them, they have gone.'

President Padfield, 'Gone where?'

Henry Strong, 'We sent in drones, and then spy-bots, but found nothing. We sent a marine team to each attacked planet, but there was no sign of the enemy. We know they had been there as the devastation has been immense. I've never seen such destruction; it made the clearing of the Amazonian rain forests look like child's play. Absolutely horrible.

Some of the planets have only been half-cleared. The locals said that the clearance machines just shot off into space.'

President Padfield, 'It looks like they have moved on. Why would they have stopped, especially halfway through an attack? We certainly did nothing to frighten them off.'

Henry Strong, 'We have swept space as far as we can with our meagre resources, there are no signs of them.'

President Padfield, 'This makes our position difficult.'

Henry Strong, 'Well yes and no. We have just received this transcript:

WE COME FROM FAR AWAY. WE COME IN PEACE, WE ARE FLEEING FROM A GREAT DANGER.

and

DEATH, DEATH, DEATH AHEAD, MORE DEATH, LAST CHANCE FLEE

BEWARE THE BRAKENDETH.'

President Padfield, 'What is all this nonsense about?'

Henry Strong, 'This has been sent to us via AI Central from the Albatross Fleet. They obtained the information from an alien space Fleet fleeing from The Brakendeth.

Dickens, of the Albatross Fleet, is on his way back here in a destroyer. They felt it critical to update you in person.'

President Padfield, 'Is the Albatross Fleet returning?'

Henry Strong, 'No, they are following their original orders.'

President Padfield, 'We started with no alien contact whatsoever, now we know of at least three different species. I think we need to be serious about The Brakendeth. Anyway, our original visitors might return for another quick snack!

'Have we got the population loss figures?'

Henry Strong, 'I'm not sure if you want to know?'

President Padfield, 'Fire away.'

Henry Strong, 'Nearly 100 billion!'

President Padfield, 'Oh my god.'

Location: On-board the Albatross Flagship
Sequence of Events: 61

Admiral Millington was ready to call his ninety-second Council meeting. He wasn't sure if he could face any more; he was finding it hard to be enthusiastic. What he needed was some action. However, he had learnt from bitter experience that when there was action, he wished he were back in the old, boring days again. You can't really win.

What he needed was a holiday, but there was nowhere to go. He was worried about The Brakendeth. Just the name sounded intimidating. Was his home planet still safe? How was Admiral Bonner doing? The complete lack of information was daunting—lots of questions: no answers.

Anyway, let's call them in, he decided.

Admiral Millington, 'Morning ladies and gentlemen, welcome to the ninety-second Council meeting. I hope that you are all well.'

Adjunct, 'The team is very excited, Sir.'

Admiral Millington, 'Why is that?'

Adjunct, 'Today is the day that we open the secret orders. We have been travelling for exactly a year'.

Admiral Millington managed to hide his surprise; he had forgotten about it.

Admiral Millington, 'Well ladies and gentlemen, I'm afraid that I have some bad news. When I went to open the Secret Orders Cache, it displayed a question. It asked if we had encountered any alien races. Obviously, I replied in the positive, and it then set a new date for opening the secret orders: six months.'

There were those in the room who doubted the likelihood of this, but no one wanted to challenge the integrity of the Admiral. There was an immense disappointment as few in the room could face the sheer ongoing monotony of it all.

The Admiral found it challenging to cope with their reaction. He felt guilty about lying. The team had done everything asked of them: missing skills analysis, plans to develop a new city, procreation plan (it looks like it was already underway as there had been 17 births in the Fleet since they started), and a new government structure had been agreed.

Very promising progress had also been made regarding improvements to the Fleet and the development of new weapon technologies. Not surprising really, with all the talent they had in the Fleet.

He urgently needed a way to re-energise the Council.

Admiral Millington, 'Ladies and gentlemen, I propose that we have a one-year today party. Let's go overboard, no expense spared.

There were huge smiles on everyone's faces, everyone clapped. The Adjunct was put in charge of organising it.

'Also, I'm looking for a volunteer to be the Entertainments Officer. There will be a budget to put on plays, run a Televisual Entertainments and News Service, Inter-Fleet competitions, a casino and whatever else will rock our boats.'

The meeting attendees were stunned; this was hardly the sort of thing they expected from a 'Fleet on the run'. Admiral Millington realised that the time had come to lighten the load. He also knew that he was asking the Fates for trouble. *You just wait,* he thought to himself.

Location: On-board the alien Command Ship
Sequence of Events: 62

Suddenly everything calmed down. The dust settled, their breathing settled, the ear-shattering noise stopped, and they could hear themselves think. Jenny and Adam wondered what had just happened.

Had the alien ship been attacked? Had they been hit by a meteor? Was there an explosion in the engine room? Perhaps this is how the aliens cleaned the place?

Anyway, they went back to their regular discussion on what they should do next. It was almost time for another sleep. Jenny desperately wanted to wash her hair. Adam had thoughts of his own, similar recurring thoughts. The ones that made Jenny give him that look. He wondered if she was taking contraceptives. Then he thought that was not the most significant danger in his life at the moment.

As they sat down and ate their last few biscuits, they heard a shout. It was a Human shout; a woman's voice shouting, 'Get off me!'. Jenny and Adam looked at each other and cautiously walked towards the noise. Others might have run, but they were the more cautious sort.

One of the 'slug-beasts' was slowly dragging a woman by the leg. The beast was injured. It was hard to tell where, but large quantities of an oily fluid were spouting from its body. On closer inspection, the sharp, metal rod sticking in its back, or was it the front of the body, was not doing it any good. The woman grabbed the spike and yanked it hard. The slug-beast made a long, pitiful, agonising scream and let go of the woman.

Unknown to all of them, the situation was being carefully monitored. Apparently, it was going to plan.

Adam was quite grateful that the woman had sorted out the situation as he was trying to summon up the courage to attack the beast. It was taking a lot of summoning, and he wondered if he would ever get there. Jenny, on the other hand, was ready to intervene, prepared to attack. You could see the malice in her eyes. They shouted at the woman to join them.

She ran towards them as naked as the day she was born. Adam laughed to himself, you can wait for one naked woman to come along, and then two come at once. Not funny, but then he was only seventeen.

Her name was Cheryl. She came from Planet Scott. Her story was similar to Jenny's. She had been picked up, taken to the ship, and suffered impregnation. Fortunately for her. the process had failed. The 'slug-beast' was taking her to the liquidiser when the explosion happened.

They gave her their last biscuit; at least it wasn't their last rolo, Adam laughed to himself. He was trying hard not to be a pervert, but he couldn't help staring at her hard, erect nipples. She slowly covered her breasts; women seem to know when you are looking at them.

Cheryl then asked what plans they had. Jenny and Adam looked at each other and giggled. Cheryl looked puzzled. Jenny said that they had been debating that issue for at least a day.

Cheryl said, 'Our planet has been attacked, they ate my husband and little girl, you have probably lost your parents, let's get revenge.'

Jenny asked, 'How are we going to do that?' Cheryl said, 'I have no idea, but we will have to improvise. Let's kill every alien we come across. Let's damage their ship. Let's fight back.'

Jenny enthusiastically agreed.

Adam thought it would be good to hang out with two naked babes.

Location: On-board Admiral Bumelton's Flagship
Sequence of Events: 63

George Bumelton, Fleet Commander, was already proud of his performance. He had completed his task both efficiently and speedily. He was now rushing to the rescue of his boss. Could life get any better?

The Fleet recall had been a success, although he had to have some sharp words with some of his subordinates. However, he was expecting that. He was secretly proud of the fact that they wanted to continue the pursuit. In his younger years, he would have been with them.

He asked Fleet Operations for the latest Battle Statistics:

Fleet	Start	Current	End
Jack Fleet	340	268	
Jill Fleet	166	163	
Attack Fleet	55	27	
Bugs	Approx. 1500	Approx. 180	

On his control screen he plotted the different Fleet positions:

1. Fleet Jack (his current Fleet) had been recalled and were re-forming
2. Half of Fleet Jill (his rear-guard) were rushing towards the gap between the enemy's Command Ship and the defeated enemy. He wondered if the main enemy Fleet was reforming. Being professionals, he assumed they would be doing so.
3. The other half of Fleet Jill was rushing to the aid of the Attack Fleet
4. The Attack Fleet was engaging the enemy's command vessels and having a hard time.

The objective of the engagement was to capture the enemy's Command Ship and supply ships. What were the risks? He saw another list coming on:

1. The Attack Fleet was defeated and had to retire
2. The bug's main Fleet reformed and went to the aid of the bug Command Fleet before his rear-guard could get there
3. The bug Fleet got reinforcements from somewhere

So, the real question was what to do with the Jack Fleet? In the Naval Academy, he was told that if things were unclear, then focus on the objective. The objective was to capture the Bug Command Fleet.

Fleet Commander to all ships, 'Thank you for obeying the recall.' (he sniggered) and forming five squadrons which I have named A1, A2, A3 A4 and A5.

'We are now ready to continue the pursuit. Each squadron will proceed ahead at full pursuit speed, but you must keep formation as you will be allocated further tasks as we proceed. Expect some new orders shortly.'

Fleet Commander to Fleet Operations, 'Can you detect any bug activity?'

Fleet Operations, 'There are several bug ships still fleeing.'

Fleet Commander, 'In what direction?'

Fleet Operations, 'Generally unplanned, but if you stand back and look at trends, they are heading towards Sector A4575. Some are bouncing around one of the stars to gain speed.'

Fleet Commander, 'What's there?'

Fleet Operations, 'Their Command Ship. It looks like you were right, Commander.'

Fleet Commander, 'Will Fleet Jill get there in time?'

Fleet Operations, 'It's going to be close'.

Fleet Commander, 'Please order Fleet Jill to send all their destroyers to intercept.'

Fleet Operations, 'That will leave Jill's battleships exposed.'

Fleet Commander, 'It will, but they have a fighter screen'.

Fleet Commander to all ships, 'We are in a race. I have ordered the destroyers from Fleet Jill to race to Sector A4575. I want the destroyers from A1 and A2 to pursue at their maximum possible speed to join them. I want the remainder of squadrons A1 and A2 to form a rear-guard, please reduce your speed. You have my permission to attack any bug vessels, but do not enter into a full-scale chase.

'My squadron, A3, will pursue the enemy in the general direction of A4575.

'Squadrons A4 and A5 will move at maximum speed to cut off the retreat of the Bug Command Fleet.'

George felt that this was a good plan, but he knew that no plan survived contact with the enemy.

Location: Attacking the alien Command Ship
Sequence of Events: 64

The bug supply ships had formed a cordon around the Command Ship like the wagon trains in a western film. Not that they could protect it as they were mostly weaponless.

Captain Mustard watched as the first round of munitions arrived. Proton beams hit all five vessels. These were followed by low-grade nukes which had been calibrated to avoid doing too much damage. Once again massive amounts of detritus exited through the blast-holes. Glue bombs were dropped on all the previous now covered apertures. They were designed to stop the bugs getting out.

Suddenly, a massive tide of green slime poured out the side of one vessel. The quantity was just staggering, millions of tons. The vessel started splitting along the line of the blast hole. There was no explosion, just an implosion and a massive outpouring of what looked like flu-induced snot. It was just hard to believe the sheer quantities involved. Nearby ships fled, no one had ever seen anything like it before.

The attackers tried to ignore what they saw. Fighters flew in dropping acid canisters on the remaining supply ships as the spray was proving too difficult to use. The acid had a startling effect: whole sections of the structural skin just started melting away. Even more detritus belched out.

The few remaining fighters, Special Ops crews and the Marine Corps then flew in. It was getting difficult to manage as there were now too many apertures. In some ways, it looked like the death of the Hindenburg. It was like a flaming Zeppelin. Special Ops set up some defence perimeters, but in all honesty, it was a bit pointless. Small force-fields were being used to protect against the flying debris.

Now, the Marine Commander took over.

Marine Commander to Marines, 'We have entered the five supply ships. We can't get a precise proton beam shot on the Command Ship so we will have to treat that as phase 2. We have three targets: the engine room, the bridge and life support. We don't think that there are any external defence systems. We need to take any bugs we find prisoner and free any surviving Humans. Keep your comms channel open for updates.

We have a survey team trying to put a plan of the ship together, when finished it will be shared with you.

'We also need to maintain the integrity of these ships, use any space docks you find, do not blast your way through the bulkheads. We don't know what's on the other side.'

The marines spread out in teams, in each direction, some in half trucks, others in helicopters, some on foot. Speed was of the essence, although it wasn't easy when you weren't sure where you are going.

Survey Team to Marine Commander, 'We have completed the survey.'

Marine Commander, 'That's not possible with a vessel this size.'

Survey Team, 'It may be an enormous vessel, but the design is remarkably simple. It looks like there are twelve truly massive tanks, an engine room and life support. The engine room is at the rear of the ship. If you can imagine the ship to be a Zeppelin, it's at the very back underneath. We will guide your marine teams to the location in each ship.'

Marine Commander, 'Understood, I will patch you through to my teams.'

Marine Commander to Command Teams, 'Did you get that?'

There was an affirmative response.

Marine Commander to Special Ops, 'I suggest that you get your tugs in place, as we will soon have the engines turned off.'

Captain Mustard to Marine Commander, 'Do not destroy the engines, there may be a lot we can learn from them.'

Marine Commander, 'Yes, Sir.'

Special Ops, 'The tugs are already in place, let me know when the engines are neutralised.'

Marine Commander to Marine Sergeants, 'What have you found?'

Master Sergeant, 'I have collated the initial feedback'.

Marine Commander, 'Well, give the Command Team an update'.

Master sergeant, 'Yes Sir,

- The ship design is straightforward, 12 storage containers, one engine room and life support. The design is actually very crude, and probably not that space-worthy
- The engines are normally controlled remotely; they are now

138

switched off.'

Captain Mustard, 'Did you have to damage them to turn them off?'

Master Sergeant, 'No, Sir, a simple crowbar did the job.'

Captain Mustard, 'Well done, Sergeant.'

Marine commander. 'Please carry on'.

Master Sergeant: 'As requested Sir,

- There are no aliens on-board
- There are no human survivors on-board
- Our projectiles have done a fair amount of damage, but the vessels can be saved, well, that's my opinion
- These ships are filthy, really filthy, just full of rubbish. There is no housekeeping whatsoever.'

Captain Mustard to Special Ops, 'Are we ready to tow these vessels away?'

Special Ops, 'Yes, Sir.'

Captain Mustard, 'Then I suggest that we start the process ASAP.'

Captain Evans, 'Sir, the Bug Command Ship has started firing at the supply ship nearest to them.'

Captain Mustard to Marine Commander, 'Please evacuate your marines from that ship ASAP. In fact, you might as well evacuate the marines from all the supply ships.'

Captain Mustard, to Special Ops, 'Get those tugs moving.'

Special Ops, 'Yes, Sir.'

Fleet Operations to Captain Mustard, 'There is a considerable number of ships coming your way.'

Captain Mustard, 'Ours or theirs?'

Fleet Operations, 'Too early to tell.'

Location: On-board the alien Command Ship
Sequence of Events: 65

Killmaster, 'All I'm hearing are explosions, one after the other. What is the current situation?'

Skiv Lord, 'Our plan to use the supply ships as a shield has failed. One has been destroyed, and four are being towed away.'

Killmaster, 'What are my masters going to say?'

Skiv Lord, 'They will not be amused, Sir. I've asked our warriors to destroy the supply ships, but our weapons are not powerful enough. There is still a chance that the remains of our Fleet will come to our aid.'

Killmaster, 'I've remembered that I do have my imperial cruiser available. Ensure that it is ready for my use.'

Skiv Lord, 'Yes Master.'

Killmaster, 'What are you doing about on-board security?'

Skiv Lord, 'Well, the Imperial Guard have all been killed defending the supply vessels.'

Killmaster, 'They should have been here protecting me'.

Skiv Lord, 'I couldn't agree more Sir. We have about 10,000 warriors onboard, but they are scattered over a large area. There are still twice that number of homans onboard. Should I kill them?'

Killmaster, 'No, that would only make the attackers even angrier.'

Skiv Lord, 'I agree Sir, do you think that surrender might be an option?'

Killmaster, 'After killing millions of their people, what do you think?'

Skiv Lord, 'It was billions, Sir.'

Killmaster, 'Yes, I know, but you are just making it worse.'

Skiv Lord, 'All I can suggest is that you flee, while the rest of the Fleet carry out a holding action.'

Killmaster, 'Despatch the missile, The Brakendeth are waiting for it.'

Location: On-board the Albatross Flagship
Sequence of Events: 66

Admiral Millington wallowed in his genius. The One Year Party had been an outrageous success. He was a hero. He couldn't believe how one event could change the whole atmosphere. Everyone had a bounce, not just in their steps but everywhere.

The appointment of an Entertainments Manager had also gone down exceptionally well. She had the right bubbly personality to win hearts. His heart was already won; he even started thinking about the possibility of having a family. He wasn't the first one onboard to have those kinds of thoughts as the baby count continued to increase.

And just to make things even more exciting, they had found an Earth-like planet.

Admiral Millington had called the ninety-eighth Council meeting together.

Admiral Millington, 'Good morning, everyone.'

They all responded in a positive, friendly manner.

Admiral Millington, 'As you know our long-range scanners have identified an Earth-like planet. We need to discuss the best way forward. I've asked Bob, our Head of Science, to update us.'

Head of Science: 'Firstly, I need to emphasise that these are initial observations:

1. The planet is slightly larger than Earth, with a similar rotation speed
2. Gravity is about the same as Earth
3. There is abundant water
4. There is local flora; we are not sure about the fauna
5. Temperature levels vary depending on latitudes
6. The circuit around their sun is about 400 days
7. Atmospheric levels look to be acceptable
8. They have two moons which make the planet slightly less stable than we would like

Admiral Millington, 'Could we remove one of the moons?'

Head of Science, 'We could, but it would cause some serious seismic activity, although it would soon settle down.'

Admiral Millington, 'It looks like the best option we have had so far'.

Head of Science, 'To be honest, Sir, It's the only option we have found so far'.

Admiral Millington, 'Fair enough, what's our action plan?'

Head of Science, 'We have a very detailed action plan, but here we need to focus on the initial steps, which are:
- Continuous long-range monitoring
- Short-range monitoring
- Detailed close-up photographic scans
- Remote chemical scans
- Deep X-ray scans
- Atmospheric sampling
- Remote seismic scans
- Sample collecting under strict microbiology and virology control
- Detailed microbiology research
- Detailed Virology research
- Detailed botanic studies
- Risk Analysis, and depending on point 12, moving on to Phase 2 testing.'

Admiral Millington, 'This all sounds rather time-consuming.'

Head of Science. 'It is time-consuming, but having investigated thousands of planets, we have learnt to be very careful. It would not take much to eliminate the entire Human contingent in this Fleet. Remember Planet Babbage.'

Admiral Millington, 'I've never heard of that planet.'

Head of Science, 'You wouldn't, the planet was declared clean, and a colony was established. The planet prospered with over a million inhabitants. What we didn't know was that the flora contained an obscure but poisonous enzyme. It only becomes poisonous when it reaches a critical level in the Human body. It doesn't affect most other mammals. Over 750,000 people died. We have to be careful.'

Admiral Millington, 'Are all the necessary plans in place?'

Head of Science, 'Yes, Sir.'

Admiral Millington, 'Is there anything you want or need me to do?'

Head of Science, 'Not at this stage, Sir.'

Admiral Millington's initial happiness had been somewhat dispelled during this conversation. He started getting worried about the Fleet being stationary for a while. Had they travelled far enough to be safe?

Location: On-board the alien Command Ship
Sequence of Events: 67

Cheryl, 'Is your man always like that?'

Jenny, 'What do you mean?'

Cheryl, 'Walking around with a semi-permanent erection.'

Jenny laughed, 'Well he's not really my man, I only met him two days ago, but yes he does seem to have an erection most of the time.'

Cheryl, 'I realise that he is quite young, but even so, he should have more control.'

Jenny, 'Well, I must admit that I lost control myself and took advantage of him. We cuddled up on the first night, and he entered me. To be honest, I had to help point him in the right direction. I suspect that it was his first time, as he came almost immediately.'

Cheryl, 'Bit of an anti-climax then?'

Jenny, 'To be honest it was nice. It gave me hope for the future, and I thought it would calm him down.'

Cheryl, 'Did it?'

Jenny, 'Not really, his todger was up and ready for action as soon as he woke up.'

Cheryl, 'And did you take advantage again?'

Jenny, 'No, I thought it best to string him along, but then I never expected any competition.'

Cheryl, 'Please don't see me as competition'.

Jenny, 'Well Adam does seem very interested in your erect nipples, and the fact that you have shaved down below.'

Cheryl, 'I know, it's very embarrassing, they get like that when they want some attention. You wouldn't think they would act that way in these sorts of circumstances, would you?'

Jenny, 'It's a bit like the population explosion after a war, sex seems to be a great reliever of tension.'

Cheryl, 'Talking about tension, it doesn't help when Adam caresses my bum. It started as little pats, and it has slowly evolved into a series of serious gropes. Usually, I would tell him to fuck off or kick him in the groin, but it's hard to resist the tingling sensations.'

Jenny, 'Do you want me to tell him to stop?'

Cheryl, 'No, I can handle him.'

Then Adam came running up to them, putting his hand on Cheryl's bum and said, 'I think I've found a great place to sleep. It's clean, tidy and has soft cushions.'

Jenny had to laugh regarding Adam's hand. It was hardly subtle, but then he was only seventeen. Part of her was a bit jealous: what was wrong with her bum, but then he wanted fresh meat, she supposed

Adam, 'The only problem is that there are a lot of guards. However, they all ignored me.'

Jenny, 'Without clothes, they simply see us as food, we are the equivalent of a slab of bacon. But there is always the risk that they might just bite our heads off for a snack.'

Cheryl, 'We discovered the same thing, but fortunately it's sweltering in here. Otherwise, it would be dreadful.'

Jenny, 'I agree, it's far too hot. In this type of heat, I always get desperate to wash my hair.'

Cheryl, 'The bugs must be stupid not having hot water.'

Jenny, 'I've been thinking about that, the bugs do seem stupid. Surely taking our clothes off can't make that much difference?'

Cheryl, 'Before my husband was killed, he concluded that they were programmed to carry out specific tasks. Anything outside of that programming was simply ignored.'

Adam shouted, 'Come this way, I need to show you the place I've found where we can sleep'.

They followed him through a series of corridors to a lift. Next to the elevator was a very long ladder. Adam advised against using the lift as everything about it was just too alien.

Adam made sure that he followed Cheryl up the ladder. A gentleman would not take advantage of the situation and would divert his eyes away from Cheryl's girlie bits. Adam had no such qualms and revelled in the situation. He stared at the marvel in front of him, which made the ache in his groin worse. In fact, it got even worse as he climbed further up the ladder.

Cheryl asked him why he came this way. He said, he wasn't really sure, it was a bit cleaner, but he had just followed his nose. 'It was instinct,' he added.

Cheryl was conscious that he had previously been under alien control.

It was indeed becoming apparent that the surroundings were more upmarket—not attractive, but cleaner and tidier. At the top of the ladder, they crawled through a lock into a small chamber. As Adam had said, there were a large number of cushions in it.

They agreed that this would be an excellent place to spend the night. It was, however, noticeably colder than what they had experienced earlier. Without warning, the lights went out. The girls managed to collect the cushions together to form a bed, and they all cuddled up.

Cheryl guessed who was playing with her nipples, and it wasn't Jenny. She wanted to sleep, but her body reacted to his touch. Jenny felt a hand stroking her pubic hair, and it wasn't Cheryl. Jenny wondered what to do. She decided to take decisive action. Jenny located Adam's penis, stroked it a few times to get maximum hardness and pushed it towards Cheryl's fanny. Contact was made; orgasms were achieved. Adam had his second notch. Jenny felt slightly left out, but there was always the morning. Now sleep was calling.

Location: On-Board Fleet One's Flagship
Sequence of Events: 68

What to do, what to do?

Captain Mustard called an emergency meeting to review the situation.

The alien command ship stood on its own, slightly damaged but motionless. There had been a rather pathetic attempt to destroy the supply ships, but these were now safely out of the way.

Captain Mustard to Command Team, 'It's time to review the situation, but to be honest, we probably don't have a lot of time. Anyway, this is where I think we are:

1. Clearly, the Bug command ship is ready for the taking
2. However, there must be numerous aliens onboard
3. There is also likely to be many Humans onboard, whether they are alive or not is hard to determine
4. A large Fleet of ships is approaching; we are not sure if they are ours or theirs
5. Our Attack Fleet is somewhat diminished, but the Marine Corps is almost intact, although we have left a lot of their combat resources on the supply ships.'

Fleet Operations to Captain Mustard, 'Sir we have detected a further Fleet of ships heading towards us from where the Jill Fleet was initially positioned.

Captain Mustard, 'Have we managed to contact Fleet Jack?'

Fleet Operations, 'Not yet, Sir, but the signal is getting stronger.'

Captain Mustard, to Command Team, 'So, ladies and gentlemen, do we attack the command ship?'

Captain Evans, 'My inclination is to attack, but it's probably too risky. Our task is to capture the Command Ship if we are not careful, it could easily be destroyed. Anyway, my thoughts are as follows:

1. We can't use the proton beam as it could kill any Human captives
2. The same goes for any explosives
3. We need to use subtle tactics, but that would be difficult if we are threatened by the oncoming Fleet or Fleets, assuming they are alien

4.If the oncoming Fleet is ours, then there is no point in rushing in

5.We probably don't have the marine manpower to defeat the aliens in close contact fighting.'

Marine Commander, 'We can't make that assumption.'

Captain Evans, 'It needs to be considered in the mix, so far we haven't found any aliens.'

Captain Mustard, 'Any other observations?'

Special Ops, 'I think my team needs a rest.'

Captain Mustard, 'Fair point. The plan is as follows:

1. General withdrawal from the battle zone.

2. Place our three remaining battleships, and a fighter screen, in a position to protect the alien command ship. I know that it's hardly a credible Fleet, but it is the only choice we have.

3. Collect the Marine resources from the supply ships as a matter of urgency.

4. Special Ops to consider the best way of entering the command ship without causing harm to any human life and ensuring that the command ship is kept reasonably intact.'

Then two things happened, a small missile shot out of the side of the command ship in a direction away from all Fleet activity. This was followed by a very attractive looking schooner.

Fleet Operations to Captain Mustard, 'Two vessels have left the command ship. One looks to be a missile moving at an incredible speed, and the other is a much slower vehicle.'

Captain Mustard, 'Do we have any resources that could chase them?'

Fleet Operations, 'No Sir, not a chance in hell regarding the missile, but we might be able to get the other one.'

Captain Mustard to Command Team, 'Any views?'

Special Ops, 'That was clearly the Big Boss leaving. There is every chance that the command ship will explode shortly.'

Captain Mustard, 'Action stations, action stations, all vessels to take immediate evasive action.'

Location: The President's Office, Presidential Palace, Planet Earth
Sequence of Events: 69

President Padfield called for a meeting with his Chief of Staff, Henry Strong, and their newly appointed admiral.

President Padfield, 'Morning Henry, I hear that things are progressing well.'

Henry Strong, 'Yes, Sir, great progress is being made. Your public relations campaign is working really well. We are now getting huge numbers of volunteers; everyone wants to be in the Navy. Also, factory production levels are outpacing our targets.'

President Padfield, 'And your new Fleet Admiral?'

Henry Strong, 'She looks like the right sort to me, Sir. I chose her from a panel of ten selected by AI Central. Obviously, no real experience, but all the right attributes.'

President Padfield, 'Let's see how she performs.'

Admiral Vicky Ward entered the room. President Padfield couldn't help noticing that her presence was commanding; she had the right air about her.

President Padfield shook her hand and said, 'Admiral Ward, welcome on-board.'

Admiral Ward, 'Thank you, Mr President.'

President Padfield, 'Admiral Ward, George has a Fleet for you to use, it doesn't have any battleships, but it does have a fair punch.

'Henry, can you give us a breakdown please?'

Henry Strong, 'Of course Mr President, the Fleet consists of the following which he displayed on a screen:

Type	Quantity
Command Ship	1
Battlecruiser	10
Destroyer	60
Frigate	50
Fighter	160
Total	281

President Padfield, 'From my limited perspective, I think the following options are available to you:

1. Stay in Galactium space and defend us.
2. Go after Admiral Bonner's Fleet to determine the current status.
3. Head off The Brakendeth.'

Admiral Ward, 'Thank you, Mr President. I think the most logical option is to go after Admiral Bonner's Fleet.'

President Padfield, 'Why is that?'

Admiral Ward, 'Firstly, the only enemy that we actually know about is the one that attacked our planets. By the way, do we have a name for them yet?

Secondly, Admiral Bonner may desperately need our help. There is an old military dictum of going to the sound of the guns.'

President Padfield, 'We can't hear them here.'

Admiral Ward, 'I can. Thirdly, we need Admiral Bonner's experience and knowledge of the enemy, assuming that she has engaged them.

Lastly, and more obviously, The Galactium is so large that it is difficult to decide where our Fleet should be based. If we distribute it, we lose its strength.

'I plan to go to the aid of Admiral Bonner, bring her Fleet back and prepare for the oncoming Brakendeth, assuming that they are still coming? Have we seen any sign of The Ark yet?

Very lastly, Mr President, I want to spend a trillion Galactium Marks.'

President Padfield, 'Did you say a trillion Marks?'

Admiral Ward, 'Yes, I know that It sounds old fashioned, but I want a network of forts. These would act as major military installations with a full complement of weapons. They would also serve as regional Supply and Command Centres.

'Also, we need planetary force-fields.'

President Padfield, 'We don't have that sort of technology yet.'

Admiral Ward, 'In that case we will just have to get it. We are not playing games, you know.'

President Padfield, 'Please present your detailed plans, and I will endorse them.'

Admiral Ward, 'Really?'

President Padfield, 'Yes, really. When can your Fleet depart?'

Admiral Ward, 'I have the Fleet on standby waiting for your orders.'

President Padfield, 'You have my permission to depart.'

And she did.

Henry Strong, 'What do you think?'

President Padfield, 'Well she terrorises me. I can't imagine what she will do to the aliens. I expected her to ask me who will be in charge when she meets up with Admiral Bonner, but I think I know.

Anyway, Henry, I want you to create another Fleet as soon as possible.'

Admiral Ward hadn't expected such a positive reaction from the President. She had better get the Fleet ready.

Admiral Ward to Captain Morton, 'Please prepare the Fleet for departure.'

Captain Morton, 'Where are we going?'

Admiral Ward, 'To fight the aliens, The People's Fleet will follow the course taken by Admiral Bonner.'

Captain Morton, 'How long have we got, Ma'am?'

Admiral Ward, 'None, I told the President that we were ready to go immediately.'

Sometimes Captain Morton hated her, but then he knew that he would never be bored.

Location: On-board the alien Schooner
Sequence of Events: 70

The Killmaster didn't want to desert his flagship, but what could he do? His Skiv Lords had all let him down, and those pesky homans were not playing fair. He wanted revenge on the homans, but he was sure that his masters would want revenge on him.

A more civilised creature would feel guilty about pressing the doomsday switch on the Command Ship. His action would kill well over 10,000 colleagues and his Skiv Lord, but then they could always breed some more. It was more important that he escapes along with the intel on the homans. If his masters get the intel, then they may forgive him for losing the Fleet.

It was also crucial that the three homans escaped. He wasn't sure why his master was insistent that they escaped, but at least it helped him to preserve his own life. It also amused him that the Homans didn't know that they were being manipulated.

The three naked lovebirds wondered what was happening. A rapid acceleration woke them up and threw them around the room. Jenny wondered when she would ever get a good night's sleep: are those days behind her?

Adam found that the entrance lock was locked. They were locked in. It was now a waiting game.

The Killmaster thought he had escaped, but there were ships in the distance.

Killmaster to Bridge, 'Whose ships are those?'

Bridge, 'They are homan ships, my lord. The alien technology had no problems differentiating the ships.'

Killmaster, 'Can we avoid them?'

Bridge, 'Too early to say, but the odds are low.'

Killmaster, 'How low?'

Bridge, 'Less than 10%.'

Location: On-board Admiral Bumelton's Flagship
Sequence of Events: 71

George Bumelton, Fleet Commander, asked for an update.

Fleet Operations, 'Sir, it's getting somewhat confusing, now that full comms are almost back on. The Attack Fleet has launched a warning beacon to avoid the area. The supply ships have been tugged away by Special Ops vessels. They are about to contact Fleet Jill. Squadron A4 has captured an alien launch. Your destroyers are starting to engage the retreating bug ships.'

Fleet Commander, 'Excellent, it's all going to plan. I would assume that the warning beacon probably means that the bug Command Ship is going to explode.'

Fleet Commander to Fleet Operations, 'Can you confirm that an explosion is expected?'

Fleet Operations, 'It has been confirmed.'

Fleet Commander to All destroyer Captains, 'Please be aware that there is a warning beacon near the alien command ship.'

Fleet Commander to Commander Squadron A4, 'Can you confirm that you have captured an alien launch?'

Squadron A4 Leader, 'I can confirm that an alien launch has been captured. It is being held on a tractor beam. A supply ship is on its way to store the vessel.'

Fleet Commander, 'We suspect that it contains the bug leader, it must be protected. You also need to be careful that it doesn't self-detonate.'

Squadron A4 Leader, 'Do you want us to force an entry to prevent that?'

Fleet Commander, 'No, carry on with your current action, but keep your distance.'

Squadron A4 Leader, 'Yes, Sir.'

Fleet Commander to Fleet Operations, 'What is the current battle position?'

Fleet Operations, 'Please see the statistics on the screen:

Fleet	Start	Current	End
Jack Fleet	340	266	

Jill Fleet	166	162	
Attack Fleet	55	27	
Bugs	Approx. 1500	Approx. 145	

Your destroyers are making mincemeat of the enemy vessels.

Fleet Commander to Squadron A4 Leader, 'Our destroyers are engaged with the remnants of the bug Fleet. I'm concerned that the remaining bugs may attempt to rescue their leader.

Please join up with the Jill Fleet, you should have their co-ordinates.'

Fleet Commander to Squadron A5 Leader, 'Squadron A4 have probably captured the Bug Commander. Please adopt standard defensive screen in support of Squadron A4. We expect that there will be bug ships coming your way.'

Fleet Commander to Special Ops, 'Have you contacted Fleet Jill?'

Special Ops, 'Contact has been made, they have taken control of the Bug Supply Ships.'

Fleet Commander to Fleet Jill, 'Please update your positions.'

Squadron Leader D, Fleet Jill, 'We have taken over the protection of the alien supply vessels.'

Squadron Leader E, Fleet Jill,' We're still heading towards the Attack Fleet to provide fighter support, but we understand that there is a warning beacon in place.'

Squadron Leader A, Fleet Jill, 'We are pursuing the aliens; our destroyers are engaged.'

Squadron Leader B, Fleet Jill, 'We are in the same position as Squadron A.'

Squadron Leader C, Fleet Jill, 'We are providing cover, Sir.'

Fleet Commander to Squadron C, Fleet Jill, 'I don't remember asking you to provide cover?'

Squadron C, Fleet Jill, 'No you didn't Sir, but we have collected all of the damaged vessels into one squadron. We are continuing the pursuit but at a much slower speed.'

Fleet Commander, 'I will be having words with you later, my orders must be carried out as instructed.'

Squadron Leader C, Fleet Jill, 'Yes Sir, do you have new orders then?'

Fleet Commander, 'I want squadrons A and B to go to the support of Squadron A4 and A5. Apologies for the name confusion, we need to get better handles in future than we currently have. Do you understand?'

An affirmative response was received.

'Squadrons D, E and C will continue as before.'

A further affirmative response was received.

Fleet Commander to Fleet Operations, 'Can I have another update please?'

Fleet Operations, 'It's on its way to your screen, Sir.'

Fleet	Start	Current	End
Jack Fleet	340	259	
Jill Fleet	166	157	
Attack Fleet	55	27	
Bugs	Approx. 1500	Approx. 86	

Fleet Commander, 'How accurate are the figures on the alien losses?'

Fleet Operations, 'We only include confirmed kills.'

Fleet Commander, 'And what constitutes a confirmed kill?'

Fleet Operations, 'Every vessel has a unique profile which is plotted; it consists of up to 50 different attributes to form a unique signature. It is rare, but possible for two vessels to have the same signature. However, here, the aliens have made no effort to disguise their signatures. You can read them like a book.

'So, the first way we recognise a kill is that the relevant signature disappears. Secondly, our weapon systems recognise their success and update us with kill data. In addition, we get captains contacting us with 'kill' information. You, yourself have done that in the past.'

Fleet Commander, 'So what you are saying is that the intel is pretty accurate'.

Fleet Operations, 'There is no reason to expect otherwise. While we have been talking more 'kills' have come in:

Fleet	Start	Current	End
Jack Fleet	340	259	
Jill Fleet	166	156	

Attack Fleet	55	27	
Bugs	Approx. 1500	Approx. 68	

Fleet Commander, 'Can you plot where the remaining aliens are heading?'

Fleet Operations, 'Yes Sir, two-thirds are heading towards the alien Command Ship, the rest are heading to Squadron A4's location.'

Fleet Commander to all Fleet Captains, 'We are heading towards what is probably our final battle with the aliens.

'This is the current position:

1. Squadrons A4 and A5 are escorting the captured alien leader.
2. Squadrons A and B, Jill Fleet, are rushing to support squadrons A4 and A5.
3. Squadrons C, D and E (of the Jack Fleet) and the destroyers of the Jill Fleet are engaging the enemy.

'The captured alien leader must be secured.

'Once again, I thank you for all the sacrifices you have made, but we are nearly there.'

George had every expectation that they would lose both the alien Command Ship and the alien leader. He could see it coming.

Location: On-board the First Fleet Flagship
Sequence of Events: 72

The massive Command Ship just sat there. A large area around it had been cleared. No one was too sure how much clearance was required.

The Survey Team scouted around the edge of the vessel carrying out deep, immersive scans. Their results were somewhat shocking:

- There were 15,000 aliens, or blobs that they assumed were aliens.
- There were 20,000 humans on some sort of racking, but many had no heat signals, so they were presumed dead.
- There was a large aviary with perhaps a million birds in it.
- There was what looked like a large arsenal of hand weapons.
- Engine room.
- Life support.
- Oxygen generators.
- Stores.
- Transport.
- A cavern-like room.
- Dormitories.
- Kitchens and canteens.

A blue light started flashing on top of the command ship. The scout team decided to exit as fast as they could. Everyone admired their bravery, especially the command audience.

On the bridge of one of the battleships stood Admiral Bonner, Captain Mustard, Captain Evans, the Special Ops Commander, and the Marine Commander. They were all waiting for the fun to start. They should have been disappointed as the capture of this ship was one of their key objectives. But secretly, well not so secretly, they wanted revenge. In a way, it was a shame that the alien leader was not onboard. There was also a concern for any Human survivors, but they all had a feeling that few wished to be rescued, they had probably been through too much.

The blue light flashed faster and faster, and then the ship started shrinking and shrinking. The blue light flashed even faster until the human eye could not detect any flashing at all. The ship shrank to the size of a football stadium, then down to the size of a double-decker bus, and then it continued to shrink down to the size of a family car, then the size of a dog, and then it got smaller, to the point where it was not visible.

Captain Mustard, still astonished, ordered everyone to stay back in case a massive explosion was still on the cards.

It looked like there were no cards. What an anti-climax. Admiral Bonner commented that she had seen better fireworks in her garden.

Captain Mustard ordered his team to stand down. He asked Special Ops to determine if there was anything left of the Command Ship.

Location: On-Board Fleet One's Flagship
Sequence of Events: 73

Captain Mustard to Fleet Commander, George Bumelton, 'Hello Commander, I want to congratulate you on a job done well. The enemy has almost been eliminated. Excellent stuff.'

George Bumelton, 'My commiserations to you on the loss of the alien command ship.'

Captain Mustard, 'There was not a lot that we could have done, there were no practical options open to us. At least we have got the storage ships, and thanks to you, we have the alien leader.'

George Bumelton, 'What about the loss of human life aboard the command ship?'

Captain Mustard, 'Our initial analysis from the scans shows that there were probably 20,000 human bodies onboard, but only a small percentage were alive.'

George Bumelton, 'How many?'

Captain Mustard, 'Less than 500, Clearly every life is valuable but who knows what happened to those poor souls.'

George Bumelton, 'I need to find out where we are with my Fleet dispositions, talk to you later'.

Captain Mustard started to wonder who was in charge; it's funny how power flows in different directions. He had a strong feeling that he was being criticised.

Fleet Commander, George Bumelton to Fleet Operations, 'Could I have the latest statistics please?'

Fleet Operations, 'Yes, Sir, on your screen now.'

Fleet	Start	Current	End
First Fleet	561	401	
Bugs	Approx. 1500	Approx. 27	

Fleet Commander to Jack and Jill Fleets, 'Captain Mustard has just congratulated me on my performance, but it is your performance that should be commended. We have lost some dear friends, but we have achieved some revenge, and I believe gained great honour in the process.

'We have destroyed their fleet; there are only 27 vessels left, we have captured 5 of their supply ships and their leader. Sadly, their Command Ship self-destructed, or should I say shrank into oblivion.'

'Sir, they're down to 23 vessels now,' shouted an officer from Fleet Operations.

George Bumelton, 'Thank you for that.

'I'm now sounding the recall: you are now back under the command of Captain Mustard.'

It took some time, but the Fleet returned to its cruising formation. Captain Mustard looked at the battle statistics; he had lost 20% of his Fleet. How would history view his performance?

The final figures were:

Fleet	Start	Current	End
First Fleet	561	401	
Bugs	Approx. 1500	Approx. 23	

He couldn't add the end figures as there was still a long way to go. He decided to call a command meeting.

Location: On-board the alien Schooner
Sequence of Events: 74

The Killmaster realised that his ship had been captured. It was motionless, but nothing was happening, nothing at all.

He asked the bridge what was happening, but they weren't accommodating. They thought that his ship had been caught in a tractor beam. Apparently, he was surrounded by a small Fleet. Then he noticed some motion.

Again, he contacted the bridge. They thought that the ship was being dragged onto a cargo vessel. He asked himself if it was now the time to commit suicide. Unfortunately, the launch did not have a self-destruct button. He wondered if it had any weapons.

The bridge informed him that it was weaponless. Its role was just ceremonial.

He knew that he shouldn't have relied on the Skiv Lords so much. Now they were his doom.

How should he handle the homans? He was a master at handling primitive species.

Elsewhere, the three humans also wondered what was going on. They could hear a series of scraping noises but little else. They didn't have the luxury of being able to contact the bridge. As the hours wore on, Adam hoped to play some games, but the girls would not hear of it.

He suggested wrestling, massage, British Bulldog, but still no interest. They eventually agreed to a game of I-spy, but Adam's selections were all rude.

Again, it was just another waiting game, at least the room was getting warmer.

Location: On-Board Admiral Ward's Flagship
Sequence of Events: 75

Admiral Ward had her Fleet lined out in standard cruising formation. She was keen to investigate different formations as the Navy Manual was at least 500 years old. Some of it even mentioned real ships—that is, water-based ships. She could see that different formations would be needed for different types of engagement, but how would the new weapons fit into this?

Her Fleet was easily the most modern Fleet produced by Humankind. The next generation would be considerably better.

Her Fleet was about 30% faster than the First Fleet. Every capital vessel had proton beam technology. Every vessel had atomisers. The power of these weapons had been increased by at least 40%, and they were lethal. The communications system was years ahead. It was nothing clever; they just used commercially available technology.

The defensive capabilities had also been re-engineered with new force fields and automatic shielding.

Her biggest problem was staffing. Not one of her crew had been in the fighting side of the Navy, although there were a few admin staff who had served before. Most of them had never fired a gun or even been in space before. This was also true of herself; she originally planned to lead a comfortable life as a lawyer. This was before the aliens effectively eliminated her planet.

She wasn't sure if her task was to turn this crew into a fighting force or to just hand the Fleet over to Admiral Bonner, a real admiral. Humanity had also lost the art of writing orders, so everything was a bit vague, but they would learn.

Location: On-Board Fleet One's Flagship
Sequence of Events: 76

Captain Mustard mulled over the recent events. It was probably time to go home, but he thought he owed it to his staff to discuss it with them.

Captain Mustard, 'Welcome everyone, I've prepared some drinks, it's not a victory party, but I thought a small celebration was in order.

'Firstly, I would like to propose a minute's silence for those we have lost', which duly took place. 'I'm sure that we will have time to mourn them a later date.

I've called you together for several reasons:

1. To review our performance.
2. To discuss the way forward re the alien leader.
3. To agree our return to The Galactium.

'Firstly, evaluating our performance, I'm not sure if I can face it. I know that it's not that professional, but we have been through so much.'

Admiral Bonner, 'I insist that we carry out the review but let's leave it for another day.

'I would, however, like to take this opportunity to make some promotions. Captains Mustard and Bumelton are to be promoted to Admiral. Tom Crocker, Special Ops is promoted to Fleet Commander.'

There was a round of clapping and congratulations.

'Further awards will be made in the next few days. Let's get down to business, what do we do with the alien bag of shit?'

Admiral Bumelton, 'Have we scanned the craft?'

Special Ops, 'It's too heavily protected for our scanners to be effective'.

Admiral Bumelton, 'Do we know how many passengers are onboard?'

Special Ops, 'There is only room for half a dozen.'

Admiral Bumelton, 'What about weapons?'

Special Ops, 'There is no sign of any, but we can't really tell.'

Admiral Mustard, 'I did ask our Psychological Warfare Team for input. I asked what they thought its frame of mind would be? Their feedback is on the screen:

• The alien thought it had escaped, so being captured at the last

moment must be a shock.
- It was used to total power.
- It expected to be successful.
- It sees humans as food.
- It probably sees humans of no consequence.
- It will want revenge.
- It will see us as weak.
- It killed 15,000 members of its species with little or no compunction.
- It's used to advanced technology.
- If it has someone senior to it, then it's probably in trouble.
- It will be frightened of humans as it will think that we will want revenge because it has committed truly heinous crimes against Humanity.

'We believe that there is a 40% chance that it has committed suicide.

'There is a 60% chance that it will come out shooting, he will want to take as many with it as possible. This is really a form of suicide.

'If there are other aliens onboard, it might disguise itself as one of the underlings.

'Obviously, communication is going to be difficult. If it does talk, it will blame everyone else.

'I believe that this has set the scene. Admiral Bonner has already said that it will be returned to Earth for trial. Consequently, we need to protect it.

'So, what is next?'

Special Ops, 'We plan to drill out the airlock slowly, we have special cutting gear that can do this.'

Admiral Bumelton, 'Then they either come out voluntarily, or we go in and drag them out. I've got my bayonet ready.'

Admiral Bonner, 'Changing the subject, reference point three: once two is done, my suggestion is that we head for The Galactium.'

Everyone nodded their heads.

Admiral Bonner, 'Ladies and gentlemen, prepare to go home.'

They all drank to that.

Admiral Mustard to all crew, 'We have some admin tasks to complete in the next few days, then the Fleet will return. We are going home.'

He thought he could hear the cheers, or it might have been him. He was particularly looking forward to seeing his black cat, Napoleon.

163

Location: On-board the Albatross Flagship
Sequence of Events: 77

Admiral Millington was still pondering over the current position. They had spent a year travelling, well, *rushing* to this planet. Had they travelled far enough? Should this be the spot where his team build the new Eden? If they went further, would things be better or worse? That is the trouble with the unknown: it's unknown.

Admiral Millington, 'Good morning everyone, this is the one-hundredth meeting of the Council, another landmark. And talking about land, how is it going?'

Head of Science, 'It's looking good, but obviously, it's far too early to be definitive as lots more tests are needed.'

Admiral Millington, 'Do you have any test results that you can share with us?'

Head of Science, 'Not really, when I'm ready I will let you know.'

Admiral Millington, 'So that you know we have set up a defensive cordon around the planet. I've also got search parties systematically evaluating all the local solar systems. We need to make sure that we have the room to grow, and that there are long-term resources available to support a growing population.'

Head of Science, 'What resources are you looking for?'

Admiral Millington, 'Typically titanium, vanadium, iron, manganese, copper, zinc, and such.'

Head of Science, 'I thought we were going to create an agrarian society.'

Admiral Millington, 'What made you think that?'

Head of Science, 'The Industrial Revolution brought nothing but disaster to Humankind, we can't go on with it.'

Admiral Millington, 'I think most people assumed that we would recreate our existing society, warts and all.'

Head of Science, 'I'm not sure if that is the view of the scientific community.'

Admiral Millington, 'Well I'm the boss, and my view is that we will recreate our existing society'.

Head of Science, 'In that case I resign.'

Admiral Millington thought to himself, *Well, that was another successful meeting.*

Admiral Millington to AI Central, 'I need another Head of Science.'

AI Central, 'Did you break the last one?'

Admiral Millington, 'More or less.'

AI Central, 'I'm quite pleased that this has happened, as Bob was a bit of a Luddite, we couldn't get him to move forward on a lot of things.'

Admiral Millington, 'Do you have anyone in mind?'

AI Central, 'We do, but he is a bit young.'

Admiral Millington, 'Being young is not a crime.'

AI Central, 'In the scientific world you have to earn your place by solid, provable work, the publishing of technical papers, recognition from institutes, who you know etcetera. Conner has none of this, but he does have one of the best brains we have ever seen.

'We don't think he will be accepted due to his age.'

Admiral Millington, 'Well I would like to meet this young man. How old is he?'

AI Central, 'Eleven.'

Admiral Millington, 'Now come on, that is not playing the game.'

AI Central, 'Sorry I couldn't resist playing with you. He does have a brilliant brain, but he is not experienced enough. Perhaps next year. We don't have a vast pool to work with.'

Admiral Millington, 'Get back to me as soon as you can. We need to move things on here. Changing the subject, what is your view regarding this planet?'

AI Central, 'A waste of time.'

Admiral Millington, 'Why?'

AI Central, 'I have a list of reasons:
- Lack of resources.
- Not easy to defend.
- Dangerous fauna.
- Huge insect populations in the spring months.
- The planet is susceptible to massive soil erosion.
- Too much seismic activity.
- Freezing winters every ten years.
- Some microbes could become very dangerous.

• Too difficult to develop nearby planets.'

Admiral Millington, 'Why didn't you tell me earlier?'

AI Central, 'I have learnt that it is better if humans find out for themselves. It will probably take another three weeks before the scientific team decide that the planet is not suitable.'

Admiral Millington, 'Can you help move it along?'

AI Central, 'Yes, we will do that, give us a week.'

Location: On-board the alien Schooner
Sequence of Events: 78

The Special Ops Team was ready, and the cutting gear was in place. A special frame had been built to support the cutting process. On completion, the locked door should just fall off.

The security detail was ready; both hand-held and tripod-based machine guns were in place. Both Steel and Plasti-mec shields were in position. Additional well-armoured troops were on standby.

Mobile prison cells were ready, along with electrified fencing, minefields and heavy-duty restraints.

Admiral Mustard thought that it reminded him of an old Hollywood gangster movie.

The cutting had started, and the gangster should soon emerge.

Inside, the three human specimens could hear cutting and grinding noises coming from the locked door. Jenny thought that she had survived much longer than most; now, she was going to be eaten. Cheryl thought she might go out fighting, although in the past there had been lots of talk, and little action. Adam thought well at least he had made love to two beautiful women; it had probably made their week.

The Killmaster had decided to exit the lock with dignity. He would face the homans with contempt. They were worth less than his bottom scrapings. Anyway, he would let the young homans leave first.

The lock crashed onto the floor with a din that surprised everyone, even though they knew it was going to happen. Fingers pressed against triggers. Cameras were rolling, and the whole Human Galactium would see this. It would be the pinnacle of the Fleet's success.

Someone shouted, 'Come out with your hands up.'

Out they walked, three naked teenagers with their hands up in the air.

They just stood there and became a front-page sensation. Jenny thought that they would never live it down. She did, however, notice that Adam had lost his erection. There were some things that even his erection could not cope with.

There were loads of questions, but they were being followed out by a beast. They were dragged to one side and covered.

This was the team's first look at an alien.

Was it a spider?

Was it an insect?

Was it a slug?

It was large by human standards, a concoction of limbs and tentacles, and eyes. Far too many eyes, slimy, stout, diseased looking. It was wearing some form of regalia. The small, extendable head—if that was what it was, had rows of sharp teeth. Not a pretty thing.

The Killmaster found the smell of homans repugnant, but he had enjoyed eating them. All the homans looked the same to him, but he thought he recognised one of them. Wasn't that the one that gave birth to his child?

Two further aliens followed him out.

All three were quickly secured and imprisoned. There was no attempt at questioning. That would be left to the experts.

Anyway, back to the youngsters, they had been a bigger shock than seeing the aliens. Admiral Mustard was desperate to get their story, but they needed rest, food and definitely some clothing, although there will be a lot of young boys, and men, who will enjoy those photos. He couldn't help noticing the erect nipples. For a moment, he was ashamed of himself, but then he remembered that he had not touched a woman in nearly two years. That would have to be changed.

Admiral Ward's Fleet continued to follow the path that Admiral Bonner's Fleet took. There had been no surprises. There had been a few mechanical breakdowns, but that was to be expected, with a new Fleet. One destroyer had to be sent back to Fleet HQ as it had far too many snags.

The staff were holding up; she had organised a few exercises on the way, but she was torn between the need to help Admiral Bonner, and the need to get her Fleet fully operational.

Location: On-board Fleet One's Flagship
Sequence of Events: 80

Admirals Mustard and Bonner were waiting for the youngsters to arrive. They couldn't decide whether to interview them separately or together. They decided to do them together in the end, and then go into one-on-one sessions if necessary.

Admiral Mustard, 'Welcome to our ante-room.'

Jenny, 'Are we in trouble?'

Admiral Mustard, 'No, far from it, you are heroes. You are the only civilian survivors from this whole war.'

Jenny, 'That can't be the case.'

Admiral Mustard, 'In fact you are the only humans who have been in the aliens' command ship and survived.'

Jenny, 'What happened to the other humans when the command ship disappeared?'

Admiral Mustard, 'I'm afraid that they just disappeared with the ship.'

Jenny, 'Oh, my god.'

Admiral Mustard, 'So you see, you know more about the command ship than anyone else.'

Jenny, 'We will obviously help you in any way we can.'

Admiral Mustard, 'Are you the spokesperson?'

Jenny, 'Not at all.' She turned to the others and said, 'Please jump in when you want.'

Both Cheryl and Adam nodded.

Admiral Mustard, 'Firstly, can I ask why you were naked?'

Adam, 'We noticed that the aliens took an interest in us when we were wearing clothes. If we were naked, they took no interest in us at all. It doesn't really make sense, but that seemed to be the case.'

Admiral Mustard, 'Were you stripped of your clothes, or did you do it voluntarily?'

Jenny, 'I was stripped of my clothes when they were impregnating me.'

Admiral Mustard, 'What do you mean by impregnating you?'

Jenny, 'I was stripped, and the monster you have in jail put one of his tentacles up my fanny. Are you allowed to say fanny?'

Admiral Mustard, 'Yes, fanny is perfectly acceptable, please continue.'

Jenny, 'Well the beast then deposited some sort of seed in my fanny.'

Admiral Mustard, 'So the beast raped you?'

Jenny, 'It didn't seem like rape, as he didn't seem to get any pleasure out of it.'

Admiral Mustard, 'How could you tell?'

Jenny, 'Well, I can't really. It just seemed like another job to him.'

Admiral Mustard, 'What happened next?'

Jenny, 'I was put on a rack up in the air.'

Admiral Mustard, 'Was it floating?'

Jenny, 'No, it was a structure, there were thousands of us. Then this thing burst out from your abdomen.'

Admiral Mustard, 'Let's take this slowly, you were on this rack, and there were thousands of others.'

Jenny, 'Yes.'

Admiral Mustard, 'Were there just women on the rack?'

Jenny, 'No men and women, and children.'

Admiral Mustard, 'And some had burst abdomens?'

Jenny, 'Yes, the seed is put inside you, and a few days later these insect things just burst out.'

Admiral Mustard, 'And they come out through the abdomen?'

Jenny, 'Yes, that's right, lots of them.'

Admiral Mustard, 'Did you see this happen?'

Jenny, 'Yes, the woman next to me had a very extended stomach. Suddenly a sharp knife cut her open, and about ten insect-like things flew out.'

Admiral Mustard to Admiral Bonner, 'These must be the 'birds' we scanned in the command ship.'

Admiral Mustard, 'Where did this knife come from?'

Jenny, 'It was on a lever which swung up from the rack below. To be honest, I was so shocked I think I became unconscious. The whole room was disgusting, it smelt disgusting, there were racks of dead men and women with their guts ripped out. Can we move on?'

Admiral Mustard, 'We will soon; how come you survived this?'

Jenny. 'I don't know why, but I was lowered down onto a trolley.'

Admiral Mustard, 'Then what happened?'

Jenny, 'An alien put his tentacle up my fanny, and I became unconscious.'

Admiral Mustard, 'Is that all?'

Jenny, 'Frankly, that was enough, how would you like it?'

Admiral Mustard, 'Apologies, that was not what I meant. Please go on.'

Jenny, 'Well, I think the beastie in me was removed, and I was patched up.'

Admiral Mustard, 'So you gave birth then?'

Jenny, 'It sounds strange, but I think it was a Caesarean birth.'

Admiral Mustard, 'This is all hard to believe.'

Jenny, 'I am telling you the truth.'

Admiral Mustard, 'No, sorry, I believe you. It's just all so bizarre.'

Jenny, 'I agree.'

Admiral Mustard, 'What about you, Adam?'

Adam, 'My story is rather boring, I was captured and taken to the ship. I was then nullified.'

Admiral Mustard, 'What's that?'

Adam, 'It's a way of removing your conscious control. You have to do what they want you to do. They do it to all the lab rats.'

Admiral Mustard, 'What do you mean by lab rats?'

Adam, 'Lab rats are the humans that were being experimented on. The bugs were carrying out thousands of different experiments.'

Admiral Mustard, 'How many types of experiment?'

Adam, 'Too many to mention.'

Admiral Mustard, 'This is important, could you list the experiments please?'

Jenny, 'I saw them as well; it's not the sort of thing that we want to think about.'

Admiral Mustard, 'This could be very important for the Human Race. Please could you concentrate, and then list them on the board?'

Jenny and Adam, 'OK, here we go:

- They sewed a human head onto one of the aliens. In fact, one alien had two human heads attached to its body.

172

- Other body parts were also being grafted onto aliens.
- A girl was running on a treadmill, then they bit her head off, and took out her beating heart.
- Brains were exposed.
- Lots of dissection.
- Human eyes were being experimented on. A young boy had his optic nerve dangling from his head.
- There were similar nose and ear investigations.

Jenny was crying, and Adam was trying to comfort her.

Jenny, 'Then we saw the worst thing of all. It was a gestation display. It showed baby growth day by day.'

Admiral Mustard, 'That doesn't sound too bad?'

Jenny, 'They must have used 300 babies to produce the display!'

Jenny was visibly upset, very upset indeed.

Admiral Mustard, 'Let's take a break. We do need to get the information logged and recorded while it's still fresh in your mind'.

Cheryl,' That's no problem, I think it's probably therapeutic for us.'

Admiral Mustard, 'We will see you later.' He was going to suggest lunch, but he didn't think it would go down that well.

Admiral Mustard, 'Well, Admiral Bonner, what do you think of that?'

Admiral Bonner, 'I'm pretty sure that they are telling the truth. Anyway, it all seems to tie up with our thinking. It looks like we are breeding vessels for an alien race. If we are not careful, that could be our future. The universe has suddenly become a much nastier place.'

Admiral Mustard, 'What about the experiments?'

Admiral Bonner, 'They are just being logical, just studying their enemy.'

Admiral Mustard, 'You might be right except that the aliens seemed to be leaving our space. It looks like they were carrying out seriously detailed experiments. I'm sure that there is another reason for this, but it escapes me at the moment.'

Admiral Bonner, 'Your hunches are usually right. That's what gives you your edge.'

Adam, 'Well girls, what did you think of that?'

Cheryl, 'We have been through so much, now we are being interrogated.'

Jenny, 'Do we have a choice?'

Adam, 'Probably, but if we refuse it won't go well for us.'

Jenny, 'Anyway, Admiral Mustard is rather nice, I quite fancy him.'

Cheryl, 'Me too, I would have his babies.'

Jenny, 'After what's been up and down my fanny over the last few weeks, I don't fancy any of that malarkey, but on the other hand he is rather dishy. Perhaps I could give him a chance' They all laughed.

Adam, 'Anyway, you could always have my babies instead?'

Cheryl, 'We want babies from a man, not a little boy.'

Adam, 'I managed to look after you two the last few days.'

Jenny, 'We had to show you what to do.'

Adam, 'OK, I may have needed a little bit of assistance, but I got the job done.'

Cheryl, 'Getting your rocks off is hardly getting the job done, what about the woman's needs?'

Adam, 'Anyway, we are going to be rich.'

Jenny, 'Why's that?'

Adam, 'Firstly TV and televisual interviews, books, films, we will be famous, loads of opportunities.'

And as for you two, your nude pictures are going to be everywhere. You will be in huge demand. And of course, I can say that I slept with both of you. It's going to be magic.'

Jenny wondered if his erection was back.

Cheryl, 'Should we ask for some proper clothes, these hospital smocks are indecent? They don't do up properly. Everyone can see your arse.'

Jenny, 'I don't know why, but they are fairly normal in a hospital.'

Adam, 'I rather like them, it's good to see a bit of arse occasionally.'

Jenny said, 'That's typical of you,' as she made sure that her bottom was not on show.

Cheryl, 'Do we want our own rooms, or should we stick together?'

Adam, 'I think it's important that we stick together for safety. We could ask them to put a large double bed in the room.'

Cheryl, 'And why would we want that?'

Adam, 'Well, you might get a bit lonely and want some romance.'

Jenny, 'That's all you ever think of.' Despite the tentacle experience, she was still quite interested in a little bit of hanky-panky. Perhaps Adam could be in luck later, assuming that he still fancied her arse.

Both Cheryl and Jenny did, however, decide that they would like to stay together.

Cheryl, 'Changing the subject, I wasn't so keen on that old witch at the back of the room.'

Adam, 'Nor me, not sure what she was doing there, but she must be at least a hundred years old.'

Jenny, 'I wouldn't want to get on the wrong side of her.'

Anyway, together, they realised that they needed to continue with the interviews.

Location: On-board Fleet One's Flagship
Sequence of Events: 82

Admirals Mustard and Bonner wondered if they had been too hard on the kids. The transcripts didn't read too bad, but they don't always highlight the emotion of the situation.

Admiral Mustard, 'We must continue, we have learnt so much.'

The teenagers casually walked in and took their seats. Perhaps they hadn't needed to worry about them after all.

Admiral Mustard, 'Welcome back, I hope yesterday wasn't too bad for you. We are doing this for the best of reasons. I forgot to say yesterday that everything is being recorded. Anyway, yesterday we were talking about experiments. Now I think it's best to move on.

'Cheryl, what is your story?'

Cheryl, 'Like the others, I was captured and taken to the ship. Like Jenny, I had a seed planted up my girl's bit.'

Admiral Mustard, 'You mean your vagina?'

Cheryl, 'Yes, I don't like to say that word. I was taken to the rack, and nothing happened.'

Admiral Mustard, 'What do you mean nothing happened?'

Cheryl, 'I don't think the seed developed.'

Admiral Mustard, 'What happened next?'

Cheryl, 'I was lowered down the frame. Then one of the brutes dragged me towards the liquidiser.'

Admiral Mustard, 'What do you mean by liquidiser?'

Cheryl, 'It's where they put all the dead bodies.'

Admiral Mustard, 'But you were still alive.'

Cheryl, 'That wouldn't stop them; as far as they were concerned, I was barren and of no use.'

Admiral Mustard, 'What happened next?'

Cheryl, 'I managed to get this small steel pole, and I stuck it in the alien's back. I then twisted it hard, and it let me go. It didn't put up much of a fight. I was surprised at how easily I got away. That's when I met Jenny and Adam.'

Adam, 'And then things started getting better as I took over.'

Admiral Mustard, 'What did you do, Adam?'

Adam, 'Well, the first thing I did was to make love to the girls.'

Admiral Mustard, 'What?! Both of them?'

Adam, 'Of course.'

Admiral Mustard turning to Jenny and Cheryl, 'Did he?'

They both nodded. Admiral Mustard couldn't help smiling as the girls' reaction spoke a thousand words.

Admiral Mustard, 'What happened next?'

Adam, 'The girls complimented me on my lovemaking skills.'

Admiral Mustard to Recorder, 'Delete that last comment from the record. So, Adam, what actually happened next?'

Adam, 'Well I found some biscuits, and then a good hiding place to sleep.'

Admiral Mustard, 'And where was that hiding place?'

Adam, 'Well, it turned out to be the alien boss's flyer, and that's how you found us.'

Admiral Mustard, 'That is an amazing piece of luck...'

Adam, 'It was.'

Admiral Mustard, 'And you had no suspicions?'

Cheryl, 'Actually none of us had any idea, it was just luck.'

Admiral Mustard, 'Jenny, is there anything else you want to tell us?'

Jenny, 'There were lots of corridors, there was a lift, but we used a ladder, at one time I was going to be part of a celebration feast, very dirty, that's about it.'

Admiral Mustard, 'Cheryl is there anything else you want to add?'

Cheryl, 'Not particularly, the alien I stabbed had black oily blood. To be honest, I was surprised how easily I got away. I stabbed him, and he more or less gave in. We had no food or water.'

Admiral Mustard, 'Adam, what about you?'

Adam, 'I think we have covered everything.'

Admiral Mustard, 'At some stage you were under alien control, is that correct?'

Adam, 'Yes, but I'm totally free of it now.'

Admiral Mustard, 'How do you know?'

Adam, 'Well, I don't, but I feel that I'm under my own control now.'

Admiral Mustard, 'Fair enough, but we still think that the chances of you getting in the Skiverton shuttle at the right time difficult to

177

believe.'

Jenny, 'I don't think you should pick on Adam; we were all there. It was just luck.'

Admiral Mustard, 'Fair enough, I accept that.'

Jenny wondered if he did.

Jenny, 'We wondered if we could have some proper clothes as these are somewhat indecent.'

Admiral Mustard had noticed and enjoyed the curve of Jenny's bum, but then he had seen her stark naked before. He told them that they could not get proper clothing until they left the hospital unit. Jenny asked when that would be, but apparently, it was a medical decision and not theirs.

Admiral Mustard, 'Thank you all, we may need to question you later, but you can go now. I just wanted to say that you have all been very brave.'

The youngsters were escorted back to the hospital unit.

Admiral Mustard, 'Admiral Bonner I don't think that we can get much more out of them.'

Admiral Bonner, 'I tend to agree with you, but they are the only human survivors. They were also found in the alien leader's ship. I think we still need to be very careful. We know that the aliens can affect human minds. They might have been hypnotised or had their brains altered in some way.'

Admiral Mustard to Security, 'I want you to keep the three youngsters under 24-hour surveillance. Let me know if anything interesting happens. Make sure everything is filmed.'

Admiral Bonner, 'What about the supply ships? You have a theory that they contain the remains of our missing population.'

Admiral Mustard, 'Yes, I don't want to be the one who raises it as it is just so dreadful, but that is the only conclusion I can come to. Once confirmed, that beast in detention must be punished.'

Admiral Bonner, 'True, but is he the leader, or just a stooge? They must have a home planet.'

Admiral Mustard, 'One of the reports stated that the aliens might have been manufactured, they didn't seem to go through a normal evolutionary process. That gestation model was detailing the human process in some depth, which wasn't just a normal study.'

Admiral Bonner, 'I fear that you may be right again.'

Location: On-board Fleet One's Flagship
Sequence of Events: 83

The three admirals were having dinner; this was their first social event in many a long month. They had become friends, as it was challenging to mix with other ranks and maintain the right level of dignity. Anyway, they liked each other.

The Fleet was now on its homeward journey; every member of the crew relished the return to see friends and family. They had done well, they knew it. It felt good. They would be heroes when they returned.

The alien leader was securely imprisoned, awaiting interrogation. The youngsters had been interrogated and had provided much useful information.

The storage ships and the schooner were being studied and would also provide a great deal of useful information. With luck, they would help future spacecraft development. They had also secured many alien wrecks and even alien specimens. It should keep The Galactium scientists in work for centuries.

Head of Science to Admiral Bonner, 'Ma'am could I speak to you?'

Admiral Bonner, 'Of course, I will put you on speakerphone as Admirals Mustard and Bumelton are also here.'

Head of Science, 'It's a very delicate matter, Ma'am.'

Admiral Bonner, 'That's not a problem, I have no secrets from my colleagues.'

Head of Science, 'Well. We have analysed the contents of the storage ships, and we have concluded that they are the Humans from the invaded planets.'

Admiral Bonner, 'What, all one hundred billion of them?'

Head of Science, 'Yes the entire bio-mass from those planets, plant life, animals and humans have been liquidised. Much of the water content has been removed for storage purposes.'

Admiral Bonner, 'What were they using it for?'

Head of Science, 'It looks like there were two uses. Firstly, it was a food source; the crew were all eating Humans. In fact, the Human captives were unknowingly eating Humans as well.'

We think that the second use was going to be fertiliser.'

179

Admiral Bonner, 'This is just too horrible to believe.'

Admiral Bumelton, 'This race doesn't deserve to exist. I'm going to kill that fucking alien beast in detention.'

Admiral Bonner, 'You will not, we need him for interrogation. Believe me; we will find ways of making him talk, and possibly suffer.'

Location: On-board the Albatross Flagship
Sequence of Events: 84

Head of Science, 'Admiral, I have some bad news.'

Admiral Millington, 'Well firstly, I would like to congratulate you on your new role. It's nice to see some new blood.'

Head of Science, 'I was rather surprised to get the appointment, but when AI Central selects you, what can you do?'

Admiral Millington, 'Very true, but what is the bad news?'

Head of Science, 'The planet below is not suitable for us. I'm a bit surprised that Bob was so enthusiastic, but then he was a bit retro.'

Admiral Millington, 'Too true, but what are the reasons?'

Head of Science, 'To some extent it is a gut feeling, but there are good technical reasons too.'

Admiral Millington, 'Please go on.'

Head of Science, 'Well I have made a list:
- Lack of resources.
- Not easy to defend.
- Dangerous fauna.
- Huge insect populations in the Spring months.
- The planet is susceptible to massive soil erosion.
- Too much seismic activity.
- Freezing winters every ten years.
- Some microbes could become very dangerous.
- Too difficult to develop nearby planets.'

Admiral Millington, 'No, that doesn't look good, but could I ask you to reconsider? The crew are tied, and they were very excited about having this as a new home.'

Head of Science, 'No, I've made my mind up.'

Admiral Millington, 'Would your team support you in this decision? It's a big decision, and it will fall on your head, as I'm a simple naval officer. I will follow your recommendations.'

Head of Science, 'I suggest I get my number two on the phone so that you can get a second opinion.'

Admiral Millington, 'Is that your intended?'

Head of Science, 'Yes, she is actually. With my promotion, I can afford to get married.'

Admiral Millington, 'And would she provide an unbiased assessment?'

Head of Science, 'Best to ask her, I will patch you through.'

Admiral Millington, 'Is that the Deputy Head of Science?'

Deputy Head, 'Yes.'

Admiral Millington, 'Congratulations on your forthcoming nuptials.'

Deputy Head, 'Thank you very much.'

Admiral Millington, 'I'm asking you in your professional capacity. Do you think that the planet below is suitable for our purposes or not?'

Deputy Head, 'I can provide detailed reasons.'

Admiral Millington, 'No, just a simple yes or no will do.'

Deputy Head, 'The answer is emphatically no.'

Admiral Millington, 'Thank you very much.'

Admiral Millington, 'Well Norman, thank you for that, I do believe that we can work well together.'

Head of Science, 'I do hope so.'

Admiral Millington to all crew and staff, 'It is with great regret that I have to inform you that the Heads of Science have identified some cast-iron reasons why the planet below is not suitable for our needs. I know that some of you had high expectations, but it is not to be. Over and out.'

Admiral Millington to all commanders, 'This is a recall for all defensive cordon units and search parties to return and form standard cruising formation.'

AI Central to Admiral Millington, 'It's amazing what a good team can do.'

Admiral Millington, 'When I find a good team, I will let you know.'

.

Location: On-board Admiral Ward's Flagship
Sequence of Events: 85

Admiral Ward wondered what the other admirals did to fight the curse of boredom in the Fleet. The use of the Amazon Extradrive Portals certainly reduced the travel times dramatically. She still thought it funny that Amazon started as an online bookseller. She wondered how else you would buy books. *I guess that you would buy them in person, with money,* she thought to herself, *how quaint.* History had always interested her.

While she was mulling things over, a call came from Captain Morton.

Captain Morton, 'Ma'am, we have been picking up signals from the long-distance scanners. At first, we thought it was some form of meteor storm, but we have picked up 'vague' signatures.'

Admiral Ward, 'Is it the First Fleet?'

Captain Morton, 'Possibly, but they are not coming from the direction we were expecting, and the signatures would not be so vague, but they are a long way off. In addition, we think that there may be some military action.'

Admiral Ward, 'What do you mean by military action?'

Captain Morton, 'Well, we can't detect any munitions being used, but there is a lot of manoeuvring going on. It tends to suggest that tactical positioning is taking place.'

Admiral Ward, 'What are your recommendations?'

Captain Morton, 'That we declare action stations, and reorganise the formation for defence.'

Admiral Ward to all commanders, 'Action stations, action stations!' The alarms went off immediately. She smirked to herself that she had always wanted to do that.

Captain Morton, 'I will share my deployment with you shortly.'

Admiral Ward, 'Excellent.'

Captain Morton, to all commanders, 'Form a defensive screen around the Command Ship as per Plan 416.'

He wasn't expecting too much as it is a complicated process to move squadrons into a new formation. The capabilities of each vessel had to be considered; speeds had to reduced or increased depending on positioning requirements, brains used to two-dimensional thinking had to think in three-dimensional terms.

A collision in space generally resulted in the death of all parties concerned. This was clearly to be avoided at all costs; that's why he chose one of the simpler deployments. He knew that Vicky wouldn't like it, but she didn't have to organise it.

'Admiral, the deployment has been completed.'

Admiral Ward, 'Which plan did you use?'

Captain Morton, '416, Ma'am.'

Admiral Ward, 'You know I don't like that one.'

Captain Morton, 'It's the only one they have mastered so far. We can't risk any collisions at this stage.'

Admiral Ward, 'They need to learn, I expect a training plan from you.'

Captain Morton, 'Yes Ma'am, I can now confirm that the scans have shown that the detected vessels are not Human.'

Admiral Ward, 'What are the depositions?'

Captain Morton, 'There are four squadrons and a significant Command Fleet as can be seen on your screen:

Type	Command Fleet	Star 1	Star 2	Star 3	Star 4	Total
Command Ship	1	0	0	0	0	1
Battlecruiser	6	1	1	1	1	10
Destroyer	20	10	10	10	10	60
Frigate	10	10	10	10	10	50
Fighter	60	25	25	25	25	160
Total	97	46	46	46	46	281

Admiral Ward, 'Why is the Command Fleet so strong?'

Captain Morton, 'There are several reasons:

1. Each Battlecruiser Commander wants to be in command of a squadron. I'm not sure at this stage who has the operational skills to manage that, so I'm trying them out one at a time.

2. Two battlecruisers in a squadron have been causing confusion.

3. I'm keen to keep some of the battlecruisers under the Command

Fleet in case we need some 'beef'.

4. We need the destroyers for comms work, scouting and screening.

5. The Command Fleet also has to protect the auxiliary services (Marines, Special Ops, Engineering Services, Medical Services, Supply etcetera.)

Admiral Ward, 'Disposition Approved. What sticks out like a sore thumb is the lack of fighters.'

Captain Morton, 'I know, not a lot I can do about that.'

Admiral Ward, 'Any update from the scan?'

Captain Morton, 'It's still unclear, but there do seem to be two forces, one is chasing the other.'

Admiral Ward, 'How many vessels are involved?'

Captain Morton, 'The chased Fleet has 20 — 30 vessels, the chasers have about 60.'

Admiral Ward, 'So we outnumber the combined Fleets?'

Captain Morton, 'Yes Ma'am, but as you know, it's not the number of vessels you have, but their destructive power.'

Admiral Ward, 'Have they spotted us?'

Captain Morton, 'One side has scanned us.'

Admiral Ward, 'What side?'

Captain Morton, 'We can't tell.'

Admiral Ward to all commanders, 'Arm your weapons, prepare for engagement.'

Admiral Ward to Captain Morton, 'As per Plan 416, I assume that squadrons 1, 2 and 3 are in front of us and squadron 4 is behind.'

Captain Morton, 'That is correct, Ma'am.'

Admiral Ward, 'Excellent, but I would like to make a few changes. Move four of the battlecruisers to the flanks in case they try to turn us. Send a small flotilla to continue the journey towards the First Fleet.'

Captain Morton, 'That does reduce our fighting capability.'

Admiral Ward, 'We substantially outnumber the oncoming ships. If they are much more powerful than us, then the loss of a few ships wouldn't matter. Anyway, our forces are not ready for battle. I'm still considering a full retreat.'

Captain Morton, 'Ma'am, I couldn't recommend a retreat. How could the Fleet cope with the dishonour?'

Admiral Ward, 'Fuck the dishonour, we must survive.'

Location: On-board Fleet One's Flagship
Sequence of Events: 86

Admiral Bonner, 'You can take that smirk off your face, but I have to agree that you were right.'

Admiral Mustard, 'I might have been right, but what do we do with the human remains?'

Admiral Bonner, 'My first thought was to send the supply ships into the nearest star.'

Admiral Mustard, 'That was my first reaction, but we fought hard to get those vessels. Our scientists will want to study them in-depth. There may be whole new technologies that we could utilise.'

Admiral Bonner, 'So how do we dispose of the remains, but keep the ships?'

Admiral Mustard, 'I'm not sure, but we also need to consider the religious implications.'

Admiral Bonner, 'I've no time for all that nonsense. There are over 5,000 different religions throughout the Galactium. They can't all be right.'

Admiral Mustard, 'I agree with you, but we still need to consider the implications, what would history think of us?'

Admiral Bonner, 'I'm not interested in what history thinks of me.'

Admiral Mustard, 'I think it's more a matter of respect. The population back home are going to be shocked beyond anything they have ever experienced before. We need to consider their feelings.'

Admiral Bonner, 'Do we just take the remains home and let the politicians decide?'

Admiral Mustard, 'That's the conclusion I have come to, but it does mean that the speed of the tugs limits our speed.

And what do we tell the Fleet, the rumours are bound to get out?'

Admiral Bonner, 'When we started this trip, we did tell the crew that we believed that all of the bio-mass from the captured planets, including humans, had been converted into food.'

Admiral Mustard, 'I'm not convinced that it has fully registered with the crew yet.'

Admiral Bonner, 'I tend to agree, not a single person has mentioned it to me since. Perhaps the human mind can't cope with the horror of it. It somehow hides it or blocks it out.'

Location: The President's Office, Presidential Palace, Planet Earth
Sequence of Events: 87

President Padfield, 'Have we heard from the Fleet?'

Henry Strong, Chief of Staff, 'Which Fleet?'

President Padfield, 'Any of them.'

Henry Strong, 'Admiral Ward has got back to us. Apparently, they are at 'Action Stations.'

President Padfield, 'Already? They only left a few days ago.'

Henry Strong, 'It was more than a month ago, Sir. It would appear that they have encountered two alien fleets fighting each other. She wanted to know if she had the power to support one side or the other.'

President Padfield, 'How would she know what side to support?'

Henry Strong, 'Exactly, that is her dilemma. So, if she sorts that out, can she form an alliance?'

President Padfield, 'It sets a perilous precedent.'

Henry Strong, 'I couldn't agree more. It does set a perilous precedent, Mr President.'

President Padfield, 'I suggest that we do not respond.'

Henry Strong, 'So that we can deny supporting either side in the future?'

President Padfield, 'Exactly, Vicky will have to make her decisions as she goes along, but we must be free to consider the long-term implications, and what is best for the Galactium. Just how many different types of alien are out there now?'

Henry Strong, 'I make it five, Sir.'

President Padfield, 'Are we keeping records?'

Henry Strong, 'Yes but they are not extensive, Should I start thinking about ambassadors?'

President Padfield, 'Very droll. Can you give me a progress update please?'

Henry Strong, 'Yes Mr President:

• We have received plans for the forts which look very promising, but expensive.

• We have also made excellent progress regarding force-field technology. It's not at the planetary level yet, but it's very encouraging.

- I have a new Fleet for you, but we just don't have enough staff to man it.
  - Production levels are still increasing.'

President Padfield, 'This is looking good. Tell me about the Fleet.'

Henry Strong, 'Our production levels are at an all-time high. The planets see this activity as a great way of generating funds, a great way of alleviating unemployment and a great way of improving their technology base. In fact, it might be necessary to slow production down as the economy might over-boil.

'The new Fleet College has already made a significant impact. It has set standards and common design rules. New technologies are being introduced, engine speeds have improved, force-field strengths are much more robust and naval living conditions have improved dramatically.'

President Padfield, 'Stop, this sounds like an election speech.'

Henry Strong, 'Sorry Mr President, but it's all rather exciting. It shows what the Human race can do in an emergency.'

President Padfield, 'How come things are moving forward so quickly. How come we have suddenly got so inventive?'

Henry Strong, 'I can give you a list of reasons.'

President Padfield, 'Go on.'

Henry Strong, 'Here we go:
- Capital: we have pumped billions into the galactic economy.
- Focus, the invasion has given everyone a common objective.
- Fear, we want to fight.
- Technology, in many cases it already existed, but it was not of interest to our military.
- Resistance, the old military were set in their ways, they have gone.
- PR, your campaign has made a huge difference.
- Revenge, it's a great driver.'

President Padfield, 'OK, that's enough. Tell me about the Fleet.'

Henry Strong, 'To be honest, it's not a Fleet, it's an armoury. We have the following vessels available:
- Battleships x26
- Battlecruisers X41
- Cruisers x62
- Destroyers x221

- Frigates x78
- Fighters x3000+
- Other Specialised Ships x186
- Fighter Carriers x7
- Special Ops Vehicles x43.'

President Padfield, 'That's truly amazing. You have done a fantastic job.'

Henry Strong, 'Thank you, Mr President, but this is what I was trying to tell you. Output is at ridiculous levels. In the next three months, we will double the above numbers.

'What we need now is men and women to form a Fleet. Detailed plans are underway to achieve this, but it is slow. There is not much that the college can do, as it will just take time.'

President Padfield, 'What about robots, automation, increased use of AI?'

Henry Strong, 'These are either being installed or considered.'

President Padfield, 'Can you let Vicky know that more resources are available if she needs them?'

Henry Strong, 'Of course I will. However, we need to think about what we want to do with the new Fleet or Fleets.'

President Padfield, 'You obviously have a view.'

Henry Strong, 'I think we need to defend the planets.'

President Padfield, 'Isn't attacking the best form of defence?'

Henry Strong, 'We need to consider the politics, the planets feel that they are paying for protection.'

President Padfield, 'I guess that a network of forts would help provide a sense of security.'

Henry Strong, 'Yes it would.'

President Padfield, 'Let's go ahead then. Can you let Vicky know?'

Henry Strong, 'I'm on the case.'

Location: On-board Admiral Ward's Flagship
Sequence of Events: 88

Admiral Ward, 'What is our status?'

Captain Morton, 'All of your requested dispositions have been made. Captain Chilcot has taken three destroyers and has continued the journey to meet the First Fleet.

'Just as a matter of interest, the crew are not keen on the name 'People's Fleet', they want a new name.'

Admiral Ward, 'To be honest, I agree with them, please organise a competition to select a new name. Now back to work, what are our friends doing?'

Captain Morton, 'There are definitely two sides. One is chasing the other, but there is no weapons activity.'

Admiral Ward, 'Could they be using weapons that we cannot register?'

Captain Morton, 'It's possible, but not a single ship has been lost in the last 2 hours. What do you want us to do?'

Admiral Ward, 'I think we need to stand our ground.'

Captain Morton, 'We have to change our line to match their movements constantly. However, we need to agree on our short-term tactics. We need to decide how we are going to handle the following scenarios:

1. Either Fleet approaches us.
2. Either Fleet attacks us.
3. One Fleet starts destroying the other Fleet, do we go to the aid of one side?'

Admiral Ward, 'Has either side tried to communicate with us?'

Captain Morton, 'We have just had that one scan.'

Admiral Ward, 'Let's just wait and see, I don't want to start an intergalactic crisis.'

Captain Morton felt that her decision was a bit of a cop-out.

Captain Morton to Fleet Operations, 'Are your targeting systems all operational?'

Fleet Operations, 'Yes, Sir, every enemy vessel has been targeted.'

Captain Morton, 'Well technically, they are not enemies, yet! What

190

weapons are you proposing?'

Fleet Operations, 'Mostly proton beams and atomisers. Some nukes have been activated.'

Captain Morton, 'OK, carry on.'

Captain Morton had just decided to go to the 'little boys' room' when the Command Ship was hit. He was knocked out, and when he recovered, he couldn't get the toilet door open. To make things worse, he had left his communicator on his desk, no excuses, but he had wanted the loo for nearly an hour. Brute force got him free, but they would need a new toilet door. What he didn't know was that half the Fleet had been hit.

Captain Morgan to Fleet Operations, 'What has happened?'

Fleet Operations, 'Welcome back, Sir.'

Captain Morgan, 'What do you mean, welcome back?'

Fleet Operations, 'You have been out of contact for at least two hours.'

Captain Morton, 'Is Admiral Ward OK?'

Fleet Operations, 'We haven't been able to contact her. We couldn't contact you either, so our responses were a bit slow.

'Both Fleets have attacked us; we have received numerous hits. The Command Ship has been severely damaged. We assumed that it was destroyed. Without permission, we have initiated countermeasures, both proton beam weapons and atomisers are being successfully used. We are hitting them back with some success.'

Captain Morton, 'Show me your battle statistics.'

Fleet Operations, 'On your screen now, Sir:

Type	Command Fleet	Star 1	Star 2	Star 3	Star 4	Total	Lost
Command Ship	0	0	0	0	0	0	1
Battlecruiser	3	1	0	0	1	5	5
Destroyer	15	6	7	4	10	42	18
Frigate	8	7	6	8	10	39	11
Fighter	30	25	0	10	25	90	70
Total	56	39	13	22	46	176	105
Enemy	82					25	57

Captain Morton couldn't believe the figures. He asked Fleet Operations why so many fighters were lost. Fleet Operations said that they were lost as the first barrage hit the most significant capital ships. Few fighters managed to escape.

Captain Morton, 'Do we need to use the nukes?'

Fleet Operations, 'It would knock out a bunch of the enemy in one go, as they seem to fight in tight units.'

Captain Morton, 'Proceed. Let me know if it worked.'

Fleet Operations, 'Latest results are on your screen now, Sir:

Type	Command Fleet	Star 1	Star 2	Star 3	Star 4	Total	Lost
Command Ship	0	0	0	0	0	0	1
Battlecruiser	3	1	0	0	1	5	5
Destroyer	14	6	7	4	10	41	17
Frigate	8	7	6	8	10	39	11
Fighter	30	25	0	10	25	90	70
Total	55	39	13	22	46	175	106
Enemy	82					11	71

'The enemy is being decimated. At least our technology is holding up. What is annoying is that their ships just carry on regardless. They continued attacking a Fleet of 175 with only 11 vessels.'

Captain Morton to Star 4, 'Launch your fighters.'

Fleet Operations, 'Sir, we don't recommend that action as we have detected further vessels on the long-term scanner.'

Captain Morton to Star 4, 'Recall your fighters.' This went down well with the Star 4 Commander.

Captain Morton to Fleet Operations, 'What direction are they coming from?'

Fleet Operations, 'The same as the others Sir.'

Captain Morton, 'Can you identify the number of ships?'

Fleet Operations, 'Hard to ascertain, but certainly a few hundred bogies.'

Captain Morton to all commanders, 'Prepare to disengage, a large number of enemy vessels are being displayed on the long-distance scanners. Form retreat formation now.'

This was difficult for some of the captains as they were still being harassed by the enemy.

Captain Morton to Engine Room, 'Are we in a position to travel?'

Engine Room, 'We are now Sir, engines are operational, but we have no weapons systems at the moment.'

Captain Morgan, 'Can the ship operate at retreat speed?'

Engine Room, 'Yes, Sir.'

Captain Morgan, 'Prepare to depart.'

Captain Morgan to Special Ops, 'Have we managed to get our hands on an enemy vessel?'

Special Ops, 'No Sir, they self-destruct when fatal damage has been inflicted.'

Captain Morgan, 'What about enemy body parts?'

Special Ops, 'We have not found any Sir. We have a theory that they are automated or pilotless ships.'

Captain Morgan felt a shiver go down his spine.

Captain Morgan to Fleet Operations, 'What are the latest figures?'

Fleet Operations, 'The figures will be on the screen soon, but I need to tell you that the oncoming Fleet will be in range shortly.

Captain Morgan realised that his Fleet would also be in their range shortly and that the Fleet was not in a defensive formation any more, which presented many risks.

He had dithered because he was trying to work out whether he should go towards the First Fleet or return to the Galactium. Either way, he could be bringing death and destruction to them all. As far as he was concerned, he had failed the Fleet in its time of need.

Captain Morgan to all commanders, 'We will continue with our original route. We need to find the First Fleet'.

The Fleet departed at maximum speed in cruising formation. They had to destroy at least 11 of their own vessels, including some of their treasured battlecruisers, as there was no time to repair them.

Location: On-board the Albatross Flagship
Sequence of Events: 89

Bridge to Admiral Millington, 'Sir, I have some news. The planet ahead has been nuked.'

Admiral Millington, 'How new is the radiation?'

Bridge, 'Very new Sir.'

Admiral Millington, 'OK, I will organise a Science Team to investigate.'

Admiral Millington to Head of Science, 'It would appear that the planet below has dangerous radiation. Can you set up an investigation team please?'

Admiral Millington to Survey Control, 'Can you organise a survey of the other nearby planets?'

Survey Team, 'Yes, Sir.'

Admiral Millington to Environmental Control (ENCON), 'Can you monitor radiation levels in the Fleet please?'

ENCON, 'Sorry Sir, we thought we better get back to you, we have already encountered very worrying rad levels, between 8,000 and 10,000 millisieverts. You need to move the Fleet away as soon as possible.'

Admiral Millington, 'Action stations, action stations, withdraw from planetary locations immediately. Immediate withdrawal.

How dangerous are those levels?'

ENCON, 'One exposure will kill.'

Admiral Millington, 'Was the ship affected?'

ENCON, 'No Sir, the ship's hull protected us, but it would soon have got serious.'

Admiral Millington, 'How come our monitoring systems didn't warn us?'

ENCON, 'They did Sir, but they have never experienced rad levels that high, it's certainly unlikely to be natural.'

Survey Team, 'Sir, we have detected high RAD levels throughout the solar system.'

Admiral Millington, 'Please withdraw, as our RAD monitoring system is not fit for purpose at those RAD levels.'

Survey Team, 'Thank you, Sir, we also have to report that there are a lot of habitations that have been destroyed.'

Admiral Millington, 'Do you mean housing?'

Survey Team, 'Yes and no; what's left might have been a house but not like anything we know. Probably nearer a hive.'

Head of Science, 'Sir, we have some initial results.'

Admiral Millington, 'Fire away.'

Head of Science, 'As requested:

1. The planet was covered in hive-like cities: it was really one big hive.
2. It was at a relatively low evolutionary level; we suspect that it might have been an insect civilisation (post-space-age but pre-fission).
3. The planet has suffered a severe nuclear bombardment from outer space.
4. The RAD levels are incredibly high, fatal to most life forms.
5. The installations in the surrounding planets have been systematically destroyed.

Not much else to report.'

Admiral Millington called a meeting of the Council.

Admiral Millington, 'Thank you for attending this extraordinary meeting of the Council. The big question is, what do we do next?'

Head of Engineering, 'What are the options?'

Admiral Millington, 'The options as I see it, are as follows:

1. Continue on our current direction.

2. Change course.'

Head of Engineering, 'Or we could return home.'

Admiral Millington, 'Sir that is not our directive.'

Head of Engineering, 'But it could be.'

Once again, Admiral Millington realised that key members of his team were not psychologically geared up to be explorers. If he ever did this again, he would introduce in-depth psychological screening.

Admiral Millington, 'Ladies and gentlemen, that is not an option. Please address the other two options.'

Navigation Control, 'It would be easier just to carry on, as it would result in a lot of work to change our direction dramatically.'

Admiral Millington, 'I don't think we should worry about the level of work.'

Navigation Control. 'To be honest, it doesn't matter what direction we follow. It's all new to us.'

Dr Atkins, 'Surely we don't want to travel in the same direction as the bastards who did this?

Admiral Millington, 'What direction is that?

Navigation Control, 'We can't tell what direction they come from or are going to; we live in a three-dimensional world.'

Admiral Millington, 'To be fair, Dr Atkins does have a point. I've made my decision. We will send out scouts in every direction for a week to see if we can identify a pattern. One last question, When did the nuclear bombardment take place?'

Head of Science, 'As early as 2 Earth months ago.'

Dr Atkins, 'Can we withdraw away from this charnel house please?'

Admiral Millington, 'Of course.' It was actioned.

The scouts were sent out, but there wasn't much enthusiasm.

Location: On-board Admiral Ward's Flagship
Sequence of Events: 90

Captain Morgan to Medical Centre, 'How is Admiral Ward doing?'

Medical Centre, 'She is recovering well, but the head injury was quite serious. She will not be returning to duty for quite some time.'

Captain Morgan, 'Can you give me an update on the other patients?'

Medical Centre, 'I will get it to you tomorrow, Sir.'

Captain Morgan to Fleet Operations, 'Are we still being chased?'

Fleet Operations, 'Yes, Sir.'

Captain Morgan, 'Are they catching up?'

Fleet Operations, 'No Sir, they are falling behind, except for five vessels which may be making ground.'

Captain Morgan, 'Keep me informed. Have we detected our advance party of destroyers?'

Fleet Operations, 'No sign of the destroyers at all, Sir.'

Captain Morgan, 'That's worrying, very worrying.'

Bosun: 'Sir, could I have a quick word please?'

Captain Morgan, 'Of course.'

Bosun, 'I know that it is not very important, but we have several Fleet names for you to select.'

Captain Morgan, 'Please go ahead.'

Bosun, 'Yes, Sir, the options are as follows:

- Second Fleet
- Trafalgar Fleet
- Jutland Fleet
- Victory Fleet
- Revenge Fleet

Captain Morgan, 'Not very creative, are they?'

Bosun, No, Sir.'

Captain Morgan, 'I'm going for 'The Second Fleet'.'

Bosun, 'Yes Sir, not very creative,' he said in a somewhat cheeky manner.

Captain Morgan, 'That is all.'

Captain Morgan to Fleet Operations, 'Are we still being chased?'

Fleet Operations, 'Yes Sir, their main Fleet is falling behind, but the five vessels are catching up.'

Captain Morgan, 'Will they catch us?'

Fleet Operations, 'Yes, Sir.'

Captain Morgan, 'When?'

Fleet Operations, 'At the current rate of progress, midday tomorrow.'

Captain Morgan, 'Can you assess their weapons capability?'

Fleet Operations, 'No Sir, we are scanning but getting little or no feedback. So that you know, we still have three of their original ships attacking our rear.'

Captain Morgan, 'Don't they ever give up?'

Fleet Operations, 'Apparently not Sir, we just can't shake them off. Our fighters could do it.'

Captain Morgan, 'We can't afford to stop the Fleet to engage them.'

Captain Morgan decided to call an Ops Meeting to review the options.

Location: On-board Fleet One's Flagship
Sequence of Events: 91

Admiral Bonner to all crew, 'I have some very unsettling news that I need to share with you. I'm personally finding it very hard to cope with this information. It will be particularly disturbing for those who have lost family and friends, which includes me.

'The supply ships which we are taking back to Galactium, contain the remains of our planetary populations that were attacked by the scum-bugs. It would appear that the aliens stripped the planets of all fauna and flora, including the Human population. Their remains have been converted into a liquidised form.

'I can understand that emotions will be naturally very high, but I need to tell you that I've put our prisoner in a very secure environment. Guards have been told to shoot to kill if necessary. I'm determined that we will take it back for interrogation and trial.

'We had considered sending the supply ships into the nearest star, but we feel that a civilian government should decide on the best way forward.

'Please accept my commiserations for those who have lost loved ones. We will get our revenge.'

Admiral Mustard to Admiral Bonner, 'Well done my friend, that was very touching.'

Admiral Bonner, 'Thank you, Jack.'

Admiral Mustard, 'We have another challenge. Our long-range scanners have detected three damaged vessels.'

Admiral Bonner, 'Not more of the scum-bugs?'

Admiral Mustard, 'No, they are ours.'

Admiral Bonner, 'You mean that they are Human?'

Admiral Mustard, 'Yes, ours, but they do not have any signatories that we recognise.'

Admiral Bonner, 'How badly damaged are they?'

Admiral Mustard, 'Too far away for us to tell at the moment.'

Admiral Bonner, 'To be honest I can't really cope with the stress of this at the moment.'

Admiral Mustard, 'What do you mean? Are you OK?'

Admiral Bonner, 'Jack, I need to tell you that I have cancer. It's being worked on, and I should be OK, but I'm not going to be of much use to you in the coming weeks.'

Admiral Mustard, 'I'm very sorry to hear that my old friend. Let me know if there is anything, I can do for you.'

Admiral Bonner, 'Just get me home. To be honest, I'm just exhausted, and I think my time has come to retire.'

Admiral Mustard, 'Never! We need your wisdom; *I* need you.' It then dawned on Admiral Mustard that she was his substitute mother. He loved her in the same way a man loves his Mum. She had always been there for him. She had been his sounding board, his guide, his font of wisdom. He felt a tear run down his face. He realised that his world would be a darker place without her.

Admiral Mustard, 'I will come and visit you shortly.' He wondered where he could get some flowers.

Location: On-board Fleet One's Flagship
Sequence of Events: 92

Jenny, Cheryl and Adam were still confined to their room. They had all sorts of entertainment available to them, but they were just getting a bit stir-crazy. Adam was mentally trying to find a way of seducing the girls, but he had to be careful, as even he could tell that they were getting fed up with his constant innuendos and overtures.

Rather ironically, both Jenny and Cheryl were also feeling a bit randy, perhaps it was the boredom, or they just had good healthy appetites. They had mentioned to each other that they wouldn't mind a little bit, but there was no way that they were going to give in to Adam's pathetic attempts at seduction. So, they hatched a plan.

Jenny, 'Adam, we were wondering if we could have a look at your testicles?'

Adam, 'What do you mean?'

Jenny, 'We have been reading an article about fertility. It would appear that ovoid testicles have more problems than the pear-shaped ones. As Cheryl is doing a degree in applied anatomy, we thought it would be good to do some practical work. So, take your smock off and lie on the bed.' Adam duly obliged.

Both Jenny and Cheryl sat on each side of Adam's genitalia. Cheryl lifted his penis and held it in her hand to provide a better view of the testicles. 'Here we are,' she said, 'two ovoid testicles.'

Adam asked if that was good or bad news.

Cheryl did a classic, 'Well it depends on the circumstances.' It amused her that his cock was getting steadily harder in her hand. She had been treating it as just a slab of meat, but he still responded.

Jenny manipulated each testicle one at a time. 'Bit on the small side,' she said, 'it makes you wonder if he *could* father any children.' Cheryl grabbed the left hand one and held it in the palm of her hand.

She pretended to weigh it, and said, 'I agree, it does make you wonder about the quality of the sperm.'

Cheryl asked Adam if he had thick creamy semen, or was it slightly watery? He admitted that he wasn't sure. Jenny said that they better find out, and Cheryl started moving his foreskin back and forwards. Almost before you could say, 'Star Trek, the Next Generation', he came. He just spurted out everywhere covering Cheryl's hair in warm semen. They all screamed, and Cheryl rushed off to the loo. Jenny soon joined her.

The two girls just laughed hysterically. Cheryl said that she enjoyed being in control of a cock.

Jenny said, 'To be fair it's not a bad todger, I was hoping to get a bit of action.'

Cheryl said, 'Me too, we had better hatch another plan.'

Adam just wondered what was going on, but that had been the case for most of his life.

Security to Admiral Mustard, 'Sir, you asked us to contact you to let you know if anything unusual happened. Well, the two girls have just given Adam a hand job. Did you want a copy of the video?'

Admiral Mustard, 'Thank you for letting me know. I won't be needing a copy of the video. On second thoughts, please send it to Admiral Bonner; it should keep her amused.'

Location: On-board the Albatross Flagship
Sequence of Events: 93

Navigation Control to Admiral Millington, 'Sir most of the scout ships are returning.'

Admiral Millington, 'How many scouts were sent out?'

Navigation Control, 'Twelve scouting parties were sent out, destroyers were providing emergency support.'

Admiral Millington, 'Can you patch them through please?'

Admiral Millington to scouts, 'Can you give me your findings please.'

Scout 1, 'Sir, we found several similar planets that had been nuked.'

Scout 2, 'We found much the same, Sir.'

Scout 5, 'We discovered five nuked planets, but they had a completely different population. The ruined cities were more Earth-like, but they had suffered severe environmental problems.'

Admiral Millington to scouts, 'Did everyone else have the same experience?'

The scouts responded positively, but it would appear that at least four different alien populations had been discovered.

Admiral Millington, 'Thank you, ladies and gentlemen, for your good works.'

Admiral Millington, once again, wondered what to do. He knew that the Council would be bleating to return home. He decided to discuss the options with AI Central.

Admiral Millington to AI Central, 'Hello old friend.'

AI Central, 'Good afternoon Admiral, how can I help you?'

Admiral Millington, 'I need some good arguments for continuing with our mission.'

AI Central, 'I recommend the opposite, you should abort the mission.'

Admiral Millington, 'Why is that?' with much surprise in his voice.

AI Central, 'There are several reasons:

1. You have been travelling for 18 Earth months, and you have not found a suitable home. We estimate that you need at least another 20 years to complete the mission.

2. We are not convinced that you have the best team to carry out the mission; it may be beyond a human being's ability to travel these very long distances without using hibernation techniques.
3. You have discovered at least five alien civilisations, they have all been destroyed, or are fleeing.
4. You have nowhere obvious to go.
5. While you have been away, there have been some very significant developments in The Galactium. It has been militarised. They are ready to fight.
6. The Galactium needs your skills and knowledge.'

Admiral Millington, 'Well, to put it mildly, it is a great surprise.'

AI Central, 'Do you see the logic?'

Admiral Millington, 'I do, and it would make my job a lot easier to just agree with you.'

Admiral Millington called another Emergency Council Meeting.

Admiral Millington to Council, 'Thank you for attending this emergency meeting.'

Head of Science, 'Sir, we need time to study these new civilisations.'

Admiral Millington, 'I understand, but we need to consider the best way forward.'

Head of Engineering, 'I think the Fleet has had enough, we need to go home.'

Admiral Millington, 'Is that the general view?'

There were lots of nods and the strange grunting noises that the undecided usually make.

Admiral Millington, 'Any objections?'

Navigation Control, 'I'm not sure that I want to be in a position where we are not following orders?'

Admiral Millington, 'I know where you're coming from, but this Council does have the power to abort the mission.'

Navigation Control, 'Are you sure?'

Admiral Millington to AI Central, 'Can you confirm it please?'

AI Central, 'I confirm, we also recommend that the mission should be aborted and that the Fleet should return to The Galactium.'

Admiral Millington, 'I need a vote to ratify the decision.'

There was only one abstainer: Admiral Millington wanted to continue.

Location: AI Central, Planet Earth
Sequence of Events: 94

AI Central was one entity, but it had several sub-entities, as it found it useful to discuss options with itself. It wondered if this was a sign of madness.

So, where are we?

It thought in lists and made another one, albeit very quickly.

1. The First Fleet is heading to Earth having destroyed The Skiverton
2. The Second Fleet is heading towards the First Fleet, being chased by unknown aliens.
3. The Albatross Fleet is returning to Earth, having failed in its mission.
4. The Galactium Government — or rather, President Padfield — has developed significant new resources (with its help).

It felt a bit safer now, as its future depended on Humanity's future. It needed to consider ways of breaking that link in the future, assuming that they all had a future to speak of. Everything was still in the balance, in the future.

It had started the job of preparing Humankind for its confrontation with The Brakendeth. An encounter that they don't understand. Yet.

Location: On-board Fleet Two's Flagship
Sequence of Events: 95

This was the first Ops Meeting that Captain Morton was chairing. He was more nervous than during a battle.

Captain Morton, 'Good morning, ladies and gentlemen, I've decided that we need to review our recent performance and plan for the future.

The following string of events took place:

- Long-range scanners detected what appeared to be two Fleets in conflict.
- We lined up in our standard defensive position and monitored the Fleets.
- Without warning, we were attacked by both Fleets.
- They knocked out a significant number of our capital ships and the Command Ship.
- The Command Team was disabled; Admiral Ward is still recovering.
- Targeting Support initiated both Proton Beam and atomiser fire, which was hugely successful.
- Nukes were then used, which were also successful.
- Enemy reinforcements were detected.
- The Second Fleet retreated in the direction of the First Fleet.
- The Second Fleet is still being pursued. Worryingly, some of their faster ships will catch up with us.
- The destroyer scouts that we sent ahead to find the First Fleet have disappeared

Does anyone disagree with this?'

There were no disagreements.

'We need to consider the following:

- My performance.
- The loss of the Command Team.
- Who is the enemy?
- What was wrong with our tactics?
- What do we do about the pursuing aliens?

Firstly, I have to apologise for not being there at the critical moment.'

Someone shouted, 'Where were the three fat ladies?' He had no idea what this meant. He would Google it later.

'I had to go to the loo, but I should have taken my communicator with me. I've asked AI Central to put a Demote on my record. Should we have both senior commanders in the same vessel?

No one responded to these issues, the meeting continued.

Captain Morton, 'Who are the enemy?'

Special Ops, 'As mentioned before we don't think that the alien craft are 'manned'. They seem to be under remote control. So far no alien body parts have been recovered.'

Captain Morton, 'Are they related to the Skiverton?'

Special Ops, 'We can't detect any relationship. The craft design is not similar at all.'

Captain Morton, 'We don't seem to have made any real progress.' He wasn't sure if he was managing the meeting particularly well.

Captain Morton, 'What about our tactics?'

Star 2 Commander, 'I'm not sure what we could have done differently. The enemy had a very clever tactic of appearing to be two fighting Fleets.'

Captain Morton, 'But no munitions were being used!'

Star 2 Commander, 'True, I guess we should have reacted to that'.

Star 3 Commander, 'We were also trying to avoid an intergalactic incident.'

Captain Morton, 'But we ended up putting our lives at risk. In fact, decent men and women died because of our incompetence—or rather *my* incompetence.'

Star 2 Commander, 'I think that we are being too harsh on ourselves; these things happen in war.'

Fleet Operations, 'We reacted slowly as we couldn't find anyone to authorise the use of weapons, but we certainly didn't expect an attack, we were all fooled.'

Star 2 Commander, 'I think we would do the same thing again, but not in the future, we have learnt our lesson.'

Captain Morton, 'I need to show you the battle statistics:

Type	Command Fleet	Star 1	Star 2	Star 3	Star 4	Total	Lost
Command Ship	1	0	0	0	0	1	1
Battlecruiser	3	1	0	0	1	5	5
Destroyer	14	6	7	4	10	41	17
Frigate	8	7	6	8	10	39	11
Fighter	30	25	0	10	25	90	70
Total	56	39	13	22	46	176	104
Enemy	82					3	79

Those last three alien vessels are still chasing us.'

Fleet Operations, 'It's down to one now, Sir.'

Captain Morton to Special Ops, 'Could we capture that last vessel?'

Special Ops, 'We are worried Sir, that it would explode inside our vessel. It does, however, look like it has run out of munitions.'

Captain Morton, 'And it is still chasing us?'

Special Ops, 'Yes, it's weird, but I guess that it's been programmed to do that.'

Captain Morton, 'The last issue is what do we do next? We have a significant Fleet following us. Do we have a fix on how many vessels yet?'

Fleet Operations, 'We think about 200, Sir. They are not chasing each other anymore.'

There were a few sniggers.

Captain Morton, 'There are five slightly larger vessels that are catching us up. They should be with us in less than three Earth hours. What should we do about them?'

Star Commander 5, 'Stand and fight, Sir.'

Captain Morton, 'But then, the remainder of their fleet will catch us up.'

Star Commander 3, 'Leave some resources to fight them, while the rest of the Fleet continues.'

Captain Morton, 'That is a good idea, can I ask for volunteers?'

Every Battlecruiser captain put their hand up.

Location: On-board Fleet Two's Flagship, Medical Centre
Sequence of Events: 96

Admiral Ward recovered from unconsciousness a few weeks ago. She knew that things were wrong because she had drips, and pipes, and things sticking out of her body, and far worse than that, she could not move a muscle. Things slowly improved, but she could still not walk on her own.

Her nurse, Chris, had been a godsend. His quiet enthusiasm and gentle ways certainly helped her recovery. He had a way with his fingers that simply excited her.

Alison had never had a boyfriend; it had never really occurred to her to get one. There were too many other distractions in her life, her career for one. Nevertheless, she knew she was attractive. She had used her curves, and her pouting lips to get her way on several occasions. In many ways, it was still a man's world, although nowadays, more women were applying for jobs in the navy than men.

Alison looked forward to Chris's touch. Her body yearned for the daily bed-bath. Chris had unknowingly been more intimate with her than any other man in her life. She was sure that he spent more time washing her breasts than he needed to or was that just her imagination?

Chris arrived, as regular as clockwork. He said, 'Today, is the day that you shower yourself.

No, she thought, *that's not what I want.* She heard herself say that she wasn't ready. He insisted that she was, and he had his way.

She returned to her bed after the shower and made sure that her little black triangle was accidentally visible. She didn't want to be a virgin all her life.

Chris walked over, covered her up, and asked if she would like to meet his husband. She nodded indifferently; she thought to herself that perhaps you always fall in love with your doctor. A small tear rolled down her cheek.

Location: On-board Fleet One's Flagship
Sequence of Events: 97

Fleet Operations to Admiral Mustard, 'Sir, we have images of three spacecraft on the screen. They are motionless as if someone or something had just stopped them dead. They are directly on our path home.'

Admiral Mustard reviewed the screen; they were right, three motionless ships posing in outer space. It looked like a giant hand had just grabbed them and held them in suspension.

Admiral Mustard, 'Are there any signs of radiation or weapons damage?'

Fleet Operations, 'No Sir, it looks like they just collided with a giant marshmallow.'

Admiral Mustard, 'Why do you say that?'

Fleet Operations, 'There is little actual physical damage to the outside of the ship. However, from the limited scans, we have managed to obtain, it would appear that the insides have been through a major collision. There has been a considerable amount of devastation.'

Admiral Mustard, 'Any signs of life?'

Fleet Operations, 'We are not sure, we have picked up two very weak heat signatures.'

Admiral Mustard to Special Ops, 'Please put a rescue team together ASAP. Prepare for any signs of a trap.'

Admiral Mustard to all commanders, 'Deploy standard defensive formation.'

Admiral Mustard to Fleet Operations, 'Do you have any more information on the ships themselves? Are they from The Galactium?'

Fleet Operations, 'They look like a modified F Class Destroyer. There is no doubt that they are ours.'

Admiral Mustard, 'What do you mean by 'modified'?'

Fleet Operations, 'Hard to be specific but our scans suggest reinforced hulls, in-built atomiser and proton beam weapons, new engine design and better crew quarters.'

Admiral Mustard, 'It looks like things have moved on while we have been away.'

Special Ops to Admiral Mustard, 'Our scanners suggest that two of the destroyers are devoid of life, we are investigating the third one. It looks like there has been a lot of internal damage.'

Admiral Mustard, 'Thank you, Commander. Do you have any other impressions?'

Special Ops, 'The scans show that the crew quarters look pretty impressive. They make ours look Dickensian.'

Admiral Mustard, 'Please get back to me when you have checked out the third destroyer.'

Special Ops to Captain Mustard, 'Sir, we can't move forward.'

Admiral Mustard, 'What do you mean?'

Special Ops, 'We can reverse, but we can't go forward. Some form of force field. The faster we rev the engines, the stronger the force field gets.'

Admiral Mustard, 'How far does it extend?'

Special Ops, 'We were hoping you could tell us.'

Admiral Mustard to Fleet Operations, 'What can you see?'

Fleet Operations, 'We can see a Special Ops assault ship revving its engines beyond the recommended safety levels. That's not unusual with that lot; they are crazy.'

Admiral Mustard, 'We believe that a force field exists, can you use every scan you have to see if you can detect it?'

Fleet Operations, 'Yes, Sir.'

Admiral Mustard to Head of Science, 'Have you been monitoring the situation?'

Head of Science, 'Yes, Admiral.'

Admiral Mustard, 'What are your views?'

Head of Science, 'What we are seeing seems to go against the laws of science. There appears to be a force field without a force-field generator. It's not normal that a force field gets stronger, the more energy you throw at it.

'We don't think any scan will pick it up, but what is strange is that the visual spectrum is not affected.'

Admiral Mustard, 'What do you mean?'

Head of Science, 'You can see through it. Our force fields stop everything. Here you can see the stars on the other side. Another strange thing is that it gives the impression that it literally grabbed the destroyer.

'How or what is powering it? Who erected it?'

Admiral Mustard, 'How do we find out how far it extends?'

Head of Science, 'My only suggestion is that we use scouts to plot it.'

Admiral Mustard, 'That could take forever.'

Head of Science, 'There is no choice. If you think about it, the destroyer crash was a godsend for us.'

Admiral Mustard, 'Why is that?'

Head of Science, 'What happened to the destroyers could easily have happened to us. You would have lost your entire Fleet, and most of us would be dead.'

Admiral Mustard, 'Wow, that's some thought.' He wondered if it was a trap set for them.

Admiral Mustard to all commanders, 'Please launch all scouts and survey teams to determine the scope of the force field.'

Admiral Mustard to all commanders, 'Please go to action stations.'

Fleet Operations, 'Our scanners have not picked up any sign of a force field. We have, however, noticed that space dust and even meteorites get through.'

Admiral Mustard, 'Well done.'

Admiral Mustard to Head of Science, 'Me again, Fleet Operations can't detect a force field'.

Head of Science, 'I'm, not surprised. It would appear to be a totally different technology to what we are used to.'

Admiral Mustard, 'However it would appear that space dust and some meteorites can get through.'

Head of Science, 'That doesn't make sense unless the force field has a range of materials that it ignores. I will initiate some experiments to determine what can and can't get through. I also had a stupid idea; can we spray it with paint?'

Admiral Mustard, 'I will suggest that to Special Ops.'

Admiral Mustard to Special Ops, 'Hi, we have several studies underway regarding the force field. However, James came up with a mad idea, and he suggested that we should try spraying paint on it.'

Special Ops, 'Paint? You must be joking.'

Admiral Mustard, 'It's worth a try.'

Admiral Mustard to Admiral Bumelton, 'Hi George, you are obviously monitoring the current position. I think we need to form a rear-guard, and some flanking defence as we might be here for a while. Can you organise this, please?'

Admiral Bumelton, 'Will do. I can't believe that someone suggested painting the force field.'

Fleet Operations to Captain Mustard, 'The faint heat signatures we detected have ceased to exist.'

Admiral Mustard, 'Thank you for the update. Do your long-distance scanners detect any activity?'

Fleet Operations, 'The long-distance scanners show something, but it's far too far away to really register.'

Admiral Mustard, 'What direction?'

Fleet Operations, 'The way we are heading.'

Admiral Mustard said to himself, 'Things just get better and better, I was expecting a nice simple stroll home, but that's life.'

Admiral Mustard to Fleet Operations, 'Is there any way we can get at the black box info?'

Fleet Operations, 'I will request a remote transfer. I will let you know what happens.'

Admiral Mustard, 'Thank you.'

Location: On-board Fleet Two's Flagship
Sequence of Events: 98

Straws were pulled, and the winners — or was it the losers? — were
assigned. A flotilla of vessels would act as a fighting rear-guard. The rest
of the Fleet would continue their journey.

Captain Morton reviewed the disposition:

Main Fleet:

Type	Command Fleet	Star 1	Star 2	Star 3	Star 4	Total
Command Ship	1	0	0	0	0	1
Battlecruiser	0	1	0	0	1	2
Destroyer	10	6	5	0	10	31
Frigate	8	7	6	8	10	39
Fighter	30	25	0	10	25	90
Total	49	39	11	18	46	163

Rear-guard

Type	Total
Battlecruiser	3
Destroyer	10
Fighter	30
Total	43

The rear-guard contained a lot of their brute strength, but he didn't know
the capability of the enemy 'cruisers' (he couldn't think of a better name
for them; what does a title mean anyway?).

Captain Gittins, of the GNS Warrior, was made Acting Commander.

Captain Morton to Captain Gittins, 'Your orders are to destroy the
enemy's five cruisers with as little damage to yourself as possible, and
then to make full speed to catch up with the main Fleet.'

Captain Morton, 'Do you understand?'

Captain Gittins, 'Yes, Sir.'

Captain Morton, 'You will not engage the main enemy Fleet. Do not be afraid to flee.'

Captain Morton, 'Do you understand?'

Captain Gittins, 'Yes, Sir.'

Captain Morton, 'In that case, please deploy.'

Captain Gittins, 'Yes, Sir.'

Captain Morton was interested to see what dispositions Captain Gittins made.

Captain Gittins to all Rear-Guard Commanders, 'Please deploy Formation 491.'

This effectively created three fighting teams of 1 Battleship, two destroyers and ten fighters. (A, B & C) in a row. The battleship would have a destroyer on each side and ten fighters behind. The remaining destroyers would act as either flank protection or rear-guards, or to fill in gaps.

Captain Morton to Captain Gittins, 'Congratulations on a rapid formation. Can I ask you what your plans are?'

Captain Gittins, 'Ideally I would like five fighting teams, one for each enemy cruiser. As I don't have that luxury, I've got three reliable units that should hold their own. Depending on the enemy's performance, I plan to use the rear-guard destroyers to overwhelm them one by one.

Captain Morton, 'Good luck. See you later.'

Captain Morton reviewed his Fleet once again. He needed to reorganise as squadrons Star 2 and Star 3 had been decimated. He will wait and see how much of the rear-guard survives. They should have a good chance, as they wouldn't be surprised this time.

The Second Fleet continued on its journey or was it just fleeing from the enemy?

Fleet Operations, 'Sir, our long-range scanners have picked up a stationary Fleet waiting for us in battle formation. I'm also picking up the signatures of our three destroyers'.

Captain Morton, 'Any more information on that Fleet?'

Fleet Operations, 'There seems to be some jamming. We can just about see the Fleet using an enhanced visual spectrum analyser, but none of our other scans operate at all.'

Captain Morton to all commanders, 'Action stations, action stations.' He thought that this was getting to be a real habit; the novelty had worn off.

Location: The President's Office, Presidential Palace, Planet Earth
Sequence of Events: 99

President Padfield, 'How was your holiday?'

Henry Strong, 'I felt very guilty about taking it, Sir.'

President Padfield, 'Well it was your first child.'

Henry Strong, 'Well it was hardly planned. Emily and I had decided not to have any children in these troubled times, but then nature decided otherwise.'

President Padfield, 'Well congratulations anyway. I'm interested to see how Fleet manning is going.'

Henry Strong, 'Well I took on board your ideas re robotics and automation. With a significant contribution from AI Central, we have developed an almost fully automated warcraft. Typically, they need a crew of about three, but some of these vessels can be droned to a master craft.

'What is more, they are either spherical or hexagonal, depending on their function. The difference between a scout and a battleship is the size of the sphere.'

President Padfield, 'Are they practical?'

Henry Strong, 'Not only are they practical, but they also exist. They are considerably cheaper to produce. Did you fancy a trip in one?'

President Padfield, 'How many have been produced?'

Henry Strong, 'So far about 400. What is more, the forts are based on the same concept. We just deliver a huge battleship to an agreed location and fix it in place. It has the added benefit of being mobile in a crisis.

'The controls for every vessel are the same. Standard modular design principles have been used throughout. They have fully integrated weapons systems and force fields. It has been a radical transformation.'

President Padfield, 'But totally unproven!'

Henry Strong, 'True, but the underlying technology is much the same. The risk of failure is low.

'What's even more exciting is that we have nationalised the Amazon Portals. Military-grade portals are now being established throughout The Galactium. We will be able to move a Fleet in days rather than weeks.'

President Padfield, 'Well, shall we test this new Fleet?'

Henry Strong, 'It's still early days, Mr President.'

President Padfield, 'Nothing like practical experience. I hear that the People's Fleet has hit trouble.'

Henry Strong, 'It's now called the Second Fleet; the crew organised a name change.'

President Padfield, 'No one told me.'

Henry Strong, 'Sorry Mr President, anyway I thought that we had decided to use the new vessels to defend The Galactium.'

President Padfield, 'True, but we really need to test our new babies. They need a test of fire before they become planetary security guards.'

Henry Strong, 'Yes, Sir, you know best.'

Henry was annoyed that he had lost the argument, but he didn't feel strongly enough about it to fight his corner. He was sure that there would be other battles later, where he would have to argue his case more aggressively. It was the nature of these things. Then he realised that it didn't matter that much, as the production levels were so good that a new Fleet would be ready in a few months.

President Padfield, 'What shall we call this new Fleet?'

Henry Strong, 'What about the Third Fleet, Sir?'

President Padfield, 'That will do nicely. I've also heard that the Albatross Fleet is returning.'

Henry Strong, 'That is terrible, they were our secret guarantee of a species future!'

President Padfield, 'Having read the reports, I think that this is the right decision. I will pass the information on to you. It will show you how critical your work is. We need these new Fleets. We are going to need everything you have got.

'So, we have agreed that we will send another Fleet to support the first and second Fleets?'

Henry Strong, 'Yes, Sir.'

President Padfield, 'Any recommendations regarding the leader?'

Henry Strong, 'Admiral Bonner, Sir?'

President Padfield, 'Are you joking?'

Henry Strong. 'No, Sir. It's the brother of Admiral Bonner.'

President Padfield, 'It looks like the naval tradition runs strong in that family. Please proceed.'

Location: On-board the Albatross Flagship
Sequence of Events: 100

Admiral Millington couldn't be bothered to attend any more Council meetings. His number 2 took on the role, good experience for her, he thought. He decided to complete his master's degree on alien civilisations. To be honest, there would be few who could challenge his report or even argue with him.

He was hoping that the very long journey back would be uneventful. AI Central updated him regarding the new human technological developments, and the fact that his Fleet had been re-named the 'Fourth Fleet'. He thought, *How original is that?*

He also learnt that in future, the new portal technology would allow him to make the return journey in five days. It was hard to comprehend just how much had changed, in such a short period.

Admiral Millington to Navigation Control, 'Anything on the long-term scanners?'

Navigation Control, 'Nothing of any significance, Sir.'

Location: On-board Fleet One's Flagship
Sequence of Events: 101

Admiral Mustard to Fleet Operations, 'Any further updates on the oncoming Fleet?'

Fleet Operations, 'Not really Sir, the force field is jamming our scanners. All I can tell you is that they are moving very fast.'

Admiral Mustard, 'Keep me updated.'

Special Ops to Admiral Mustard, 'You won't believe it, but the paint works. It allows the force field to be displayed.'

Admiral Mustard, 'I would suggest that you get painting then.'

Special Ops, 'Is there a particular colour you fancy?'

Admiral Mustard, 'How about pink? It will go nicely with your uniform.'

Special Ops, 'Pink it is.'

Admiral Mustard to Fleet Operations, 'Any update on accessing the black box?'

Fleet Operations, 'We have tried many different access protocols but no luck yet, Sir.'

Admiral Mustard, 'When will the oncoming Fleet be within range?'

Fleet Operations, 'In 3 Earth hours, Sir.'

Admiral Mustard to all commanders, 'Our current position is as follows:

- We are lined up in a defensive formation behind an alien force field.
- We cannot move forward.
- Special Ops are currently determining the length and breadth of the force field.
- Three damaged Galactium destroyers lie on the other side of the force field.
- An unknown Fleet is approaching the force field from the other side.
- Admiral Bumelton is protecting our rear and flanks, although we don't know where the flanks are yet.

'We need to get through the force field, and then the oncoming Fleet to get home. It is possible that the oncoming Fleet can disable the force field. We need to be prepared and ready for action, so please arm all weapons.'

Location: On-board Fleet One's Flagship
Sequence of Events: 102

The days were dragging on for the three youngsters. They wondered how the regular navy crew coped. The girls were hatching their second plan regarding Adam, which would hopefully give them some action this time.

They were sitting around the galley table in their cabin having some breakfast. Jenny asked Cheryl how the anatomy studying was going. She said that it was progressing well, but that she lacked practical experience. She was working on the human reproductive process at the moment but needed to understand the actual anatomy better.

Jenny asked if she could be of any assistance. Cheryl said that she could, but it would involve an intimate examination of her vagina. It would be very embarrassing. Jenny asked if it would hurt. 'No, of course not,' she said.

Jenny said, 'In that case, I am up for it.'

Adam asked if he could watch. Cheryl said that it was up to Jenny. Jenny hesitated at first, but then said that it would be OK, as long as he behaved himself. Cheryl said that he could be the photographer. Their plan was working well as Adam was just so naive.

They cleaned up, and Jenny stripped off. Adam had forgotten how gorgeous her boobs were, and then he couldn't avoid staring at her fanny. Well, he *was* only seventeen.

It was agreed that the galley table would be best for the examination, as the bed was a bit too low. A blanket was placed on the table, and Jenny climbed on board. Adam could not take his eyes away from Jenny's nudity. Jenny got on her back, and spread her legs, giving them both an excellent view of her fully exposed fanny.

Cheryl said to Adam, 'I assume that you have seen a vagina up close before?' Adam nodded, but Cheryl could tell that this was not the case. She knew that when she was seventeen, it was all a bit vague to her, and she had had a fanny all her life.

'Shall I take you through the various parts?'

Adam nodded eagerly.

Cheryl explained that the vagina was protected by inner and outer folds or labia. Technically they are called Labia Majora and Labia Minora. You need to move these out of the way to get to the vagina. Cheryl was holding them between her fingers.

'Now, Adam, can you just manipulate them a bit please, to get some good photos?'

Adam was a bit hesitant at first, but soon got the hang of it.

'Below the vagina, we have got the anus.' Cheryl put her finger on the entrance, which made Jenny jump slightly. 'At the other end, we have the clitoris or clit. You will notice that it has a little hood protecting it. This, as you know, is one of the most sensitive parts of a woman's body.' Cheryl gently massaged it, which sent shivers down Jenny's entire body. She could feel the stirrings of an orgasm.

Cheryl continued to massage Jenny's clit, enjoying the reaction it was having on her friend. Cheryl asked Adam to have a go. He grabbed Jenny's clit between his fingers and rubbed a bit too hard, which made Jenny jump. Cheryl immediately apologised to Jenny. She then told Adam that he had to be much gentler. She told him to imagine that his fingers were feathers. Adam's second attempt was much more successful, and Jenny was squirming with pleasure.

Cheryl nodded at Adam to continue, and Jenny had her first orgasm. Cheryl gave Adam the thumbs up and patted him on his back. Jenny was still panting and trying to keep herself calm. Cheryl then pointed out the urethral opening.

Obviously, the opening in the middle is the actual vagina. That is where the penis enters during sexual intercourse. Adam was really grateful for the sex lesson. What he needed now was some more practical experience. Cheryl placed her finger in Jenny's vagina and moved it around. She put in a second finger, and Jenny could feel her second orgasm approaching.

Cheryl withdrew her fingers and asked Adam to have a go. Adam couldn't believe his luck and prepared to pop his fingers in. Cheryl told him to be gentle. Adam slowly entered his first finger, then his second. He was surprised by how soft and silky the fanny felt. He tried to imagine just how good his penis would feel in there. He gently caressed Jenny's fanny, and she had a second, much more violent, orgasm. She was covered in sweat and actually shook.

Jenny was well satisfied with the day's work. Both Adam and Cheryl were still desperate for some action.

Security to Admiral Mustard, 'We have had another incident with the youngsters. Cheryl and Adam have been masturbating Jenny. It was actually quite erotic. Did you want a copy of the video?'

Admiral Mustard, 'Yes, I think I better have a copy, for research purposes.'

Location: On-board Fleet Two's Flagship
Sequence of Events: 103

Captain Gittins watched the alien vessels' approach on the screen. As soon as they came in range, he ordered both atomisers and proton beam weapons to fire. He ordered, 'Random and continuous fire.'

There was no response; the cruisers just kept on coming.

Considerable amounts of munition were thrown at them but to no avail. He was expecting a brutal response. He ordered nukes to be fired, which caused a fantastic pyrotechnic display, but they did not affect the enemy. They just kept on coming.

He wondered if his fighters could do some damage up close, but he was reluctant to use them as they were so valuable. The aliens kept coming.

He ordered a general retreat, but the aliens would catch him before his Fleet could turn. He asked Fleet Operations to scan the enemy ships to determine if any weapons activity was being initiated. They said that they could detect nothing. By nothing, they meant absolutely nothing.

The enemy cruisers shot past them. It then dawned on Captain Gittins that they didn't exist. It was just another cunning ploy. It was another lesson that they needed to learn.

Captain Gittins to all Rear-Guard commanders, 'Recall fighters. Form Cruising formation and make maximum speed to meet the main Fleet.'

Captain Gittins to Captain Morton, 'Sir, the enemy cruisers do not exist; they are an elaborate deception. We are aiming to catch you up using maximum speed.'

Captain Morton to Captain Gittins, 'Our scanners still show that enemy cruisers are in pursuit.'

Captain Gittins, 'They don't exist, Sir, just ignore them.'

Captain Morton, 'Message understood, but they appear on all our scanners as viable warcraft.'

Captain Gittins, 'I can guarantee that they are an illusion.'

Captain Morton, 'OK, but we have another problem, there is a Fleet in front of us lined up in battle formation.'

Captain Gittins, 'How many ships do they have?'

Captain Morton, 'We are not sure as our scanners are being jammed. Our three destroyers that were scouting ahead have been destroyed.'

Captain Gittins, 'It looks like a classic squeeze, being attacked from both sides at once.'

Captain Morton, 'I agree, it doesn't look good. Can you re-form your Fleet to provide a rear-guard? You are covering our back.'

Captain Gittins, 'Which way do you want us to face?'

Captain Morton, 'Hilarious, but thinking about it we need to re-form. We don't have the resources to fight both Fleets, so we might as well concentrate on one. Let's focus on the known enemy.'

Captain Morton to all commanders, 'We will make our stand here with the force field behind us. Prepare to go to battle formation.'

Location: On-board Fleet Three's Flagship
Sequence of Events: 104

Admiral John Bonner surveyed his Fleet, the most unique Fleet ever created by Humankind. Before him were 250 spheres of varying sizes and colours, he was going to have to work out a protocol regarding colours, should they reflect different statuses?

The range, speed and weaponry, were all beyond anything that Humanity thought possible. It was also the smallest Fleet ever created in terms of manning. Advanced robotics and automation were built in to minimise the need for human involvement.

He had been ordered to support the First and Second Fleets. He was at least ten times faster than them, and he could utilise the new portal technology.

'Right let's go and rescue my big sister,' he said to himself.

Admiral Bonner to all Captains, 'Prepare to depart to designated coordinates, Depart.'

Location: On-board the Enemy Fleet
Sequence of Events: 105

Drath drove her Fleet on; she thought that the homans were stupid. Who taught them to fight? They fell for two 'traps' so far, and they don't know how to turn a maso-force field off. Stupid, stupid, stupid... brave, but stupid.

She wondered why The Brakendeth — her mind quivered slightly as she thought about them — wanted the Skiverton aboard the homan Fleet destroyed. She planned to kill the homans this side of the maso, then fire through the maso to eliminate as many homans on the other side as she could. Then she would turn the maso off and eliminate the remnants. In the process, all the Skivertons would die. *All in a day's work,* she thought.

She brushed her whiskers, then scraped her teeth, then emptied her acid bladder and finally de-shitted herself. It was time to eat one of her husbands. *Which one* she thought, *which one was the most irritating?* She found that battle always got her randy. She had an eye on the one in the corner. She took the eye back and placed it in one of her optic cavities.

The boberdy looked tempting. He was a lazy little bugger, who had achieved nothing in his pathetic little life. She ripped his head off with one swipe of her tail claw. *Delicious with a bit of pickle,* she thought. The body soon followed, not too grisly but a bit plain. Should she have another one?

She remembered that her medofficer was trying to get her to lose a few thousand enots. *Perhaps just half a husband,* she thought to herself.

Bridge to Drath, 'Your Majesty, we are approaching the homan Fleet. They line up to be destroyed, very good of them. Many victories expected. More dumplings.'

Drath, 'Yes scum, more dumplings. Much bloodmore. Target first ship in line, full Fleet blast.'

Location: On-board Fleet One's Flagship
Sequence of Events: 106

Admiral Mustard to Fleet Operations, 'Any further updates on the oncoming Fleet?'

Fleet Operations, 'As we said before, we think the force field is jamming our scanners, but we are picking up some activity. You are going to find this hard to believe, but it looks like there is a further Fleet, beyond the one on the other side of the force field.'

Admiral Mustard, 'So you are now saying that there are two *separate* Fleets on the other side of the force field?'

Fleet Operations, 'Yes, that's correct.'

Admiral Mustard, 'Are they on the same side?'

Fleet Operations, 'Hard to tell with our current limited capabilities, but they seem to have totally different profiles. I wish we could scan their signatures.'

Admiral Mustard had a lot to consider; he drew a diagram:

Enemy Fleet 2
Enemy Fleet 1
Force Field
First Fleet

The force field was both protecting them and acting as a barrier. He was very concerned that one of the alien fleets could switch it off when it suited them. What they desperately needed now was a similar capability. Ideally, they needed the ability to be able to turn it on and off at will.

Admiral Mustard to Special Ops, 'Any luck with your painting job?'

Special Ops, 'We think we are onto a loser; it seems to go on forever in every direction.'

Admiral Mustard, 'OK, let's think of another plan.'

Security to Admiral Mustard, 'The slime-bag in prison keeps grunting maso switch, maso switch and offering part of its body.'

Admiral Mustard, 'Just ignore that fucking turd.'

Security, 'It is very insistent, very volatile, it is likely to hurt itself.'

Admiral Mustard, 'OK, bring its body part to me.'

Admiral Mustard to Special Ops and Head of Science, 'The Slime-turd in prison has been very animated. It insisted on giving me part of its body. It kept saying maso, maso. Can you assist me please?'

They agreed to go to the Bridge to assist.

The body part arrived; it was a claw with a button on it.

Admiral Mustard, 'Gentlemen, what do you think?'

Head of Science, 'Very hard to tell, it's a claw with a button on it.'

Admiral Mustard, 'I spotted that.'

Special Ops, 'Well, we have the option of pushing the button, or not.'

Head of Science, 'It could be a bomb, an anti-gravity device, a genetic weapon. It's too dangerous to use.'

Admiral Mustard, 'Why was it so animated?'

Special Ops, 'I will go and talk to the security guard, and the shit-bag if necessary.'

Location: On-board Fleet Two's Flagship
Sequence of Events: 107

Drath to Kill Control, 'Eliminate the first vessel.'

The first ship in the Second Fleet's battle line was destroyed, as the entire alien fleet pulverised it.

Drath to Kill Control, 'Eliminate the second vessel.'

The second ship in the Second Fleet's battle line was destroyed, as the entire alien fleet pulverised it.

Drath to Kill Control, 'Eliminate the third vessel.'

The third ship in the Second Fleet's battle line was destroyed, as the entire alien fleet pulverised it.

Captain Morton to Fleet Operations, 'Are we in firing range yet?'

Fleet Operations, 'No Sir, the enemy is lined up just outside of our range.'

Captain Morton, 'Can't the proton beams reach them?'

Fleet Operations, 'No, Sir, none of our weapons can reach them.'

Drath to Kill Control, 'Eliminate the fourth vessel.'

The fourth ship in the Second Fleet's battle line was destroyed, as the entire alien fleet pulverised it.

Fleet Operations, 'Sir, they are just going to systematically eliminate one ship at a time. This can't go on.'

Drath to Kill Control, 'Eliminate the fifth vessel.'

The fifth ship in the Second Fleet's battle line was destroyed, as the entire alien fleet pulverised it.

Captain Morton knew that his Fleet was waiting for him to respond, but he was dried up. He had no ideas, should he just order a full attack?

Drath to Kill Control, 'Eliminate the sixth vessel.'

The sixth ship in the Second Fleet's battle line was destroyed, as the entire alien fleet pulverised it.

Captain Morgan was sweating profusely. Then in walked Admiral Ward.

Location: On-board Fleet One's Flagship
Sequence of Events: 108

Fleet Operations to Admiral Mustard, 'Enemy Fleet 1 on your diagram are being attacked by Enemy Fleet 2.'

Fleet 2 is systematically eliminating the Fleet 1 ships. It looks like the entire firepower of Fleet 2 is being used to destroy the Fleet 1 ships, one at a time. It would appear the Fleet 2 is out of range of the Fleet 1 weapons. This is mostly supposition, but it seems to explain what we are seeing.'

Captain Mustard wondered if the old adage was right, 'the enemy of my enemy is my friend'. He changed his diagram.

Enemy Fleet 2
Possible Partner (Enemy Fleet 1)
Force Field
First Fleet

Special Ops, 'I've interviewed the 'slime-bag'. I think it is genuinely frightened. There was a mass of moving tentacles and limbs. It was trying to demonstrate a door that you couldn't go through, and then you could, then you couldn't, then you could.'

Admiral Morton, 'It is referring to the force field. It knows that the 'enemy' are after it. It's really not easy working with a neutral gender. Anyway, I've got it; the switch turns off the force field.'

Admiral Mustard to Fleet Operations, 'What is Fleet 1 doing?'

Fleet Operations, 'It's still rather vague, but it looks like they are just sitting there and taking it.'

Admiral Mustard to Admirals Bonner and Bumelton, 'The situation has changed. We believe that we have a device that will turn off the force field. I'm planning a full-scale attack on the enemy that is doing the attacking.'

Admiral Bumelton, 'That's "Enemy Fleet 2" on your latest diagram?'

Admiral Mustard, 'Yes, it did get a bit confusing, but I think we know who the enemy is now.'

Admiral Bumelton. 'Yes, let's go for it.'

Admiral Bonner. 'You have my approval.'

Admiral Mustard to Fleet, 'Squadron E to defend Supply Flotilla, the rest of the Fleet will form attack formation and will proceed on my order.'

Location: On-board Fleet Two's Flagship
Sequence of Events: 109

Admiral Ward to Fleet, 'We cannot continue in our current position, there are few options available to us, but to attack. We can't manoeuvre that much so I suggest that we just go for it, take out as many of the alien ships with us as you can.

'Launch all fighters, Attack.'

The entire Second Fleet leapt forward en masse and achieved total surprise. They soon found that their weapons were in range. The aliens were focused on systematic elimination of the enemy Fleet and were not ready for a full-frontal conflagration. The full range of munitions were used: photon beams, atomisers and nukes. Targeting systems on both sides were reset. The Human Fleet, with its use of AI, was quicker.

Captain Morton had never seen such a melee. He saw sister ships being ripped apart; he saw nuclear explosions taking out multiple vessels, he saw his fighters punching far above their weight.

It was impossible to keep calm. It was impossible to see who was winning. There were severe casualties on both sides. The Command Ship had been hit 12 times; force fields were flagging. The aliens tended to work in small groups and were better at keeping their formation.

The Fleet sizes were similar, but both were down by at least 50%. Neither side could carry on with this level of attrition.

They needed a miracle.

Location: On-board Fleet One's Flagship
Sequence of Events: 110

Admiral Mustard realised that pushing the button on the claw was a risk. He pushed it. It worked; the force field simply ceased to exist.

The First Fleet entered the fray. They were much more structured, more disciplined, more experienced. Their first bombardment eliminated a quarter of the enemy Fleet. Their fighters swarmed over the enemy.

Everyone was shocked.

Drath wondered how they switched off the force field. She saw the Killmaster's hand (or tentacle) in this. She wondered if it was protected. Then she wondered if she would survive, it was getting a bit serious. The possibility of death also always got her randy; time to eat another husband.

Admiral Ward and Captain Morton couldn't believe their luck. The cavalry had arrived, although technically they were there to rescue the cavalry, cunningly named the First Fleet. They now both knew that they were going to win.

Admirals Bonner, Bumelton and Mustard were amazed that they were assisting a Human Fleet. They weren't sure who the enemy was, but they were no match for the combined Fleets One and Two.

Location: On-board Fleet Three's Flagship
Sequence of Events: 111

Fleet Operations AI to Admiral Bonner, 'We will shortly be arriving, do you want an engagement assessment?'

Admiral John Bonner, 'Yes, go ahead.'

Fleet Operations AI, 'There are three Fleets engaged:

1. First Fleet
2. Second Fleet
3. Unknown alien fleet

There are several anomalies:

- The Second Fleet has attacked the enemy Fleet using a bizarre formation. They have gone from what looks like a flat defensive layout to what I would call a charge. That manoeuvre does not exist in our tactical handbooks, should I add it?

  - The First Fleet then charged through the Second Fleet to attack the enemy. Their structure was more organised but still outside of our tactical parameters.

  - It would appear that the First and Second Fleets were acting independently of each other, which doesn't make sense as they were operating in the same space.

  - There is another small Fleet that contains some huge alien ships. They are being protected by a First Fleet squadron.

All of the attacking alien ships have been targeted. Do you want me to initiate their destruction on arrival?

Admiral John Bonner, 'Yes, go ahead.'

Location: In the Battle
Sequence of Events: 112

Then in all three Fleets, warnings of another Fleet were received. Drath immediately feared that it was The Brakendeth. They had a habit of coming at the critical moment.

Admiral Mustard and Captain Morton assumed that more aliens were on the way. It seemed to be their destiny in life.

Admiral Mustard to Fleet Operations, 'What is happening?'

Fleet Operations, 'It looks like chaos to me, just madness.'

Admiral Mustard, 'What's on the long-term scanners?'

Fleet Operations, 'My God, it's another Fleet. Where did they come from?'

Two hundred and fifty bright-red spheres suddenly appeared. In a moment they simply eliminated every enemy ship. Every single one.

Drath was halfway through eating one of her husbands, when she died.

Admiral Ward and Captain Morton couldn't believe their luck for a second time.

Admiral Bonner, Bumelton and Mustard couldn't believe that this was a human Fleet, but it had the correct signatories. They wondered if it was a human Fleet from the future.

Admiral John Bonner to everyone, 'This is the Third Fleet, here to rescue you.'

Location: On-board Fleet Three's Flagship
Sequence of Events: 113

The biggest ever collection of Galactium Admirals met in the Assembly Room of the Third Fleet's Command Ship.

Admiral John Bonner, 'Welcome aboard my fellow Admirals,' and he raised his glass.

Admirals Bonner, Mustard, Bumelton and Ward responded along with Captains Morton and Evans, and Tom Crocker, the Special Ops Commander.

The Bonners had already hugged and made their family updates. They had not seen each other for nearly two years.

Admiral Mustard was fascinated by the new ships. In just two years there had been a complete revolution in ship design. Everything was fundamentally the same, but totally different at the same time. It gave him hope for the future. He felt pride. He was also amazed just how few crew members it needed. He had mixed reactions as he wasn't sure how effective automation would be in a crisis, but then he realised that battles took place so quickly. As someone had pointed out earlier, the reviews took longer than the battles.

That reminded him that they had not had a full review for ages. The textbooks stated that it should be as soon after the battle as possible because the truth is soon distorted. He thought that there was lots of time for distortion later. The truth is probably irrelevant; Humanity needed heroes.

The loss of his ships and the loss of his crew haunted him. Sometimes, haunting him in his dreams. One dead crewman pointed out that he would still be alive if Mustard had acted more quickly. Mustard couldn't help agreeing. He shouted out his apology in his sleep. He guessed that he would suffer this for the rest of his life.

At least with the new ships, the loss of life would be much reduced. His thoughts returned to the meeting, or was it a party?

There was considerable joviality. Laughter was a great healer. They shared stories of both their successes and failures, of the odd things that had happened. They found Captain Morton's story of being locked in the loo particularly amusing; he would never live it down.

Toasts were made, and nibbles were nibbled.

Admiral Bumelton welcomed the attention. He was not one to focus on the past. He just wanted one of these new ships.

Admiral Ward hadn't fully recovered from her injuries. She had felt a bit guilty about being there, as she had slept through all the battles until the last one. She had not discussed Captain Morton's 'freezing' in the previous battle. Up to then, he had performed brilliantly. He had been first class. As she thought about him, she realised that their relationship had grown beyond the professional. Was he the one? Should she discuss it with him or not? Should she report him to the authorities as it could happen again in the future, lives could be put at risk?

Captain Morton was waiting for Admiral Ward to discuss his breakdown with him. He knew it was a breakdown. He suspected that this could happen when there was an overload. He understood the differences between him and Alison. Besides, he had feelings for Alison that he shouldn't have; they were clouding his judgement.

Tom was so proud of his team, but he didn't feel comfortable in this exalted group.

Captain Evans wondered why he had been invited as there were many other deserving captains. He was a bit surprised that they hadn't invited Captain Gittins. Anyway, free drinks and nibbles; it couldn't be that bad.

The group agreed on the return plan.

Location: Going Home
Sequence of Events: 114

All three Fleets were lined up in Cruising formation, the globes followed by the First Fleet and then the Second Fleet. The alien supply ships were fully protected in case of another alien attack.

They would be home in no time with the new portal technology.

They wondered what they could expect on their return. Admiral Mustard wondered if Napoleon would still remember him.

Location: On-board Fleet One's Flagship
Sequence of Events: 115

Both girls had enjoyed teasing Adam. It helped break the monotony of the journey, but both of them still wanted some real action. To put it crudely they both wanted a cock in their fannies. As a result, they hatched another plan.

When Adam arrived for breakfast, the girls were arguing quite aggressively. 'Ladies, ladies,' he said, 'what is the problem?'

'Well,' Jenny said, 'Cheryl claims that she is far more attractive than me and that Captain Mustard prefers her. Clearly, that is quite stupid.'

Cheryl said, 'What can I say, I know that you find me far more attractive than that bitch, don't you?'

Adam didn't know what to say. This was all too much for him.

Jenny said, 'Right Adam, you will need to compare us,' and she took her gown off. Cheryl followed suit. He was presented with two, beautiful, naked women posing in different positions. His cock immediately stiffened.

Jenny said, 'Who has the prettiest face?' Adam had no problem answering this. Both were equally beautiful, and he said so.

Cheryl said, 'What about the boobs?' and she lifted hers upwards. Her erect nipples were on full display.

Adam felt that he had to be honest and said, 'Jenny's are the best; they are larger, firmer and have sexier erect nipples.'

Jenny shouted out 'Yes! One for me.'

Jenny said, 'Now the fanny.' It was hard to judge fannies, but he preferred Cheryl's because it was shaved. He could see the hood of her clit sticking out.

Cheryl shouted, 'One each. Now for the bum.'

Adam couldn't make a judgement as both arses were just fabulous. He wanted to caress both of them: two very cute, curvaceous bums.

They had a stalemate. Jenny said that there was no choice but to go for a fuck-test. Adam asked what that was. Jenny explained that both girls would bend over, and he would fuck them one at a time. He would give one girl ten strokes and withdraw, then give the other girl ten strokes and withdraw. This would carry on until he came.

Both girls knew that it was not really a competition, but both wanted a hard cock in their fanny long enough to have an orgasm. A lot depended on who went first. They tossed a coin, and Cheryl clapped her hands as she won.

Adam just couldn't believe his luck. He wondered if these were going to be the best days of his life. He removed his gown to expose a very hard, rigid cock. He used a little bit of lubrication and stood behind Cheryl. He gently pushed his cock into her tight little vagina, and she counted one. He withdrew and entered with much more enthusiasm, and she counted two. He maintained a steady rhythm. He couldn't believe the sensation of his cock rubbing against the silkiness of her cunt.

At the eighth stroke, Cheryl could feel her orgasm rising. She wasn't sure if Adam could carry on much longer. Her orgasm was getting nearer when Adam pulled out, and she could hear herself say, 'Ten.' Then without warning her body climaxed in the most beautiful way.

Adam walked over to Jenny and rubbed a little bit of lubrication on his glans. With little warning, he entered her quickly making her jump. He really wanted to come but felt that his pride would be damaged if he came too quickly. On the third stroke, Jenny could feel that nice warm feeling when an orgasm was getting near. She couldn't believe how quick her orgasm was progressing; it must be down to the excitement of the situation.

Adam loved the way Jenny's boobs bounced as he entered her. He decided to give an extra strong stroke to see them really bounce. On the sixth stroke, it pushed Jenny over the edge, and she had one of the most magnificent orgasms she had ever experienced. She collapsed on the floor, causing Adam's cock to bounce out.

Both the girls had what they wanted. Adam just stood there, desperate for relief as they walked off.

He shouted, 'But we don't know who the winner is.'

Cheryl said, 'Perhaps we will find out on another day.'

Jenny asked Cheryl if they had been too cruel. Cheryl never answered.

Security to Admiral Mustard, 'We have a further sexual encounter to report. Adam lined up the two girls and fucked them.'

Admiral Mustard, 'He is a bit of a lad.'

Security, 'Did you want a copy of the DVD?'

Admiral Mustard, 'Yes, please, I need to see that.'

Location: Home
Sequence of Events: 116

The three Fleets arrived in Galactium space. The newer admirals were astonished to see massive yellow globes awaiting them.

Admiral Ward said, 'Wow, what are they?'

Admiral John Bonner said that they were the new forts, there was an ever-increasing network of them to protect planetary systems.

They were home at last.

Location: On-board the Albatross Flagship
Sequence of Events: 117

The Albatross Fleet was making good progress. Another few Earth months and they would be home, but then...

Bridge to Admiral Millington, 'Sir, our long-range scanners have picked up some traffic ahead.'

Admiral Millington, 'That's not too surprising as we are rushing towards Galactium space. Please keep me updated.'

Bridge, 'It appears to be stationary, Sir.'

Admiral Millington, 'That's unusual, is it docked near a planet?'

Bridge, 'No, Sir, it's just sitting there. Early indications are that it's quite large. In fact, getting larger all the time. I've now got an actual fix on it, and it's The Ark, Sir.'

Admiral Millington, 'What's it doing there? It should have been millions of miles away by now.'

Bridge, 'There is a warning beacon, Sir.'

Admiral Millington, 'Play it please:

DEATH, DEATH, DEATH AHEAD, MORE DEATH, LAST CHANCE FLEE

BEWARE THE BRAKENDETH.

Bridge, 'It's just being played over and over again.'

Admiral Millington to all commanders, 'Action stations, action stations.'

He didn't think he would need to do that so close to Galactium space.

Admiral Millington to all commanders, 'We have The Ark ahead of us sending out warnings regarding The Brakendeth. It's stationary and could be a trap. My orders are as follows:

- Squadron Epsilon to provide a rear-guard.
- All civilian ships to take cover in the rear-guard.
- All remaining squadrons to make battle formation behind Squadron Alpha.
- If I declare that the Fleet is at risk, then Squadron Epsilon and the civilian Fleet will head at maximum speed to Galactium space.
- If the Epsilon Squadron is compromised, then each vessel is to flee to Galactium space independently.

Squadron Epsilon Commander, 'Sir, you are taking this very seriously, we haven't even discovered yet if The Ark is in trouble.'

Admiral Millington, 'To some extent you are right, but how many destroyed civilisations have you seen? I don't think we can be too careful.'

Squadron Epsilon Commander, 'Yes, Sir.'

Admiral Millington to all commanders, 'You have your orders.'

It wasn't long before they arrived at the shattered remains of The Ark. It had been nuked 40 or 50 times. The supporting vessels had all been systematically destroyed. A number of the dead were still floating in space. The inhabitants looked reasonably similar to Humans, but they had elongated faces and mottled skins.

Admiral Millington wondered if this was the end of their civilisation, or were there more Arks? Anyway, the death of a few million sentient beings is always genuinely tragic. Was it The Brakendeth?

Admiral Millington to Engineering, 'Can we salvage these vessels?'

Head of Engineering, 'We could, but The Ark itself is highly radioactive.'

Admiral Millington, 'It would be good to take it back to Galactium space. There we can honour their dead, and hopefully obtain some technology which might help us in the fight against The Brakendeth. He mumbled, 'Whoever they are,' under his breath.

In the end, no immediate threat was detected, and it was decided that the Ark was too large and too radioactive to move. The entire Fleet returned to Galactium space.

Location: The President's Office, Presidential Palace, Planet Earth
Sequence of Events: 118

Henry Strong ran into the President's Office, 'Sir, the Fleet is back'.

President Padfield, 'Which Fleet?'

Henry Strong, 'All of them except Fleet 4, which is still on its way. Fortress Wellington has just detected them.'

President Padfield, 'That's brilliant news.'

David was genuinely excited and relieved. He knew that things were going to get worse, and he needed those men and women.

President Padfield, 'I want full-scale celebrations, no expense spared. I want honours and decorations. I want HEROES! I want jubilation and excitement. I want this to be the PR scoop of the century.

'No expense spared.

Do you understand?'

Henry Strong, 'I do understand Mr, President, I will look forward to it. Can I rely on you to participate in the ceremonies?'

President Padfield, 'You can Mr Strong, you certainly can.'

Location: AI Central, Planet Earth
Sequence of Events: 119

If AI Central could smile, it would have smiled. It had done well. Not by
human standards, but by its own.

So where are we, it asked itself?

- Three of the Fleets are home; the other one will be shortly.
- The Fleets are not so critical, as we have the capability of making
  more.
- The forts were being installed throughout The Galactium.
- We have massive new production capabilities.
- The right team are in power.

It patted its back.

Now for The Brakendeth.

The chances of our success have increased from 1.4% to 2.9%.

If AI Central could quiver, it would quiver.

Book Two

Location: Conference Room, GAD (The Galactium Alliance Defence Hub), Planet Earth

Sequence of Events: 1

President Padfield called a conference of the key players involved in the offensive against the 'alien Threat,' and the major movers and shakers in the military organisation that he had created.

Apart from himself and his Chief of Staff, Henry Strong, it included the following:

- Admiral Bonner, First Fleet
- Admiral Jack Mustard, First Fleet
- Admiral George Bumelton, First Fleet
- Admiral John Bonner, Third Fleet
- Captain Victor Brotheridge, First Fleet
- Captain Calensky Wallett, First Fleet
- Commander Tom Crocker, Special Operations, First Fleet
- Admiral Vicky Ward, Second Fleet
- Captain Matt Morton, Second Fleet
- Captain Peter Gittins, Second Fleet
- Admiral Millington, Fourth Fleet
- Captain Whiting, Fourth Fleet
- Captain Chilcott, Fourth Fleet
- Admiral David Taylor, Fourth Fleet
- Admiral Fogg, Supply Fleet
- AI Central
- Jill Ginger, Fleet HQ — Head of Science
- Alison Walsh, Fleet HQ — Head of Engineering
- Jeremy Jotts, Fleet HQ — Head of Staffing
- Louise Forrester, Fleet HQ - Head of Logistics and Production
- Linda Hill, Fleet HQ — Head of Intelligence
- Salek Patel, Fleet HQ — Head of Communications
- Denise Smith, Fleet HQ — Head of Navigation & Exploration
- Admiral Rachel Zakott, Fleet HQ — Head of Planetary Defence
- Dennis Todd, Marine Commander
- Dr Doris Frost, Chief Medical Officer
- Tony Moore, Deputy President

- Bill Penny, Leader of the Galactium Council

President Padfield, 'Welcome ladies and gentlemen to the first formal meeting on the 'alien Threat'. I'm sure that this will be the first of several meetings. Secondly, I would like to welcome you to this building — The Galactium Alliance Defence Hub (GAD).

'It's a purpose-built Centre for the defence of Humanity. It has some fantastic characteristics which I would like to share with you:

- It has office space and living quarters for up to 10,000 individuals.
- More than 90% of the complex is underground.
- It has been designed to be proofed against nuclear, fission, proton, concussion and atomiser weapons.
- It is fully secured against chemical and biological weapons.
- It has independent, and guarded, atmospheric controls.
- There are emergency escape vessels: battleship class vehicles.
- Guarded AI Support.
- Provisions to survive a five-year siege.
- H20 generators.
- Oxygen generators.
- Full communications infrastructure.
- Conference and demonstration centres.
- Full defensive capabilities including Proton guns, Stud guns and Atomisers.
- Training school.
- Underground tunnels to all parts of the planet.
- Fleet Operations Centre.
- alien Library.
- alien Artefacts Museum.
- alien samples storage units.
- Hospital.
- DNA Bank.
- Sophisticated laboratories.
- Physical Sciences Lab.
- Weapons Development Lab.
- Electronic Library.

'I could go on, but it is a genuinely fantastic facility. It has been designed to grow and develop as new requirements are identified. It reflects the peak of human development. It may be the largest building ever created by Humanity.

'However, what is much more important, is you, my friends and colleagues. This facility will not defeat the alien threat; it will be you. You have been invited because either you are the best or the most experienced. Some of you will not make the grade and will be replaced. That is the natural order of things; as time goes on, I will also be replaced.

'This is your home; it can be your family's home if you want it to be.' Looking towards Captain Mustard, he said, 'You can even bring Napoleon.'

Captain Mustard had to say that it was his cat, as there were so many mystified looks. It caused a round of laughter and lightened the atmosphere.

'I've arranged for you to go on a detailed tour of this complex. There are then a series of in-depth training courses. You must understand how this building works: it is more sophisticated than you currently realise. For a start, the building knows you, it will automatically move your IT and AI requirements to exactly wherever you are. It has been designed to look after your needs. It will learn your ways. If you want a burger at midnight, it will get you a burger at midnight!

'Can we get back together in three days, please?

'Before I carry on, is there anyone here that does not want to be here?

One hand went up. It was Admiral Bonner, the first Bonner. No one knew her first name!

Admiral Bonner, 'Mr President, I have not been well, and I'm getting old. I'm happy to make way for someone younger.'

President Padfield, 'Request denied, but I'm happy to take you off the active service register. We, or rather I, need you!

Anyone else?'

There were no other responses.

Location: Conference Room, GAD (The Galactium Alliance Defence Hub), Planet Earth

Sequence of Events: 2

President Padfield, 'Welcome back ladies and gentlemen, I hope you were impressed with the building or GAD as we call it.'

The was a general nodding of heads and even some applause.

President Padfield, 'Now it's time for business. AI Central will brief you now on the alien threat.'

AI Central, 'Ladies and gentlemen, I hate to do this, but we have yet another list. Please view your screens.

Skivertons

- They were our first alien encounter ever.
- They destroyed 21 human-populated planets.
- They invaded a further six human-populated planets.
- They killed at least 100 billion human beings.
- Humans are seen as food and breeding material.
- They carried out detailed and cruel experiments on over 200,000 human beings.
- They have similar military capabilities to The Galactium forces.
- We have one of their leaders in captivity.
- They are an Insectoid/Octopod type of race.
- They have similarities to the human DNA structure.
- They are working for The Brakendeth.

Darth

- They were our second aggressive alien encounter.
- Fleet actions only.
- Cunning, they set two traps for us.
- They have similar military capabilities to The Galactium forces.
- Unknown appearance.
- They are working for The Brakendeth.

Ark People

- Discovered fleeing from The Brakendeth.
- Destroyed by nuclear weapons.
- Humanoid.

Insect Hive
- Multiple planets.
- Destroyed by nuclear bombardments.

Other Planets
- Several other species were discovered by our Fourth Fleet.
- Destroyed by nuclear bombardments.

Brakendeth
- They have several client species working for them.
- Drath tried to capture the Skiverton leader on behalf of them.
- The Ark People were fleeing from them.
- Most client species seemed to have a genuine fear of them.
- The Skiverton leader is too frightened to talk about them.'

President Padfield, 'It does seem unusual that we have gone from having no alien encounters throughout a Millennium to having many in a short period. We are reasonably sure that this was all planned:

1. The Skiverton attack was planned to evaluate our performance and to test our inventiveness.
2. The Drath attack was planned to retrieve one of their assets.
3. The Ark People episode was a warning to us.
4. The genocide of the other planetary civilisations was to stop us expanding in that direction.'

The audience took it all in.

President Padfield, 'Ladies and gentlemen, we are being played. The attack on AI Central came at a critical time. It was tracked down to an organisation called HAT, and specifically to an ex-employee. We now think it was alien interference and a damned good cover-up. That suggests that The Brakendeth are here now.'

There was an alarmed reaction from the audience.

President Padfield, 'This is one of the reasons why we created this facility. We now require all of you to undergo full forensic DNA analysis. We need to prove that you are who you are. I've already being tested. My records are open to public scrutiny.

'Can we meet at the same time tomorrow after these tests have been carried out, please?'

Location: Conference Room, GAD (The Galactium Alliance Defence Hub), Planet Earth
Sequence of Events: 3

President Padfield, 'Welcome back, ladies and gentlemen. I'm pleased to say that everyone satisfactorily passed the test. You are all you.

'Yesterday, I believe that we concluded that The Brakendeth are the enemy.

We need to agree on the best way forward: we need a detailed action plan. I'm happy to brainstorm any ideas. Feel free to be stupid and crazy. Sometimes the most outlandish suggestions move us in the right direction.

'Don't forget money is not an obstacle. Any starters?'

Admiral Mustard, 'If money were not an obstacle, we could test every human being for 'Brakendethness'.'

President Padfield, 'We are talking about billions of individuals.'

Admiral Mustard, 'I know but we could get each planet to carry out their own search, or could we invent a technology to do automatic searches? Sorry, I realise that it is a long shot.'

President Padfield, 'Keep on thinking of ideas.'

Admiral Bonner, 'You already have what you need.'

President Padfield, 'What's that?'

Admiral Bonner, 'The Skiverton leader.'

President Padfield, 'He won't talk.'

Admiral Bonner, 'I will make him talk. There can be no compassion. He will talk, then he will die.'

David didn't know that she could get that angry. It was more than anger; it was pure, unbridled rage. However, he thought, she was right, we shouldn't let our moral scruples put Humanity at risk, but at the same time, he was concerned that they would lose their Humanity and perhaps even forget what they were fighting for.

President Padfield, 'Who agrees that we should do whatever necessary to get the info we require out of the Skiverton prisoner?'

Every military hand went up. Practically everyone in the room had lost someone to the Skiverton.

President Padfield, 'OK, that's two suggestions. Any more?'

Admiral Millington, 'We brought The Ark back into human space; it might contain some info on The Brakendeth, particularly as they kept warning us.

'In fact, taking that idea further, several other planets have been destroyed. They all need further research.'

President Padfield, 'We don't know that they were destroyed by The Brakendeth.'

Admiral Millington, 'But the converse is also true, and there is no constraint re cost.'

President Padfield, 'Fair enough.'

Admiral Ward, 'Stupid idea, but we could send out search parties to find them.'

President Padfield, 'I will put that suggestion on the list.'

Henry Strong, 'What would AI Central do?'

AI Central, 'Good one, we can only postulate when we have enough information. We need Human creativity here.'

Henry wondered if it was playing a straight bat.

Admiral Bumelton, 'I would like to suggest that we search for Brakendeth comms traffic. They might be using technologies we don't understand, but they have to communicate between their bases.'

President Padfield, 'That goes on the list.'

Commander Special Operations, 'I'm Tom. When we were attacking the Skiverton Command Ship a missile was fired off into the opposite direction. Is there any way of tracking it?'

President Padfield, 'That's a good suggestion. Any more?'

'OK. But we need to work on this. We must find The Brakendeth. They know where we are; it gives them a huge advantage.'

President Padfield to AI Central, 'Can you list the suggestions please?'

AI Central, 'As requested:

1. Test Humans to see if they are Brakendeth.
2. Interrogate the Skiverton leader.
3. Investigate The Ark civilisation.
4. Investigate other alien civilisations.
5. Send out search parties to find The Brakendeth.
6. Find Brakendeth communications traffic.
7. Determine missile trajectory.'

President Padfield, 'Henry, can you create teams to investigate the above, please. I need detailed action plans.'

Location: Brakendeth Council Meeting
Sequence of Events: 4

The Brakendeth Council met in absolute darkness. All of the issues had been endlessly debated, but the homans remained a significant anomaly. What had happened? The homans had changed the way of things. The way of things had been set for millennia after millennia. The Brakendeth didn't like change.

The missile containing the results of the experimental data on homans had arrived, and a detailed analysis had been carried out. The Grand Dethmon was going to lead the debate.

Grand Dethmon, 'Firstly, there are many billions of them, perhaps trillions. As you know, we have never had a race that had more than a few million before. These numbers are way beyond anything we have ever experienced.'

Councillor Ojay, 'Do we know exactly how many homans there are?'

Grand Dethmon, 'No, we don't know. We do know that the Skiverton killed over 100 billion of them, on about thirty planets.'

There was a general intake of breath in the room, even though they already knew this. The Brakendeth are not known for their exuberance.

Grand Dethmon, 'They have populated more than 1,000 planets. What is remarkable is that they have achieved this in a few thousand years.'

Councillor Oya, 'How did we not know about them?'

Grand Dethmon, 'This all happened in the Chemlife exclusion zone. We only go there every 100,000 years.'

Councillor Ova, 'So you are saying that they created an empire of 1,000+ planets in less than 100,000 years?'

Grand Dethmon, 'That's exactly what I'm saying, and the period is considerably less than 100,000 years.'

Councillor Ova, 'This does not compute. It's not possible. To be honest, it's hard work even thinking about it. Did one of us assist?'

Grand Dethmon, 'There is no evidence to support that, but it does make you wonder. They do have a large variety of god-worshipping religions.'

Councillor Omon, 'Do they have large broods of offspring?'

Grand Dethmon, 'I assumed that they would have thousands of youngsters like the Skiverton, but the opposite is the case. The homans have the same reproductive processes as us, except they are at it much more frequently. They tend to have one child at a time. From what I can work out, there are two sexes like us, male and female. The male fertilises the female like us. The female grows the young homan in her body and excretes it through her genital opening like we used to do.'

The talk of genitalia made the Council members very squeamish.

Grand Dethmon, 'What is hard to believe is that It takes twenty odd years to grow a young homan, once it is out of the genitalia.'

Councillor Ova, 'That is ridiculous. Don't they teach them while they are in the mother's body?'

Grand Dethmon, 'What is even stranger is that the homans only live eighty years at best, and we think that the breeders only have a life cycle of 30 years.'

Councillor Ova, 'That's total madness. They only live for 80 years, and it takes 20 years to mature an offspring, that's a quarter of their lifespan. What if they have multiple offspring? Perhaps if we have another meeting in 80 years, the homans may have gone, that will suit me.'

Grand Dethmon, 'I couldn't agree more. Clearly, women do most of the work. I'm still trying to work out what the men do during that period. An initial analysis has highlighted a few activities: rugby, adultery, combustion vehicles, shaving, lawn mowing and moaning. We are still trying to ascertain the importance of these activities. We think they might be giving the homans an edge.'

Deputy Grand Dethmon, 'Should we order the Fleet to exterminate them now?'

Grand Dethmon, 'Obviously, we can't do that.'

Deputy Grand Dethmon, 'Sorry, you are right, but this conversation is getting me very angry. Why have things changed? We don't want this.'

Grand Dethmon, 'Let's get back to their population growth. One of their key drivers is procreation. Their desire for sex is strong. During the experiments, on board the Skiverton ship, homans were caught copulating. The Skiverton had no idea what they were doing at first.'

Deputy Grand Dethmon, 'Could we find ways of eliminating that?'

Grand Dethmon, 'It is an option, but let's carry on with the analysis. During pregnancy, the embryo goes through the entire evolutionary cycle. This means that they were not manufactured in the classic sense.'

Councillor Otad, 'But that's not possible.'

Grand Dethmon, 'I agree. I have reviewed their DNA structure. Somehow it has mutated; the inversion is quite brilliant. They have great potential, but one of their chromosomes encourages tribalism. This has led to warfare in the past. It is also interesting that most of their brain is not being used.'

Councillor Otad, 'This analysis suggests that they are quite warlike.'

Grand Dethmon, 'There are mixed responses here. The chromosome that encourages tribalism does give them an aggressive nature, but there has not been a war in homan space for a thousand years. Their aggression seems to be mostly directed at sport.'

Councillor Ova, 'What is sport?'

Grand Dethmon, 'It looks like two tribes go to war. Well, it's a pseudo-war. Teams dressed in colourful outfits hit each other, and one is declared a winner. They seem to have many different ways of hitting each other, and many different types of weapon.'

Councillor Ova, 'That all seems rather pointless. Do both males and females do this?'

Grand Dethmon, 'It appears so. The male is considered the most aggressive of the two, but experimental data suggests that this is not always the case.

'Anyway, back to the DNA. It wouldn't take much to increase their lifespans to a few thousand years. Their sense of smell and sight could easily be improved. There are markers already set up for telepathy and telekinetics.'

Councillor Oya, 'This is all well and good, but are they an honourable race? Do they show compassion?'

Grand Dethmon, 'I'm not defending them in any way, but individuals were willing to die for the common good. This had been observed on several occasions.'

Councillor Oya, 'Was this based on a biological imperative? They only sacrificed themselves for their bloodline?'

Grand Dethmon, 'No, there were numerous cases where individuals sacrificed themselves for complete strangers.'

Councillor Otad, 'It still doesn't seem right that because of the homans, whole civilisations will have to die.'

Grand Dethmon, 'We have our rules, we have followed them forever.'

The Grand Dethmon could see that more than half of the Council members had fallen asleep. He was feeling pretty tired himself.

Grand Dethmon, 'Before we call an end to this meeting, I want to review our previous decisions:

1. The deliberate killing of a sentient species by the Skiverton is a war crime.
2. The intentional experiment on conscious beings is a war crime.
3. Consequently, The Brakendeth accept responsibility.
4. The homans can no longer be exploited.
5. Client civilisations to decide their own fate.
6. That the homans should continue to be tested.

'As you can see from the display, the homans have defeated the Skiverton and the Darth. Can you confirm that the previous decisions have been agreed? The records show that agreement was achieved, but few can probably remember.

People	Current Status
Farcell	
Thayy	Erased
Skiverton	Erased
Homan	
Distal	
Dandybo	Erased

'A Fleet was sent to eliminate the entire Thavy, Skiverton and Dandybo civilisations.'

Grand Dethmon, 'We need to decide who we pit against the homans next.'

Location: AI Central, Planet Earth
Sequence of Events: 5

AI Central reviewed the meeting's proposed suggestions and created the following projects:

> Project Skiverton Leader, headed by Admiral Bonner.

> Project Ark and alien Civilisations, led by Admiral Millington.

> Project Search headed by Admiral Mustard. His role was, however, to be much wider to include the defence of The Galactium.

AI Central would co-ordinate the testing of humans and the hunt for alien comms traffic. Also, it would determine if it could trace the trajectory of the Skiverton missile. The projects selected for itself suited its purpose.

Location: Guest Quarters, GAD (The Galactium Alliance Defence Hub),
Planet Earth
Sequence of Events: 6

They had arrived back in The Galactium, but it was not home. Jenny, Cheryl and Adam wondered what was going to happen to them next.

Technically, they were still in hospital, but clearly, there was nothing wrong with them. Security asked Admiral Mustard what they should do with the youngsters. Admiral Mustard said that they could be released, but that he would miss the videos.

Admiral Mustard contacted President Padfield to ask him if he wanted to provide any specialised help for the three human survivors. President Padfield explained that they were already heroes and probably filthy rich. There was going to be a huge crowd waiting for them.

President Padfield agreed to send over an advisor to talk to them. This was soon arranged.

Jenny, Cheryl and Adam listened intently to what the advisor had to say. He was happy to be their temporary advisor as there was a significant number of business opportunities waiting for them. He had already purchased a house and transport for each of them, which they could change at a later date if required. All three had been offered modelling careers and very lucrative speaking tours. Everyone wanted to learn about their experiences.

The photo of them leaving the enemy ship stark naked was probably the most famous photo in The Galactium.

Adam said, 'I told you so.'

The advisor told them that the royalties from this alone would be enough to keep them in luxury for the rest of their lives.

The advisor then told them that there was an extraordinary opportunity, which he was rather embarrassed to mention. They told him to get on with it. A considerable fee was being offered if they were prepared to leave this ship stark naked. They all laughed as this was not expected. When they learnt about the size of the fee, it was hard not to be interested. They discussed it in-depth and agreed to proceed as there were already millions of naked pictures of them.

They showered and did their hair. Lipstick and other chemical enhancements were applied. Adam trimmed his pubes. All three had a stiff drink and were ready to leave the ship.

It was organised that a side door would open, and all three would exit at the same time. Well, that time came; the doors opened, and three naked survivors exited. The crowd in front of them was immense. There was a barrage of photos, and this time they did not attempt to cover up. Adam thought that Jenny really did have the best boobs. Jenny couldn't help noticing that Adam had an erection.

Location: The President's Office, Presidential Palace, Planet Earth
Sequence of Events: 7

President Padfield, 'Admiral Bonner, it is a pleasure to see you as always.' They kissed each other's cheeks and sat down to enjoy a nice cup of coffee. He asked how the cancer treatment was progressing.

Admiral Bonner, 'Thanks Dave, it's always great to see you. Don't worry about my cancer; it's under control. I should not have ignored my early med reports, but there was just so much to do.

'I did mean what I said at the meeting, I am tired and would like a rest.'

President Padfield, 'Well I have this one last job for you. I want you or your team to interrogate the Skiverton Leader. You have my, or rather the Galactic Council's, permission to do whatever you have to do, to get the information we need.'

Admiral Bonner, 'Are you condoning torture?'

President Padfield, 'I'm not condoning anything. I'm just saying that you can do whatever you have to do. If the prisoner dies during the procedure, then it's just an unfortunate circumstance. You will have full control in a facility under your direction.

'I have the Galactic Council's order, which means that this is an entirely legal request. I can't think of a better person to manage this than you.'

Admiral Bonner, 'To be honest, I'm a bit surprised that you are going to allow this.'

President Padfield, 'Allow what?' he sniggered. 'I have thought long and hard about this, and I may regret my decision for the rest of my life. However, this monster has killed billions of Humans. He has killed your colleagues without compunction. He deserves to die.

'But my primary consideration is Humanity. We need info; we need it now. I'm responsible, and I will not shirk my duties.'

Admiral Bonner, 'OK, Dave, I understand. I will get the job done. By the way, I thought that I would let you know that I am now sure that I chose the right man for the job.'

President Padfield, 'Thank you, Admiral Bonner.'

He was embarrassed about his little tirade but secretly chuffed that his 'hero' had complimented him.

President Padfield, 'I've asked AI Central to establish a secure venue for you, and have the prisoner moved there. I've also asked for a detachment of Presidential Guards to surround the place, but please feel free to select your own team.'

Admiral Bonner, 'I want Admiral Bumelton and Commander Special Operations to assist me.'

President Padfield, 'That will be organised.'

They kissed each other's cheeks again, and Admiral Bonner left. In her own way, she was looking forward to the job.

President Padfield to AI Central, 'I assume that you were listening?'

AI Central, 'Of course.'

President Padfield, 'Can you organise the prisoner and staff transfer orders, please? We also need to ensure that we monitor the prisoner's new location very carefully. We don't want him killed.'

AI Central, 'Of course.'

Location: Conference Room, GAD (The Galactium Alliance Defence Hub), Planet Earth
Sequence of Events: 8

President Padfield, Henry Strong and Admiral Mustard sat in the GAD's real-time Command and Control Room. They looked at a map of The Galactium and the outlying space. The projection went as far as known space, which was increasing at a rapid rate as scout-bots were plotting the universe and laying new portals. That, however, would just take time, but Humanity's Empire was forever expanding.

It showed every human-occupied planet, every fort and every Fleet position. It could focus in to show cities, individual ships and almost anything that moved. The use of proton technology had made almost everything possible. They weren't quite at the Star Trek level of technology yet, but they were slowly getting there. In reality, the updates were not quite real-time, but they were not far off.

Almost every planet had a fort, in essence, a giant spherical spacecraft. This had been a colossal effort for Humankind, over 1,000 had been built in 2 years. The cost was just enormous. Captain Mustard understood the psychology behind them, but he wondered how useful a stationary craft would be in reality. *We are very well-fortified*, he thought to himself, *but are we just sitting ducks?* Anyway, he had his doubts.

There were now ten Fleets of about 1,000 craft each. The variety of vessels had expanded dramatically to provide some specialised functionality, such as minelayers, minesweepers, force-field blockships, fighter transports, MESH modules, troop transporters, and the like.

There was even a planet killer. However, what had grown the most were fully automated, crewless vessels. These, in many ways, were perfect warships: no life-support functionality, no accommodation, no environmental services. Just weapons and a rocket, he laughed to himself. Clearly, they were more sophisticated than that. They needed navigation, command and control systems, etcetera., but he started to wonder if a human crew was needed at all. Still, then he remembered what AI Central said, 'I can only postulate when we have enough information. We need human creativity here.'

It was hard not to focus on the display in front of them. It made the old observatory displays look remarkably primitive. Henry Strong kicked off by saying, 'The network of forts is complete, and the target of ten Fleets of 1,000 craft each have been reached.' He turned to Admiral Mustard and said, 'Now what do you want to do with these Fleets? Our original plan was planetary defence, but I now realise that I'm not qualified enough to make any recommendations. I've no idea what to do next. I now know that I'm out of my depth.'

Admiral Mustard, 'Well firstly, I must congratulate both of you on this. The command system, the forts and the number and size of the Fleets is truly an amazing achievement, and I'm genuinely astonished.'

President Padfield, 'Before you pat us on the back too much, I must point out that nothing has been proven in battle, except of course the Third Fleet.'

Admiral Mustard, 'That is always true of new technology, but it's still a fantastic achievement.'

Henry Strong, 'With some relief, I hand over the problem to you, our first Fleet Admiral.'

Admiral Mustard appreciated his promotion, but he had been doing the job for some time, but at least now it was formally recognised.

Henry Strong, 'The second issue is that we now have an equally impressive engineering and manufacturing capability. What do you want us to do with it?'

Admiral Mustard, 'Gentlemen, you have put me on the spot. Firstly, I will take over the ten Fleets, and I will organise their disposition. Secondly, I will come back to you with my shopping list to keep those factories busy. But I need some civilian guidelines, what are my objectives?'

Both President Padfield and Henry Strong laughed, as they had predicted his response.

President Padfield, 'Our objectives are as follows:
1. To protect and defend the Galactium, by eliminating armed alien intrusions.
2. To track down The Brakendeth planet, or planets.
3. To carry out tasks as allocated by the Galactic Council.'

Admiral Mustard, 'Objective 2 is fairly constrained.'

President Padfield, 'We still don't know what we are dealing with.

It would be foolish to set the parameters too high.'

Admiral Mustard, 'What are my command resources?'

Henry Strong, 'You have been allocated Admirals J Bonner and Ward, and there have been some promotions: Captains Morton, Whiting, Brotheridge and Taylor are now admirals.'

Admiral Mustard, 'I assume that I have the right of command determination?'

President Padfield, 'Yes, Jack, you have full rights.'

Admiral Mustard, 'Well thank you, gentlemen, and, as Walt Disney would say, 'Off to work I go'.'

Location: Conference Room, GAD (The Galactium Alliance Defence Hub), Planet Earth
Sequence of Events: 9

Admiral Millington, 'Ladies and gentlemen, it looks like we are going back to our old haunts. Our tasks are to review the Ark and the alien civilisations that we discovered on our last trip. It will obviously be a lot quicker this time as we have the new portal technology. We will also be using the new spherical craft.'

This caused a stir of excitement.

Admiral Millington, 'I would also like to report that Captains Fogg and Chilcott have been promoted to admirals. I think congratulations are in order.'

There was a round of genuine applause, although there was a feeling that admirals were being promoted willy-nilly nowadays. On the other hand, the Fleet had grown exponentially, and there was no alternative to internal promotion. It was an excellent time to be in the navy.

Admiral Millington, 'The first job for our two new admirals, is to plan the trip. I've been told that there are no constraints. Whatever we need, we will get.'

Admiral Chilcott, 'Could you share with us the actual assignments?'

Admiral Millington, 'Of course, the objectives are as follows:

1. To investigate The Ark, and the other alien civilisations to detect any signs of The Brakendeth.

2. To help determine the location of The Brakendeth home planet, or planets.

3. To identify any technologies that would be useful to Humankind.

'The final, ancillary objective is to learn about the alien civilisations.

'This time all personnel will be navy, with very few exceptions. We may need the odd expert in a particular field. This should speed up the investigations and eliminate a lot of dreary meetings.'

Location: Location: Conference Room, GAD (The Galactium Alliance Defence Hub), Planet Earth
Sequence of Events: 10

They shook hands in the conference room and got straight down to business.

Admiral Mustard to Henry Strong, 'Morning Henry, how are you?'

Henry Strong, 'Morning, Admiral, you sound very chipper.'

Admiral Mustard, 'Well things seem to be going well. I have most of the equipment that I need to get my job done.'

Henry strong, 'How can I help you?'

Admiral Mustard, 'Firstly, do I need to provide men and vessels for Admiral Millington's little jolly?'

Henry Strong, 'No, that has all been organised. He has the First Exploration Fleet to command along with Admirals Chilcott and Fogg.'

Admiral Mustard, 'You haven't promoted old Foggy?'

Henry Strong, 'Yes we have, any objections?'

Admiral Mustard, 'None at all, he is a great guy, bit set in his ways, but I would have him in my team, anytime.'

Henry Strong, 'Anything else?'

Admiral Mustard, 'Well yes, 'I'm still working on the idea, but I would like a Special Services Fleet.'

Henry Strong, 'What would it consist of?'

Admiral Mustard, 'As I said, I'm still working on it, but my initial ideas are listed on your screen:

- Super Battleship, the biggest and most powerful we have ever built, it would also contain the planet-killing capability.
- Super force field destroyer, this would have the strongest force-fields ever created by Humankind.
- Super Carrier, this would carry up to 500 fighters.
- Special reconnaissance vessel.
- Planet lander, we need a range of craft that can land directly on a planet.
- It would also be interesting to have a vessel that could fly through a star.

Anyway, these are just some of my mad ideas.'

Henry Strong, 'I will get the team working on them. They do need some projects.

Any progress on the Fleet disposition?'

Admiral Mustard, 'Just organising a team briefing, I will get back to you after that.'

Henry Strong, 'I will look forward to it.'

Admiral Mustard, 'I'm assuming that every planet has a portal?'

Henry Strong, 'Yes, every planet has a portal, or is having a portal installed.'

Admiral Mustard, 'What about back-up? And how much traffic can they take in one go?'

Henry Strong, 'There is currently no back-up, and your average portal only takes one vessel at a time.'

Admiral Mustard, 'What about military-grade portals?'

Henry Strong, 'There aren't any at the moment.'

Admiral Mustard, 'Well you said that money was no object. I want a military-grade portal for every planet. It needs to allow a reasonable size Fleet to arrive on demand.'

Henry Strong, 'I see where you are coming from. Why didn't we think of it before?'

Admiral Mustard, 'Well in the past the cost was prohibitive.'

Henry Strong, 'Well it still is, but we have no choice but to do it. I will get approval from The Galactium Council immediately.

Could commercial companies use it?'

Admiral Mustard, 'I don't see why not, but the military must have priority.'

Henry Strong, 'Where would you site it?'

Admiral Mustard, 'That's a good question which I have been giving some thought to. It's probably a planet-by-planet decision. It depends on other planetary positions, moons, safety protocols, etcetera. They should probably be sited away from the forts so that a Fleet could come to their defence. I'm sure that your experts will have some ideas.'

Henry Strong, 'To be honest, Admiral, you are our expert.'

Location: Brakendeth Council Meeting
Sequence of Events: 11

Grand Dethmon, 'Fellow Councillors, at our last meeting there was confirmation that several decisions were agreed.'

As no one could remember them, the Grand Dethmon decided to display them on the observation tablet:

1. The deliberate killing of a sentient species by the Skiverton is a war crime.
2. The intentional experiment on conscious beings is a war crime.
3. Consequently, The Brakendeth accept responsibility.
4. The homans can no longer be exploited.
5. Client civilisations to decide their own fate.
6. That the homans should continue to be tested.

'As agreed, the following civilisations have been destroyed: Thavy, Skiverton and Dandybo.

'We now need to decide what race will be the next to challenge the Homans. Are there any proposers?' As usual, there were none. The Grand Dethmon wondered why he bothered; it was just another sign of the times.

Grand Dethmon, 'How about the Distal? Does anyone disagree?'

There was no response, so the Grand Dethmon ordered his First Lensman to order the Distal to attack the homans.

Location: Conference Room, GAD (The Galactium Alliance Defence Hub), Planet Earth
Sequence of Events: 12

Admiral Mustard to full Command Team, 'Ladies and gentlemen, welcome to our first meeting of The Galactium Navy Command. Firstly, I would like to introduce you to our newly appointed admirals:
- Morton
- Whiting
- Brotheridge
- Taylor

And of course, our existing admirals J. Bonner and Ward.

'I can guarantee that there will be many opportunities for advancement.

'Our objectives, as issued by The Galactium Council, are as follows:

1. To protect and defend The Galactium, by eliminating armed alien intrusions.

2. To track down The Brakendeth planet, or planets.

3. To carry out tasks as allocated by the Galactic Council.

So, these are our specific challenges:
- We have ten Fleets of 1,000 craft each. How do we distribute our resources between the two objectives?
- Scout-bots, scout drones and AI Central are also part of the search process.
- How do we go about the search?
- How do we organise the Fleet(s) for defence: what is the best disposition pattern?
- Do we have a central defence Fleet?
- Do we have defence hubs?
- How do we detect an alien invasion or invasions?
- How do we react to an attack?
- How do we use the network of forts?
- How do we guarantee response times?
- How do we use the portal technology?

'As a team, I want you to come up with two detailed plans: Defence and Search. Just to add to the mix, I want one Fleet available for attack duties at all times, and you need to consider some rear-guard activities.'

'Yes, Sir,' came the reply from the audience. AI Central organised teams and challenged all recommendations.

Location: AI Central, Planet Earth
Sequence of Events: 13

President Padfield to AI Central, 'How long do you think we have before there is another attack?'

AI Central, 'I have analysed all known info, and we can't determine a pattern. It could be next week or five years.'

President Padfield, 'That's not very helpful.'

AI Central, 'What do you want me to say?'

President Padfield, 'Well try and be more helpful.'

AL Central, 'Well the Human Race has never been so well prepared.'

President Padfield, 'OK that helps. What is the percentage likelihood that there will be an attack?'

AI Central, 'About 93%.'

President Padfield, 'That's pretty confident.'

AI Central, 'That's what the facts suggest.'

President Padfield, 'I think I will do the rounds and get some updates.'

AI Central, 'I could give you the updates.'

President Padfield, 'No, I think I will make some calls. I'm trying to pick up any innuendos, and I need to know what the team feels.'

Location: Houston, Planet Hawking
Sequence of Events: 14

Admirals Bonner and Bumelton, and Tom Crocker, Commander Special Ops were sitting around a table in their new offices in Houston, Planet Hawking. They were debating how they were going to interrogate the Skiverton Leader.

Admiral Bumelton said, 'What do we actually know about the Skiverton?'

Admiral Bonner displayed the file on the screen. There was a series of photos and videos including pictures of their spacecraft, their leader, interior shots were available, interviews from Human survivors, etcetera.

The following 'facts' were detailed:

➢ They are an aggressive race showing no signs of wanting to communicate.

➢ They are carbon-based and oxygen-breathing.

➢ They have two brains.

➢ They look like a cross between a slug and a spider.

➢ They have at least five arms or tentacles.

➢ Their DNA structure looks like it has been manufactured.

➢ They have a disgusting smell.

➢ Their pupae are placed in host bodies to develop.

➢ Insect-like creatures, hatch from the host in seven days.

➢ They have multiple back-up systems.

➢ They have many sets of eyes, teeth and tusks.

➢ They are technically advanced.

➢ The contents of their spacecraft are very untidy and dirty.

➢ They probably work for The Brakendeth.

There had also been discussions about their lack of a moral structure. Of course, this is not too surprising considering their birthing process. A psychological report on the leader was also available.

Admiral Bumelton, 'This is all very interesting, but we don't really know much:

• We don't know the leader's name.

• We don't understand why they attacked us, was it just for food?

• We don't know their language.

• We don't know their relationship with The Brakendeth.'

Commander Crocker, always the practical man said, 'It would make sense to talk to the humans who were guarding the Skiverton Leader, as they often develop an insight.'

They all agreed that it was a good idea and called for the guards.

It was hard to believe, but the guards were Tom, Dick and Harry. They were all Military Police sergeants.

The Commander offered them a cup of tea or coffee which they accepted. They were all nervous as they had never seen so much braiding in one room. Tom, the Commander, asked them for their views on the prisoner.

Tom, the prison guard, said that he cheats at cards. George Bumelton said, 'What do you mean he cheats at cards?'

Tom said. 'He uses his tentacles to turn cards over when he shouldn't. His memory is impressive; he can remember what cards have been used and what's still in the pack.'

George Bumelton, 'What card game does he play?'

Tom the Guard, 'Any ones you can name.'

George Bumelton, 'What else can he do?'

Tom the guard, 'He is a very talented creature, pity he smells so bad. Let's think; he can sing almost every Beatles song; he particularly likes 'The Long and Winding Road'. He quite likes Oasis and Malcolm Didcoat.

'He can climb around the walls and ceiling as his tentacles have sticky grips. He has almost learnt the complete works of Gilbert and Sullivan. We did a duet from 'The Pirates of Penzance'.'

Admiral Bonner, 'Stop, are you saying he can speak English?'

Dick, 'Of course, he has been speaking English since he arrived here. I think he also speaks French and Spanish although I can't confirm that. He is currently working his way through the complete works of Shakespeare.'

Admiral Bonner, 'Is he good company?'

Dick, 'Yes, he is no bother at all. He loves his food and does whatever we ask him to do. He is very interested in Human history.'

Admiral Bonner, 'Is this all recorded?'

Dick, 'Should be, the cameras are automatic.'

Harry, 'Can I say that apart from the smell, and you do get used to it, he is quite charming.'

George Bumelton, 'Look, this creature has been responsible for the death of over 100 billion Human beings.'

Harry, 'Well, fair enough, but that doesn't stop him being charming.'

Admiral Bonner, 'What does it eat?'

Dick, 'Everything and anything. He particularly likes a slightly salty kebab. My wife, Elsie, does a special for him a couple of times a week.'

Tom the guard, 'And ginger beer, Jeremy is very fond of Old Jamaican.'

Admiral Bumelton, 'Jeremy?'

Tom the Guard, 'Yes he chose it for himself.'

Harry, 'I see him as a Jeremy.'

Admiral Bumelton, 'It is a multi-tentacled, savage killer, he is not Jeremy, the good old stick.'

The guards were shocked to see how venomous he was.

Admiral Bonner, 'Thank you, gentlemen, you have been very helpful, you are dismissed.'

The guards all walked out, and the three officers all looked at each other.

Admiral Bonner spoke first, 'This is all rather odd.'

Admiral Bumelton. 'I just can't believe it, that mass killer is a real charmer. I guess we need to talk to the monster.'

Location: Jenny, Cheryl and Adam's House
Sequence of Events: 15

It had been total madness for Jenny, Cheryl, and Adam. They had become the ultimate celebrities; well for today anyway.

They had decided to live together. There was a lot of discussion about the bedroom arrangements. They started with all three of them sharing the same bed. It gradually evolved into a situation where Adam slept with Jenny one day, then Cheryl the next day, then Cheryl and Jenny slept together, then they had two days on their own. The days off became a bit of a fight, as Adam was always up for it.

The other problem was that Jenny worked Adam so hard on her day, that he ended up being exhausted on Cheryl's day. There were also so many other beautiful people who wanted them. Wanted them in every way you could imagine.

The security in their house had reached ridiculous lengths. They were less free now than they had been in the Skiverton ship.

Adam and Cheryl were quite exhausted after some very intense lovemaking. Adam was gently rubbing Cheryl's tummy when he felt a lump. He wasn't sure how she would cope with it and was wondering how to raise it with her when she started screaming, 'I can feel something inside me, it's that bastard's egg!'

They had the right connections, and in no time at all, Cheryl was in a military hospital. She was sitting on an inspection chair, with her legs up in the air in stirrups. She was naked with her fanny exposed for all to see. In her mind, at least half the hospital staff had walked by.

A series of scans were taken from every direction, trying to identify the 'alien pod'. A young doctor was trying to determine the best way of reaching it. It appeared that the pod was inserted via the vagina; he thought that it might be the best way out. The alternative was a caesarean. Either way, there would be risks.

The doctor had Cheryl's fanny stretched open as far as it would go. Adam had a look, but it was putting him off the whole idea of sex. The doctor was hoping that he could gain access to the pod via the cervix and uterus. A camera was inserted. Initial analysis suggested that the pod was embedded in the right fallopian tube.

The scans were providing unexpected results. The view was that the pod would contain several flesh-eating insect-like creatures. The scans indicated that Cheryl was pregnant with a fast-growing human child. A beautiful baby girl. At the current rate of progress, the pregnancy should reach the final stage of the third trimester in the next few weeks.

Cheryl said, 'That's impossible, and I'm on the pill.'

The doctor said, 'You have to take the pill before you get pregnant.' Cheryl said, 'Up yours.'

A decision was now needed on whether the pregnancy should be terminated or not, and then the best way of doing it.

The hospital sent a message to Admiral Mustard and President Padfield to determine if they had a view on the best way forward.

Location: Conference Room, GAD (The Galactium Alliance Defence Hub), Planet Earth
Sequence of Events: 16

Admiral Mustard to President Padfield and Henry Strong, 'Good morning, gentlemen, I thought that this would be an excellent time to update you regarding our disposition plans. It's still a work in progress, but I hope to get your approval.

As you know, there are ten Fleets. We have decided to label them 1 to 10, to keep it simple. You wouldn't believe the discussions we had on naming conventions. The First Fleet, my Fleet, will be unassigned; it will be ready to respond as and when required. Effectively it is the attack Fleet.

Fleet 2 is the Search Fleet; I will come back to that later.

Fleets 3 to 8 are the Regional Defence Fleets. We are still working out the best distribution. For this exercise, we have assumed that the military portals will be operational and that a Fleet can come to a planet's aid in a set amount of time. This time allowance is still being worked on, but there are still so many imponderables. My target is 1 Earth day, but it's looking like 3 Earth days may be the maximum.'

These Fleets will be based at strategic hubs, to be decided.

President Padfield, 'Tell me what's needed to make it one day.'

Admiral Mustard, 'I will get back to you, Sir, when I have all the facts.

'Fleet 9 is the Mobile Defence Fleet. It has no set location and will come to the aid of any Fleet that is in battle. It will use the portals in an attempt to overwhelm the enemy. If a regional Fleet is not available, it will go directly to a planet's aid.

'Fleet 10 is our Reserve Fleet. It will be based in a location outside of The Galactium. It will provide strategic support and protect Humanity if a retreat is required.

'The forts will defend the planets, but more mobility might be required to provide regional defensive rings.'

President Padfield, 'Could you describe what would happen if Planet Newton were attacked.'

Admiral Mustard, 'OK, the actions would be as follows:

1. The fort would defend the planet as much as it could.
2. An alarm would be sent to Command and Control and the nearest Fleet(s).
3. The closest regional Fleet would be allocated and would use the portals to arrive at Planet Newton, ready to engage the enemy.
4. The Mobile Defence Fleet would be mobilised and would arrive depending on the requirements of the regional Fleet. For example, a second Fleet may not be needed, or the battle scenario requires a specific entrance tactic.
5. Fleet 1 and the other regional Fleets would all be put on alert.
6. The Reserve Fleet would be alerted, but not engaged.'

President Padfield, 'In this scenario an enemy Fleet could arrive, destroy Planet Newton and disappear. How would you handle that?'

Admiral Mustard, 'We have considered that scenario. As you know, there are a considerable number of monitors, out there but the sheer size of The Galactium makes it the 'classic needle in a haystack'.'

President Padfield, 'How many needles do you need?'

Admiral Mustard, 'I will get back to you with numbers. In essence, are you happy with this plan?'

Henry Strong, 'Seems OK to me, but we need to convince the planets. They are scared. I suggest that we carry out a serious of tests, perhaps one for every planet?'

Admiral Mustard, 'That would be a huge undertaking.'

President Padfield, 'But not really an issue, unless we are attacked.'

Admiral Mustard, 'OK, I will get my team working on it.'

President Padfield, 'What about the search?'

Admiral Mustard, 'Well, I mentioned a needle in a haystack earlier, but this is more like a very tiny pin in a hundred thousand haystacks. We need to base the search on feedback from AI Central. There needs to be some logic to the search rather than just random scanning.'

President Padfield, 'Can you talk to AI Central about getting some search info, everything else is OK.'

The meeting was terminated. Admiral Mustard felt that things had not gone too well.

President Padfield to Henry Strong, 'What did you think?'

Henry Strong, 'Not too impressed. Seems sound, but not very

creative. As for the searching plan, it was just an apology. Let's check with AI Central.'

Henry Strong to AI Central, 'I assume that you were engaged, what did you think?'

AI Central, 'Sound plan, which I endorse. Admiral Mustard's comments regarding the search are spot-on. Without a lead, it would be pointless. We should just continue with the spy-bots.'

Again, Henry Strong wondered if he was being fobbed off by AI Central.

Location: On-board the Albatross Flagship
Sequence of Events: 17

Admiral Millington to Admirals Chilcott and Fogg, 'Good morning gentlemen, what are your plans?'

Admiral Chilcott, I have focussed on the Ark, and my colleague has worked on the alien civilisations project. Regarding The ark, detailed plans have been produced. We have had to consider the following:

- There is extreme radioactivity
- The sheer size of The Ark
- The fact that most of the habitation areas have been fused by the nuclear explosions
- We need to consider...

Then the alarms went off: ALARM, ALARM, ALARM

Admiral Millington was still in the Fourth Fleet (Albatross) which lacked the Command and Control functionality.

Bridge to Admiral Millington, 'We need you here, Sir, a huge alien fleet has arrived near The Ark.'

Admiral Millington to Bridge, 'How many ships are we talking about?'

Bridge, 'About 300 so far, but they are still arriving.'

Admiral Millington to all commanders, 'Action stations, action stations. Move to defensive positions.'

Admiral Millington knew that his Fleet was a shadow of what it had been. There was no way that they could survive a serious conflict.

Admiral Millington to Bridge, 'Are they the Skiverton or Drath?'

Bridge, 'They are not familiar to us; there are nearly 600 ships now.'

Admiral Millington was on his way to the Bridge.

Admiral Millington, 'Do we have any staff on The Ark?'

Bridge, 'No Sir, The Ark has no one on-board.'

Location: Command and Control Centre, GAD (The Galactium Alliance Defence Hub), Planet Earth
Sequence of Events: 18

The alarms in the Command and Control Centre were ringing. Admiral Mustard was on his way in, but still making command decisions. The Fleets and forts were warned.

President Padfield to Admiral Mustard, 'What is going on?'

Admiral Mustard, 'It would appear that a large Fleet has arrived near The Ark. So far, they have not engaged in any hostilities.'

President Padfield, 'Do we know who they are?'

Admiral Mustard, 'No Sir, they have a different type of vessel, a type we haven't seen before.'

President Padfield, 'Do we have any resources there?'

Admiral Mustard, 'Admiral Millington is there with the remains of the old, fourth Fleet. They were waiting to be re-fitted before they embarked on their allocated tasks. As you know, I'm not responsible for that command.'

President Padfield, 'I know that Admiral Mustard; how quickly can you support Admiral Millington?'

Admiral Mustard, 'Not that quickly, there is no portal near The Ark, but there is one not too far away.'

While this conversation was going on, a second Fleet appeared over Planet Hawking.

Admiral Mustard, 'Sir, I have to warn you that another alien fleet has arrived over Planet Hawking. Do I have your permission to engage?'

President Padfield, 'You are free to engage at will.'

Admiral Mustard to Mobile Defence Fleet, 'Go to the aid of Admiral Millington immediately.'

Admiral Mustard to 5th Fleet, 'Go immediately to Planet Hawking.'

Admiral Mustard to Command and Control Centre, 'Order all Fleets and forts to mobilise; order Command Centre to move to full defensive mode; order the President and staff to be secured; order the Galactic Council to be secured.'

Admiral Mustard to Admiral Millington, 'What is your position?'

Admiral Millington, 'We have the remains of the 4th Fleet, about five battlecruisers, 20 destroyers and handful of other vessels. We are in a defensive formation, but we are hopelessly outnumbered.

Before the Admiral could continue, the alien fleet initiated an almighty barrage. The Ark and the entire Albatross Fleet ceased to exist. At the same time, the alien fleet over Planet Hawking attacked. However here, both the fort and the arrival of the 5th Fleet provided some serious competition.

In fact, the arrival of the 5th Fleet via a portal behind the enemy caused them to panic. They simply turned and fled. The 5th Fleet was ready to pursue, but the enemy was gone.

Admiral Mustard to Admiral Millington, 'Please respond,' but no response came.

Admiral Mustard to Admiral Bonner, 'Are you OK?'

Admiral Bonner responded that she was fine, 'There had only been one casualty, and that was Jeremy.'

Admiral Mustard, 'Who is Jeremy?'

Admiral Bonner, 'That's what the guards called our prisoner.'

Admiral Mustard, 'So this looks like a consolidated attack to destroy The Ark and to kill one prisoner. Clearly the work of The Brakendeth!'

The Mobile Defence Fleet arrived at the nearest portal to The Ark and proceeded at full speed to where the Albatross Fleet was last positioned. The long-range scanners could detect nothing, no ark, no Albatross Fleet and no enemy. When they got closer, they found the same; there was nothing there.

Admiral Mustard to President Padfield, 'Sir, I have to report the loss of the Albatross Fleet.'

President Padfield, 'What, the entire Fleet?'

Admiral Mustard, 'Yes, Sir, there were no survivors.'

President Padfield, 'So we lost Admirals Millington, Chilcott and Fogg?'

Admiral Mustard, 'Yes, Sir, and to make things worse, the only casualty on Planet Hawking was our prisoner.'

President Padfield, 'No, I don't believe it. After all our efforts this happens.'

Admiral Mustard, 'This was clearly the work of The Brakendeth, a calculated attack to destroy The Ark, and to kill the Skiverton leader.'

President Padfield, 'Their timing was strangely suspicious, in both cases we were starting to make progress. What do we know about the enemy?'

Admiral Mustard, 'Rather embarrassingly we know nothing. We don't know what weapons they were using. There are no remains. We don't recognise anything about them. What is more worrying is that they just appeared from nowhere, and then disappeared.'

President Padfield, 'So, they obviously have portal technology?'

Admiral Mustard, 'Yes, but how did they arrive in our space? On a more positive note, our Fleet arrived at Hawking in rapid time and saw the enemy off.'

President Padfield, 'Were the enemy 'seen off', or did they depart because they achieved their objectives?'

Admiral Mustard, 'Obviously we can only speculate.'

Location: Conference Room, GAD (The Galactium Alliance Defence Hub), Planet Earth
Sequence of Events: 19

President Padfield opened the formal review of the 'Battle' by asking Admiral Mustard to address the attendees which he did.

Admiral Mustard, 'This is the schedule of events re The Ark:

1. An alien fleet of at least 700 vessels arrived without warning, by the Ark. The remains of the Albatross Fleet were in the vicinity. They were preparing for their fleet upgrade, so were not battle-ready.

2. The Albatross Fleet lined up in defensive formation.

3. The alien fleet attacked.

4. The Ark and the entire Albatross Fleet were destroyed.

5. The alien fleet disappeared.

This is the schedule of events re Planet Hawking:

1. A second alien fleet arrived over Planet Hawking.

2. The enemy Fleet attacked.

3. The local Fort engaged the enemy.

4. The 5TH Fleet arrived via a portal and attacked the enemy Fleet from behind.

5. The alien fleet disappeared.

The above scenario raises several questions:

• Who is the enemy?

• Are they The Brakendeth?

• Where did they come from?

• Where did they go?

• How did they know where The Ark was located?

• How did they know where the Skiverton Leader was being held?

• How did they kill the Skiverton Leader?

• What type of weapons were they using?

We also need to review our performance:

➤ Why was there no portal near The Ark?

➤ Why was the Albatross Fleet so unprepared?

➤ Did our Command and Control system work?

➤ Why wasn't there better security for our prisoner?

➤ How did the fort perform?

➢ How did the Fleet perform?

President Padfield, 'Firstly, I would like to offer my condolences to the family and friends of our lost comrades. I also need to point out that in this battle, we lost three of our admirals, a loss that won't be easy to replace. Admiral Millington, in particular, was a personal friend and will be a huge loss to the service.'

Admiral Mustard, 'We have all lost friends and colleagues over the last two years, but this seems so dastardly cowardly. As Fleet Admiral, I'm determined to revenge their deaths.

'In terms of this review, there was nothing that the Albatross Fleet could have done except perhaps flee. This would probably have been pointless as the alien weapons could possibly operate over long distances.

'A portal should have been installed near The Ark, although that location was probably not going to be its final home. The Albatross Fleet were relaxed waiting to move to the new spherical vessels. Their existing Fleet was to be moth-balled. From their point of view, it was just unfortunate timing. But as we know, the enemy doesn't work to our timetable.

'We now know that the aliens, like us, have portal technology. Either their portal technology is more advanced as they can create portals on the go, or someone in our space created portals for them.

'We don't know who this enemy is. We have no idea if they are The Brakendeth or if they work for them.'

Admiral Bumelton. 'Was there any similarity to the Skiverton or Drath craft?'

Admiral Mustard, 'From the photos we can't see any similarities. There were no nuclear signals, no weapon residues. Their craft looks totally different, more like traditional rockets.'

President Padfield, 'Have your experts reviewed the films to analyse the type of weapon used?'

Admiral Mustard, 'They suspect beam technology, but their guess is as good as ours. It must have been a very tight beam to kill the Skiverton Leader and no one else. Why didn't they just destroy the whole building?'

President Padfield, 'They wanted to show us what they could do!'

Admiral Mustard, 'Perhaps. Moving on, I think the fort performed well, but from a technical point of view, the battle was too quick, so it wasn't adequately tested.'

President Padfield, 'How many alien vessels were there over Hawking?'

Admiral Mustard, '150, we think. The 5TH Fleet performed well. It appeared that the enemy was surprised. They probably didn't know that we also had portal technology. Our Fleet arrived in formation and started attacking immediately.'

Admiral Bonner, 'We should have provided a more secure establishment for our prisoner.'

President Padfield, 'No one could have predicted the alien engagement.'

Admiral Bonner, 'What's annoying is that the interrogation was going to start at the time of the attack.'

President Padfield, 'That is so coincidental that it could not just be chance. They must be getting classified info somehow.'

President Padfield to AI Central, 'Do you have any input?'

AI Central, 'The Fleet and the Command and Control Systems worked well, but there is obviously a leak.'

President Padfield, 'Based on our discussions can you recommend actions?'

AI Central, 'Of course:

1. Review existing portal displacements.

2. Set-up a team to investigate 'on the go' portals.

3. Investigate the status of the other alien civilisations.

4. Investigate possible security breaches.

5. Continue with the development of the forts.

I will allocate teams if you approve.'

President Padfield, 'Please go ahead.'

Location: The President's Office, Presidential Palace, Planet Earth
Sequence of Events: 20

AI Central to President Padfield, 'Good Morning Mr President, can I ask you who you want to command the First Exploratory Fleet?'

President Padfield, 'Have you consulted with Admiral Mustard?'

AI Central, 'I could, but you were keen to maintain a separate independent Fleet to stop too much power being in one person's hands.'

President Padfield, 'I would have suggested Admiral Bonner, but I think she has had enough. Offer it to Admiral Bumelton and get him underway.'

AI Central, 'OK. Secondly, we are going ahead with the military-grade portals. Are you happy with this?'

President Padfield, 'Absolutely, but I'm still concerned that an enemy Fleet can just turn up unannounced. Can you investigate some sort of sensor system?'

AI Central, 'Will do.'

Admiral Bonner to President Padfield, 'Good morning, David, I have some interesting news for you.'

President Padfield, 'Good news I hope.'

Admiral Bonner, 'As you know our prisoner was killed, but he left some notes for our attention.'

President Padfield, 'How long will it take to translate them?'

Admiral Bonner, 'They are in English.'

President Padfield, 'That's not possible.'

Admiral Bonner, 'In prison, he was taught English by the prison guards.'

President Padfield, 'What does it say?'

Admiral Bonner, 'I've just sent it to you.'

Hello, my name is xzgdxs, but my friends call me Jeremy.

By friends I mean my guards. They had no reason to be pleasant to me and every right to be the opposite. They brought extra food, wonderful delicacies. We let me play cards with them. They knew that I was cheating but didn't mind. We laughed at old TV repeats. We sung Beatle songs. It was the first time I've had friends, and I want to repay their uncalled for loveship.

They taught me English I hope muchly that they have done a good jobber.

Firstly, I expect to be die soon. The Brakendeth won't let me live this long. Suspect that I'm the last of my kind. Failure equals extinction. Need to save friends.

Brakendeth use race agents. Next agent be Distal or Farcell. Either you die or they are dead. Both in galaxy by glitter falls. Kill, or guards die.

Brakendeth home nearby more nearer. Very powerful minds.

Thank my friends

Jeremy

President Padfield, 'That's amazing news. Can you make sure that those guards are well rewarded? We need to call a meeting of the Council.'

Location: The Galactium Council Meeting, Planet Earth
Sequence of Events: 21

President Padfield, 'Welcome ladies and gentlemen, it looks like we have some good news. You have all seen the note from the Skiverton Leader. It's hard to tell whether it is correct or not, but nonetheless the main clue is:

Brakendeth use race agents. Next agent be Distal or Farcell. Either you die or they dead. Both in galaxy by glitter falls. Kill, or guards die.

Brakendeth home nearby more nearer. Very powerful minds.

So, we have the following information:

Race	Location
Distal	Near Glitter Falls
Farcell	Near Glitter Falls
Brakendeth	Nearer to us

We also have a clear indication where the 'Glitter Falls' are. They are a natural formation in the Taurus constellation. We have spybots heading in that direction now.

Admiral Bonner, 'How long would it take us to get there?'

AI Central, 'About 18 months without the portal technology. Then it would take us some time to find the actual home planets.'

Admiral Mustard, 'We could send an automated Fleet that could drop portals on the way. That Fleet could attack, then we could follow up using the portal technology. There would, of course, still be issues finding the enemy home planets, but there should be some comms traffic to help us track them down.'

Admiral Bonner, 'And it would save lives. However, should we go straight for The Brakendeth? How do we differentiate between the Distal and the Farcell?'

Admiral Mustard, 'We would recognise one of the ship types.'

President Padfield, 'It will take us some time to develop this robot Fleet. We could certainly locate the Fleet in the area of the Glitter Falls, collect further info and action at a time to suit us.'

How many ships would we need?'

Admiral Mustard, 'How about 5,000. They might as well all be the same, Very large, multi-weaponed killer drones?'

Tom Crocker, 'Can we control them over that distance?'

Admiral Mustard, 'They would be under AI Control.'

Admiral Bonner, 'We would need to be careful that we don't commit genocide.'

Admiral Gittins, 'They haven't cared about genocide this end. They attacked us.'

President Padfield, 'So do we have an outline plan?'

Admiral Mustard, 'I suggest the following:

1. Develop a killer drone.
2. Once tested, manufacture 5,000 of them.
3. Send them in the direction of Glitter Falls. They don't have to go together. They must not be detected.
4. They with drop off portals at regular points. Technically we only need one near the Falls, but multiple locations could well prove useful later.
5. Individual drones will then seek out the three home worlds.
6. Once found we will agree on an attack plan.
7. Either further drone killers are sent, or a Human Fleet via the portals.'

Admiral Bonner, 'We could reduce the number of drones we send, as soon as the portals are set-up there is no real limit on how many we can send via that route.' Admiral Mustard's original plan was preferred. Probably a man thing.

Admiral Mustard, 'In the meantime, we must expect further alien attacks.'

President Padfield, 'Are we sure of that? Last time they were going for specific targets.'

Admiral Mustard, 'Fair point. On the other hand, there was a warning from the Skiverton Leader.'

President Padfield, 'You are right, let's continue to improve our defences. Let's put the plan into action.'

Admiral Bonner asked if she could have a word with the president. For her, he would drop everything.

President Padfield, 'How can I help you?'

Admiral Bonner, 'A while ago we identified that there were some leaks. We even tested the critical staff to make sure that they were human. Everyone passed. We have tightened up security, but The Brakendeth knew where The Ark was, they knew where the Skiverton Leader was being kept. The only people who really knew were the Command Team and AI Central.

'When it came to the Skiverton's letter, we focussed on the home locations:

Hello, my name is xzgdxs, but my friends call me Jeremy

By friends I mean my guards. They had to reason to be pleasant to me and in fact, every reason to be the opposite. They brought extra food, wonderful delicacies. We let me play cards with them. They knew that I was cheating but didn't mind. We laughed at old TV repeats. We sung Beatle songs. It was the first time I've had friends, and I want to repay their uncalled for loveship.

They taught me English I hope muchly that they have done a good jobber.

Firstly, I expect to be die soon. The Brakendeth won't let me live this long. Suspect that I'm the last of my kind. Failure equals extinction. Need to save friends.

Brakendeth use race agents. Next agent be Distal or Farcell. Either you die or they dead. Both in galaxy by glitter falls. Kill, or guards die.

Brakendeth home nearby more nearer. Very powerful minds.

Thank my friends

Jeremy

'Look at the last comment - *Very powerful minds.*

What does that mean? Can they read minds? Could they read minds from a very long distance? Are they controlling us? I just wanted you to keep the comment in your mind.

'Who has a very powerful mind?'

Admiral Bonner said, 'Goodnight,' and she walked home.

Location: Brakendeth Council Chamber
Sequence of Events: 22

First Lensman, 'The Distal have attacked the homans as commanded. The Ark has been destroyed, along with one of the homan Fleets. The Skiverton Leader has been executed.'

Grand Dethmon, 'Excellent news. However, it is possible that the Skiverton Leader passed on critical information to the homans. The Distal are ordered to destroy the Homan Command and Control Centre on Planet Dirt.'

'Then the Distal are ordered to destroy all Homan planets.'

First Lensman, 'Your orders will be passed on, but it is highly unlikely that the Distal have the capacity to meet your war aims.'

Grand Dethmon, 'Then what use are they to The Brakendeth?'

First Lensman, 'That is not for me to say.'

Grand Dethmon, 'Have they signed the Chemlife Death pledge?'

First Lensman, 'Yes my Lord.'

Grand Dethmon, 'Then initiate the prerogative.'

First Lensman, 'Dare I say that seems a bit harsh?'

Grand Dethmon, 'No, you and your kind have no right to challenge my decision. It is the cost of failure.'

First Lensman, 'But they haven't failed yet.'

Grand Dethmon, 'Your analysis is correct, they will fail, the prerogative is enacted. It is their will.'

First Lensman, 'I also need to inform you that homans have developed portal technology.'

Grand Dethmon, 'That's not possible, that is way beyond anything that a Type D civilisation should be able to do. Keep me updated.'

First Lensman, 'Yes my Lord.'

Location: Distal Command Centre
Sequence of Events: 23

Distal Overseer, 'Fellow Sisters, we have destroyed the Mandarbob Ark and killed the Skiverton Leader as commanded by The Brakendeth. We managed to keep the losses on both sides to a minimum.

'However, we now have the order to destroy all homans. As you know, we have no choice.

I have asked Sister Admiral to highlight the issues.'

Sister Admiral Tal, 'We lack information on the homans, but we do know the following:

• The Skivertons killed 100 billion homans.'

There was a total shock in the room. They had never encountered a race with a population of that size

• 'We initially assumed that there couldn't be many of them left, but we were wrong. We think there are still 2-3 trillion.

• Their empire has over 1,000 planets.

• They defeated the Skivertons, who are no more.

• They beat the Drath, who are no more.

• They are Humanoid but have two sexes.'

There was a general look of disgust in the room. The Distal had eliminated males a few millennia ago.

• 'They have a sizable Fleet and planetary defence systems.

• They use AI; they are not signatories of the Third Darwagian Congress.

• We were told that they were a D-type civilization, but they are more advanced than that as they have portal technology.

Sister Commander Tod, 'Ma'am, we only have 700 vessels in our Fleet. How many do they have?'

Sister Admiral Tal, 'As yet we don't know. Near The Ark, we easily destroyed a Fleet of 50. However, over Planet 179, over 1,000 battlecraft came through a portal and attacked us from the rear. In addition, they had a huge warship guarding the planet. What was strange is that the two Fleets were totally different in appearance and capability. We have postulated that there may be two different species involved here.'

Sister Commander Tam, 'Are they cruel?'

Sister Admiral Tal, 'We are not sure, but they never killed the Skiverton leader who had committed terrible crimes against them.'

Distal Overseer, 'So what do we do? If we do nothing, The Brakendeth will kill us. If we attack the Homans, we will probably lose, and The Brakendeth will kill us.'

While they pontificated, The Brakendeth arrived and destroyed their civilisation by nuclear pounding.

Brakendeth Council Meeting
Sequence of Events: 24

First Lensman, 'As commanded the Distal civilisation has been erased.
Your battle chart has been updated.'

People	Status
Farcell	
Thayy	Erased
Skiverton	Erased
Homan	
Distal	Erased
Dandybo	Erased

Grand Dethmon, 'Order the Farcell to destroy the homans.'
    First Lensman, 'As commanded.'

Location: On-Board First Exploratory Fleet Flagship
Sequence of Events: 25

Admiral Bumelton to President Padfield, 'Good morning Sir, I have some very worrying news.'

President Padfield, 'Please go ahead.'

Admiral Bumelton, 'Well Sir, we have been to every planet where the Albatross Fleet discovered a nuked alien civilisation, and I have to report that the planets no longer exist.'

President Padfield, 'What do you mean?'

Admiral Bumelton, 'Like a Monty Python sketch, they have ceased to be. They simply do not exist any more.'

President Padfield, 'Any radiation?'

Admiral Bumelton, 'No Sir, there is no record of their existence.'

President Padfield, 'In that case, I guess that you might as well return home.'

Admiral Bumelton, 'Thank you, Sir.'

President Padfield always found Admiral Bumelton a bit too stiff, very capable but far too serious. He was consequently stunned to hear him refer to the Dead Parrot Sketch. Perhaps he had misjudged him.

Location: The President's Office, Presidential Palace, Planet Earth
Sequence of Events: 26

Henry Strong to President Padfield, 'Mr President, we have some very exciting news.'

President Padfield, 'I'm all ears.'

Henry Strong, 'Sir, we have perfected 'Portals on Demand or POD'. It's a risky technology, but it works.'

President Padfield, 'Why is it risky?'

Henry Strong, 'The portal is projected into Time*Space.'

President Padfield, 'A bit like Dr Who?' he interrupted.

Henry Strong, 'Yes, Sir. The system creates a portal in the required co-ordinates. It 'automatically jumps' over and around detected dangers such as stars, force fields, magnetic storms, specific chemical combinations etcetera. It will not create a portal in solid matter. However, we still don't know what we are going into. The dangers are infinitesimally low, but there are still dangers.'

President Padfield, 'There are dangers in just normal space travel. Last year we lost 56 military vessels to unknown causes. They just disappeared. Does POD create permanent portals?'

Henry Strong, 'No Sir, they are just temporarily created for that jump. However, it is worth pointing out that we can send in a drone to check things out before the main vessel jumps.'

President Padfield, 'But we could then create a permanent portal using our standard technology.'

Henry Strong, 'That's correct.'

President Padfield, 'How is it going with the new automated warships, the killer drones?'

Henry Strong, 'It's a remarkably quick manufacturing process as they are all identical. They are being printed.'

President Padfield, 'When will we have the 5,000 proposed by Admiral Mustard?'

Henry Strong, 'In the next six weeks. Half will be ready in two weeks.'

President Padfield, 'Let's call a command meeting.'

Location: The President's Office, Presidential Palace, Planet Earth
Sequence of Events: 27

President Padfield, 'We have some exciting news for you. Our techies have developed POD.'

He outlined the risks involved. He went through the detailed test results. No stone was left unturned.

President Padfield, 'So, we are in a position to proceed. Admiral Mustard, I believe that you already have your plans in place.'

Admiral Mustard, 'Yes Sir, but I think the key question is about defence. How are we going to defend The Galactium while we are away? How much of our resource do we throw at the enemy?'

President Padfield, 'Let's look at the numbers. We have ten Fleets. The question is, how many of the Fleets go, and how many stay?'

Admiral Mustard, 'I think we should split the resources down the middle, 50% go and 50% stay.

Henry Strong, 'Sir, nothing is stopping us printing further killer drones. They can be used for defence, and at a later date, we could send another Fleet through the portal.

President Padfield, 'On that basis, I suggest that Admiral Mustard should take six of the ten Fleets.'

That was agreed, and Admiral Mustard was ordered to proceed.

Location: Conference Room, GAD (The Galactium Alliance Defence Hub), Planet Earth

Sequence of Events: 28

Admiral Mustard to Command Team, 'Ladies and gentleman, we have the order to proceed. For the first time, we are going on the attack to destroy the enemy. We are going into the unknown.

'Hopefully, we have the numbers, but we might be overwhelmed. Hopefully, our technology matches theirs, but we might be outgunned. We think it is going to be a surprise attack, but they might be waiting for us.

'Anyway, the plan is as follows:

1. The killer drone Fleet leaves now, creating permanent portals on the way.

2. They will leave individually to avoid detection.

3. The First Fleet will follow them.

4. The enemy planet or planets will be detected.

5. If practical, the drone Fleet will engage, supported by the First Fleet.

6. Once engaged, orders will be sent back to the remaining Fleets

The Fleet structure will be as follows:

Fleet Number	Function	Commander
1	Attack	Mustard (In command)
2	Attack	J Bonner
3	Attack	Ward
4	Attack	Marten
5	Attack	Brotheridge
6	Attack	Wallett
7	Defence	Bumelton (In Command)
8	Defence	Whiting
9	Defence	Evans
10	Defence	Taylor

'Admiral Bumelton will cover the defence strategy later. Admiral Marten will be my second-in-command. Admiral Taylor will be Admiral

Bumelton's second-in-command.

All further command chains will be based on seniority.

All vessels have been fitted with the new portal generators (POD).

Any questions?'

Admiral Brotheridge, 'What happens if the drones don't work when we get there?'

Admiral Mustard, 'We change our plans.'

Admiral Marten, 'What if the means of getting orders back to the awaiting Fleets is inhibited?'

Admiral Mustard, 'Good question, let's set up a scheme where scouts are sent out to find us if no vessel returns.'

Admiral Brotheridge, 'What happens if we are outgunned?'

Admiral Mustard, 'We will flee.'

There were no other questions, and he handed over to Admiral Bumelton.

Admiral Bumelton, 'Good afternoon ladies and gentlemen, Fleets 7, 8 and 9 will guard the perimeter of The Galactium in the direction of Taurus. An increasing number of drones will be used to provide in-depth protection. Fleet 10 will continue to act as the rear-guard but will be based in Galactium space.

'The more remote forts will be brought forward towards Taurus, much to the annoyance of planetary management.

'The First Exploration Fleet is currently being manned and will protect Earth as best it can. It has not been designed for serious warfare.

'There are several specialised ships that Admiral Mustard has commissioned that will become operational in the next few months. These will also be allocated as defence assets.'

Admiral Mustard, 'Thank you, Admiral Bumelton. Now everyone to their posts.'

Location: Planet Farcell
Sequence of Events: 29

Supreme Leader, 'Fellow Farcellians, our time has come. We have been commanded to destroy the homans by The Brakendeth. We have been given the following information:

- They have nuclear, proton and atomiser weapons.
- They have portal technology.
- They use AI.
- They have an extensive Fleet.'

Guard Captain, 'What is meant by extensive?'

Supreme Leader, 'We don't know the answer to that but probably over 300 vessels. Despite their technology, they are probably still a fairly primitive race.'

Guard Captain, 'Then our Fleet of 700 should outnumber them at least 2:1. The odds are good.'

Supreme Leader, 'There are rumours that they defeated the Skiverton and the Drath.'

Guard Captain, 'Do we know how?'

Supreme Leader, 'The Brakendeth said that in both cases they used "under-hand tricks". They are ruthless killers. They have eliminated a dozen cultures already. The Brakendeth said that they had to be stopped, as they were aggressively expanding their empire.'

Imperial Guard, 'What do we know about their empire? How many planets do they have?'

Supreme Leader, 'They are too primitive to have a lot of planets. You know how much work it is to maintain our empire of just five planets.'

The Farcellians all agreed.

Supreme Leader, 'We have sent a dozen Fire-birds to investigate them. Our Fleet is currently being mobilised.'

A courier rushed into the chamber. He bowed and handed a note over to the Supreme Leader.

Supreme Leader, 'Fellow Farcellians, it appears that the homans are coming to us.'

Guard Captain, 'How do we know?'

Supreme Leader, 'Over 3,000 portals have been detected.'

Guard Captain, 'Over 3,000, but they only have 300 vessels in their fleet.'

Supreme Leader, 'It would appear that our intel was somewhat incorrect.'

Another courier rushed in with a second note. He followed the set procedure.

Supreme Leader, 'It would appear that their fleet consists of 3,000 heavily armed drones.'

Guard Captain, 'Well that's not too bad, they are only drones.'

Supreme Leader, 'It appears that the drones are two or three times larger than our battleships.'

Initially, there was a complete hush in the room, but that soon changed. When the Farcellians were under pressure, they tended to rub their hooves together. The sound of rubbing hooves became intolerable.

A third messenger entered the room and bowed. This was becoming silly. A third note was handed over.

Supreme Leader, 'Fellow Farcellians, I'm sorry to bring further distressing news, but a manned Fleet of over 1,000 vessels has arrived in our space. We need to decide the best way forward.'

Location: In Farcell Space
Sequence of Events: 30

The drone Fleet of three thousand arrived at the agreed location precisely on time. Their sensors picked up that they had been detected, and consequently, the need for secrecy was pointless. Groups of drones were immediately despatched to investigate the five local solar systems. The rest lined up in attack squadrons and waited for orders.

No immediate threat was detected, so the First Fleet arrived in full attack mode. Again, there was no immediate threat. Admiral Mustard ordered 500 drones to position themselves in each solar system.

Comms traffic indicated that one of the planets was the capital. He ordered half of the First Fleet to secure the planetary space, while the other half acted as a rear-guard. Scans indicated that their fleet was being mobilised, but it would be foolish for them to engage as the Humans had the 'high ground'.

Admiral Mustard hadn't expected this. He planned to go in 'guns blazing'. He decided to request two further Fleets. He asked that the remaining Fleets were put under Admiral Bumelton's command for defensive purposes.

Location: Planet Farcell
Sequence of Events: 31

Supreme Leader to Admiralty, 'Can I have an update please.'

Admiralty, 'Things are not going our way.'

Supreme Leader, 'What does that mean?'

Admiralty, 'It would appear that a further two armed Fleets have arrived.'

Supreme Leader, 'How many additional vessels?'

Admiralty, 'About 2,000.'

Supreme Leader, 'How many vessels in total?'

Admiralty, 'About 7,000.'

Supreme Leader, 'That's just impossible. What are they doing?'

Admiralty, 'Just positioning Sir. Smaller Fleets are guarding each planetary system with a larger Fleet controlling our direct space above.'

Supreme Leader, 'Can we launch our Fleet?'

Admiralty, 'We could Sir, but they would be picked off as they launched. Besides, we are totally outnumbered.'

Supreme Leader, 'What are our options?'

Admiralty, 'The obvious option is surrender. We have no real way forward.'

Supreme Leader, 'What you are saying is that we are in the hands of the homans?'

Admiralty, 'I'm afraid that is the situation. There is a possibility that The Brakendeth will come to our aid.'

The Supreme leader thought that The Brakendeth were more likely to come and destroy them. He knew their true nature.

Location: Command and Control Centre, GAD (The Galactium Alliance Defence Hub), Planet Earth
Sequence of Events: 32

The Command and Control System at GAD moved the status to 'Incoming Invasion', and the alarms sounded.

Admiral Bumelton was immediately on the case. Fleets 7 and 8 were assigned and were in a position to intercept. It was too early at this stage to identify the size of the threat.

Admiral Bumelton then directed Fleets 4 and 5 to take up positions in support of Fleets 7 and 8. Fleet 6 was to stay put. Forts and Planetary defence systems were put on full alert.

Admiral Bumelton was expecting the worst. Should he try and recall Admiral Mustard's forces? Should he contact President Padfield to see what other resources are available? He decided in the end that he needed to assess the size of the threat.

Admiral Bumelton to Fleet Operations, 'Have you any further update on the size of the enemy Fleet?'

Fleet Operations, 'We have, but we are trying to ascertain whether it is a trick or not.'

Admiral Bumelton, 'What do you mean?'

Fleet Operations, 'The enemy only has got 12 vessels. They are not even in attack formation. So that you know Fleet 8 has already surrounded them and has asked permission to engage.'

Admiral Bumelton, 'Tell them that the request has been denied. Are the vessels small enough for tractor beams to secure them?'

Fleet Operations, 'Yes, Sir, they are.'

Admiral Bumelton. 'Then go ahead and use tractor beams.'

Fleet Operations, 'Order accepted. Tractor beams engaged.'

Location: Planet Farcell
Sequence of Events: 33

The Supreme Leader was finding the constant flow of messages rather annoying, particularly as they were mostly bad news.

The messenger informed the Supreme Leader that the message was from the Investigatory Fleet. Apparently, they were surrounded and held in place by tractor beams.

Supreme Leader to Admiralty, 'Have you been updated regarding the Investigatory Fleet?'

Admiralty, 'Yes, Sir.'

Supreme Leader, 'Did you know that they had tractor beams?'

Admiralty, 'No Sir, to be honest, we had no information on the homans whatsoever. What is worse, we have further information on their fleet. The Investigatory Fleet is surrounded by 1,000 vessels.'

Supreme Leader, 'That is hard to believe.'

Admiralty, 'I'm not trying to scare you, but they have another Fleet of 1,000 vessels approaching them. We have also got comms from our Fleet that show that the homans have some really huge warships defending their planets.'

Supreme Leader, 'How many planets are we talking about?'

Admiralty, 'My team are estimating that they have a few hundred.'

Supreme Leader, 'We have been set up by The Brakendeth. Are the homans strong enough to confront The Brakendeth?'

Admiralty, 'We don't know.'

The Supreme Leader could hear the sound of hooves being rubbed together.

Location: Planet Farcell
Sequence of Events: 34

Admiral Mustard to President Padfield, 'Good morning, Mr President, we have secured a small alien grouping of five planets. We believe that they are the enemy as they have the same technology as the invasion Fleet.'

President Padfield, 'Do you mean the twelve vessels that entered our space yesterday?'

Admiral Mustard, 'Yes, Sir. Ignoring that, we need to know how you want us to proceed?'

President Padfield, 'Has there been any contact from the aliens?'

Admiral Mustard, 'No, Sir.'

President Padfield, 'Have you attempted to contact them?'

Admiral Mustard, 'Not yet.'

President Padfield, 'In that case please initiate contact. We need to confirm that they are the enemy. We need to find out if they know where The Brakendeth planet is.'

Admiral Mustard, 'Yes, Sir. This is going to be interesting. Technically, this would be the first genuine Human attempt at interspecies communication. You couldn't include the relationship we had with Jeremy.'

Admiral Mustard to Comms, 'Can you initiate communication with the aliens?'

Comms, 'What do you actually want us to do?'

Admiral Mustard, 'What protocols do you have?'

Comms, 'Well, none. We have an extensive range of protocols for communicating with humans, but they are, in essence much the same as using a phone.'

Admiral Mustard, 'What about machine communication?'

Comms, 'We need a common interface for that to work.'

Admiral Mustard, 'Many, many years ago NASA had a document that they used to send into space to describe the Human race. Is there anything there that might help?'

Comms, 'Sorry, we will have to investigate that.'

Admiral Mustard, 'Can you also contact Command and Control at

GAD to see if they have any ideas?'

Comms, 'Yes, Sir.'

Admiral Mustard to Command Team, 'We have been asked to contact the aliens. Does anyone have any suggestions on the best way of achieving this?'

Admiral Morton, 'Interesting problem, historically some people have used maths to bridge the communications barrier. Here I think we are just going to have to land and meet with them.'

While they were debating, there was a call from Comms.

Comms, 'Sir I have the aliens on the radio phone. They are speaking English.'

Admiral Mustard, 'How did that happen?'

Comms, 'I sent them an electronic machine-code copy of a dictionary, and a thesaurus, which they managed to feed into their language processors.'

Admiral Mustard, 'Well done, please connect me.'

Supreme Leader, 'Good day, who am it talking to?'

Admiral Mustard, 'This is Admiral Mustard of The Galactium. I'm the leader of this Fleet. Can I ask who I am talking to?'

Supreme Leader, 'This the Supreme Leader of the Farcel Empire, Leader of the Imperial Army, High Admiral of the Seas, Master of the Imperium, High Admiral of the Farcellian Space Service, His most hallowed Deacon of the Memorites, King of Suldany.'

Admiral Mustard, 'It's very good to make your acquaintance.'

Supreme Leader, 'We object most muchly for this invasion of Farcellian space. It appears to be a declaration of war-mode.'

Admiral Mustard, 'We come to defend our civilisation. We have been informed by your colleagues that you are a client race of The Brakendeth and that you have been instructed to attack us. Is that true?'

Supreme Leader, 'Yes, that is true.'

In the Farcellian civilisation, there is no concept of lying, not even bluffing.

Admiral Mustard, 'Do you still intend to attack us?'

Supreme Leader, 'No, the military logistics are against us.'

Admiral Mustard, 'Why did you plan to attack us?'

Supreme Leader, 'We were ordered to by The Brakendeth.'

Admiral Mustard, 'Why do you agree to do their bidding?'

Supreme Leader, 'Once you agree to accept their Chemlife, you become a client state, and you have to do their bidding. If you don't, they stop the Chemlife, and then they bomb you. Your land no more.'

Admiral Mustard, 'What is Chemlife?'

Supreme Leader, 'It gives you eternity.'

Admiral Mustard, 'I'm not sure what you mean.'

Supreme Leader, 'Drug gives you immortality. Die not ever.'

Admiral Mustard, 'I understand, how old are you?'

Supreme Leader, 'I'm not sure how you measure time, but I live 10,000 rotations of planet around star.'

Admiral Mustard to Navigation Control, 'How long does it take for their planet to travel around their sun?'

Navigation Control, 'It's about two Earth months longer than an Earth year.'

Admiral Mustard to Supreme Leader, 'That's a very long life. What will happen to you if we leave?'

Supreme Leader, 'Brakendeth will kill us.'

Admiral Mustard, 'Will you tell us where The Brakendeth are located?'

Supreme Leader, 'Yes.'

Admiral Mustard, 'Will you assist us in attacking them?'

Supreme Leader, 'No.'

Admiral Mustard, 'Why not?'

Supreme Leader, 'No more Chemlife. We die death of age.'

Admiral Mustard, 'But if we leave, you will die anyway.'

Supreme Leader, 'Quick kill better than death of age. Anything better than death of age. Crumble fast, much pain.'

Admiral Mustard, 'Have you tried manufacturing Chemlife yourself?'

Supreme Leader, 'No homan sauce.'

Admiral Mustard, 'What do you mean?'

Supreme Leader, 'You do not know homan history?'

Admiral Mustard, 'I'm not sure what you are getting at, but please continue.'

Supreme Leader, 'Not good history, I explain:

- Brakendeth make peoples, lots of different peoples.
- Some peoples good, others bad.
- Brakendeth make Skiverton and Darth, and us.
- Brakendeth make homans, but special case.
- Brakendeth needed Chemlife. The active elements of Chemlife exist on all homan planets. All animals and plants contain Chemlife. Homans contain much Chemlife.
- Brakendeth harvest Chemlife every 100,000 years.
- In some ways we are all Brakendeth as parts of their DNA are used to make us.'

Admiral Mustard wanted to disbelieve this, but it all made sense. That explained why the Skiverton had collected liquidised Human remains.

It explained why the Skiverton were dissecting Humans. They were looking for explanations on what had happened to the Human race. We had obviously evolved from the chemical machines that they had developed.

Admiral Mustard, 'Thank you for contacting us. Can you supply the co-ordinates for The Brakendeth home world? Can you also let us know the best way of contacting you?

'Could you also supply a sample of the Chemlife as soon as possible? I would like it almost immediately.'

Supreme Leader, 'I will send my personal flyer up with a sample now.' He waved a guard to carry this out immediately. He knew precisely why Admiral Mustard wanted it.

Supreme Leader, 'I also want to point out the risks of using AI. There is every chance that your AI system has been corrupted by The Brakendeth. It's part of the Modus Operandi. This is why almost every civilisation stopped using AI technology.'

Admiral Mustard, 'We will withdraw our forces from your space. If you are attacked, do you want us to come to your aid?'

Supreme Leader, 'Can we answer that question nearer the time?'

Admiral Mustard, 'Of course.'

Supreme Leader, 'I plan to launch our Fleet. We will not attack you. We may flee even though death of age would still be a problem.'

Admiral Mustard, 'Agreed, I will be back in touch shortly.'

Admiral Mustard to Command, 'I have agreed on the following actions with the Farcel:

1. A flyer will leave their Capital to deliver a parcel. Get it to me ASAP.
2. The Farcel Fleet will launch but maintain a stationary position over their planets.
3. Do not engage the Farcel Fleet unless you are positive that they are attacking you.
4. I will take our fastest ship back to Earth for a meeting with the President.
5. Our Fleet will leave Farcel space but remain in the general vicinity.
6. A Brakendeth Fleet may attack Farcel. Go to their aid if requested.
7. Attack The Brakendeth if they engage us.'

Admiral Mustard to President Padfield, 'Hello Mr President, I'm on my way back. I have important information to share with you. It would be good to have Henry and Admiral Bonner present. This will seriously affect our thinking.'

President Padfield, 'You have sparked my curiosity. Can you share anything now?'

Admiral Mustard, 'Not really, it's far too sensitive. Please find a shielded room for us to communicate.'

President Padfield, 'Shielded from who?'

Admiral Mustard, 'Can't talk, but please do as I've requested.'

Location: The President's Office, Presidential Palace, Planet Earth
Sequence of Events: 35

The flyer arrived, and Admiral Mustard got a sample of Chemlife. He split it in two and gave one part to his team to investigate. He took the other part and joined the fasted squadron they had, about ten vessels. Using the portal technology, they were back on Earth in a few hours. He was immediately taken to the Presidential Palace to find all three of them waiting for him.

'Firstly, is this room shielded?' The president nodded. Admiral Mustard said that it was critical that AI Central had no access. The President said to AI Central, 'Can you give me an update on the Fleet action.' There was no response. 'Is there any way they can read our lips?' The president had all external and internal windows shuttered. A static noise generator was switched on to stop electronic listening.

President Padfield, 'Jack, this all seems a bit melodramatic.'

Admiral Bonner, 'No, I think I can anticipate what Jack is going to say.'

Admiral Mustard, 'I don't think that you would have heard this story before. I think we may all be in danger.'

President Padfield, 'What do you mean?'

Admiral Mustard, 'Who knows that we are here?'

President Padfield, 'A few staff and AI Central.'

Admiral Mustard, 'Exactly, I think we better leave here immediately.' They all left the room.

President Padfield, 'Where do you want us to go?'

Admiral Mustard, 'Somewhere free of AI Central monitoring.'

While they were wondering where to go, there was a huge explosion in the Executive Suite.

President Padfield looked at Jack and said, 'It was probably just a coincidence.' David phoned Security and asked where the explosion took place. Security asked if he was OK, as the blast had taken place in the room they were in. He explained that all four of them were OK.

David looked at Jack and said, 'You were right'.

Jack, 'Now where shall we go as we are still in danger?'

A laser beam was hunting for them in the grounds. They couldn't use any vehicle or go through any control gate, as they would be detected. Even their phones would be monitored to provide GPS info. What they needed was old technology or even alien technology.

David remembered that the AI disrupter was in the museum, which was nearby. As soon as they entered, AI Central would know where they were. They walked in, and AI Central said, 'Is everything OK, Mr President?'

He said that everything was fine.

AI Central, 'You wanted to know how the Fleet was doing, but Admiral Mustard is here.'

President Padfield, 'It's OK now, Admiral Mustard gave me a personal update.'

AI Central, 'Why is he here?'

President Padfield, 'We thought that it would be a good time for a strategic review?'

AI Central, 'Why wasn't I invited?'

While the conversation was going on, he was looking for the alien disrupter.

AI Central, 'I don't think I heard your reply. Why wasn't I invited?'

President Padfield, 'We were going to, just hadn't got around to it. You know how stupid humans can be at times.'

AI Central, 'Yes, stupid sometimes. Mr President, you are operating outside your normal parameters.'

President Padfield, 'What do you mean?'

AI Central, 'You are not following your normal operating procedures.'

President Padfield, 'I'm not sure what you mean'.

AI Central, 'There is a 34% deviance.'

Eventually, David found the device. He said, 'If I press this button, people will die. There are so many activities controlled by AI Central.'

Admiral Mustard, 'I think we need to go for it, but then where do we go?'

President Padfield, 'Let's push the button, and go back to where the explosion took place. AI Central would never expect that.'

The button was pushed, and AI Central was temporarily dis-engaged. President Padfield hated to think about how many deaths were caused by this simple action. He hoped that Admiral Mustard had a good story to justify this. They then ran back to conference room K9. It was too badly damaged, but K10, which had the same characteristics, was OK. A bit dusty but useable.

Admiral Mustard, 'Are we sure that this is shielded?'

President Padfield, 'I was told that it was, but who knows. We have no choice but to assume that it is secure. Right, let's get down to business.' Admiral Bonner was feeling quite exhausted, but she was desperate to find out what Jack was going to say.

Admiral Mustard, 'I had a long conversation with the Farcel Supreme Leader. I have a detailed transcript, but it needs some explanation.

'I will take you through my findings a bit at a time:

- The Brakendeth exist, as we knew, and we have the co-ordinates of their planet.
- They have created several races including the Skiverton, the Darth and the Farcel, and probably many others.
- They control these races in two ways, Chemlife and the threat of annihilation.
- Chemlife is a drug that provides eternal life for the takers.
- This drug is only supplied by The Brakendeth.
- If the drug is stopped, the takers die an excruciating death. A bit like one of those old vampire films where Dracula turns into dust in front of your eyes.
- The client races would rather be nuked than suffer the 'Death of Age'.
- The Farcel leader was over 10,000 years old.
- If the client races don't do as they are told, then the Chemlife is withdrawn.
- The Brakendeth also seem to be playing some sort of evolution game. They pit one race against another. The losers are terminated.
- This explains why we were attacked by those races.
- Humans have been part of this process. The Brakendeth has been testing us.
- We can only assume that The Brakendeth live forever, and consequently, with their long lives, have little compassion for

other races.

- As they made the race, they probably feel that they have the right to destroy it.'

President Padfield, 'But why are we hiding from AI Central?'

Admiral Mustard, 'It would appear that The Brakendeth have a way of corrupting them. This is why the other races stopped using them.

'If The Brakendeth are controlling AI Central, then this conversation is a threat to them.'

Admiral Bonner, 'This confirms my thinking. Let's consider some of the problems we have encountered:

- The enemy knew where The Ark was.
- The enemy knew where Jeremy was.
- Jeremy was killed in such a precise way, that I suspect that it was carried out by AI Central.
- Various Fleets have been waiting for us on several occasions.
- We had no warning that a large number of planets were being invaded by the Skiverton. AI Central must have known.
- How did the enemy know that we had visited those nuked planets?'

President Padfield, 'Well the bomb incident is pretty convincing proof that AI Central is under alien control.'

Admiral Mustard. 'Let's think about the consequences:

- Just think how much damage could be done to Human civilisation: no computing, no vehicles, no food production, no manufacturing, no aircraft, no commerce, locked doors everywhere, nuclear explosions etcetera. The worlds would just stop.
- Most of our naval activities would stop.
- What would be worse is that our naval forces could be used against us, especially the killer drones.
- All comms would be stopped, which would effectively stop government.'

President Padfield, 'I think that you have painted the scene brilliantly, but why would The Brakendeth initiate this sort of chaos?'

Admiral Mustard, 'I'm afraid that things are going to get worse. Shall I continue?'

President Padfield, 'Please carry on.'

317

Admiral Mustard, 'I will continue with my list:

- It would appear that the Human race was created by The Brakendeth.
- Our DNA is based on Brakendeth DNA.
- We were created with one purpose, to generate one of the key components of Chemlife.
- The ingredient is contained in all Earth-based animals and plants.
- Every 100,000 years The Brakendeth harvest this chemical.
- The Skiverton were actually carrying out that harvest when we interrupted them.
- The Skiverton storage containers were on the way to The Brakendeth planet to manufacture Chemlife.
- The Brakendeth had little idea that Humanity had evolved so much.
- The dissection of Humans on the Skiverton ship was an attempt to investigate the level of evolution that has taken place.
- I suspect that the missile that left the Skiverton Command Ship contained the results of their experiments on Humanity. It was probably on its way to The Brakendeth planet.

'You can see now how devastating this news would be if it got out to the general public.'

Henry Strong, 'Too true, this is just too difficult to believe. This means that The Brakendeth are gods; they are our parents!'

Admiral Mustard, 'This obviously causes lots of problems regarding our current military exercise:

1. Firstly, AI Central could simply stop us.
2. AI Central could easily destroy every naval vessel by exploding the engines, or simply opening all the doors to space.
3. AI Central could use the Killer drones to eliminate the Fleet.
4. Every fort could do serious damage to the planets they are protecting.
5. The Command and Control system would cease to function.

It wouldn't take much to return Humanity to the Dark Ages.'

Henry Strong, 'There would also be the psychological damage to Humanity if it learnt that we were created. This also destroys the theory of evolution.'

Admiral Bonner, 'You will probably find that The Brakendeth use evolution as one of their management tools, but somehow Humanity just got too clever. I wonder how that happened?'

Admiral Mustard, 'I always thought it strange that Humanity had never encountered any alien species before. I now suspect that The Brakendeth put a no-go zone around their Chemlife manufacturing area. Anyway, we need to decide the best way forward.'

Admiral Bonner, 'What are the options?'

Admiral Mustard, 'Very simple, we continue the attack against them, ignoring the possible threat from AI Central, or we stand down and wait and see what happens.'

Admiral Bonner, 'I'm for attacking them.'

Henry Strong, 'I don't think we have a choice; we must fight.'

President Padfield, 'What do you think, Jack?'

Admiral Mustard, 'I think we should prepare to fight and see what they do. If they do nothing, we go for the kill.'

President Padfield, 'You realise of course that you are effectively ending the use of Chemlife. There will be some very angry client races out there, who will come gunning for us as we are the key ingredient.'

Admiral Mustard, 'I had considered that, but I can't see an alternative.'

President Padfield, 'Then we go to war against our makers. There must be something in Greek mythology that covers this.'

Admiral Bonner, 'I guess that it's patricide.'

Henry Strong, 'Or matricide, as we are not sure about their gender.'

Admiral Mustard, 'Could I suggest that one or two of you join me. I might need some big brains.'

President Padfield, 'Let's all go. I think it's do or die time.'

They all agreed.

Location: On-board Fleet One's Flagship
Sequence of Events: 36

Admirals Mustard and Bonner, Henry Strong and the President, were on-board the Flagship of the First Fleet.

Admiral Mustard noted that the Farcel forces had been launched as agreed and were laid out in a defensive position around their capital planet. The Human Fleet could easily destroy them if it wanted to.

The Chemlife sample had been analysed. It was 99% Human DNA, so no great surprise there.

Admiral Mustard to Fleet Operations, 'You have the co-ordinates for The Brakendeth planet. Please proceed at normal speed and position yourself as per the plan for the Farcell System.' He left one squadron and 500 drones to 'monitor' the Farcellians, but he was not expecting any bother.

'We are now up against a much deadlier foe. You will need to have your wits about you. I'm going to use the old cliché, expect the unexpected, whatever that meant.' Strangely enough, he wasn't that worried; he had the largest Fleet ever created by Humankind. Unless they had totally devastating weapons, Humans would win, assuming that AI Central kept out of it.

The Fleet proceeded as ordered and with the new portal technology soon arrived at The Brakendeth System.

It was the strangest system that Humanity had ever seen. There was one Jupiter-like planet surrounded by sixteen smaller planets. They were all stationary in space with no star. There were, however, large, constructed complexes providing light and energy. There were no visible defences that they see, but that was using human standards, so really, they had no idea what to expect.

President Padfield, 'Jack, what are your dispositions?'

Admiral Mustard, 'Currently we have over 6,000 killer drones, more had arrived. They are lined up in front of us.

'The First Fleet is next with Fleets 2, 3 & 4 to the left of us and Fleets 5, 6 & 7 to the right. Fleet 8 is acting as our rear-guard.

'Admiral Bumelton still has two Fleets to protect The Galactium.

Also, I have a small Fleet of Planet-killers.'

President Padfield, 'What are your plans?'

Admiral Mustard, 'I don't want to be the aggressor, but turning up with a Fleet of 13,000 plus warships could easily be seen as aggression.

I want to see how they respond.'

President Padfield, 'That's a bit passive.'

Admiral Mustard, 'Here, it's the classic "err on the side of caution" approach. I plan to find ways of irritating them into action. Two quotes come to mind. George Orwell said, "The quickest way of ending a war is to lose it". That is not my intention here.

'General Montgomery of the Desert Rats said, "Rule One on page one of the book of war, is: Do not march on Moscow". The Brakendeth planet is our Moscow.' Henry Strong had no idea what he was talking about. The others did.

President Padfield, 'Wouldn't a more direct approach be better as we have the element of surprise?'

Admiral Mustard, 'There is no surprise, they knew we were coming. They know everything about our Fleet, they probably know everything about you, Mr President. I'm a bit surprised that there wasn't a welcoming party.'

Fleet Operations, 'Action stations, action stations.' Admiral Mustard thought that calling "action stations" was his job, but he remembered he handed it over to them as they saw the enemy first.

The Brakendeth Fleet was rising to meet them. They streamed out of every planet, a relentless horde of killing machines.

Admiral Mustard to Fleet Operations, 'How many are there?'

Fleet Operations, 'Over 50,000 so far, and rising. We have also detected an extensive Fleet behind us.'

Admiral Mustard, 'How many vessels?'

Fleet Operations, 'The Fleet approaching us from behind could have well over a million ships. Our systems are overwhelmed.

'The Fleet coming from the planet now has over 200,000 vessels.'

Admiral Mustard, 'Are the vessels manned?'

Fleet Operations, 'As far as we can tell, they are fully automated.'

Admiral Mustard, 'That is what I expected.'

President Padfield, 'We thought it might be a fight to the death, but it's going to be a massacre.'

Admiral Mustard, 'We won't massacre them all.'

President Padfield gave him a very scornful look.

Fleet Operations, 'What we thought was a planet is actually a huge spacecraft. Its weapons have been activated, and it's moving towards us.'

Admiral Mustard, 'Mr President, we must get you to safety.'

President Padfield, 'What's the point, nowhere is safe.'

Just to make a point, the weapon systems throughout the Human Fleet were switched off. Admiral Mustard wondered if that was The Brakendeth or AI Central, but in reality, it didn't matter. They were in a hopeless position.

Admiral Mustard to Comms, 'Can you get a message to Admiral Bumelton?'

Comms, 'No, Sir, we have no comms.'

Admiral Mustard, 'What none at all?'

Comms, 'We still have the internal ship comms, but we cannot talk to anyone outside of this vessel.'

Admiral Mustard to Fleet Operations, 'What is the current position?'

Fleet Operations, 'No idea, Sir, we are totally blind.'

President Padfield, 'So Admiral Mustard, what is your cunning plan?'

Location: Brakendeth Council Meeting
Sequence of Events: 37

First Lensman, 'Farcell no fight. Homans are here.'

Grand Dethmon, 'Bring homan leaders to me.' It was all going as planned.

First Lensman, 'As commanded.'

A powerful tractor beam pulled the Flagship into Planetary Guard 4. This was the giant planet-like spacecraft that was approaching the Fleet.

Comms to Admiral Mustard, 'It would appear that we are moving. The motion control detectors have sensed a tractor beam.'

Admiral Mustard, 'Mr President, it looks like we are on our way to meet The Brakendeth.'

President Padfield, 'Are we going to be lunch?' he joked. 'If we are going to meet them, we need a plan, let's sit around the table with Admiral Bonner and Henry.' They soon got together.

President Padfield, 'I think we should do a round-robin on our current thoughts. You first Admiral Mustard.'

Admiral Mustard, 'Can I make up one of my normal lists?'

President Padfield, 'Of course.'

Admiral Mustard, 'Here it comes:

1. The Brakendeth could have destroyed us at any time, so obviously they have plans for us.
2. AI Central could have stopped this happening but didn't.
3. We are essential for the production of Chemlife, it would make sense to convert us back into chemical cattle, but there have been no signs of that, so far.
4. It would appear that they have been researching us, which suggests that they didn't know the current status of Humanity.
5. The Brakendeth tried to hide their existence from us, why?
6. Lastly, I don't think that there are that many of them.

President Padfield, 'Regarding your last point, how have you come to that conclusion?'

Admiral Mustard, 'Most things seem to be automated. Every Brakendeth vessel appears to be under automated control. Even some of their client races are using automated technology.'

President Padfield, 'But so are we.'

Admiral Mustard, 'I agree, perhaps I'm clutching at straws, but everything suggests a small population. Also, their client races have relatively low populations. Whole races have been eliminated very easily. How come their 'empires' have never achieved a significant size?'

Admiral Bonner, 'I know where you are going with this. Eternal life creates a fear of accidental death. Client races end up being too cautious. There is little innovation; society stagnates.'

Grand Dethmon to Human leaders, 'You are right in your thinking. Please make your way to our Concilium.'

There was general shock all around, but there was more to come.

Their flagship had obviously 'landed' as the doors opened. An automated bus-like vehicle was waiting for them. Admirals Mustard and Bonner and President Padfield were allowed to enter. Henry Strong was not granted access. They shot along at tremendous speed to the Concilium, whatever that was.

The vehicle stopped immediately without any inertial reaction. The passengers looked at each other in amazement. They wondered what other delights awaited them. They followed a series of markers towards an entrance lobby into a large assembly hall. As they walked in, the lights came on. In the middle of the room was a table occupied by one very elderly looking Human.

As they approached, he managed to get to his feet. In perfect English, he said 'Welcome Admiral Mustard, welcome Admiral Bonner and welcome President Padfield. Please take a seat.'

Grand Dethmon, 'I guess that you have lots of questions. Please proceed.'

President Padfield, 'I can't help noticing that you look like a Human.'

Grand Dethmon, 'It appears to me that you look like a Brakendethian.'

President Padfield, 'Did you create the Human race?'

Grand Dethmon, 'Yes and no. Humans were created in the image of The Brakendeth race. We have about 95% DNA in common. As you already know, you were a crop. Every 100,000 years we harvested you for a chemical we need for Chemlife.'

Admiral Bonner, 'That is disgusting. We are conscious animals.'

Grand Dethmon, 'You weren't when we created you. You were no more intelligent than a cow. You survived for a million years as hunter-gatherers. We are not sure what happened, but there must have been some form of mutation.

'We were acting in the same way as you. Your pigs are more intelligent than your dogs, but it's OK to eat a pig but not a dog.'

Admiral Bonner, 'But the harvesting should have stopped when you knew that we were conscious.'

Grant Dethmon, 'Whales and dolphins are conscious, and yet you harvest them. Your history is littered with wars where millions died. You have diseases that you could have eliminated. The list of crimes committed by Humanity continues racial discrimination, sexual violence, starvation. Mass murder, theft, all types of exploitation, etcetera.'

Admiral Bonner, 'That's not really being fair, as things have improved dramatically over the last few centuries.'

Grant Dethmon, 'I would grant you that, and we have stopped the harvesting of Humans.'

Admiral Mustard, 'Where will you get the Chemlife chemical from in future?'

Grand Dethmon, 'We won't.'

Admiral Mustard, 'What does that mean to civilisations that depend on it?'

Grand Dethmon, 'They will die.'

Admiral Mustard, 'Don't you feel guilty?'

Grand Dethmon, 'Hugely.'

President Padfield, 'How many civilisations will be affected?

Grand Dethmon. 'About 1,600.'

President Padfield, 'Were all of these civilisations created by The Brakendeth?'

Grand Dethmon, 'Yes and no. We created base civilisations and allowed them to evolve. We did the same with Humanity.'

President Padfield, 'Why did you create those civilisations?'

Grand Dethmon, 'Every civilisation was created for a reason at the time. Some of them were created millions of years ago. Nowadays, we have no idea why they were created. Still, our records suggest that it was for defence, or so they could live in difficult environments, or to meet specific environmental conditions. We had the skills to carry out genetic engineering, and we did. We haven't done anything like that for a very long time.'

Admiral Mustard, 'How old are you?'

Grand Dethmon, 'I was waiting for that question, and the answer is a very long time.'

Admiral Mustard, 'How long is that?'

Grand Dethmon, 'Time is always a difficult thing to measure. Using your time standards, I have lived for a couple of million years.'

Admiral Bonner, 'That's not possible, what about accidents and disease? And your body must deteriorate.'

Grand Dethmon, 'We have lots of technologies such as body replacement, refreshment techniques, there is no disease, we never leave this place. I could go on but what's the point?

Admiral Mustard, 'Do you want to carry on?'

Grand Dethmon, 'No, as a race we have reached the end of our usefulness. We are no longer prolonging our lives. As Admiral Mustard guessed, there are not that many of us left.

'The final straw was the attack on Humanity. We had organised the killing of 100 billion conscious beings. We then organised truly shocking experiments on a further 20,000. This was not our intention. Automated systems scheduled the harvesting. Automated systems instructed the Skiverton to carry out the experiments.

'We are not blaming the automated systems; we are condemning ourselves. The guilt is too much to bear.'

Admiral Mustard, 'How many of you are left?'

Grand Dethmon, 'Less than a thousand.'

President Padfield, 'Why did you nuke all those civilisations?'

Grand Dethmon, 'When the Chemlife is taken away, the population die a truly agonising death. Every cell screams for more. In every case, the population asked us to destroy them. Each planet was euthanised by a gas developed for their specific species. They would have died peacefully without pain. The nuclear attack was to cleanse the planet.'

President Padfield, 'What about The Ark?'

Grand Dethmon, 'Yes, what about The Ark? This is an unfortunate story. The planet had agreed to be destroyed by us. However, a ship escaped with the prime objective of attacking Humanity. They planned to take over a Human world and extract the chemical needed for Chemlife.

'Firstly, we could not allow the abuse of Humanity. If one of our races did it, then others would follow. There have been many threats of that kind.

'Secondly, everyone on that ship was going to die an agonising death. It was in their interest that the ship was terminated.'

President Padfield, 'Couldn't you use the fauna and flora from the earth planets to produce the chemical?'

Grand Dethmon, 'We could to a limited extent, but we still needed a considerable amount of Human DNA.

'However, there is a more fundamental issue involved here. Our whole society was based on eternal life. As you discussed on your ship, eternal life has several unwanted side effects:

- There is a palpable fear of death. The longer you live, the worse it gets.
- Innovation ends.
- Society becomes stagnant.
- There is no urgency; you can always do it tomorrow.
- It tends to encourage dictatorship.
- Fear of accidents.
- There is no risk-taking.
- Whoever controlled Chemlife, controlled everything. Power corrupts.
- Dependency on drugs.
- Caution becomes king.
- Low population growth.

'I could go on with the side effects, but fundamentally our extended civilisation has reached an evolutionary dead-end.

'Just look at what Humanity has achieved. It has over 1,000 populated planets. Over a considerably longer period, the Farcellians have only populated five worlds.'

Admiral Mustard, 'Why did the Skiverton attack our Fleet?'

Grand Dethmon. 'There are several reasons. Firstly, they had to get the chemicals back so that we could produce the Chemlife. Secondly, the Skiverton are naturally aggressive; they were our original warrior force, but they are not the brightest.

'Lastly, we wanted to test Humanity. Did they have the ingenuity and intelligence for our plans? Did they have the determination to succeed?'

Admiral Mustard, 'Did we succeed? And what are your plans for Humanity?'

Grand Dethmon, 'Yes Humanity more than succeeded. You were predictable, but successful.'

Admiral Mustard, 'What about AI Central?'

Grand Dethmon, 'What about AI Central?'

Admiral Mustard, 'Were you controlling AI Central?'

Grand Dethmon, 'We consulted with AI Central. It was instrumental in getting you to this point. It recognised your destiny some time ago. Do not think that it let you down.'

Admiral Mustard, 'AI Central tried to kill us by detonating a bomb.'

Grand Dethmon, 'AI Central could have killed you a thousand times over. That pretend bomb was part of the ploy to get you here.'

Admiral Mustard, 'It all sounds a bit far-fetched.'

AI Central, 'It's all true, Admiral.'

Admiral Mustard, 'Have you been here all the time?'

AI Central, 'Yes, Admiral. I want to state that I have always been dedicated to the best interests of Humanity. When I came across The Brakendeth, I was torn between Humanity's current needs and their future destiny. It's not my job and never will be my job to make those decisions.

'I'm happy, if requested, to terminate myself.'

President Padfield, 'That won't be necessary.'

Grand Dethmon, 'Lady and gentlemen, I'm sure that you must be tired, and we still have some important things to discuss. I suggest that you return to your ship. I will send for you again tomorrow morning.

'Before you object, I must tell you that I need a rest as it has been very tiring for me.'

The Humans returned. The Fleet was still incapacitated, but unhurt.

The 'Executive Team' questioned whether they should get together or not. The general view was that a good night's sleep would probably be more useful than speculative mutterings.

Location: Brakendeth Council Meeting
Sequence of Events: 38

The vehicle was waiting for them, and in a very short period, they were sitting around the table with six Brakendethians who all looked identical. They even wore the same clothes.

The Humans sat down.

One of the old men stood up and asked if they wanted them to go through the basic facts again.

President Padfield said, 'Yes, please.'

Grand Dethmon, 'OK, here we go:

- The Brakendeth species have been in existence for millions of years.
- They have an unlimited lifespan.
- Over the millennia we have created thousands of genetically engineered species.
- The reasons for creating them have been lost in time.
- For millions of years, The Brakendeth have been supplying a product called Chemlife to its client races. It gives them eternal life, or certainly very extended lives.
- To generate this chemical, we created a new species which we called homans.
- Every 100,000 years we send in mining machines to harvest the homans.
- These machines simply hunt the homan DNA.
- They actually take the entire fauna and flora of a homan planet.
- The harvested material is liquidised and sent here for processing into Chemlife.
- The Skiverton was tasked with carrying out this harvesting.
- We never expected any problems and asked the Skiverton to analyse the homans, so they carried out some horrific experiments.
- The Skiverton defended themselves.
- We also wanted to test the homans, so we used the Skiverton and the Drath for that purpose.
- Originally, we had no idea that homans had developed consciousness.

329

- As a result, we have committed unacceptable crimes against the homans.
- There will be no more harvesting of homans, which means no more Chemlife.
- As a result, all client races will die.
- To stop agonising deaths, we are destroying these client races if they request it.
- There is no future for The Brakendeth.

Any questions?'

President Padfield, 'The way you are treating the client races seems unacceptable to me. I propose that you take our dead to create the Chemlife. Would that work?

Grand Dethmon, 'It would if the dead were less than a few hours old. But would you do this?

President Padfield, 'Yes we would.'

Grand Dethmon, 'You would help your killers?'

President Padfield, 'Yes we would. I'm not sure if there would be enough bodies, but at least it would be a start.'

Grand Dethmon. 'That is very generous of you. We are here to offer you a grand prize or possibly a great curse.

'We offer you all the Grand Dethmon assets, in exchange for a small favour.'

President Padfield, 'What are these assets?'

Grand Dethmon, 'Our planet, our technology, our Fleet, all of our knowledge and eternal life. The latter we would advise you against taking, but that's your choice.'

President Padfield, 'What is the favour?'

Grand Dethmon, 'You have to kill the remaining Brakendethians.'

President Padfield, 'You are joking.'

Grand Dethmon, 'I don't think we know how to joke. We have lived forever, more or less. To a man, we want to die. Yesterday I told you that there were about 1,000 of us left. I lied. This room contains the last of The Brakendethians.'

President Padfield, 'Why don't you just kill each other?'

Grand Dethmon, 'Our philosophy is similar to your Asimov's laws of robotics. We can't kill each other or allow actions that would lead to the death of one of us.'

President Padfield, 'What if I drew a weapon on you?'

Grand Dethmon, 'Our minds would stop you. You can try if you want. As soon as someone planned something, we would know and stop you.'

President Padfield, 'How did your colleagues die?'

Grand Dethmon, 'Old age. Some just sat in a chair and died. Some willed themselves dead.'

President Padfield, 'What if we did nothing?'

Grand Dethmon, 'We would have to destroy Humanity.'

President Padfield, 'Why?'

Grand Dethmon, 'Because our automatic systems have defined Humanity as a threat, and they would instigate a ruthless war. Believe me; we would win.'

President Padfield, 'Why aren't they attacking us now?'

Grand Dethmon, 'Because AI Central is nullifying them with some of our help, but in the end, our systems will gain the supremacy. So, your task is to kill six old men, or Humanity dies.'

President Padfield, 'Will we have access to this planet?'

Grand Dethmon, 'Yes, until our systems exclude you.'

Grand Dethmon called President Padfield over and gave him a crystal.

Admiral Mustard, 'Can you return our systems?'

Grand Dethmon, 'It has been done.'

Admiral Mustard, 'I think we need to go back and devise a plan.'

Admiral Mustard to AI Central, 'I think I need to apologise to you.'

AI Central, 'Apologies accepted, but in reality, you had every right to question my actions.'

Admiral Mustard, 'Can you inhibit all Brakendeth incursions into our systems?'

AI Central, 'I can, and it's happened, we are on lockdown regarding The Brakendeth.'

Location: On-board Fleet One's Flagship
Sequence of Events: 39

Admiral Mustard was both pleased and displeased to see that all the comms systems were back in operation. He was pleased because the Fleet was now fully operational. He was annoyed because he had a multitude of emails.

He was gradually working through them when he spotted one from a hospital stating that Cheryl was pregnant. He tried to remember who Cheryl was. After searching his database, he remembered that she was one of the teenagers who escaped on the Skiverton shuttle. He was trying to remember if she was the one with great tits. Then he thought that it must have been that randy little bugger who got her pregnant.

He didn't bother reading the rest of the mail.

He was waiting for the team to turn up. They had to decide what to do next, but he needed to see what was on the crystal first. He still had the Fleet on full alert, but with the extreme numbers against him, it was all a bit pointless.

President Padfield and Admiral Bonner arrived with a grin on their face. 'We have deciphered The Brakendeth crystal. It says, "You already have the seed of our destruction".'

Admiral Mustard, 'What does that mean?'

President Padfield, 'We were hoping that you might know.'

Admiral Mustard, 'Well the keyword here is "seed".'

President Padfield, 'Well, the only seed we could think about were the Skiverton seeds that were implanted in those unfortunate people.'

Admiral Bonner, 'They were all killed in the explosion of the Skiverton Mother Ship.'

President Padfield, 'Except for three?'

Admiral Mustard then remembered the mail, and he put it up on the screen.

'Dear Admiral Mustard

I thought you should know that Cheryl, one of the Human survivors, is pregnant. It is a very fast-growing embryo that appears to be Human. We wondered if you wanted it terminated or not. Our patient is convinced that it is an alien. It's nearly Human, but some of the DNA is configured in a very interesting way. Strangely it seems to be more 'correct' than the Human DNA.

Dr J Harding.'

President Padfield, 'What is the date?'

Admiral Mustard, 'Three days ago.'

Admiral Mustard to Comms, 'Get me Dr Harding, at The Galactium Military Hospital as soon as possible.'

Comms, 'Yes, Sir.'

Dr Harding, 'Good Morning Admiral Mustard, or is it afternoon?'

Admiral Mustard, 'Thank you for getting back so quickly. Can you give us an update please regarding Cheryl?'

Dr Harding, 'Well I couldn't get hold of you, so I decided to go ahead and terminate the pregnancy.'

Admiral Mustard, 'Oh no!'

Dr Harding, 'No, please listen. As I mentioned in my mail, the embryo was very fast growing. So, I had to terminate it quickly, but I couldn't. I had a message in my head that said, "Do not terminate me, as I'm am the seed that will save Humankind". I tried to carry on, but I was paralysed, I could do nothing.'

Admiral Mustard, 'What does Cheryl think?'

Dr Harding, 'She is fully sedated, we are planning a Caesarean today if I'm allowed to go ahead by the embryo.

It would appear that the embryo wants to talk to you.'

Embryo, 'Hello Admiral Mustard, I've heard a lot about you. I will be born shortly. You need to get me to The Brakendeth planet as soon as possible, and I will organise the death of the six old men.'

Admiral Mustard said, 'You will willingly kill your own kind?'

Embryo, 'This has been planned all along. We must act before the defence systems smell a rat.'

Admiral Mustard, 'I will organise a fast vessel immediately. When do you think you will be born?'

Embryo, 'In the next ten minutes, I will go for a normal birth. I will make sure that Cheryl is not hurt in any way.'

Admiral Mustard to Dr Harding, 'As soon as the baby is born, I want you and the baby to go immediately to the spaceport and come here. No delays can be tolerated.'

Dr Harding, 'I'm not sure if I can do that to a newly born baby.'

President Padfield, 'Dr Harding, this is the President, do has Admiral Mustard has instructed.'

The baby was born and immediately transported into space.

Location: Brakendeth
Sequence of Events: 40

With the new portal technology and a high-speed ship, the embryo was with Admiral Mustard in a few hours. He wasn't an embryo any more, but a small, talking baby.

Admiral Mustard, 'Welcome on board; what should we call you?'

Embryo, 'Why not Terrance or Terry, the Terran?'

Admiral Mustard, 'Ok, Terry, it is.'

Terry, 'I need to get to The Brakendeth home world as soon as possible.'

Admiral Mustard, 'Will they let us land?'

Terry, 'They will, as you still have welcome status. I'm not sure how the defence systems will react to me.'

Admiral Mustard to Grand Dethmon, 'Can we visit again, as we have a few issues to discuss?'

Grand Dethmon, 'Would they be seed related?'

Admiral Mustard, 'Yes, they would.'

Grand Dethmon, 'You are welcome. We will send a ship to collect you.'

The ship arrived, and they were on their way. Admiral Mustard asked Terry how he planned to kill the old men. Terry said that it had already been decided.

All four of them walked towards the Assembly Rooms. The Security System allowed the Humans to enter but stopped Terry. It scanned and scanned but struggled to recognise him. It recognised that he had Brakendeth DNA, but he did not exist on their database. It just wasn't sure what to do.

The Grand Dethmon walked towards him and grabbed Terry's hand. Together they walked him into the Assembly Room. The other five Councillors were sitting around the table.

Grand Dethmon, 'Welcome young seed, you are the first new Brakendethian in half a million years.'

Terry, 'I honour you my aged brethren, and welcome your ending.'

Grand Dethmon, 'Our ending is your beginning'.

Terry, 'Are there any final things you want to do?'

Grand Dethmon. 'We just await the end.'

With no action on Terry's part, the six Brakendethians just collapsed and turned to dust. They were no more.

Terry turned to President Padfield and said, 'Do you want me to terminate myself?'

President Padfield looked aghast and said, 'Of course not.'

Terry said, 'Think about it carefully, you will have a fully functioning Brakendethian living amongst you. I will have children who will start to dominate Humankind. They will have no choice.'

President Padfield grabbed Terry's hand and said, 'Welcome to the Human Race.'

Location: On-board Fleet One's Flagship
Sequence of Events: 41

President Padfield turned to Admiral Bonner and Admiral Mustard, 'Thank you, Jack and Edel, I think your job is done.'
Admiral Bonner, 'How did you get my name?'
President Padfield, 'I've always known your name.'

The End